Children of Maya

by Christopher Vastag

It is not death that a man should fear,
but he should fear never beginning to live.
Marcus Aurelius

FENRIS
™

This is a work of fiction. All characters, events, and locations portrayed within are fictitious.

CHILDREN OF MAYA

Published by Fenris Publishing
Flagstaff, Arizona
https://www.fenrispublishing.com

ISBN 978-1-62475-155-4
Printed in the United States, United Kingdom, or Australia
First trade paperback edition: August 2021

Cover art by Irbeus
Edited by David M. Sula

For my father's mother. No one else showed me more love or a better understanding of the joy of learning.

Special thanks to Hannah Sandoval for her assistance in the editing and rewriting process.

CHAPTER ONE
Scraps of Gold

Maria

My shoulders burned as the pickax swung in a broad arc beside my head, averting my eyes from the guard strolling by with whip in hand. The workday was, at last, coming to a close. My familiar friend, hunger pains, warned me that if I didn't hold my focus on the vein of gold snaking through the dark rock in front of me, my weariness might earn me a few good lashings.

A rhythmic ringing of metal on stone tapped out the time like a metronome. *Clang, clink, clang, clunk.* A nugget came free and bounced at my feet. I blinked through the dark tunnel, lit only by a few swaying oil lamps. If the overseer allowed me to work in my animal form, I'd have an easier time finding them in the dim, but I was left to scrounge half-blind. I tossed the retrieved gold into my pail and took a precious moment to peel a few locks of my thick, black hair from my sweating neck.

The driving blows of my pick flicked debris around me. Each time I found anything that might hold gold, I tossed it into the pail. Children scurried around gathering the chipped rock before, eventually, hauling off the filled pail—more fuel for the greed of petty nobles feuding for control of the kingdom.

Clang, clink, clang, clunk. Another nugget in the pail.

"Well, do you have anything for me?"

I whirled to find Lukas, a miner from the men's camp. His large eyes darted down the tunnel where a guard's lamp glowed.

"Lukas, go away before someone sees us."

"No one's looking. I made certain. But hurry up," he whispered. "Something small, easy to hide." He held out a cupped hand.

"Oh, by the goddess, when is Gomez going to give up this foolish plan?" I picked a large pebble of ore from my bucket and examined it.

"It's not foolish, and you agreed to help us, so thank you." He twitched his fingers, urging me to hurry.

"Yes, well, you also agreed to tell the men *my* plan."

"Don't worry. Paul and I are spreading the word. But not everyone is convinced."

"Here." I plopped the rock into his hand. "Tell Paul I said hello and I miss him." I couldn't recall how long it had been since I'd spoken with my brother. Last time we'd been put on work duty together, I'd been shocked to see he was growing a beard. He had become a man down here in the dark, away from our mother and sisters.

The damp, the dark, and the swing of the ax were all I'd ever known. The work itself wasn't the source of misery here. I didn't mind the burn of my muscles. I'd swing my pick with all my might again and again, all day long, if it meant I'd save others from the whip. But my body craved the sunlight it had never known, the sunlight *The Words of Maya* spoke about so sweetly.

I found my rhythm again as one of the guards headed back my way. But a great *boom* made us all jump. With a crack and a rumble, the ceiling split into thin branches, spilling rock dust onto my head. I looked to Bridget and Nadia on either side of me and saw my fear reflected in their eyes. Bridget transformed with me, her ears elongating at the tips. The rabbit features first transposed over her human face—pink rabbit nose and whiskers overshadowing her freckles—and then overtook it completely.

Her red hair became auburn fur, and she shrank several feet in height.

On my right, Nadia breathed in short gasps. As I felt my own ears grow, my body falling forward onto paws, I yelled, "Run!" But Nadia was frozen. My transformation complete, I rose on my hind legs and slammed my paws into her back, spurring her forward. I ran alongside Bridget, looking back at Nadia who was sprinting behind us through the steeply-sloped tunnel, her frail human body unable to keep stride with our springing legs.

Rocks fell around us, pebbles at first, but the rumbling was a roar now, and the ground beneath my paws shook. A boulder the size of a collection bucket crashed to earth between Bridget and me, and the shock knocked me off my feet. Bridget paused to help, but I shouted, "Keep going!"

The fluffy white underside of her tail bounced away as I righted myself, only to be pummeled into the ground again by a guard, now in bloodhound form, sprinting toward the tunnel exit. Nadia hoisted me onto my paws with her hands under my forelegs. The two of us scrambled forward, fighting the vibrations of the earth. A boulder struck Nadia's shoulder and sent her sprawling. I skidded and spun to help her. Another large rock fell on her hand as she attempted to push herself up. Her scream of agony set my rabbit heart racing, begging me to flee, but I fought the instinct. As the back of the tunnel crumbled in a wave of choking dust, the cracks deepening as they raced toward us, I used my back legs to kick the boulder off of Nadia. I tried to push my body under her uninjured shoulder and help her get to her feet, but she fell on top of me, moaning.

"Go, go, Maria! Save yourself," she said.

"Transform!" I yelled over the roar of the collapse. "It's your only hope."

As Nadia concentrated, gritting her teeth through the transformation of starving, pale human into brown rabbit, I looked to the exit. Only twenty feet. We could make it. The heavy panting of a massive dog made my fur stand on end. It was Christian, one of the few guards whose name I knew. The sleek, black hound grabbed Nadia by her scruff and ran with her toward the exit, her legs kicking in fright. I raced at Christian's heels, leaping through the exit. I lay on my side and coughed thick dust from my lungs. Christian dropped Nadia beside me and ran back into the tunnel, looking for more rabbits.

Breathing a little easier, I righted myself and tried to go after him, to help my clan members. But as I reached the tunnel entrance, Christian came barreling back out, a white rabbit in his mouth, and the last half of the tunnel fell with a *boom* that shook the whole mine.

"Thank you. Thank you," the white rabbit whispered, the fur of her back leg stained crimson.

"Yes, thank you, Christian," I said softly.

The hound only inclined his head, his eyes distant, and I guessed he was thinking the same thing I was. Saving our lives had likely just cost him his.

* * *

Gunpowder ignited and muskets roared their brief but vicious staccato. My arms trembled as I hugged myself, but I refused to close or avert my eyes, even as the smoke cleared. I watched Christian until his body buckled and collapsed into a carriage below the wooden platform. I hoped it was me Christian had looked down at from the grisly scaffold, hoped he saw the gratitude reflected in my eyes before the guns fired. A sullen silence descended over the group of slaves as we lamented the death of another decent man.

The overseer raised his paw toward the sepulchral ceiling of the "Cathedral," the immense cavern crammed with barracks we were meant to call home. The fox seemed to fancy himself a serious priest as he sent up praises to the black wolf god, Khaytan, with reverence in his oily voice. "To You, we send this tribute, oh Khaytan, Prince of Predators, to bless our work here. This changeling hath angered thee with his interference in the natural order, and so we offer up his blood." Bricriu turned his beady eyes on us, gazing down his red muzzle from the scaffold. "That is all it takes to appease our mighty god. Gold... or blood. Today, your sloppiness cost this mine a good deal of gold, and so we must repay Khaytan with blood."

It was the wolf king who had coined the phrase, "No amount of gold or blood will ever be enough." The first lesson any prey changeling learned was that neither Khaytan nor the Blood Counts who worshiped him would ever be satisfied. Only in death did our service end, despite the multitudes already sacrificed.

While the firing squad reloaded their matchlocks, another group of guards forced a score of haggard, terrified slaves onto the platform. Unlike us, the guards of Marburg Mine were muscular and well-fed. They stood in precise rows to one side of the spectators, wearing silver breastplates and red jackets with blue tunics underneath. Their spectacular presentation couldn't hide who they were. We knew better. Those men were hounds, Canum, something as clear to me as if they had shifted into animal form before my eyes.

They had seized all the workers who were injured in the collapse, including those Christian had saved. I saw Nadia at the front, her hair hacked close to her head, the locks offered up so that we could knit the soft strands into blankets. She cradled her mangled hand to her bosom, and tears glistened on her cheeks.

"I want you all to remember Guard Christian," said Bricriu. "Because neither Lord Khaytan nor His representatives on Kaskilia are willing to forgive such betrayal."

I could tell he'd indulged in a goblet of wine to heighten his enjoyment of this moment. Spirits always took his high-pitched voice up a notch. Only a changeling who spent most of his life in his animal form could stand on his hind legs while drunk without swaying. Most changelings couldn't stand upright at all, but Bricriu never gave up his fangs.

With his mouth, Bricriu grabbed the chain attached to the steel collar around Nadia's neck and yanked her onto the platform. Then he took the chain in his paws, though his grip was clumsy like a toddler with a spoon.

Mother put her hand on my shoulder. We shared a brief look. Her eyes were the same shade of silver as her hair, and her wrinkles were deep. I could see she was growing old, and it pained me to think of what tomorrow might bring. At any moment, she could be murdered and hauled away to feed insatiable aristocrats and their lackeys.

"Transform!" said Bricriu, snarling at Nadia.

Blood dripped from the remnants of Nadia's crushed hand, and her face contorted with pain, but she still managed a brave affect as she looked at the overseer.

"Why? Would it soil your conscience to murder me in my human form?" she said.

The only thing it would soil is his appetite, I thought. Still, I was impressed with Nadia's gall in the face of death.

Bricriu's eyes went wide, but his surprise only lasted a moment before he flashed his fangs. He raked his claws across her face in a vicious slap.

"Insolent girl! I don't care if you die from a soul shock; you are useless to your king in your human form. Transform, now! Or I'll flay the flesh off your worthless bones."

He snapped his jaws centimeters from her face, and she whimpered. She looked so small. Even in her human form, she stood face to face with the upright fox. Eyes averted, she shook her head in defiance.

Bricriu lunged for her throat, his jaws encircling her neck below the chin, squeezing just hard enough to draw pricks of blood. He growled out something that sounded like, "Now!"

I choked off a scream. Nadia's face paled, her eyes vacant and her mouth gaping as her form began to shift and shudder. Her ears grew and shrank, grew and shrank. Her body shrank and hunched. Soundlessly, I prayed for her. The transformation was chaotic, fur growing in random patches, her eyes bulging to twice their normal size, her nose shrunken and twitching, but still distinctly human. Blood suddenly gushed from one nostril, and her sharp scream echoed through the subterranean walls as she went limp. Bricriu was left holding an abomination in his mouth, neither human nor rabbit. He carelessly threw the deformed carcass onto the cart below, then turned to the remaining chained Lepores.

As he stared his victims down, each changed, falling onto four paws. Their long ears drooped. Changeling rabbits were significantly larger than the wild rabbits professed to exist in the world above, those not blessed by Maya with a human soul. When upright, our eyeline still only came up to the waist of most human adults, which was enough of a disparity of size to put us at a phsycial disadvantage to most other changelings, predators and prey alike.

After a short nod from their master, the Canum guards hoisted the Lepores by their hind feet, tying them upside down from ropes dangling overhead. A metal bucket was placed under each slave before the guards drew hunting knives across their throats.

If the sight of their feeble thrashing wasn't enough, the sound of the blood cascading into the buckets really turned my stomach. This place they called a temple was nothing more than a slaughterhouse.

Bricriu licked his lips; no doubt, he would want first pick of the slaughtered rabbits. He gave a theatrical bow. "And so the ceremonial curtain comes down, and another show is over. Guards, send the slaves back to their dwellings." As he turned, he swished his black robe around him, flashing the emblem of a white stag pierced by three arrows straight through the neck.

The guards closed in, swords and spears drawn to push us into lines. Some of them shifted, their faces elongating and eyes drooping as they became massive hounds of all colors and patterns. They snapped at stragglers' heels, herding us and separating the men from the women.

Shunted and bullied into designated groups, Mother and I branched off into our assigned barrack, lining up next to our stinking bunks, stuffed with a few inches of old straw. Each barrack held more than a hundred of us, but the crowding didn't bother our kind. The warmth of companionship in our little makeshift "burrows" brought us some small shred of comfort.

After the guards walked down the rows of bunks, searching anyone they suspected might be carrying contraband, most of the Lepores, including Mother, transformed into rabbits and gathered their garments around themselves. It lessened the crowding, made the bunks more spacious, and reduced the chill of the constant draft drifting through the barrack's shoddy boards. But unless I wanted to end up like poor Nadia, I would have to stay in human form tonight or risk draining what little energy I had left. I had already transformed twice today. A strong changeling could shift four times in a single day, but the bones poking against my skin warned me I did not meet that standard.

Mother hopped forward as many of the rabbits crawled onto their bunks, yawning and stretching their hind legs. Mother was the matriarch of our clan, and most in this barrack were her sisters and daughters. She thumped her back foot, and all eyes swiveled to her.

"We should hold a sermon for all those who died today, including the Canum, Christian," she said. "Maria, please fetch me the book."

Mother hopped onto one of the few rickety benches in the center of the room as I retrieved the old tome from the floorboards beneath her bunk. *The Words of Maya* was etched into the cracked leather and dyed a brilliant gold that was now almost entirely faded. I placed it, open, on the bench next to her and sat cross-legged on the floor. Mother turned the pages delicately with one paw. As she read, using her rabbit eyes to see the small words in the darkness, I followed her sweet voice like a melody. Listening to her was like dreaming with my eyes open, and at least for a while, I could forget where we were.

She had only read the first lines of a prayer honoring the dead when one of the girls cut in. "Forgive me for interrupting, Valorie, but I've been quiet for far too long. I must speak."

A younger Lepores by the name of Stephania pawed at her bent left ear, trying to make it stand up like the other. When Mother turned her steady gaze on the golden rabbit, Stephania cast her eyes to the ground. She had only been with us for a few months, and to me, she seemed so... untouched. I hoped she would be spared most of this place's daily violence, so she could remain that way.

"What do you want to say, dear?"

"We have to stop these sermons. Dispose of the book. It's far too dangerous keeping it around."

My jaw dropped at such sacrilege, and I could only manage an inarticulate grunt deep in my throat.

Others around me whispered and gasped, too, but not Mother. "Stephania, come here," she said evenly.

Stephania moved cautiously to sit in front of the bench. Mother sat back on her hind legs, her eyes bright with emotion as she glared down at Stephania.

"You listen to me, you ignorant child. If we forget our traditions, our ancestors' legacy, then we are nothing! You think this slavery is the life we want for ourselves? No!" Stephania flinched under Mother's rage, and Mother leaned forward so that her nose was almost touching Stephania's. "This book is worth more than all of our lives. It is how we hold on to our one last shred of freedom." Mother's voice, rich with reverence, hardened with fury as she said, "Respect the book, or leave my sight."

Stephania shrank back and spoke through sniffles. "Is that what you think? That our lives are worth less than a few printed pages?"

"They are not just bits of paper, girl! They are the *Words of Maya*, our one remaining hope, which deliver us into the goddess' four arms when we die. Without them, we will suffer a fate worse than death or this mine."

"So we continue risking our lives, praying for Maya to release us? Can't you see She's abandoned us?" Stephania turned to address us all. "Or has today's bloodshed not proved this to you?"

Silence... followed by soft murmurs. I saw doubt in some of the downcast, tearful eyes. They had lost loved ones today. I could see Mother's fury and feelings of betrayal in the wild flicks of her ears. I went to her and rubbed my hand over her soft back. We could not lose our heads, not when we were so close to putting our plan into action.

"Mother, please remain calm," I said before turning to Stephania. "I know you're upset, Stephania; we all are. But we must not deceive ourselves. The predators would have us believe we are meant only for slavery, that Khaytan is the supreme god, that His prey brother Sammael is a weakling, and Mother Maya is nothing but an aged, helpless woman. Mother is right. They have imprisoned our bodies, but they cannot imprison our minds... unless we trade away our faith."

Heads throughout the barrack nodded, and someone softly said, "Amen."

"I wonder," said Stephania, head tilted, "would you say the same if you were in the hands of an Inquisitor? Would you still champion Maya when they shaved your fur and put their instruments to your flesh?"

I held her gaze and stood, rising above my cousins and sisters and friends. I needed them to see my human face, to gauge the full range of my emotion as I said, "Let them try and break me. I will never renounce the Great Mother."

Stephania huffed. "No matter how loudly you sing Her praises, Maya is not going to help us. You and your mother will get us all killed harboring this book and organizing a rebellion."

Anger rose in my chest, but I pushed it down.

"I'm not the only voice questioning your insane plan," said Stephania. "Not all of the men are convinced. Bricriu will find you out for certain. He has spies everywhere. Even Gomez is working with him," she said, referring to the elder Lepores who acted as a patriarch for the men of our clan.

I couldn't hold back a gasp. Milten, my friend who worked in the smelting room, had told me he'd heard whispers: Gomez's plan to hide stolen gold nuggets wasn't actually designed to bribe guards for better living conditions as he claimed. Milten said he'd heard that Gomez and Bricriu had secret meetings and that my brother Paul was beginning to suspect the gold was actually for Bricriu. But no one could prove it, and most didn't want to believe it.

"How do you know that for certain?" I asked.

"How do you know it's false?" asked Stephania. "You can't know. Bricriu has his grimy paws in everything that goes on here. He probably already knows what you're planning."

I looked to the keen ears of my fellow Lepores for a hint of any noise outside our barrack. Certain no guards were listening, I said in a low voice, "Bricriu doesn't trust his own men. Why else would he sacrifice Christian for merely protecting the mine's assets? He keeps them living in fear of him. Why? Because they could easily overpower him. Just like we can. We outnumber the guards five to one, and Bricriu knows it. So he seeks to frighten us, beat us down, to instill discord between us. He has divided us from the moment he became overseer. And you are allowing him to win. I will not allow it anymore."

"The only thing your words prove is that he is far more cunning than us," said Stephania.

I stamped my foot. "He is a coward. And we have Maya on our side."

"If our only advantage is a silent, distant goddess, I'll take my chances in the mine and stay in the good graces of the fox."

Gasps filled the barrack, and my mother's strongest supporters gnashed their teeth in anger. Mother leaped from the bench and kicked her legs in a violent warning. "Blasphemer! Coward! You poison us all with your disbelief."

My aunts surged forward, nipping at Stephania, lashing out with kicks.

"Stop this at once!" I cried as loud as I dared, pressing myself against the golden rabbit to shield her. The guards were bound to have heard the discontent. My aunts froze, but the anger in their eyes remained. "You ought to be ashamed. We are all children of Maya. Stephania may be misguided, but it is her right to speak her mind. Will you take that small remaining freedom from her when you know well what that feels like?"

A few of my aunts hung their heads and moved back. Mother still allowed her front teeth to show in anger, but she said, "Maria is right. We have been too brash. But I will not allow this coward-ly girl to blaspheme the goddess here."

Stephania sniffed back tears. "As you wish."

"Maria's plan is still in motion," said Mother. "If you will not join us in our fight for freedom, that is your choice, but you will speak no word of it outside these barracks."

Stephania scoffed. "Despite what you think, I am not a fool. I would be punished the same as any of you." She shook her head and gave a watery sigh, saying bitterly, "Yes, let us all revolt. What does it matter if most of us die trying to make it out alive? At least the rest of us will be free to be hunted, imprisoned, and brought back here to work again."

"Enough," said Mother. "You've said your piece."

"Stephania, I know you are afraid," I said, giving her side a soft rub. "But we endure the fear and misery of this mine together, and *together*, we can overcome it and earn our freedom."

Her face softened. "You speak with kindness, but I simply cannot justify the loss of so many lives as a divine plan. It is too much like Bricriu. Nadia... Nadia was my cousin, but her life did not matter to him. She and many of the others could have easily recovered from their injuries, but they were nothing but fodder for the king. I will not be fodder for your daydream." She turned hard eyes on Mother. "There. *Now* I have said my piece."

I saw her pain in her animal form, and it cut at my heart. "Nadia did not deserve to die." I sighed. "But what you must come to understand, Stephania, is that dying on that sacrificial platform is very different from dying for what you believe in. If we stay, Bricriu's sacrifices will take more innocents. All of us will die here, in bondage. Would it not be better to meet our ends reaching for the light?"

Stephania studied the dirt floor. As she raised her head and opened her mouth, Mother cut her off with a gasp, ears flicking.

"They are coming," Mother hissed, her face already shifting with the transformation back into womanhood, her fur shrinking back into her cheeks and hairline, the skin appearing in a wave from head to toe, like melting wax dripping down a candlestick.

"Quick, Maria, we must hide the book." She reached for the book before her paws had even fully become hands. The whole clan was shifting if they could, not wanting to be caught in rabbit form when a group of angry hounds appeared.

Mother shoved the book into my hands, and I dove across the tight space toward the loose planks. I shoved it inside its hiding place, and a trio of younger girls covered it with straw as everyone scrambled for their bunks.

I leaped into my bed and rolled over to see Mother's foot snag on a lost shoe. She stumbled against a support beam. The door flew open, and two guards entered in human form, catching Mother in the light of their torches, alone.

The guards parted, and Bricriu stepped into the room, paws pressed together in front of his chest, a malicious grin pulling up one side of his jowls. He sniffed the room, feral eyes on Mother. "You! Why are you out of bed?" he demanded. "Guard, grab her."

One of the Canum yanked Mother up by her hair. She looked so tiny next to him, her face level with his chest. He shook her head like hounds were inclined to do with their prey, ripping strands of her hair free. Even in human form, he began to salivate.

Mother's eyes glazed over, her human side jarred by the violent shake, and her rabbit side frozen in terror at being in the clutches of a predator. Only after the Canum shook her again and threw her at Bricriu's feet did her expression change. She looked startled, as though momentarily unsure where she was. She looked to Bricriu with wide eyes.

"Answer me," ordered Bricriu, brushing dust off his embroidered robe. "My guards alert me of a ruckus in this barrack, and you're found out of bed? You are always causing trouble, it seems, Valorie."

I lay there, silent, watching the exchange through a curtain of black hair. I could not attract too much attention; the book was too close to my bed. I held my tongue, wrestling with visions of violence. I wanted to smear his fancy robes with mud and wipe that smirk from his face. Our most prized possession was a good pair of shoes, and he had an entire wardrobe. He and his fellow predators had never been branded as property, forced to bear a tattoo of their species on their necks.

"Forgive me, milord," said Mother. "The commotion was me. I was having a nightmare. I called out in my sleep. The others tried to wake me, but I fell out of bed."

The bastard fox slapped Mother, his claws leaving thin, bloody lines from temple to chin. I looked away, a hand over my mouth. Watching only served to egg him on.

"You lying whore," he hissed at Mother. "You're a troublemaker, Valorie. I can't have troublemakers whispering falsities in my workers' ears, riling them up." He addressed us all, eyes glowing in the firelight. "You've all been up, plotting. I will discover what." He leered at Mother. "You will tell me."

"There is nothing to tell, milord," said Mother.

"Shall I ask an Absolver to beat it out of you?" he asked, using the predator word for the king's vile torturers, whom we more appropriately called Inquisitors.

Mother shook her head. Her fist was balled in a familiar signal, tucked behind her back: Don't move. Don't draw attention to yourself.

Bricriu grabbed the front of her tattered tunic. "Then you will talk to me."

Mother said nothing.

"If you will not talk, perhaps you've outlived your usefulness. You're getting old, Valorie," he said, running a clumsy paw over her grey hair. "Perhaps a knight or noble might like to taste you. I'm half-tempted to do it myself!" His tongue lolled out of his mouth as he smiled.

"I can still work, sir. I have never fallen short of your requirements."

Bricriu's lolling tongue stretched out and licked the bloody lines he'd left across her face, leaving trails of saliva dripping down her cheek. Mother shuddered, and I bit down on my tongue.

"You taste so sweet for such a bitter liar," said Bricriu. "Such behavior cannot be tolerated." He turned toward the door but looked over his shoulder at the guards. "Seize her. We have much to discuss."

The Canum grabbed Mother by the arms, lifting her small frame so that her feet trailed in the dust as they dragged her toward their master. Bricriu put his paw under Mother's chin. "I have a remedy for nightmares, sweet Valorie," he crooned. "A cold shower, and a few warm blows from the whip!"

I stirred in my bed as the guards dragged her away, ready to leap up and pull her back, beg Bricriu for mercy. But I only clutched at the scratchy, lice-ridden blanket, knowing any action on my part would worsen her punishment. Bricriu gave the barrack one last look. "This place is a shithole. I expect you to clean it tomorrow. I will return for an inspection."

Only when the door slammed behind him did I free my tears, wondering if I would ever see Mother again.

"Maria, what do we do?" my younger sister Diane whispered through a sob from the bunk next to mine.

"We trust in Mother's strength, and we pray for help," I said, trying to hide my tears. I put my hands together and bowed my head. "Sammael, Son of Maya, Great Guardian of Prey, I call on You now. Please watch over Mother tonight. Wrap her in Your wool, protect her with Your horns, and bring her safely back to us. Guard her health, her life, and her soul as she endures the evils of predators."

A weight on my bed startled me, but I sank back on the straw mattress when I recognized my older sister Lillian in rabbit form. She had the same black fur as me, but a white patch traveled down her chest. I shifted over so she could snuggle her warm, furry body against my back. She placed a paw on my side and whispered, "It's all right, Maria. She *will* be back."

I rolled to face her. Her fur did not grow around the two deep bite marks on her face and neck, inflicted by a guard for fighting back when he tried to rape her. The scarring was much worse on her human features, pulling down one eyelid and disfiguring her entire right cheek. I tried to remember what she used to look like. With so many violent men around, beauty felt like a curse.

When Annabelle had been overseer, there were far fewer assaults. She had been a Vulpecula like Bricriu—I had even heard they were related—but she punished any guard caught attacking slaves. Under her supervision, we were still slaves, but at least we were treated decently. But the silver vixen had not held the position long. She was there one day and gone the next. No explanation. Only Bricriu's grinning muzzle, assuring us that the inefficiencies tolerated by the former overseer would be remedied.

I could not sleep. Visions of Bricriu, Mother, Annabelle, Lillian, Nadia, and Stephania bounced around my mind until the wee morning hours. The door burst open, and two hounds flung Mother onto the closest empty bunk before turning to leave without a word. Lillian and I rushed to her side.

"It's fine, darlings, I am still alive." She stroked my cheek. "Leopold was even kind enough to give me his cloak, though I'm sure Bricriu will reprimand him for it later," she mumbled, referring to the guard captain.

I looked her over, my nose stinging with the scent of blood on her whipped back. Anger threatened to choke me, but I held my tongue and placed some extra burlap sacks over her trembling body.

"I'll get you some medicine, Mother."

"No, we have too little medicine as it is. I'll survive. Please, go to sleep."

"But, Mother..."

"I said go to sleep, Maria. You, too, Lillian. You have only an hour before you must rise to work. We'll speak tomorrow."

We kissed Mother's cheek and did as she asked. For now, I praised Sammael for answering my prayer.

As long as Mother was still with us, we had hope.

* * *

An awful blue-black bruise appeared on Mother's face over the course of the workday. She flinched when I breathed on it, and I feared it went all the way to the bone. She had always walked tall, despite her age, but today the deep cuts on her back brought her low, hunched over her bucket. She could hardly swing the pickax, so I put half my nuggets in her pail, filling both. My shoulders were screaming by midday. When the nearest guard called fifteen minutes left until supper, I felt as though my spine might snap.

Lukas hadn't approached me for gold. He must have been assigned another tunnel.

"We're almost done, Mother," I whispered. "Just a few more—"

A cry of surprise and pain cut me off. Two buckets over, I saw Stephania rising to her feet, cradling her hand to her chest. Her pail was overturned, spilling out chunks of gold-embedded rock. I rushed to her, and she turned panicked brown eyes on me.

"They're broken," she whispered, revealing her swelling ring finger and crooked pinkie. "I... I slipped in the water, fell oddly. I think my pickax crushed them."

A steady trickle of water from an unseen underground spring poured down the wall and pooled on the stone floor where Stephania was working.

"What's going on down there?" asked a guard, a hand on his sword hilt.

Stephania's face turned grey and green. "They'll kill me," she said. At that moment, I could see how young she was, even through the grime. "They'll kill me like they killed Nadia."

I put a hand against her cheek, brushing aside her blond hair, and felt her trembling.

"They won't," I whispered. Then I turned to the approaching guard and said, "Just an overturned bucket." I squatted and started to collect the spilled ore. "I figured it would go faster if I helped. Besides, mine is full, and no one has been by to collect."

The guard stopped. Stephania kept her back to him, piling ore in the bucket with her uninjured hand.

"Get back in line," said the guard, jabbing a finger at me.

"Sorry, sir," I said, shrinking back to my spot. I locked eyes with Stephania and mouthed, "It's okay."

She nodded, though her expression said she didn't believe me. The guard watched Stephania for a moment and then grew bored, returning to his rounds. Stephania straightened up and held her pickax as best she could. I saw her grimace each time she swung, but there was no deviation in her form. As long as the guards didn't get too close, they wouldn't see the injury.

After that nerve-wracking fifteen minutes, the guards finally called for us to drop our pickaxes and leave the tunnel for the dining room. They herded us together, making sure no tool was unaccounted for and that none of us slipped anything in our pockets when we dumped our final haul into the ore cart stationed at the tunnel exit.

I kept Mother and Stephania close to me, guiding them with a hand on each of their backs. I put Stephania on my right side so that she could hide her wounded left hand between our bodies. "Thank you," she whispered over and over. She kept her head dipped low, and I could see the panic in the wide whites of her eyes. She was terrified. That had been clear from her speech last night, but her moxie had vanished, cracked like her fingers. She stared ahead, not seeing anything except the grim specters of what might happen now. Even though I was still angry at how she had spoken to Mother last night, I knew she needed me. We all needed each other. Pain had a way of softening people.

The dining hall was better lit than our barracks, but the musty cave was still a poor excuse for a living space. Long, rickety wooden tables stood in rows. Many of the benches were sagging with decay, and you were likely to get a splinter if you put your elbows on the table. We stood in line for our food—a small bowl of grain porridge and seeds, a bit of stale bread, a serving of wilting lettuce, and a scoop of corn—and then the three of us sat together, along with a few of my sisters. The food was never enough, even on the rare days when we got a slab of cheese or a half-cooked egg.

Mother sagged in her seat and put all of her energy into bringing her utensils to her mouth. I rubbed her back and then turned to Stephania.

"Keep your hand under the table," I said as I eyed the few guards posted on walkways carved into the upper level of the chamber. She obeyed, and I gave her a hunk of hard bread. "Bite down on this. I'm going to try and set that pinkie finger." I washed away the blood from her crushed knuckles with water from my cup and then took the pinkie firmly between two fingers. "Ready?" I asked her.

She looked at me with wide eyes, but she took a deep breath and nodded, the bread clenched in her teeth.

I popped the dislocated joint back into place with one swift yank and a stomach-churning crack. Stephania whimpered around the bread, a tear leaking from her eye. I ripped a small shred of cloth from my tunic and tied her middle, ring, and pinkie fingers together, covering the swelling and the nasty cut.

"I'll get you some medicine when we're back in the barracks. Change into rabbit form as soon as you're finished eating. Those fingers will be far less noticeable when you have paws."

"Thank you, Maria," said Stephania. "But how will I keep it hidden tomorrow when I have to work all day like this?"

"Keep close to me. Make sure you get the bucket next to mine," I said. "I'll help you."

A smile breached her face for the first time since I'd met her. It was a mite sad, but it plumped her cheeks and livened up her eyes. "You truly practice what you preach, Maria," she said. "I can't say I've met many people like you."

I didn't know what to say, so I squeezed her shoulder and smiled back.

"Thank you," she said. "So much."

"You're welcome."

She looked like she was about to say something else. Her mouth opened, but she hesitated when she saw my smile fade. We all looked to the door where Milten was leading my friend Donna into the dining room. Her eye was swollen and black.

"I'll be back," I told Stephania. I zigzagged through the milling bodies, and Milten saw me coming.

He was a little man, even for a Lepores, but his arms were lean and strong from pounding ore into shape in the smelting room. He had an uneven black beard and a rather bulbous nose, but his eyes were beautiful—deeply set and a rich, gorgeous brown with flecks of gold.

"Maria, good to see you," he said, but his smile didn't reach his eyes.

I nodded to him, then asked, "What happened?" I hugged Donna to me, and she cried into my shoulder.

"It was Jayson and his pal Edward," she said. "I was last to the ore cart, and they... they pulled me back into the tunnel."

I knew those names. All the women did. They were always together, always leering, and always ready to drag any unsuspecting Lepores into dark corners. I hugged her tighter, knowing words couldn't help right now.

"Milten heard me scream when they grabbed me," she said. "He ran to get Captain Leopold, and he stopped them, but not before they..." She dissolved into sobs.

"I was passing by the tunnel on the way here," said Milten. "I wish I could have done more myself."

"You did everything you could." I took his hand. "Thank you."

"No need to thank me."

I guided Donna to our table and inspected her bruise. "Those bastards. At least it's not broken. The swelling will go down before too long."

"At least we don't have it as bad as some of the men," said my eldest sister, Sarah.

I scowled at her. "She doesn't need to hear about who has it worse right now," I said. "Her pain is no less than that of anyone else who's gone through this."

"I'm only saying," said Sarah with a shrug.

Stephania leaned forward. "You mean that rumor about...?"

Sarah only nodded knowingly. No one seemed to want to voice the rumor. It had surfaced when the men had started coming to us for stolen gold. Some said they were collecting the gold for bribes so that they didn't have to whore their bodies out to the guards for extra food anymore. The rumor was Gomez had started the prostitution ring, like he'd started the gold-hoarding scheme. He was an idea man, Gomez.

Sarah turned around in her seat. "Seems like Gomez's new plan is working pretty well for him... and only him," she said. "Look at that." Sarah motioned to where Gomez was leaving the food line with his tray. Somehow, he had cheese and eggs that no one else had on their plate.

"If Bricriu finds out, he'll have the hides of everyone involved," said Lillian, turning in her seat beside Sarah. "I don't understand how they've continued this long. I mean, I know we've kept *our* plan secret, but our plan takes one day to execute. They've been skimming gold for two months now."

"Well, they must be bribing the guards who catch them to keep quiet," said Sarah.

"It's as Stephania said last night. Gomez has some special arrangement," I said. "How else is he always so comfortable while the men who execute his schemes remain the same?" Gomez was looking rather grey these days. If my memory served, he was in his late fifties, yet he had thick muscle and a full stomach, unlike any of us.

"Those hounds don't care about their master," said Mother, startling us all. "But they do fear him. I suppose some could be bribed, but... for how long?"

"If they're caught, they could ruin our chances," said Stephania. "Bricriu will crack the whip."

"*Our* chances?" said Lillian. "I thought you weren't taking part in our plan."

Stephania looked sidelong at me and then at her ruined hand concealed beneath the table. "I've changed my mind. I need to leave here. We all deserve to be free of this place. And..." She locked eyes with me. "And I've decided you're someone worth following, Maria."

I beamed at her and took her uninjured hand in both of mine. "Thank you."

She shrugged as if it was no large matter, but I saw her smile down at her food. I wanted to say more, but my mind was reeling.

"Gomez should have been retired from the population a long time ago, don't you think?" I asked.

Sarah and Lillian nodded. Most Lepores were "retired" by their forties, at the latest. Mother was one of the rare exceptions, and I had long suspected that the only thing keeping her alive was her status as a beloved matriarch. Bricriu knew retiring Mother would cause an uproar he wasn't prepared to deal with.

"He couldn't possibly mine very well, what with all his missing fingers," said Lillian.

"I'm beginning to think Paul's suspicions are right. Maybe he's never been caught because Bricriu already knows what he's doing," I said, mostly to myself.

"Huh?" asked Sarah.

I didn't respond. I'd picked my brother Paul out of the throng. He was in animal form, hopping toward the wall, looking worn and upset. His ears hung low, his white fur matted with slurry and dirt. I excused myself, grabbed my tray, and made my way to him at an even pace so as not to attract attention.

"Hello, Maria," he said, his ears perking up a little.

I flicked my eyes up at the nearest guard surveying the room and whispered, "Walk with me."

I headed toward the carts where we were meant to leave our trays. Paul hopped along beside me at a slight distance, acting as though he was looking for someone else.

"How many are willing to follow us?" I asked in a soft voice I knew his powerful ears could detect.

"More than half," said Paul, and I strained to hear him. "But Gomez's inner circle isn't budging, and he has a lot of influence. Most of the boys have lost their fathers, and Gomez treats them well."

"How is whoring them out treating them well?" I said, anger heating my face.

"I've seen no evidence of that," said Paul. "I've heard the rumors, sure, but only from guards' mouths. But Gomez and a few of his closest friends are getting special treatment and extra food, so something's amiss."

"Milten told me you suspect Gomez could be working with Bricriu."

"Until a week ago, I would have called that insane," said Paul, "but I saw him and Bricriu talking in an abandoned tunnel. I couldn't make out much, but it was strange. Milten saw something similar."

"What if the prostitution rumor was started by Bricriu to explain why Gomez and some of the others were getting special treatment..."

"When they're really getting it because Gomez is smuggling Bricriu his own private fortune?" said Paul, finishing my thought.

I nodded.

"If that's true, and we can prove it, that will turn the others to our plan for certain. But how are we going to get that proof?" asked Paul as I tossed my empty tray on the cart.

"One step at a time. First, we have to make sure we're right," I said. "Right now, I don't know enough to prove anything either way. All I know is he's become a serious problem. We must all be united in this plan, and he's preventing that."

"I'll see if I can find out more," said Paul.

We parted ways, and I returned to my place between Mother and Stephania.

"What did your brother say?" asked Mother.

"Gomez is still swaying a number of the men against our plan. Paul and I think he might be conspiring with Bricriu, that the gold-hoarding plan is actually Bricriu's. I'm going to confront him tomorrow."

"Who? Gomez?" asked Stephania.

"Yes."

"That old coot won't listen to a thing you say. He's comfortable. Even if he isn't Bricriu's stooge, he won't agree just because you talk to him nicely. You'd have to do something for him. Give him something Bricriu can't."

"I'm giving him the chance for freedom."

Stephania rolled her eyes. "That speech isn't going to work. It didn't work on me. Actions speak louder than words."

"Maybe you're right, but I still have to try."

CHAPTER TWO
Blood of the Fallen

Maria

I knew I was dreaming when I opened my eyes and found myself cradled in the thick, tickling grasses of a lush meadow. I had never seen such beauty. Never seen grass. Never seen the purple flowers that dotted the landscape. And yet those words, "grass, meadow, flowers," came to me from memories of *The Words of Maya*, whispered into my brain. I could feel the soft blades on my skin, but I could not smell anything, nor hear the splash of a fish leaping from the pool of crystal-clear water to my left. Yes, it had to be a dream.

Gone was the shadow of death cast by wolves and foxes, and the simple joy of living filled me like a cup overflowing. But like all good things, there was an end, and as I rose from my knees to splash in the pool, my dream became a nightmare. The water vanished as I approached, as if slurped by the earth itself. The grass shriveled around my feet, and the decay spread through the valley. I looked down the barren slope and beheld a sea of rabbits. They nibbled at the last of the flowers, chewed wads of grass in their fat cheeks until there was nothing left.

"Stop! Stop!" I cried, racing toward them, but my pounding

feet made no progress.

A great hunger overcame me, forcing me to stop, clutching my belly. The rabbits below me diminished until their bones poked through the skin. They fell on their sides in the thousands, gasping for air. My tongue called for water, and I turned toward the dust-filled pool. A towering woman garbed in a dress of red satin stood at its center with Her four arms outstretched toward me. Her dress' gold-embroidered patterns of plants, predators, and prey shifted as She approached. Gold-thread rabbits jumped into hedges, chased by foxes. Embroidered bears took to their hind legs and danced. Golden bison dipped their heads to protect their young from wolves as She stopped before me. She wore a grand headdress of flowers, bones, feathers, and fur, all painted gold and fashioned like a crown, and I knew Her at once. Great Mother Maya.

As She bent to take me into Her four arms, I saw the silver sheen of Her skin. As I turned my head into Her bosom, hiding from the horrors of death laid out before me, my forehead brushed the obsidian collar She wore around Her neck, hung with gold ornaments.

"Do not look away," She said, gently pushing my face toward the dying Lepores, "for this is your world without predators."

I understood, as if our minds were linked. This was the circle of life, and our struggle... was eternal.

"But Maya, do You not see?" I said. "In the now, predators hold dominion, and while they grow fat, we only weaken."

"Yes, but in your heart, you do not seek balance. You seek to conquer, to earn back all you have lost, but you must remember, to tip the scale too far in either direction leads only to death."

I pondered Her words and the destruction and starvation around me. I nodded. "I understand. I will not forget." I bit my lip and steeled myself before meeting Her emerald eyes. "But something must be done. We must take a stand if we are to restore balance. How would You have me do it?"

"When you accepted their peace, you accepted enslavement. To win back your freedom, first, you must sacrifice."

* * *

I awoke to a haze of darkness penetrated by a single, filmy orange light. I slammed my lids shut against the pounding in my head.

My mouth was dry, and my body trembled, but I found I could see the barracks clearly. Mother's face stood out as a pale contrast to the dark walls.

"Are you all right? You were thrashing in your sleep."

"What time is it?" I murmured.

"Work will begin in an hour." She kissed the top of my head, patted my shoulder, and said, "I have a surprise. A gift." She leaned over the end of the bunk and plucked a bowl from the floor. "Gertrude noticed my bruises and worried I needed extra strength. But you need strength more than I, and I have already had my fill."

"Praise the gods, is that spinach? I'll have to thank Gertrude," I said, taking the spoon. I eagerly emptied the bowl. It was the best meal I'd had in months. A thought occurred to me.

"Mother, what do you think of... hinting to Gertrude about our plans. If we could persuade her and some of the kinder guards to help us, we would stand a greater chance of—"

"No. One slip and we're dead before we even rise up. Gertrude might be fairly tame as badgers go, but she's still on Bricriu's payroll. Her kindness will not extend beyond slipping us finer food on occasion. She has no reason to help."

"You're right," I said. "Besides, I wouldn't want to get her into trouble. And... I received a sign last night. A message from Maya. She visited me in my dream."

Mother's eyes went wide, and as I recounted the dream in full, her mouth dropped open. By the end, she was beaming.

"You are chosen, Maria," she said, tears in her eyes as she caressed my jaw. "You will be a far better leader to this clan than I, or any other Lepores before me. I feel it."

Blinking back tears of my own, I kissed Mother's cheek. "I hope I can live up to those words."

"Do you know what sacrifice Maya spoke of? Do you know what you must do?"

"I think so... I hope so. I'll need to speak to Gomez first, and then... we'll see if our Motherly Guardian favors us."

* * *

Finding Gomez wasn't hard. He usually loitered between the newer tunnels, pretending to work while his followers did it for him.

Armed with a makeshift knife of splintered lizard bone, and guarded by Lillian and Bridget, I planned to ambush the old man when the crews were dismissed for the day's final meal. The three of us watched as he approached our hiding place around a corner, unattended by his friends. We sprung out and pulled him down a side passage where he was cornered. He cried out, and Lillian and Bridget left me to tussle with him while they headed off his men with flirtation and feigned helplessness. A bony blow to Gomez's solar plexus left him wheezing.

"What the hell do you want from me, woman?" Despite his grey hair and pudgy center, he was a tall, muscular man with a commanding presence for a Lepores. He tossed me off and looked down his bulbous nose at me.

"I just want you to keep your voice down. We need to talk."

He raised an eyebrow at me, and then a lecherous smile pulled at his wrinkled face. "Oh, I see. You couldn't wait for the mating celebrations?"

I rolled my eyes, but inwardly, I braced myself to fight. The old man had a reputation, though he was known to use bribery rather than force.

"Don't be an imbecile," I said. "Talk to me that way again, and you'll regret it." I had my knife to his throat before he could react. With my other hand, I gave his testicles a good, brutal squeeze, and he grunted in pain, eyes watering. "I may be small, but I am not helpless."

"All right, all right," he said. "You've made your point."

I released my grip and removed the knife from his skin, but I kept it pointed at his face. "Listen here, you old pervert. I want to know why you're swaying the men against my mother and I. Why will you not back our plan?"

"It is foolhardy, and I have a better one," he said with a smug grin.

"Hoarding gold? Yes, I know all about that, but what I really want to know is if the nuggets we've been slipping you are meant to benefit us Lepores or if they're going straight into Bricriu's pocket."

"That's absurd," he said, but his eyes flicked away.

"Is it? Your secret meetings have not gone unnoticed."

"There is no secrecy to my meetings. Bricriu is overseer; he can talk to whomever he pleases. He knows I lead the men, as your mother leads the women. He often tries to intimidate me so that I, in turn, persuade the men to do what he wants."

I narrowed my eyes at him. There was probably some truth in that. "And you have held out against this intimidation?"

"Of course. I hate that beady-eyed bastard."

I cocked my head, unconvinced but willing to let it slide if it meant I could use him. "I see," I said. "Well, I hope that's true. I'm certain the Lepores who've been stretching their necks over the chopping blocks for your grand scheme wouldn't be pleased if they discovered otherwise."

He harrumphed. "My plan isn't nearly as dangerous as yours."

"Perhaps not, but my plan gets us out of this hell hole. But it will only work if we are united."

He eyed the tip of my shiv. "And what would you have me do? Die a worthless death and land on some predator's platter? That is likely how it will play out. You realize that, yes?"

"Better to die fighting than to live in slavery. Whether you die in a year, or ten, or tomorrow, it makes no difference. Every day will be the same. Perhaps you're okay with that, but are you truly going to allow your sons and daughters to continue suffering after you're gone? Would you condemn our species to this forever?"

"You have a way with words, but all this grand speech-making doesn't win a battle." I scowled at him, and he waggled a finger at me, continuing, "This all stems from that gospel nonsense Valorie's been teaching you. Do you honestly believe her yarn about divine intervention?"

My lip curled in a snarl. "They are the teachings of our ancestors. You are old enough to have known life before this hell. You know the old ways, and yet you would forsake them?"

He looked as though I'd slapped him and lowered his eyes to the ground like a scolded child. I grabbed his chin and forced him to face my wrath. I hoped to look through him, to see the man I hoped existed deep beneath the shell created in the name of survival.

"Your boys, our brothers, are itching for a fight. We hear how they bicker and squabble, unable to attack those they truly hate. We learned of their lust for freedom. But they listen to you, and you are turning them away from their goddess-given rights. You must cease your sniveling and be the man they need. We have to unite against our common enemy."

His face lit for a brief moment, and then his scowl returned. "And even if we escape—what then? The king will send his armies after us. And those lucky few you think you've freed... will be made an example of." He shifted foot to foot, his face sad and tired. "You will only turn the wolf king's attention on us and bring about more death."

"Even if he sends his armies after us, I believe in my heart that some will survive. It is Maya's wish." When he scoffed, I leaned closer and said, "You've forgotten the scriptures, so let me remind you of this: And Sammael told His sons, 'All the tools my brother, Khaytan, has given His predator servants, I have given to you. All you need to survive His onslaught is a heart of steel. And that, you must find within yourselves.'"

Again, he took pause, then raised his eyebrow. "Remind me of your name, girl?"

"Maria. But that doesn't matter. It will be *your* name those rabbits remember. If you show them you have a heart of steel."

He ran his fingers through his white hair. His scowl faded into a tight-lipped look of concern. "I will think on it." I sighed and nodded. It was something. "If you do decide to help, make haste in rallying the men. Try to steal more supplies, fashion some weapons. I will find you again in three days, and I hope to hear an answer." I raised the knife to eye-level again. "And remember, should you decide to continue licking Bricriu's paws, I will find proof, and we will see how your boys feel about you then."

I turned to leave, but he grabbed my wrist.

"Wait. May I not... steal a kiss?" I tilted my head, fighting back the urge to use my blade. I needed him, but I would not allow him to think I would use my body as a bribe. The urge to mate was stronger in Lepores than many other species, thanks to our animal sides, but I wanted to appeal to his human side.

"No," I said, keeping my voice stern but my face neutral. "I will give you something better." I stowed away my knife and hugged him.

A startled sound escaped him as my arms went around his neck, but I soon felt the tension leave his shoulders as he gave me a hesitant pat on the back.

"Three days," I whispered, and left him in the passageway, his mouth agape.

To my surprise, as I rounded the corner, Stephania blocked my way, Lillian and Bridget close behind her. She'd cut herself a makeshift pocket in her tattered dress to conceal her injured hand.

"What did he say?" she asked.

"Did he admit he's working with Bricriu?" asked Bridget.

"Did he agree to help?" asked Lillian. One half of her face was eager, the brow raised and the eye flashing in the torchlight, but the half marred by scar tissue stayed indifferent.

"He admitted no guilt, but I think I may have appealed to a side of himself he thought he'd forgotten. He agreed to think things over and give me an answer in three days."

Bridget and Lillian looked hopeful, but Stephania sagged.

"Three days?" she said, looking to her concealed hand. "We're already delaying the plan too long. Bricriu is inevitably going to catch wind of our secrets. Gomez might even tell him himself. We need stronger persuasion tactics."

"We aren't going to harm him," I said, pointing a warning finger at her. "That would only turn the men against us."

Stephania bit her lip and nodded.

"Maya is watching over us," I said. "It will be all right."

Resolve smoothed and hardened her face like stone, and I couldn't explain the feeling of dread that pulled at my gut.

* * *

I tried to keep my eye on Stephania, but the next day, we were placed on separate work details. By midday, sweat was pooling between my shoulder blades. I had paused to take a drink when I noticed a male Canum guard standing by the tunnel entrance. He seemed distracted, more preoccupied with looking over his shoulder than monitoring us. As I returned to my work, I kept an eye on him. He appeared to be a lookout. But for what?

Then Stephania stepped into sight from a tight, naturally occurring crevice in the stone. She was pulling down her dress, and her curly hair was in disarray, as if yanked by a rough hand. She was frowning and hunched, but when Gomez appeared behind her, there was color high in his cheeks. He pulled her by her arm into a swift kiss. Gomez nodded to the Canum guard. The hound changeling did not look at Gomez as something shiny exchanged hands between them. Gomez then headed off into the labyrinth of tunnels with his hand on Stephania's back.

Nausea threatened to overtake me. I clenched my teeth and went back to work, wondering what on earth Stephania's motive could be. Surely she didn't find him arousing. Had she decided to ally herself with him, still fearing the consequences of rebellion? Or was this her idea of "stronger persuasion tactics"?

When at last we were dismissed to the dining area, I sought her out, finally catching up to her one tunnel away from her destination. She startled when I grabbed her shoulder.

"By the gods, Maria, you sca—"

"I saw you with Gomez," I hissed in her ear. "I'm not as naïve as you think. I know what happened. What I want to know is why?"

She pulled me to a niche where we could hide. We crouched low, and she gave me a severe look.

"Look, don't be upset, but I've told you, grand speeches aren't enough to change someone's heart. We don't have time to wait for the old man to reconnect with his faith and his youth. So, I gave him some extra encouragement."

"Stephania, you are too young for this."

"No, I am not! My mother gave her body when she was my age." She pressed her lips together and huffed.

"You didn't need to use your body as a bargaining chip. That is never the right answer. We could have found some other way to persuade him."

"No, Maria. You are too kind and too idealistic to understand. You haven't seen as much of the world as I have. A few years back, my father orchestrated an escape from Caladon Mine, just our family. But rather than lead us to safety, he looked for an honest noble to help him, as if such a thing existed. He was sold to the Inquisitors, and the rest of my family and I were brought here. You cannot get something for nothing like the predators do."

"Does he... expect you to keep doing this, or was it just the once?"

She smiled sadly at me. "You know very little of men."

"Please, explain to me, Stephania. I'm trying to look out for you. You didn't need to expose yourself to this."

"Then why didn't you do it yourself? It's the only thing we have to give. But I suppose you are too pious. That's why I took control." She raised her chin. "It worked. He has agreed to sway the rest of the men in favor of your plan. He will tell you himself in the dining area."

I opened my mouth to tell her it was not worth her innocence, but the words stuck in my throat. She extricated herself from the tight niche and walked away.

She looked over her shoulder and said, "Come on. Tonight, we, at last, have a small reason to celebrate."

* * *

Gomez made good on his promises. There were more whispers in the tunnels, sharing information. All messages from Gomez to me or my mother now came through Lukas or Stephania. We swapped plans back and forth, and with Gomez's knowledge, our preparation efforts not only picked up speed but took new shape.

Any loose piece of rope, wood, or iron from our workstations was smuggled out and hidden—concealed in hidden niches, shoved in holes dug under large rocks, tied beneath scaffolding, or buried in straw. The guards had grown complacent and bored, and we took advantage. They never physically searched us all, and Lepores in the middle were never bothered with. Too much of an effort. We were able to smuggle smaller tools this way, chisels and small hammers, meant for more delicate ore extraction. We even managed to get a handful of pickaxes, stealing them in pieces from the designated pile for broken instruments and then repairing them.

Milten was one of our greatest assets. Gomez fashioned him molds for spearheads and daggers, and with the help of his fellow smelting workers, Milten managed to pour some of the melted gold into the molds and keep them hidden in a hole beneath his work station until they cooled. We attached the gold blades to firewood and broken furniture legs whittled into handles.

Under Mother's guidance, we women had already been studying the guards' movements, patterns, and habits, judging when and where we should make our assault. We shared all our information with Gomez, and I was pleased with his adjustments to my original plan.

I was less happy with his idea to keep the date of the attack secret from everyone except himself and Mother. When I protested, Gomez sent Lukas with a message: "We can't risk loose lips whispering too close to a guard. The fewer Lepores who know the day, the better."

I couldn't fault his logic, but I still didn't totally trust the old rabbit. By the next Sunday afternoon, two weeks after Gomez had agreed to help us, I was getting antsy. We had everything we needed. The longer we waited, the more likely the guards would notice the missing tools or find our hiding places.

I sat down to breakfast with Stephania and Lillian as usual. I could always tell when Gomez had made Stephania uphold her end of the bargain by the state of her hair and the hard set of her jaw. When she caught me glancing at her, she stared me down, daring me to say anything about it. I kept my mouth shut.

Halfway through our rice and corn, a voice made us all look up from our bowls.

"It's my birthday today," said Gertrude, the badger cook.

She was a stocky woman with strong arms and chin whiskers. She pushed the sizeable grey streak at the front of her head behind her ears and held out a plate. I blinked, sure my eyes were playing tricks.

"Happy birthday," Stephania stuttered.

"Thanks," Gertrude said with a wink. "I'm thirty-three. Can hardly believe it." She placed the plate on the table. There was no denying the smell. My eyes weren't deceiving me.

"Apple pie?" I asked, salivating. "Gertrude, thank you! But you shouldn't have."

"Oh, it's nothing. I made a big one... in celebration of me!" She laughed. "Imagine a woman having to make her own birthday pie. But I'm the only one around here who can actually make it taste good. Made a huge one. Those are the last two slices. You girls look like you could use some sugar. Share it however you like."

"No, I mean..." I glanced up at the guards on their balcony, sauntering back and forth with no sense of urgency or fear. "You shouldn't have. You could get in terrible trouble for this." Christian's face filled my memory.

Gertrude studied me with dark eyes, as if she was trying to

solve a puzzle. "I'll be all right," she said. "It's just a little extra food. If the overseer says anything, I'll tell him it makes you work harder." She winked. "Sorry there isn't more. Glad you're feeling better."

As she turned toward the kitchen, I half rose from my seat, wanting to tell her I was grateful for the food she had given me during my illness, but Milten coughed loudly behind me. I didn't turn my head. As I reached to cut myself a small bite of pie, I said, "What is it?"

The other girls noticed Milten then, and their chatter quieted, though they still pretended to talk among themselves.

"Gomez has given the signal. The time of reckoning has come. We strike tonight." And with that, he was gone.

I couldn't suppress my smile as I looked around the table. I gestured to the pie, where many forks hovered, now unsure whether to partake. "It seems Maya provided a special blessing to celebrate our liberation."

* * *

I could hardly concentrate on my work. I only filled one bucket—my last, if all went as planned—before the call to cease was made.

The guards inspected us as we turned in our ore and our pickaxes. No one dared smuggle anything extra today. As we filtered through the tunnels toward the mess hall, we retrieved our weapons and hid them under our clothes as the guards splintered off, chatting among themselves. As we moved in a wave toward the dining hall, the Lepores at the head of my column pulled on a hidden rope, tripping the two guards in front of him.

The Lepores closest sprang on the Canum. All around me, weapons were pulled free as Lepores poured into the dining hall from all directions. Short spears rammed through guards' chests. Makeshift knives slit the throats of the fallen. Stolen hammers and pickaxes swung wild, embedding in stomachs and bashing heads. The stench of blood was thick in the air before most of the guards even knew what was happening. I surged forward with the rest, crammed in the middle and funneled through the small passage, unable to land a blow with my pickax.

At last, my group exploded into the dining hall as the guards rallied. On the far side of the chamber, tucked up against the kitchen, I could see the wooden stairway that led to the higher, forbidden levels of the mine, where the guards ate and fraternized. I ran for it, searching for Mother. Instead, I saw Edward, and Donna's bruised face flashed in my mind. I shifted course and charged him. He was fighting Lukas, and a single swing of his sword cut Lukas' makeshift spear in half. A war cry bubbled deep from my belly—a roar-like sound I had not known I could make—and for a second, as Edward turned toward the sound, I saw fear in the predator's eyes. I swung my ax like I did a thousand times a day, but instead of striking ore and chipping rock, the tip drove home in the soft flesh between Edward's neck and shoulder. Jayson was never far behind his friend, and I threw my full weight behind my swing as I whirled to confront him, driving the ax up into his jaw. Years of hatred burst from my mouth in a feral scream as I raced for the stairs, swinging at any Canum who dared stand in my way, screaming until my throat was raw.

A group of ten guards rallied at the foot of the steps and brandished their swords in a wall of steel. I saw the lead Lepores hesitate and slow. I mustered another cry and raced to the front. As I pushed past the foremost Lepores, I dropped into a skid, one leg out in front, the other leg bent beneath me, and slid under the guards' swords. I swung my ax, breaking the knees of two guards. A third jabbed his blade toward my heart, but a golden-tipped spear parried it. I looked up as Stephania reared back and rammed the spear into the guard's chest while Gomez protected her from the side. As Stephania helped me to my feet and the Lepores swarmed around us, heartened by our actions, a guard's blade pierced Gomez's shoulder, but he countered with a devastating hammer blow to the guard's helm.

The hounds moved with skill, but there were too many of us. Blows from all directions overwhelmed them, and our path was clear... for a moment. More guards flooded the stairwell from above. I raced up the steps, calling back, "Come, brothers and sisters! Maya is smiling upon us! Today, we see the sun!"

I met a guard's blade with my ax, and the force of his massive arms knocked me off balance. I fell backward, but hands steadied me before I plummeted to my death. It was my brother, Paul, wielding a golden blade. He slashed at the Canum's wrist while I swung high and brought the ax down in a blow that split bone. Paul's blade finished the job, but blood from a fellow Lepores splattered my face with sticky heat. I wiped the blood from my eyes and fought my way upward alongside Paul.

The guards towered over us on the high ground. I swung for knees and hip bones, and Paul dispatched those few I tumbled. At last, we reached the top of the stairs. It was brighter up here, the tunnels awash in grey rather than black. I hesitated. There wasn't a single soul in the wide, branching passageways ahead. The guards' numbers were fewer, but we could not have killed them all already.

"Follow the light." Gomez's gruff voice startled me as he passed, clutching his shoulder.

"Maria! Look out!" Lillian called from behind. I whipped around and ducked a guard's sword. A lock of my hair fell around my feet. The guard, who was bleeding profusely from a deep gash in his face, didn't stop for a fight. He fled past Gomez and around a bend.

"Correction," Gomez called. "Follow that guard!"

We swarmed the tunnels in a unit. I turned the bend just in time to see the guard's foot disappear down a right-hand passage. Gomez, Paul, and I led the others after him. This tunnel was arrow straight, and the Canum remained in plain view until he zipped into an opening to the left. We burst out of the tunnel into a vast chamber, the stone ceiling nearly as high as the Cathedral... and froze. Here, the room was bathed in soft grey light, like the color of Mother's fur. It was almost too bright. The final stairway, the set new slaves descended only once, was blocked by a platoon of guards lined up in formation, armed with crossbows and a handful of muskets (prized commodities usually reserved for the sacrifices). Behind us, Lepores in the back bumped into those in front. War cries were cut short.

Lepores and Canum faced off in ringing silence, each waiting to see what the other would do. Adrenaline made my head pound and my fingers tingle. Lost for what to do, I looked to Gomez.

"We've come this far..." he murmured.

I set my jaw and said a silent prayer. I thrust out a finger and shouted, "We will no longer be slaves!"

Gomez and Paul roared their approval, and hundreds of war cries joined in, echoing off the stone. A wave of Lepores surged from the tunnel and filled up the chamber, but I had only taken a few steps when the muskets blasted and the crossbows released their bolts with loud twangs.

A bullet whistled past my ear. Paul buckled beside me, a bolt through his head. My cry of anguish turned into a snarl as I attacked the first guard I saw. His sword blocked my swing, sending a shock up my arm. I tried to recover and swing again, but this time he twirled his wrist as he blocked, and my ax flew from my hand. He drew back his arm and thrust the sword faster than I could react. I shut my eyes, but no pain came. A gurgling made my eyes fly open. The sword tip winked at me from the middle of Lillian's back. As I screamed in horror, the Canum pressed his boot into my sister's stomach, kicking her off his blade as if she were nothing but dirt beneath his feet.

He sneered at me as he bore down, but I was already moving, running for a nearby guard who was reloading his musket. I wanted the gun. I wanted to blow a hole in Lillian's murderer's guts and watch him writhe while I tread on him with my filthy sandals. I leaped on the musket-wielding guard, wrapping my arms around his neck to try and bring him to the ground. He flipped me over his shoulder, and the air was knocked from my lungs as my back slammed against the earth. I sucked in a painful, shuddering breath and scrambled to my feet. I lunged for him again, this time grabbing directly for the gun, but he smacked the butt into the side of my head, and the world went black before I hit the ground.

* * *

Cold water shot me into a sitting position, gasping. I blinked through the droplets at a guard standing over me with a bucket. Fingers from behind me twisted in my hair, yanking my head back, and another hand squeezed my cheeks, forcing my mouth open for the second icy draught. I tried to reach up and pull the hands away, but I found my wrists bound behind my back. I fought for air as the water filled my mouth and nose, making me sputter and shiver.

The guards laughed as I looked around. Lepores surrounded me, bleeding and moaning. So few. I searched for familiar faces and saw Milten with hands and feet hogtied. I instinctively searched for the faces of Mother and my siblings, and a sob was forced from my throat when I remembered I would never see Paul or Lillian again. I couldn't find Diane, and my mind taunted me with all the ways my baby sister might have died. Sarah, the last of my siblings, was to my left, too far to touch, but our eyes met in silent mourning. We had lost our bid for freedom.

The soldiers had gathered survivors in the hollow near the Cathedral. We should not have all fit in here. How many had died... because of me?

I searched frantically for Mother and, at last, saw her bound and gagged beside Gomez, her scalp bleeding where a chunk of hair had been ripped free.

I couldn't face this. So many rabbits gone. Guards dragged corpses through the hollow, removing clothes and tools before piling the lost brothers and sisters in wagons. Their fight was over. They were free, sitting at the feet of Maya. *If I die in human form, maybe Maya might grant me an afterlife as a rabbit.*

I looked down at my scraped knees, unable to watch the carnage any longer.

A *tap... tap... tap* led my eyes to Bricriu. The fox's black robe trailed the dirt floor of the hollow as he walked upright among us, methodically flicking his forepaws so that the leather tassels of the whip he clutched slapped the floor—a lazy gesture, as if he were twirling a cane on an evening stroll under the moons, and yet each slap was a threat of great violence. His snarl wrinkled his muzzle, his teeth gleaming in torchlight. *Tap... tap... tap.* Lepores shrank away from his steps. We knew what was coming.

"You have one chance to answer me," he boomed. "Who is responsible for this?"

He scanned our faces, teeth flashing. I raised my head, fighting against the fear that set my heart pattering. This was my responsibility. My plan. I could not let anyone else suffer. I opened my mouth, but the sight of the whip and the cruel, curved blade at Bricriu's hip made the words catch. Inside, I cursed myself for a coward, while on the outside, I trembled in silence.

"That one led the charge," said a guard at Bricriu's back. I recognized him as the man who had fled the stairwell, nearly taking my head off as he went. I did not know his name, but I had seen him many times. He was a sniveling brat who'd grown drunk on the power he was allowed to wield over us smaller, weakened beings. He liked to poke and prod and jeer. He was pointing now, at me, his face twisted in a self-satisfied smirk.

Many guards nodded, some of them chiming in with, "Aye, I remember her."

I could feel my rabbit side begin to panic as Bricriu turned his canines on me, wrath blazing in his eyes. He bore down on me, and I backpedaled on my butt until I bumped into a guard's leg and toppled sideways. As Bricriu drew close, I clenched my teeth and looked away, my animal side threatening to burst from me in a transformation that would surely end in the hounds and the fox sinking fangs into my hindquarters for sport.

A guard wrestled me to my feet, and I stared at my threadbare sandals. The hard wood of Bricriu's whip handle forced my chin up.

"You," he hissed. "You're one of Valorie's wicked spawn, are you not?"

I stared back with what I hoped was defiance.

"What was your name again?" he asked.

He bent closer, and his meaty breath filled my nostrils until I wanted to gag. All I could think to do was to ignore him, turn into a statue, and place my mind on Maya. I don't know what he said next, but I was forced from my meditation by the whip handle cracking against my jaw. My head spun as I fell. With my hands bound, I landed hard, my shoulder popping and my teeth smashing together.

His impatience grew as he unfurled the deadly length of his lash, took it in his teeth, and brought it down on me—once, twice—bringing high wails from my lips. I cringed, waiting for the third strike.

"Pick up this piece of meat before I harvest her here and now."

Two guards set me back on my knees. Bricriu lowered his face to within an inch of mine. "I asked you a question, Lepores. Who is behind this foolhardy plot? You led the charge. Did you organize it?"

My human side longed to scream in his face, "Yes! Yes! And I'm proud! I would do it again, but this time, I would find you and kill you first." But my rabbit side quailed at such close proximity to an angry predator's jaws, and I hesitated, warring with myself.

No sooner had my jaws sprung free than a voice that was not my own called out, "This was my doing!"

It was Gomez, kneeling beside Mother and his wounded brethren. He stared directly at Bricriu with no trace of fear in the square of his shoulders or the half-smirk on his face.

Bricriu gaped. He advanced on the old Lepores, whip holstered but fangs bared once more. He pulled Gomez to his feet by his tunic.

"We had a deal, Gomez," he muttered through gritted teeth.

Gomez flashed a wicked grin before letting loose a spit wad that landed on Bricriu's muzzle. A strangled cry escaped my lips, unsure whether to burst into tears or laughter. Gasps and snickers filled the room.

"Your promises aren't worth shite, Bricriu," said Gomez.

The fox wiped the spittle from his face and then gestured to one of his men to approach.

"Guard, hold him."

The tall Canum hoisted Gomez off his feet by the armpits so that he could not transform and run. Bricriu got down on all fours, his red hackles rising from the collar of his robe, and gnashed his teeth.

"Go ahead and kill me," said Gomez. "My people will never tell you where your pilfered gold is hidden!"

"I know exactly where it's hidden, fool," said Bricriu, paw placed against his chest in a haughty gesture.

"Do you?" said Gomez, with that same wicked grin. "When was the last time you counted your gains, milord?"

Bricriu's eyes widened, and then, with a murderous growl, his jaws clamped on Gomez's testicles and ripped them free with one vicious yank. Gomez's screams echoed through the caverns. I fought against tears, but my eyes welled anyway, imagining what he might do to me or, worse, to Mother and the others.

The guard dropped Gomez, and the old man's knees cracked against the stone ground. Bricriu raised up on his hind legs, holding the bloodied genitals high for all to see. Then he tipped back his head and scarfed them down his gullet. I fought back vomit. He licked his jowls and bent over Gomez.

"Tell me where it is!"

Gomez only whimpered through the pain, shaking his head.

Bricriu snarled in frustration. "I will find the gold. Even if I have to turn every one of your men into eunuchs. As for you..." Bricriu lunged again, this time tearing a hole in Gomez's stomach. Our patriarch writhed, back arching as he screamed, and then he fell limp, unconscious but still breathing, as his blood seeped into the stone.

I closed my eyes and sent a prayer to Maya for Gomez's soul. What had I done? All of these deaths were on my hands, every one of them. I thought back to Edward's face, blood spraying around my pick. When I opened my eyes, I chased the shadows of death away. I would receive my punishment. I had no doubt.

But I had to stay present to protect Mother.

As I expected, Bricriu rounded on her next.

"I suppose you expect me to believe you had no hand in orchestrating this, Valorie?"

Mother glared back as a guard loosened her gag, but before she could doom herself, I said, "It was my idea to join forces with the men, Bricriu. Mine. She knew nothing of my talks with Gomez until the plans were already in place."

"Maria, no!" Mother cried, the cold hatred wiped from her face by terror. "She's lying!" She grabbed at Bricriu's hind legs as he turned toward me. "She's lying, I tell you! It was me! My idea! All of it!"

Bricriu kicked her off with a blow to the stomach, and Mother crumpled, gasping for air. His eyes darted between us. He scratched at his neck with a soft, "Hmm." At last, he smiled down at Mother, and my heart caught in my chest.

"I think perhaps I believe you, Valorie. At least, to some degree," he said.

"No! It was me!" I screamed.

"Silence her!"

A guard slapped my mouth, and my vision went fuzzy around the edges as blood pooled in my cheek.

"I do believe you," Bricriu continued, grinning at Mother. "But your girl led the charge. That much is clear. And what better way to punish the mother than to have the daughter bear the brunt of both their crimes?"

"Please," said Mother, reaching for Bricriu as she lay on the floor. "She is not responsible. Let me bleed beside Gomez. We are the responsible ones. Spare Maria."

Bricriu smiled at me. "You will receive twenty-four lashes. And when the blood is paid, we'll let you... hang around a while and look upon all that you have caused." He turned in a circle, making eye contact wherever he could. "As for the rest of you, you've earned yourselves a dozen lashes. And tomorrow, you will starve."

A guard spoke up. "What about the children, milord?"

My heart leaped to my throat. I searched wildly for the children. They were tucked in the corner. I had made sure they would stay out of the battle. None of them looked harmed... yet.

"Oh. How could I forget? Shall we have them join my little symphony, do you think, Leopold?" said Bricriu, addressing the guard.

Leopold swallowed hard and said in a careful, clipped voice, "Children don't have good lungs, overseer, and all their voices are quite high. They might ruin the melody."

"Ah, so right you are, my good man. They will not join. But they can sit on their knees and listen to the music."

Bricriu clasped his front paws around the whip and trailed the lash side to side—that lash with so much Lepores blood on it.

"You vile monster!" I screamed.

"I'll tend to you myself," he said, eyes flashing with sadistic glee. "Guards! Prepare the rest of them for their parts."

All around the room, guards shoved Lepores onto their bellies and adjusted their restraints so that their arms were bound to their sides, their backs exposed. Bricriu bit my bindings loose as he crouched over my prostrate form. He whispered at my ear, "I dare you to try and run, little rabbit."

I couldn't stop the sorrow from silently slipping down my cheeks, but I made no sound.

"Ah, there are the tears. Marvelous." He raised his voice so that everyone could hear. "I will deliver her extra blows first. As each strike falls, remember this pathetic whore is who you chose to lead you."

My people's eyes were on me; I drew a breath and restrained my fear. This was my test.

Each blow burned like fire, fanning from my back into my limbs, roaring in my brain, but I resisted the urge to cry out. Even with his mouth, Bricriu could not muster the same strength as a human's swinging arm. I had received harder lashings before. I gritted my teeth through twelve blows, and the pain was beginning to make me nauseous. I feared I would lose consciousness soon.

"What's the matter? No screaming? Nothing to say?" said Bricriu.

I swallowed, my mouth dry as the stone floor, and choked out, "You deserve nothing, Bricriu, not even my spite. Do your worst. When this is over, I will be in Maya's arms."

"Wrong! You will die of a broken heart. But until then, you will be chipping rock until your lungs are choked with dust and your bones are worn and twisted. I may even postpone my retirement just so I can wake you every now and again to remind you of this moment." He breathed hard at my ear, but when I said nothing, he calmed himself and said in a sickly sweet voice, "Perhaps you will shed tears for your family's anguish."

He passed the whip to a guard and took a seat at the front of the chamber. He raised his paws. "May the symphony of despair begin!"

The guards began whipping us in unison, following their "conductor's" gestures. I bit down on my tongue to stifle my cries, refusing to give the fox the satisfaction. I stared at Gomez's prone body, his chest no longer rising and falling. Blackness appeared at the edges of my vision. I stared at Gomez's face. *Farewell, old man. We will remember you.* As the twentieth blow fell, everything went black.

* * *

The next hours were blurred mirages of faces and sharp bites of pain. Someone hauled me to my feet, slammed me against something hard, and tied my hands around it. My wounds burned, sending heat all the way to my forehead and fingertips as someone scrubbed away the crusted blood with a rough sponge. Blackness again. Then agony in my side, my shoulder, my head. Heavy blows from all around me. My hands were still bound, but this time they were above my head, stretching my body upward so that only my tiptoes touched the ground. Something rough. *The scaffolding in the Cathedral?* I could not be sure.

"This is for *our* fallen," a voice said, and I could smell meat on the Canum's breath.

The ache in my arms was more excruciating than the blows.

Another blow, and my sweet companion, darkness, overtook me again.

Warmth on my forehead woke me next, and for a moment, I imagined it was blood gushing from my skull. But then a soft voice said, "I'm so sorry, Maria."

Mother?

No. This woman smelled of flour and boiled cabbage and... apples.

"Gertrude?" I mumbled through a fat lip.

"Yes. Have some water." She picked me up, lifting my weight off my throbbing arms as she held a bowl to my mouth.

I choked on the sudden stream, thinking, *No, no, no! She can't help me. She'll be punished.* But I didn't have the strength to say anything aloud.

Footfalls made my heart race. I knew the sound of those claws scraping dirt and stone. I had listened for it intently each night we read from Maya's book.

"And what do you think you're doing?" asked Bricriu.

My left eye was swollen shut, but I could see the angry pull of his muzzle with my right.

"I'm sorry, sir, but it was my understanding you wanted this one alive. Your men haven't brought her any water."

"It is weak predator hearts like yours that gave them the false hope that led to this rebellion. You think I don't know of your favoritism for Valorie and her children? Did you think the guards didn't see the pie you gave this rabbit yesterday?"

"Ah, but I thought you liked them to have a little hope, over-seer," said Gertrude, bitterness tingeing every syllable. "So that you can take it away again and again—each time another small death."

"You have a fine way with words, for a badger," said Bricriu. "But that lip you have on you is far too disrespectful for my tastes. Get out. You're fired." The whip snaked its way off his belt. "Perhaps I should give you a few lashings of your own for violating my laws."

"Laws?!" said Gertrude. "You hold no law over me. I am a citizen of this country, same as you. I could complain to the constable about your threats."

"Who do you think the chief constable reports to, you fat oaf? Have you forgotten how the king punishes rebel sympathizers? I am letting you off easy. Pack your things! Be gone before noon, or I will use this whip to hurry you out."

Gertrude eyed the lash and wrung her hands. "Yes, overseer. As you wish."

I watched her retreat, bent and defeated—another victim of my failures.

"What should we do with her?" inquired a guard, grabbing my hair and placing his large mouth far too close to mine. "Can't we have some fun of a different kind with her?"

"Leave her. Do not soil yourself. Besides, I don't trust you not to kill her."

The guard huffed but released me.

"She will hang there until a palace representative comes to determine what to do with her," continued Bricriu. "I sent a letter to the palace yesterday. I would not be surprised if she's brought directly to the king's table before they slit her throat. King Emmerich likes his meat fresh." The two guards chuckled along with him. Then he gave them both a stern look and said, "So tell the men to look their best, and stay vigilant."

"Aye, sir."

So, the famed Lord of Blood Counts wants my hide? Good. I'll spit in his face for you, Gomez.

I hung there for what felt like hours. Gertrude's voice pulled me free of the turmoil in my head. As she was walking by, carrying her possessions on her way out, she came close and whispered, "Don't worry, little one. Hope is stronger than fear and those who feed upon it. Trust in Maya."

I nearly gasped. I had never heard a predator use the Great Mother's name, save in contempt. And then a great peace washed over me, as though I had been drugged. My pain dulled, and I took my first deep breath since they'd hung me on their cross. At last, true sleep found me. Blessedly dreamless.

Reginald

I hated days like today. A sliver of sunlight shone in through the high windows of the corridor as I trekked toward the armory; each pillar marked my position; each statue loomed above me, reminding me of battles fought and enemies vanquished.

On my left, as I rounded the corner, a black dragon clutched a lion in its serrated teeth. The sculpted lion's defeated eyes pleaded with me. My feet slowed on the rich purple runner laid across the cold, black marble floor.

As I locked eyes with the stone beast, memory and reality merged. The obsidian dragon melted away, blown by a stiff wind like grains of sand from a dune. I was back in the desert. Beads of sweat rolled down my forehead as the lion tilted its head. Its yellow eyes became radiant and alive, its body now flesh and blood. The Karluk sultan, leader of his Leo pride, slashed dagger-like claws at me. My hand reflexively reached for a sword that wasn't there, remembering the blinding pain in my shoulder, almost feeling it at the edges of my mind. I shook away the memory, and the lion became stone again.

The Leo's fierce roar faded, replaced by clanging metal. I continued toward my destination, the acrid scent of gunpowder filling my nose. A few knights and men-at-arms saluted me as they left the weapons hall. I nodded as I passed and then spotted Thomas inside the armory.

"A blessed morning and fine day to you, my Lord Ingolf," said my messy-haired squire, small even in human form.

I raised an eyebrow at the lynx boy, his russet curls threatening to poke his strange, gold-flecked green eyes. "Calling my first name is the best way to get my attention in battle. If you can't call me Reginald now, you'll forget in the heat of swordplay. Besides, we don't want the enemy knowing who I am."

"Aye, Sir Reggie, I mean... Reginald. Got your breastplate back from the blacksmith, and I did a good job cleaning it. I'd wager you can see your reflection in it." His abundance of freckles made him look like a child, though he'd been of age for nearly two years.

"Well, I'd say you're right." I squinted into the silver-plated steel. "I think I'll have you be less thorough next time, Thomas. I can see my grey hairs," I said, scratching at the chestnut stubble on my chin.

"Nonsense, sir, your hair still looks like fresh oak seeds."

I snorted. "You're a real flatterer, kid."

"I'm only speaking the truth. A man in his thirties doesn't go grey."

"Nonsense. My father was born with grey on his head."

"Ah, an early sign from Khaytan that King Emmerich would be a great, wise man who would shoulder many burdens."

"Right," I said, dragging out the word and fighting back a laugh at Thomas' didn't-that-sound-good grin. "Hand me my gambeson and help me put this on." I tossed the breastplate into his chest. I shrugged on the navy blue arming doublet.

"Not going to put on the whole harness then, Your Highness?"

"No, little lynx. I must rush. Uncle's summoned me for an execution. Another deserter." My heart grew weary as I thought of the many men I'd put to death—men who were bound and judged, unable to defend themselves as my blade came down. I tried not to ponder too long whether or not all of them were truly guilty. Uncle's word was law, second only to Father's.

"Bloody business, that. Can I come and watch?" asked Thomas, pulling tight a strap and settling the buckle on my breastplate, sounding all too jubilant.

"No! I'd rather you didn't." I didn't intend to shout at the boy, but the whole business turned my insides, and it was beginning to unsettle me that my young squire didn't feel the same. The young man was morphing into one of my father's pawns, swayed by his blood-soaked tongue into a love of violence and a disregard for the humanity locked inside all changelings.

"Well, desertion is a serious crime," said Thomas matter-of-factly. "A man should never leave his brothers to fight and die without him."

Brothers. The boy talked like a wolf. I might have smiled, had I not been concerned by the hard conviction in his voice. Had he been tasked with this execution, he would not have asked any questions. Uncle's word would be enough to convince him entirely that a man was deserving of death. But was I any better, if my questions stayed inside my head?

"Maybe," I said, determined to make an impression on the youngster, "but I believe you should give a man a second chance—hear his story and weigh the options for a fair punishment. If it were up to me, I'd create a penal legion for such things, a committee who would not be stretched thin, and thus not rushed to make judgments."

Thomas looked thoughtful. I, however, almost laughed at myself. *What big talk, Reggie.* Uncle would have none of that. Father wouldn't even take time to listen to the idea.

"Well, when you become king, you can do all of that."

I smiled. He sounded like himself again.

"Your cuirass is all buckled up, Your Highness." I gave him a look, and he said, "I mean, Reginald."

"Thank you, Thomas. Now my sword, please."

He opened one of a dozen iron weapons chests on the left wall and took out the blade. The smell of olive oil grew stronger as I pulled it reverently from its sheath, examining it. My sturdy bastard sword had a blade that would flex but not break, and the guard had stopped a pollaxe once. It wasn't a prized ancestral killing tool with history and an allotted character—just a cold, remorseless piece of metal.

I put it back in the sheath and strapped it around my waist. I kept my emotions at bay as I made my way to the courtyard. The weather was warm, not a cloud in the sky. Silence hung in the air. One might have expected the clanging of steel as knights practiced, or the turning of wheels as carriages came to and fro.

But today, the only sound was the cawing of ravens high on the guest chambers' balustrades that hung out over the grass.

Uncle Gregory stood between two rows of armored knights on the cobblestone path that wove through the courtyard and around the grand fountain in the center. When he was in human form, one would never guess by looking at him that he was only father's half-brother, a bastard son of dear old grandfather, King Bertram the Betrayer—*the vile bastard*. Uncle and Father were the same height, though Uncle still stood spear-straight while Father now hunched forward. They had the same harsh nose, hooked in the middle, but Uncle's bore scars of a tussle with an ox. The same light blue eyes, but Uncle's were brighter.

But Uncle rarely deigned to shift into human form, and today was no exception. He preferred his Lobo side. His fur was iron-grey, while Father's was white.

Uncle waved me forward without so much as a greeting. One of my sergeants held the prisoner by a chain. He was a poor wretch of a man, leashed like a savage beast. Uncle stood over the man on his hind legs, draped in his favorite blue robe. Elite changelings like him had mastered the dexterity of their muzzles and paws to perform more difficult human movements and tasks while in animal form, and so they spent as much time in that form as possible. Part of the teachings of Khaytan included embracing our predator sides, after all, though we also had to dip into our human forms when necessary. The luxury of such robes' tailoring was already a mark of high status in Cherbourg. Clothing that fit our bodies in both forms required quite a bit of ingenuity. The lavish robes that many nobles wore permitted us to change forms without inconvenience.

"Let's hurry this along. I have other business to attend to," said Uncle, waving a slack paw at the deserter.

"Uncle, if I may speak... I think we should at least hear the man's defense." I felt like a boy, unable to meet his piercing eyes when he stared down his muzzle.

"You know the crime he's committed. Take his head and be done with it!" he said, an underlying growl making his voice husky.

The prisoner perked up like a Canum finding a bone. "Please, Lord General, if the good prince would hear my plea—" Uncle's paw silenced him with a hard blow.

"Uncle, please let him explain his reason for deserting."

Uncle snarled but acquiesced with a curt nod. I waved to the man to make his case.

"My prince, Karluk raiders attacked our tower in force, and we couldn't hold them back. We were ordered to withdraw, and I followed my captain through the escape tunnel. They pursued us; it was our lives they wanted, not the tower. The cohort was lost, and I barely survived by diving into the river. I didn't abandon them; they were slaughtered all around me. I wanted to make it back so I could make a report."

Uncle's voice boomed with righteous rage. "Lies! You went to visit your family, not me, when you returned. You only came groveling at my feet when you heard I'd sent The Crimson Guard to retrieve you. This is unforgivable! Take his head, Reginald!"

The deserter dropped his head in shame under an alpha wolf's fury.

I knew I couldn't spare the man, but perhaps I could grant him some small kindness.

"Tell me, deserter. How do you wish to die?"

"Please, Your Highness, I wish to face the gallows and keep my body in one piece." His voice trembled.

"Impossible!" said Uncle. "Take his head now, Reginald, before I lose patience with you, too."

There was no denying Uncle; I had learned that from a young age. I looked upon the prisoner's face. It was covered in cut marks from a small blade. The Absolvers had broken his fingers and ripped his nails from their beds. Those hairless beasts and their red-robed guard raised my hackles each time they crossed my path. No doubt, they had taken great pleasure in drawing this man's blood. I pitied him—punished for putting his family above royalty. What might it be like to have a family that was worth such a risk? My hatred for my own flesh and blood only grew as

I drew my sword.

"By the grace of His Majesty, King Emmerich Jorg Ingolf, Bearer of the Crimson Scepter, and by command of High Lord General Gregory Otto De Draco, I, Prince Reginald Ingolf, grant you your end."

I would have told him that I wished for his soul to go with Khaytan, but I had never believed the Emperor of the Hunt should take every soul. This man's soul would rest easier with Maya, but I dared not speak Her name in front of Uncle. My steel sliced through flesh and bone, and the head thumped onto the fountain path.

Uncle flashed his enormous, yellow canines in a smile. If his small bit of remaining humanity hadn't held him in check, he might have licked the blood right off the cobblestones. Father would have done it.

I turned to leave as the sergeant went about disposing of the body.

"Reginald," said Uncle, voice soft with reverent conviction, "harsh though it may be, discipline must be kept."

His eyes were harsh as he waited for my answer. It would not be beyond him to charge me with sedition, so I told him what he wanted to hear.

"I understand I have obligations, Uncle, and I am always happy to serve our glorious empire."

"That's more like it. If you want to be a good king, you'd best heed the advice of your father and myself, and quit clinging to your mother's skirts like a hapless boy. Your mother is a fine woman, but she is a woman still. Oh, but speaking of Emmerich—he, too, wanted to see you. I think he's in the dining room. You are dismissed."

"Yes, Uncle." He probably wouldn't have batted an eye if I'd called him general, instead. My uncle saw me as nothing but a common soldier, a grunt, after my decade of service to my father's army.

"I do care about you, Reginald. You're as much my son as you are your father's. The stability of the pack demands each wolf's undivided loyalty. Without it, the pack will fail, and so, too, will the wolf."

I left without a word, abandoning the path to march straight through the grass. Soldiers stood on each wall, walking the ramparts and manning the main gate, but I kept my back to them. The upper terrace of the courtyard was a bloody place, and I used my father's summons to turn my back on all of it.

The grand stairway to the keep was to the right of the courtyard, and the white stone of the walls sparkled in the morning light. High up on the sixth level, above the balcony where my father occasionally addressed his people, two rampant wolves held the family crest, which could be seen for miles. Grandfather had often mused, "As long as a single stone of the citadel remains, our family will endure."

Behind me, the carrion crows cawed to each other, breaking the stony silence.

Pulling my glove off with my teeth, I strode through the Grand Entry. On my left, the delicately carved lintels of the doors leading into the Great Hall depicted the god Khaytan, a dark-winged angel in His human form, gifting predators with tooth, claw, and all of our other gifts which gave us the right to rule. When I was younger, I thought the prey bowed down with love in their hearts and laid their throats open in generous acceptance of our superiority. But life turned out not to match my childhood notions, and I no longer looked at the lintels. I needed no reminders of my superiority. We predators were the natural rulers, that much was certain, but the carvings spoke of more. They showed cruelty and greed, bloodthirsty tyranny and gluttony. And for that, I looked away.

I continued past the Great Hall and other public areas and climbed the stairs toward the family's private chambers.

Father was the only person one would find in the family dining hall at this hour. He reveled in sitting at the head of the table, not to fatten himself up, but simply to relish in the grandeur of the place. Its opulence surpassed all other rooms, marking it as the place where the most influential people in all of Kaskilia sat together. In the center was a long oak table flanked by thirty chairs. A great tapestry of Silver Creek, with Cherbourg castle at the center and the surrounding countryside, hung on the wall facing the entry. Behind the chair at the head of the table was a massive, hand-carved fireplace flanked by doors into the kitchen. The mantel carvings depicted a grand hunt, where wolves sank their fangs into prey of all species, howling to each other in the jubilation of the chase.

You could burn an entire tree in its guts, and yet the size of Father's chair put the fireplace to shame—not that there was ever a seat big enough to accommodate his pride.

"Ah, Reginald, at last you've come. Please sit," said Father from his throne-like dining chair as I entered.

He was in his human form. Some naïve foreigner might have seen him as a grizzled old man with a wiry white beard, but in Kaskilia, his presence alone turned lions into lambs. He wore an elegant cardinal robe with gold embroidery, and as always, the crimson scepter was on his right. I sat on his left, as far as I could get from his royal staff with its mace-like head.

As I adjusted my seat, he sipped from his chalice and spat. "Pah! This blood is stale. Did I not ask for fresh?!" He threw the heavy cup at a servant, who dodged it expertly and then scrambled to retrieve it from the floor as the half-congealed mixture littered with ice cubes leaked onto the dark oak panels. I could tell by his neck tattoo that the man was a buck who'd had more than his antlers clipped when he came to work inside the castle. He cowered as his cleaning rag brought him too close to the king for comfort.

"Forgive me, Your Majesty," he pleaded. "It's the goat you caught not two days back."

"Clearly you haven't stored it properly. Get me a pint of fresh blood right now, or I shall open your neck and have yours!"

"Servant," I cut in, drawing Father's eyes off the buck. "Please fetch me some white wine."

"At once, my prince." He bowed and left in a hurry.

At least he was safe from Father's wrath for now, but I sure as hell wasn't.

"What have I told you about the niceties with the servants?" he snapped.

"Sorry, Father. I simply thought perhaps I would try to differentiate myself from Your Majesty, seeing as I can never hope to match your prowess."

"You fancy yourself amusing, do you?" asked Father.

"On the contrary, Father. I see nothing amusing about it whatsoever," I said, meeting his eyes with a carefully honed, indifferent, almost bored expression that I hoped made me unreadable.

"You have a smart tongue. If only your head wasn't hollow and your heart too large."

"Not too large to prevent me beheading dastardly deserters," I said with a bitter smirk.

"Oh, you can accomplish simple tasks. Well done," said Father, bringing his gnarled hands together in false applause. "I have something more important for you to do for me, for the family. Can you handle it?"

"Yes," I said, forcing myself to hold his gaze.

"Good," he said, his raised, bushy brows suggesting mild admiration for once. "You do know the Marburg Gold Mine, do you not?"

"Yes, Father. I could hardly call myself Prince of Cherbourg if I didn't know where a third of our wealth was produced."

"One would think, but I can never be too careful with you, can I?" I ignored the jab, and he continued, "Do you know who manages that mine?"

"A minor noble. That cousin of Duchess Leticia Durand." I snapped when it came to me. "Bricriu Winterhall."

"Foxes are weak-kneed cowards for the most part, and this one's certainly no exception. But they can be loyal, so I've allowed them to manage our mines... for now."

"My task involves the mine, then?"

He nodded. "Correct. A messenger came last night with a letter from the overseer. Apparently, there have been unnamed difficulties. Since the messenger made himself scarce, I don't know more than that."

I sensed one of Father's violent outbursts coming and braced myself, but instead of shouting, he let a long breath out through his nose and spoke through a tight jaw when he said, "That is one of our most productive mines, we cannot allow the work to fall behind."

"I could look at the numbers, see if it's still working optimally."

"That's not important. As long as it remains profitable, it will remain open, simple as that. But the vague nature of the overseer's letter has left me uneasy. If something unsavory is going on, you must quash it with iron fangs."

"Not to worry, Father. I shall see what the fox needs. He's likely weaseling for extra supplies or a pay raise."

"I sincerely hope he isn't wasting our time. If you find Winterhall incompetent, you have the authority to relieve him of his position. And don't forget, you are representing me in this situation. I expect you to act accordingly."

I clenched my jaw against the implications. I had few qualms over bringing Ingolf wrath down on a useless or crooked overseer, but should the slaves be involved in whatever issues Winterhall was having, I expected they had endured enough savagery already. The tales of that hell hole were never pleasant. But if memory served, there was some sort of scandal involving an overseer when I was a teen. Someone important had gone missing. Another cousin of Duchess Leticia? Or was I getting the two confused?

"Forgive me, Father, but who was Winterhall's predecessor?"

"I don't remember, and it doesn't matter. Every worker is replaceable, Reginald. Don't devote much time to remembering their names."

Normally, I would have believed him, but his eyes had suddenly found something very interesting in the far corners of the ceiling. He remembered plenty.

"Where is that servant?" he shouted and bashed his fist on

the table.

I cocked my head toward the door and heard footsteps in the corridor. "Not to worry; he's on his way."

The guard posted outside opened the door, and the servant rushed to hand Father his drink.

He sniffed it a moment, then glared at the Cervi. "From what animal is this blood?"

"A bull, Your Majesty. Very fresh. The cook is preparing its meat for your lunch." The Cervi never looked Father in the eye. Father, no doubt, saw it as a sign of respect and servitude, but I imagined it was because the buck could see the bloodlust in Father's eyes, reminding him that at any time he could become a meal.

Father sipped, and then placed the cup on the table, appearing content. At least for the moment. "Why are you making your prince wait?"

"Father, it's fine. There's no rush."

The servant poured the wine from the decanter on his tray and held out the glass with his eyes locked on my shoulder. I tilted my head so that our eyes met and nodded my thanks while Father stared into his bloody chalice.

"If it pleases you, Your Majesty, is there anything else I may get for you?"

"No, go about your other duties until I send for you," said Father, motioning the buck to be gone.

The servant bowed to Father, but when he turned to do the same to me, he looked directly at my face. This was as it should be: prey happy to attend to their predator masters. I sipped a little of my wine and asked Father where Mother had gone.

"Ecaterina is visiting your Aunt Patricia, something about womanly affairs or some nonsense," he said with a bored drawl.

"In ancient times, womanly affairs meant leading the pack. We once always had female alphas," I said, knowing I'd catch hell for it but unable to stop myself.

"You can't help but lick her muzzle, can you?" said Father, his nose wrinkled. "Some traditions die for a reason. Your mother has all the responsibility she can handle. She is soft-hearted. It is the weakness of women, and if you continue to heed her over me, you will always be a tender-footed little boy, useful for nothing but putting on parties."

I felt color rise in my cheeks, and the sudden anger made my tongue brash. "If it is she who is weak, why can she summon the courage to visit Lothar when you cannot muster the strength to speak his name?" Though I kept my eyes on the table, I sensed the fury coming off him, but I could not stop myself. "I had made plans to go see him today. Can you be persuaded to come with me?"

His hand found my neck, and I barely managed not to drop my cup. His long nails dug into my flesh as he pulled me over the corner of the table, closer to his face.

"Speak your brother's name in my presence one more time, and you shall join him! Do you understand?"

The old bastard was still mighty, and the old boyhood fear paralyzed me. "Yes! Yes, sir!" I grunted, and he released me with a jerk.

"Good. Now finish your wine and be gone."

I rubbed my neck with one hand, my breath harsh in my throat. I dared say no more, so I drank the wine in three long swallows and made my way out.

I blazed through the corridors, fuming and ashamed. I wove my way back to the courtyard, where signs of life had quickly returned after the blood had been sopped up.

Servants unloaded supply crates from carriages, the boxes exchanging hands over the splotchy, darkened stone that would forever bear the stain of death. Knights paired off to spar against each other or training dummies. I approached a pair of men practicing swordsmanship under the supervision of Sergeant Claude, whom I had fought alongside in a few skirmishes in Karluk territory.

One of the combatants was a stocky man swinging a hefty broadsword. Even with a helm over his face, I recognized my childhood friend, Albert. The red plume atop his helm and the fleur-de-lis pattern on his tabard betrayed his identity. The other man—smaller in stature and incredibly swift, though lacking in muscle mass—was clearly a Vulpecula. He wore a light cuirass over the distinctive blue Grey Lodge uniform, probably a fresh graduate who had signed on for the castle guard.

Sergeant Claude saw me approach, mouth splitting wide to greet me, but I gestured for him to be silent a moment. I stood by his side, watching the two fighters. The fox changeling moved so quickly a skilled archer might have had trouble hitting him. He swung under Albert's mighty blow, tapping the knight's unprotected armpit with his thin rapier. The sergeant declared the Vulpecula the victor, and the knight raised his visor, huffing in exasperation.

"Come on then. I want a second round against him. I know I can beat him," said Albert.

"You'll have to catch me first. I guess you forgot your training," teased the Vulpecula, tossing a stray lock of hair from his narrow forehead.

"Gentlemen, your prince is present and watching you," said Sergeant Claude.

"Ah, good day to you, Prince Reginald," said Albert, reaching out for a hand shake. His heavy mustache was redder than his dark hair and reached all the way to his jawline.

"It's been too long, Albert. Are you still working for my uncle?" I said, grasping his hand.

"Yes, indeed. We fought a few battles against the Karluk raiders in the south a month back. Sorry about that execution this morning. Bad business, that. But there was nothing else to be done with a deserter."

"Certainly not in the Lord General's eyes," I said with a wry smile. "It's either complete devotion to the cause or none at all. In all things." In that, at least, I had always admired Uncle. He held himself to the same standards he held others. He was as equally devoted to his men as he was his own family, and he was a far better father to my cousins than my own had ever been to me... or my brother.

"What's your name, soldier?" I said to the fox. "I don't believe we've met."

His ears were quite wide, and his hair was a dark mahogany—oddly dark for a fox. Not that my fawn coloring was common among wolves. He had an impressive build for a Vulpecula, as well. Most were slight and lean. This one had some muscle on him.

"Edmund Hoffman, my prince. I'm in the house guard of Duchess Durand. She paid for my schooling at Grey Lodge." He bowed low, and with a graceful flourish that I was certain endeared him to the duchess.

"Nice to make your acquaintance. Please give Lady Leticia my regards when you should return to her. The Durand family, and Lady Leticia in particular, have always been kind to me."

"I will gladly pass the message, Your Highness."

"I have an errand outside the city," I said, coming to a sudden decision. "Would you gentlemen mind coming along as my guard?"

The sergeant bowed in assent. He and Albert had a contract to serve my family, but the fox had not made similar oaths.

"If there's a bit of excitement involved, count me in," said Albert with a chuckle.

"There's a small possibility," I said, joining him in laughter.

"Never get too cocky is my advice, Albert," said Edmund, twirling his rapier before sheathing it. "That armor of yours is not indestructible."

"Pah!" said Albert with a good-natured punch to Edmund's shoulder. "Do all foxes shy from a fight? Or are you just a lightfoot?"

"Too light for you to catch with your sword," said Edmund. That shut Albert up, and the Vulpecula turned to me. "I would be honored to join your escort, Prince Reginald."

"Let's hurry off then," I said. "I'd like to reach the mine well before dusk."

"Marburg Mine?" asked Edmund.

"Yes, the overseer needs my help with some sort of issue."

"You may get your trouble after all, Albert," said Edmund, trailing behind the knight as we walked to the stables.

My stallion, Jack, sat near the washtub, scrubbing at a patch of mud on his tunic with a soapy bristle brush. Chevaux, like most prey changelings, were bound to serve one master or another. But unlike most of their enslaved kin, they were given far better treatment. Their human necks were still tattooed with the equine mark, but they were given clean linens to wear and could freely walk about their master's land.

"Jack, leave it to later," I said. "Master needs you."

He grunted and nodded in approval. Chevaux weren't small animals, nor were they small people. Jack towered over me, long and lean, and watched me with dull, obedient eyes. We liked our horses a little simple-minded and rarely taught them anything but basic manners. When their masters didn't need them, they took to playing ball games and planting flowers, which their animal sides soon ate.

Jack removed his clothing without any sense of self-consciousness and tucked the items neatly inside his saddlebag. He got down on all fours and closed his eyes in concentration. His fingers and toes morphed first, the appendages curling inward and hardening into hooves. White hair covered the flesh as the transformation moved from his legs to his body, which stretched and fattened into a long back and rounded belly, with impressive, muscled haunches. His nose and mouth lengthened into a soft muzzle.

My companions were already waiting for me when I rode him out, fully tacked. I was surprised to see that Edmund had shifted into his fox form atop his Chevaux. His fur was indeed that same rich mahogany as his hair. He was striking riding upright, back paws in the stirrups, a stretchy blue doublet covering his chest and a light helm on his head, folding down his ears. Sergeant Claude was throwing Edmund disapproving, sidelong glances, but I found the feat impressive rather than offensive.

Marburg Mine was only three hours' ride from Silver Creek, but it paid to be secure whenever I left the safety of Cherbourg's walls. My crown was a golden target, even when it was not atop my head. I always chose my own escorts, never trusting that the infantry or couriers that Father or Uncle assigned me would be trustworthy and obey my commands in a battle should they have been given alternate orders by the King or Lord General.

"You certainly took your time with him, Your Highness," teased Albert. "I guess your horses aren't as disciplined as Lord De Draco's."

"You know the rules, Albert. No mistreatment of horses."

"Aye, true. But you don't need to beat or swear at a horse to teach it to follow your lead."

"I find them to be like subservient children. Stubborn as they come," said Edmund as the castle gates opened before us. "I heard there are clans of wild horses in the northern highlands who are quite clever and fiercely independent."

"You're not wrong. Although I caution you not to make the mistake of mentioning them around my father or any of his commanders. They've been trying to conquer them for years."

"No one wants to remember having their nose bloodied," said Edmund with a crooked grin.

"Aye. And Cherbourg has quite a few enemies," said Albert. "Thank Khaytan that the Karluk sultans are at each other's throats as much as they are ours, or we would never be free of war."

"Also something I wouldn't mention to my father. They may be prone to in-fighting, but they always unite against a common enemy. I often wonder if our nobles would do the same…"

"No noble is foolish enough not to answer King Emmerich's call for aid," said Albert.

"It's perhaps your father's greatest achievement, that after thirty years as king, no one has lifted a finger to push him off his throne," said Edmund. He licked his paw and used the back to clean the tip of his nose.

"I would be careful with the political discourse, gentleman. Even if no one but us is listening," said Sergeant Claude. He'd been so silent, I had forgotten the old man was present.

"No disrespect was meant toward our high lords, sergeant." The fox turned in his saddle and looked at me. "I'm curious, my prince. If you were to be crowned king tomorrow, what would your policies be?"

"I wouldn't know how to answer that, Edmund." I flexed my jaw and studied the reins, pondering that question for the thousandth time. "I would try to patch things up with the Karluk sultans. I think there are some good business opportunities there."

"What are the Karluks like? I've never come across them," said Edmund.

"Savages, but fierce warriors. They're primarily desert hounds, but they're so tenacious that even lions occasionally join their warbands. I came across one lion who actually led the group, along with a mix of wild cats and hounds." I shifted in my saddle, trying not to linger too long on that encounter.

"I hear those wild dogs have wolf blood in their lineage," said Sergeant Claude. "If it's true, they're a disgrace to it. They ought to bow to Emmerich as their king, chosen by Khaytan."

"Who knows, Prince Reginald," said Albert, "if you open some diplomatic doors, you might find yourself marrying one of the sultan's daughters."

I gave a halfhearted chuckle and quickly changed the subject. We bantered about which fur color was most attractive and our favorite cuts of meat as we made our way past the market, toward the northern gatehouse.

Outside the walls of Cherbourg, we urged our horses into a canter on the wide, snaking dirt path. Edmund rode steady as a rock, his front paws braced at the base of his horse's neck.

"Why do you ride in animal form?" I asked.

"More comfortable," said Edmund with a shrug. "Riding in human form puts a crick in my back."

"Then you're doing it wrong," said Sergeant Claude.

"Perhaps," said Edmund, unperturbed.

I found myself wondering if the explanation was a lie to cover for his mistress. I knew for a fact that the duchess, though a woman of the noblest quality, had wild tastes. She didn't hide them, either. I thought perhaps Edmund's strange ability appealed to her, and he'd made it a habit. But thoughts of the duchess turned my mind back to the conversation with my father, and I turned my head around to Edmund again.

"The overseer of Marburg, a man called Winterhall, is your lady's cousin, yes?"

"Yes, though she'd prefer to deny it," said Edmund. "He's something of a black sheep in her family."

"Well, I thought I recalled that the previous overseer, the one before Winterhall, was related to the duchess as well, but I couldn't quite remember how. I remember some sort of trouble surrounding the appointment, but I was young and uninterested then."

"Ah," said Edmund, voice full of melancholy. "Her name was Annabelle. She was Lady Leticia's half-sister. A bastard child, but still dearly loved. She vanished. No one has ever discovered what became of her. It still brings my lady great sorrow."

"I am sorry to hear it," I said, turning from him so he would not see the tension in my brow. There was no way Father had forgotten something like that. But why had he lied?

I sighed. It was fruitless to try and figure out Father's motivations, and when they did come to light, they rarely made me feel better. I tossed the thoughts aside and studied the road ahead.

Jack kept a quick pace, and the others worked to keep up. When the path grew steeper, we slowed, and sparks lit off the steel shoes of our horses in one of the more treacherous parts of the climb. The mountains were beautiful and brimming this time of year. Birds filled every tree, mixing their songs in a chaotic but cheery celebration of life.

When we slowed, it was to take the last long rise to the entrance. I gestured for Sergeant Claude to unfurl the royal banner. Three wooden guard towers rose behind a palisade that spanned the mountainside. Armed bowmen stood in prime positions atop the towers. Our banner gained us entrance through the wall's gate without question. A hefty set of doors closed off the mouth of the mine ahead, but three figures stood outside a low structure nearby, which I guessed was an office or small barracks.

Jack stopped in front of the red fox who spearheaded the trio, and our party dismounted. Sergeant Claude stowed the flag and took charge of our mounts. Albert and Edmund flanked me as I approached the welcoming committee. I was surprised to see that Edmund didn't walk upright, but stood on all fours.

"Are you in charge here?" I eyed the other, lighter fox, surprised to find he, unlike Edmund, was an elite. I presumed he must be Winterhall, for only someone of noble blood could have afforded such a heavily embroidered robe.

"I am." The fox spared me only an inclination of the head, but it was not his insolence which brought up my dander. It was his eyes, like twin snakes hoping to embed their fangs in my hide.

"Why do you not bow before your prince, fox?" said Sergeant Claude, stepping up, his hand poised on his wheel-lock pistol.

"I'm sorry, Your Highness, I didn't recognize you." The red fox bowed only slightly, as if afraid of toppling forward in his animal form. "I am Bricriu Winterhall. It is I who requested aid. I didn't expect the crown prince."

"Thank you, sergeant, stand down."

Claude backed off reluctantly.

"You do look like His Majesty," said Bricriu, and I could have sworn he sniffed me. "I suppose you really are his son."

"Why don't you show us inside and explain the situation," I said, beginning to lose what little patience I had left.

"Yes, please. There is much we should discuss." Bricriu pulled a ring of keys from a belt pouch and walked briskly to the mine doors. His two men helped him open them.

As we passed into the antechamber and were escorted through the inner set of doors, two things occurred to me. First, the surprising silence, and second, the stench: drying blood and fresh corpses. Bricriu beckoned us down a long flight of stairs.

"Why does it smell of battle here, Bricriu?" I asked as he led us through a short series of tunnels.

"Well, Your Highness... that is why I have called you here. I am afraid there has been a minor uprising." He stopped in a chamber with a high, domed ceiling and bowed his head toward me in what was obviously meant to be an apology, but it was lost on his animal features.

My eyebrows jumped toward my hairline. "I'd very much like to know what you consider to be minor, Bricriu."

Behind his head, I noticed a support beam and knew immediately why Bricriu was my father's man. Nailed upside down to the scaffolding was an old Lepores. As I walked forward, Albert stepped between the overseer and me. The tall chevalier looked at the overseer like a cat who had cornered a mouse.

Bricriu took a quick step back, and his previously effervescent tail drooped to the floor.

I neared the gruesome display and noticed the board nailed above the corpse: "Gomez the Hero."

"Am I to assume that this was their leader?" I asked.

"Correct, sire. As you can see, I have punished him for his crime."

"This was your idea?" I asked, pointing at the plaque. I tried to sound neutral.

"In some small part, yes. Although I did take advice from my guards."

"I should like to talk to those guards." I forced a smile. "What were the casualties?"

"I am sad to say that sixty guards were killed, and another fifteen injured." He held his paws together, his head held low, but I didn't detect any real emotion.

"How many rabbits were lost?" I steeled my spine against his answer. Losing so many guards in one engagement was reprehensible enough, but the Lepores were the primary assets here.

"Of the three thousand rabbits we have working here, only five hundred and twenty-one were killed before they gave up the onslaught, and another fifty or so received minor injuries."

I let out a breath that I didn't know I was holding—a shame and not something I wanted to report. But perhaps Father wouldn't care. All the rabbits who had died in animal form would be sent straight to our kitchens. They were probably already on their way. *What a mess.*

"You need to provide the prince with the names of all the fallen guards," said Sergeant Claude. "Every one of those men were Cherbourg soldiers. Their families need to be informed and their equipment returned to the army."

I tilted my head; my attention piqued again. Across the vast room, a woman dangled on a chain tied around a stone column. Her arms were bound over her head, which hung down in utter despair. Deep, purple bruises spread out from beneath the shackles on her wrists, and her shoulders seemed half out of the sockets.

"What about her?" I asked, heading in that direction.

"Well, Your Highness, I believe she and her mother may have been the real masterminds behind this mutiny, even though the old one over there confessed."

I crossed the space to examine her more closely. They'd chained her wrists to a hook hammered into the column, stringing her up like a slab of meat set out to dry, but her frail chest rose and fell. As I drew close, an itch in my nose startled me, and I was struck by an uncontrollable urge to smell her. I had never felt my wolf side intrude so prominently into my human form.

I reached out, hesitating a moment before my hand touched her neck. I pushed aside the ebony strands of her surprisingly silky hair. Bruises had overtaken her ghostly pale skin, never kissed by the sun. I breathed her in, my fingers stroking her stenciled rabbit tattoo but not knowing why. The scent arrested my full attention, filling my head until I felt dizzy. She flinched, and a quiet whimper escaped her lips.

Her eyes moved beneath her lids, and I realized she was awake, at least to some degree. She was aware of us... of me.

"Do not show her any sympathy, my prince. She might look fragile, but she's dangerous. A cold, manipulative bitch. The others follow her and her mother, Valorie, with something like religious zeal."

"You're telling me that a few women sent you cowering under your bed, Bricriu?" I picked up her hand, examining the lines in her palm beneath deep blisters and thick calluses on her fingers.

"That's quite telling." I casually turned from her filthy, broken nails to see his reaction.

The fox's mouth contorted into a panicked grimace. He tucked his tail around his leg, eyes downcast.

I thought I heard a muffled laugh escape the woman's mouth. From the corner of my eye, I saw a smile vanish from her face as I turned her way. I found my feet drifting a step closer to her of their own accord, found myself hoping she might smile again. I prayed this sudden, strange attachment didn't show on my face.

The guards, or Bricriu himself, had punched her, and the left side of her face was badly swollen, but her beauty was still apparent on the right side.

Remove your eyes from that lowly prey spawn! Remember who you are. Be a wolf!

I turned from her so quickly I tweaked my neck. That voice. Had the wolf within me uttered it? No... it was a voice I knew well but never before had it invaded my private thoughts. It was my father's voice. Not the memory of it, either... I didn't think. But how could that be?

I breathed the woman in again, more subtly this time, determined to discover what about her was so unusual. My nose had driven me my entire life, and even in my human form, it never failed to steer me right... until today. I could detect nothing special about the scent, only that it made no sense. Dirt and sweat and blood covered her, and yet I smelled none of those things. Was it mahogany? No. Did she wear some sort of scented oil? That seemed unlikely.

I caught the others staring at me and cleared my throat.

"Are you going to tell me you summoned me to put this woman to death, Bricriu?"

"That's not required, Your Highness. I can do that. No need for you to dirty your hands." The fox licked his lips.

He was trying to indulge me, but I didn't feel flattered in the least.

"So the deaths of her confessed leader and over five hundred of her kin have not sated your bloodlust?"

I still had half my attention on the woman. When I'd asked about her death, there was no reaction. But now, tears traveled in rivulets down her cheeks. Before, I had wanted to look into her eyes, but now? I wasn't sure I could face them.

"I'm sure you understand your father's laws more than anyone, my prince," said Bricriu. "The servants cannot be permitted to defy authority."

"If you had been more careful, this would never have happened." My chest was tight with emotion I didn't dare examine, so I turned it into fury as I growled, "There is only one kind of authority that compels people to such acts of defiance. And that is one of both cruelty and incompetence."

"Pardon, prince?" the fox babbled.

"A lot is going to change around here, Bricriu, and if you want to remain overseer, I suggest you listen very carefully."

"I assure you that you've had my full attention since the moment you arrived, Your Highness."

"First things first. Release this woman immediately. And have someone tend to her wounds."

"Pardon... Your Highness?"

"Did I stutter, Bricriu?"

"No, absolutely not, prince. It's just... not what your father would want," said Bricriu, shaking his head with his nose pointed at the ground.

"Albert?"

"Yes, my prince!" The knight sprang forward at full attention.

"Can an army march on an empty stomach or fatigued legs?"

"No, my prince."

I caught Albert's eye and signaled him, twisting my hands. In one, easy movement, Albert's brawny arms went around the fox's chest, squeezing him like a vice. Bricriu whimpered like an infant.

"Mercy, Your Highness," he said. "I am nothing but a loyal servant to you and your father."

I stepped up, chest to chest with him, and snarled in his face. "Do you see my father standing here, Bricriu?"

"No, Your Highness," he said, voice trembling worse than his limbs.

"Of course you don't. Because he cannot waste his time. You do not wish to waste his time, do you?"

"No, Your Highness."

"He has left me in charge of this mess you've created. Do not defy me again."

"My humblest apologies," croaked Bricriu.

I snapped my fingers, and Albert dropped the overseer on his rump. When he stood, I grabbed his muzzle and forced his eyes up to mine.

"Your incompetence has cost my family a great deal of revenue and valued soldiers." I squeezed his muzzle tighter. "I shall be surprised if you can even get the rabbits to work at all after you've turned their leader into a martyr." I thrust his face from me.

"My prince, I am sorry for all the slain guards." Bricriu bowed low. "It was the rabbits that killed them, and the rabbits who needed to atone for their deaths. I only punished the leader to discourage the rest of his kin from rebelling again."

"A fine job that has done. Fear, abuse, and exhaustion turn little profit. I hear no mining taking place. I hear only my father's growl of rage when he finds out you've completely lost control of this place. Under Father's orders, Absolvers will have your skin. Obey *my* orders, and perhaps you will keep all your parts intact."

"Yes, Your Highness," said Bricriu, cowering.

"Did I not give you orders already?" I shouted, making him flinch.

Bricriu gestured to his two hounds. "Pull her down and take her back to the cabin. On the double!"

"And for Maya's sake, be gentle with her," I said, and then nearly bit my tongue off. I had never said the Great Mother's name aloud outside my mother's chambers. Bricriu's ears flicked my direction. Edmund shot me a puzzled look.

"You will make changes around here, and quickly," I said, too loudly. "Whipping and starvation will no longer be tolerated.

When I return... and I will return... if I find fresh whip marks on any miner's back, I shall give you a few lashings myself."

"As you wish, of course, Your Highness, but... people who are not compelled to work will simply be idle."

"Then clearly you have no idea how to compel them, Bricriu."

"What are your orders, Your Highness?"

I considered in stony silence, weighing the options. If things worked out here, then I could repeat this with every overseer in the country.

"I hope you realize that you underestimated these Lepores. They banded together against insurmountable odds because of their hate for you. So unless you want to find yourself nailed to that post, you'll need new policies. Now, how many hours of sleep are they getting?"

"Six, my prince."

"Wrong. You are to give them eight."

"Eight?"

"Don't make me repeat myself. How many meals are they given?"

"Two. But I promise you they are fed well."

"Would you say so if you were put on the same diet tomorrow?" When he stammered, I bellowed over him. "Frail bodies cannot work. You will give them larger helpings and an additional meal. Now, should I assume they work every day?"

"They did..." He studied my face with muzzle wrinkled. "Until now, my prince?"

"You're learning," I said with a grin. "You are to give them Sundays off. It doesn't mean they have to loiter. Find them less strenuous chores to keep them busy for half of the day."

"But, my prince, the king expects me to deliver gold even on Sundays."

"You let me deal with him. I've told you he's a busy man. From now on, all your reports will come to me." I kept my voice confident, but inside that boyish fear threatened to overtake me. I had never gone behind Father's back before. It was rather exhilarating, in a way that made me feel a bit like prey sprinting away from the sound of snapping jaws.

"Please, if I may speak, my prince. If production goes down under your... sympathetic rules, I will be blamed. Rabbits are incredibly dim-witted; it's hard enough to get them to work as it is."

"Rabbits, goats, pigs... I don't give a damn what species is working this mine—you will obey my orders! Question me again, and your noble blood will not save you from my wrath," I said through clenched teeth.

Bricriu's hackles betrayed his anger, but he bowed his head and said, "Yes, Your Highness. My apologies."

"You have three days to replace the servants and guards who've been lost, and get everything back in order."

"I promise I will not fail you."

"Good. One last thing. *You* will take a spade and bury Gomez."

His jaw dropped, and I thought he would protest, but instead, his whole body sagged. "As you wish."

"Very well. Sir Albert and I will see you next month for an inspection. Or maybe I should bring Angus along with me next time."

Albert burst into raucous laughter. When he'd calmed himself, he said, "Prince, please, don't be too cruel with him. Look, he's trembling like a newborn babe."

"Who's Angus?" asked Bricriu.

"Have you ever met a bear, little fox?" said Albert.

Bricriu nodded, looking especially small.

Albert gave him a roguish grin. "Well then, imagine a bear... with another bear on his shoulders. That's Angus! He'd break your slender neck like a twig."

"That won't be necessary," said Bricriu, licking nervously at his jowls.

"Let us hope not," I said. I looked around the stinking chamber with my nose wrinkled, ready to be gone. "We'll see ourselves out. You have a lot of work to do."

Maria

A pair of hands fiddled with my shackles and pulled me down. There was a blissful moment of relief, and then my arms screamed at me as feeling returned. Strong arms carried me away. Away from him... the crown prince. I tried to catch a glimpse of him. I managed to open my right eye a sliver, but I only saw a vague silhouette before a second guard blocked my view. I had no face to put to his kindness. Not even a name.

I heard the barrack door open, and they placed me on a hard, straw-covered bed. My body ached all over, but I needed to rest. My mind, too, was tired, but it was so full of questions.

I had awoken to the prince's touch, like a shock to the neck. And he had sniffed me! My rabbit side had threatened to overtake my mind. He was marking my scent, as if he expected to need to find me again. My body wanted to recoil, but I could not. And then, as he began to run his calloused fingers against my skin, I no longer wanted him to withdraw. A strange sensation, like warm water cascading over my head, moved through my body, and I felt that same painlessness, that same calm, as when Gertrude had spoken Maya's name to me.

Then *he* had spoken the Great Mother's name! "And for Maya's sake, be gentle with her," he had said. But maybe I had misheard him. Predators only worshiped Khaytan. But the prince had spared me. Was it Maya's plan? At first, I had thought Her message of sacrifice in my dream meant convincing Gomez to sacrifice his greed for our cause. Then, I had wondered if She had meant sacrificing Stephania's virtue, but that didn't seem right. So, I had told myself it must mean that I was meant to die in the rebellion, leading others to freedom. But that, too, had proved false. So, I was certain I would be sacrificed now. That I would become Bricriu's meal. Yet, I had been spared... by a wolf prince who hailed the Great Mother. What did it mean?

I nearly dozed off, contemplating things beyond my understanding, but then I heard the voice I had begun to despise with every fiber of my being. It sounded even more barbed and poisonous than before.

"You listen carefully, Maria. Just because the prince decided to show mercy doesn't mean I have to! If you ever dare to attack me again, I will destroy you and everything you care about!"

He stormed off, slamming the door behind him. His hateful presence lingered, digging in like a parasite. I had made myself Bricriu's most hated enemy. The prince might have set me free, but he was already gone. How long would I last?

I heard the door again, a quiet creaking. Soft footsteps came to the foot of my bed, and I felt a heavy presence watching over me. Through my swollen eyelids I could only make out a radiant light emanating from a towering figure, but I saw Her in my mind. Her silvery face was full of motherly love, Her eyes like onyx orbs burning with amber pupils at their center.

"Maria, my child," said Maya, Her voice filling me up. "I can see that you are weary. I have felt your pain. But you are not yet broken. You must endure. And if you persist, a far greater reward than freedom will await you. The arrogant fox is irrelevant; treat him, and all those who would deny you your rightful place, as such."

Was She really here, in the barracks, or was I dreaming? I wanted to talk to Her, to ask Her of my destiny or maybe about the Prince of Wolves. But then I felt a sting in my arm, and my body went numb.

"Your destiny is yours to make. As for the prince, you will see him again. All will be made clear in time. Have patience."

As sleep overcame me, soft lips pressed my cheek—a blessing beyond words.

CHAPTER THREE
Family Ties

Reginald

By the time I reached Cherbourg's largest cemetery, the sun had dipped behind the palace, lighting it from behind with brilliant orange tones, as if the stone were on fire. I'd left my companions behind at the city gates with my gratitude and swift goodbyes. Now, I leaned over Jack's neck to open the black gate and rode him through the rows. Only a few nobles were buried here, but their seven-foot gravestones on richly carved pedestals screamed wealth in tones of white marble and gold inlays.

In the center of the cemetery stood a mausoleum surrounded by white roses. Lamenting angels and howling wolves carved all around the structure mourned the loss of the souls inside. But the Church of Khaytan promised the way to heaven could be bought with generous donations. On the back wall of the mausoleum, wolves danced upright in finery, blood spilling from their raised cups in celebration of a guaranteed rich life after death.

The eldest Prince of Cherbourg, however, was buried among paupers, and I urged Jack toward the humble slabs of stone denoting the final resting places of those whose entrance into the afterlife was far less certain. Rabbits and bucks lay among foxes and wolves here, from days of peace and uneasy treaties long ago. I wondered how many bodies were actually in their coffins here, and how many had become meals. It was generally frowned upon to eat a fellow human, but most changelings didn't dare ask a noble what he put on his plate—certainly not a blood count (though no one would dare call a noble that to his face).

Here on the unkempt side of the lawn, many headstones were unmarked. If Father had had his way, Lothar's would have born no trace of his ancestry, stripped of all ties to the father he defied, but Mother had bared her teeth and clamped down on what little power she wielded over Father. She had insisted she be able to find her son among the blank stones.

The lilies Mother left last time we came were wilted and crumbling. I tied Jack to a nearby gnarled tree and then brushed them aside.

"Hello, brother," I said, kneeling to pull moss from the etchings of Lothar's name. "I have done something brash. You would be proud." I flashed the grave a rueful smile. "I chose to show mercy and rationality where Father would show only violence and intolerance. Of course, Father knows nothing of it." I placed my palm on the grave, struck by sudden emotion at a memory of Lothar's face, smiling over his shoulder, his hand pulling mine. He leaped into the lake, transforming in midair to splash among the reeds and try to catch fish.

"I once thought you weak," I continued. "A naïve romantic who was too foolish to see the way of things. Now I am certain you were far braver than I shall ever be." I wiped a stray tear from my jaw and rose to my feet. "I miss you very much. I wish I could ask for your guidance. There was a woman. A Lepores. She... confused me." I sighed. "Perhaps you were right. Perhaps we changelings are kindred spirits—people cursed to obey a wild nature buried within us. I... I want to be more. I want Cherbourg to be more. But I shall have to wait for my time, I suppose."

I opened my mouth once more and closed it, clearing my throat. My stomach rumbled. Maybe I could feed the human side of me with some cooked vegetables, and Father wouldn't notice. Perhaps ask the cook to fry some mushrooms with flour and crumbs and pretend they were meatballs. I did not have to be a wolf at all times.

"I'm sorry to leave you again, brother. But I promise I'll come back with Mother sometime soon. Maybe Isolde will come, too." I smiled at the tombstone and then felt foolish. He could not see me. I hoped perhaps, though, that he could hear me. If not... then I was truly alone.

* * *

When I finally returned to the castle and asked for Father, I found he was once again holed up with bishops and Absolvers. Sometimes the pope joined in, plotting new raids and grand celebrations of Khaytan. The raids intimidated the commoners into following and giving to the faith, and the festivals courted and bribed nobles to do the same. I shuddered to think of the heinous plans that passed over lips in that room. The Absolvers' bloodlust matched Father's, and there was a new raid every few months. I couldn't comprehend why. It wasn't as though anyone was fool enough to dispute that Khaytan ruled the heavens, at least not aloud. But Father had to keep his paw at the throat of resistance.

Mother had not returned from her visit with Aunt Patricia, so I began my letters to the families of the deceased guards.

A servant interrupted to announce that my parents had returned and that dinner was to be served.

Entering the dining room, I found my parents and sister all in human form, cleaning their hands while waiting for the food to arrive.

Mother looked up with a smile for me. She wore her favorite malachite satin dress and a silver circlet on her head. "Reginald, darling, I haven't seen you all day."

"Hello, Mother," I said as I embraced her.

Though her wolf's fur was still a marvelous shade of gold, her human features had withered and wrinkled faster than her time. Her blond hair had softened and was punctuated by equal amounts of goose-down grey, a result of being married to Father, no doubt. Her smile lines weren't nearly as pronounced as the crow's feet around her weary eyes or the creases in her forehead from scrunching her brow in worry. But age could not truly damage her beauty.

Isolde spared me only a brief glance before her eyes found Father again. She was the spitting image of Mother in her youth, a charming girl with golden hair, but that was where the similarities ended. For all her nobility, Mother was distinctly humble, whereas Isolde always appeared in overly embellished dresses and jewelry. Father's idea, naturally.

Father stared out the window, ignoring us all.

"Hello, Father," I prodded, hoping to get the mine business behind me as quickly as possible, before I forgot my rehearsed responses.

He grunted, eyes never leaving the window. I sat next to Mother, perplexed. I had expected him to want a full report. He seemed distracted. Had the eminent clerics managed to upset him?

Following Father's example, we ate our meal in silence, until the scratching of the forks on plates and the subtle sounds of swallowing began to grate on my nerves.

"How is Aunt Patricia fairing, Mother?" I ventured.

"She is keeping well. She told me she still goes hunting from time to time." Mother tittered. "She's younger than I am, for certain."

"I pity any wild animal or prey changeling caught in her trap," I said with a sideways grin.

"Do you now?" Father snapped, venom dripping off the words. He turned slowly to glare at me.

"You misunderstand me, Fa—"

"Tell me, son, how did your trip go?" He said it calmly enough, but he was a powder keg waiting to blow.

"Very well. Sir Albert Truman and one of Duchess Leticia's men accompanied me."

"Were you planning on giving me your report after dinner

then?"

"I suppose, unless you'd like to hear it right now."

He folded his hands against his chest. "I'm waiting."

I steeled myself, pondering how I might blaze past the beginning before he truly exploded.

"The matter was more severe than the overseer's letter suggested."

His eyes flashed, and I took a long breath so that I could get the next part out in a rush. "There was a minor insurrection, but the overseer swiftly put it down. I provided him with explicit instructions for restoring productivity. I also made sure he understood our displeasure with him, and I made it clear that if my instructions were not followed to the letter, he would feel the full wrath of the crown. He has assured me he will get everything back in order soon."

"I see..." Father looked away, but I caught that unfamiliar look of approval tug at his mouth before he did. He drummed his fingers on the table. "Details?" he said, meeting my eyes again.

"Well, sadly, sixty guards have lost their lives. I've started writing personal letters of condolence to their families."

"So, a bunch of rabbits managed to kill sixty well-trained watchdogs? How did this happen?"

"I believe they lost focus, grew lax and overly confident in their daily routine. But I told the overseer to make sure the guards get enough rest. I also told him I wanted the rabbits' quarters checked nightly, every board overturned. I made it clear the extra effort is necessary after such a costly mistake, and I'm certain I got my point across."

"Costly? Costly?! Ha, that's an understatement and a half if I ever heard one. I ought to have that fox's head on a pike!" He banged the table, splashing blood over the lip of his chalice onto the white tablecloth.

"Emmerich, please, calm yourself. It's not as if a few days of lost mining will make paupers of us," said Mother.

I cringed, wishing she hadn't gotten involved.

"If I want your opinion, woman, I will ask for it," he growled.

"If you wish to eat your fill each day in fine silks and jewelry, you will not question how I govern my assets."

"If I must forgo silks for a day, I think I shall survive," she sniffed.

"Don't take that sarcastic tongue to me, Ecaterina! You know nothing of maintaining an empire. Even the smallest of rebellions must be annihilated. We must wipe out any trace of it, any whisper, with fire and brimstone if necessary."

"And yet you remain surprised each time they rise up against you. Will you never learn?"

"Hold your tongue until I address you!"

I opened my mouth to cut in before Father truly exploded, but Isolde swooped in like a vulture who'd smelled rotting flesh. "Well I, for one, think we should do everything in our power to get that mine back in working order. Mother may survive a day without her silks, but I dare not even entertain the thought," she said with a simpering smile. "Which reminds me..." She turned to Father with golden eyelashes veiling her irises. "Father Dearest, I need a new designer. The old one's styles have grown so boring. I absolutely must enrich my wardrobe before the festivals next month."

I struggled to keep down my roast pig as Father grinned—a crooked, half-smile full of yellowed teeth that looked more like a wolf snarling out of the side of its mouth—and said, "When have I ever refused you, darling? Has that old tailor offended you? How would you have him dealt with?"

"Oh, dismissal shall be punishment enough, Father," said Isolde with a flippant wave. "He has not overstepped his bounds, but you know how things are. Once changelings find themselves working for the royal family, they suddenly think they need not improve themselves anymore. I really can't explain it."

As if she has any real talents, I thought as I forced down the last of my meal with a gulp of wine. It was time to make myself scarce before I said something I'd regret.

"Father, I'd like to be excused to finish writing my letters."

"We are still eating, Reginald," said Father, peeling his eyes from Isolde with a scowl.

I inclined my head, mouth shut tight. I had to choose my battles wisely. I sat stiff as Father and Isolde struck up a conversation of the upcoming festivals in celebration of when Khaytan was born to Mother Maya.

As I slumped back in my chair, Mother cleared her throat to get my attention. "Did you go to visit Lothar, Reginald?" she said softly, and my heart skipped a beat.

Father's words cut off as if his throat was slashed. His eyes bored into Mother, his lip curling to reveal his canines.

Each word was low and careful and brimming with fury. "You dare speak his name?"

I sensed a transformation coming on, and a horrible image of the great, white wolf leaping across the table to sink his fangs in Mother's neck drained the color from my face.

"Mother, I think it best to apologize," I said.

"No, I will not, Reggie," said Mother, raising her chin and setting down her fork. "Emmerich, just because you wish to forget our boy does not mean I will continue to fear speaking his name in my home. I was not speaking to you. You need not listen. You rarely do."

"Restrain your tongue while I can still restrain my fist, Ecaterina. My word is law, and I say that traitor is no longer our son."

"You cannot erase him like all your other failures!" screamed Mother, slamming her fork on the table as tears rushed down her cheeks. "I won't allow it. Do what you wish, but remember, I am not a peasant whore you brought in off the street. I am of noble blood, and I am your queen." She glanced between Isolde and me, both of our jaws dangling like idiots. "You are both excused. Your father and I have much to discuss."

"You're not going anywhere," said Father, lunging over the table to jab his knife and fork at us. "There is nothing to discuss. This matter ends here. Now. I will hear no more of it."

"Oh, I am certainly not going anywhere," said Isolde through a titter. "I want to watch this."

"Isolde," I said, flashing her a warning look.

"What?! I can't believe she said any of those things. I wish to see what happens. A lady should never disobey or argue with her husband."

Mother withered. Isolde stared on, as though Mother were a wounded prey animal, eyes sparkling as if she were about to lick her chops.

"At least one of my pups was born with a brain," snarled Father.

I slammed my fists on the table and toppled my chair as I rose. I stormed around the table and yanked Isolde from her seat.

"You will do as Mother says for once," I said. "This does not concern us."

"Stop that! Let me go this instant, Reggie!" she shouted as I dragged her from the dining room.

She beat at my hand gripped around her elbow and tried to plant her feet, but I led her into a secluded corridor.

"What do you think you're doing, aggravating things like that?! Do you want to see Mother hurt?"

"Not at all, Reggie." I let her yank her arm free, and she adjusted her dress with a haughty sniff. "But, if Mother's fool enough to argue with Father, she's going to lose. And I'm not going to hold her side."

"This isn't about picking sides, Isolde. You should be helping me mollify situations like that, not feeding Father's pride and sitting back with a smile each time he explodes at someone else. You're acting like a stupid little child, and until you start thinking about someone other than yourself, you'll never be anything else."

"Oh, *I'm* stupid?" she said, pressing her fingertips to her ornamented bosom with a tinkling laugh. "You say it's not about picking sides, but you've been fighting Father—and losing—for years, Reggie. If you think I'm going to follow your example, you're denser than I thought. He loves me. I have the most powerful changeling in all of Kaskilia wrapped around my finger." She twirled her pinkie with a sly grin.

"You're blind as well as stupid if you think Father loves you,

Isolde. He loves no one. Father views you as little more than a bar of gold or a bag of diamonds: beautiful, precious, inanimate, and valuable. He doesn't love you; he owns you. You're a pampered slave, and he will sell you to the highest bidder."

"Your jealousy is so delicious, brother," she said, leaning toward my face and licking her lips, her eyes cold as gemstones. "Do please tell me more."

My stomach turned, and I recoiled from her, my fingers twitching to strike her.

"You are absolutely incorrigible. You're just like Father. You only care about yourself!"

"Mother ought to have learned to take care of herself by now. I'm not going to help her dig her own grave. She grows duller and denser with each passing year."

"How dare you disrespect your mother that way?!" I said, my anger jiggling the knob of the locked door inside my head. My wolf half paced on the other side, licking his jowls, eager to be freed.

"How dare you disrespect your father?" she shot back. "You prod at him like a defiant little boy angling for his attention." A wicked grin turned her eyes feral. "Or do you actually think you might take the throne from him?" She leaned in again and whispered, "Are you planning something, brother? Should I tell Father?"

"Everything I do is because I love this family, unlike you, Isolde." I sneered back at her. "And for all the times Father and I have argued, he actually cares for me more than you. Do you want to know why?"

"Ha, this ought to be entertaining."

"Because he actually bothers to give me advice. He throws me to hungry wolves, so I can rise up and lead them. I've learned from the misery of the world, whereas you, my sheltered sister, know nothing!"

Her cheeks reddened, and for a moment, she looked truly hurt. Then her face shifted, and if she'd been in her wolf form, I might have covered my throat.

"Why should I care about the messes of the world? All I need to do is find myself a doting husband to care for me."

"You think Father will let you choose?" Now it was my turn to laugh. "He will select one of his political allies, and you will have no say. And if you think any man Father deigns worthy will not abuse you and treat you like his property, then you are more naïve than even I imagined."

She leaned in again, hatred sharpening her face, and snarled, "When I tell Father about this, you will be apologizing to me... if you don't end up like Lothar."

The wolf inside burst from his cage. My hand struck Isolde's face before I knew what I had done, the sharp smack echoing off the stone. I felt the change trying to overtake me, my wolf side begging to taste her flesh, but I choked it down and retained my humanity.

She gaped at me with her hand on her cheek. A thin line of blood trickled from her mouth, and furious tears poured down her face, running lines in her cosmetics. A stab of guilt pierced my heart, dulling the anger roaring in my brain.

"How dare you strike me?" she fumed.

"You deserved it," I said, breathing hard through my nose.

"Did Mother Dearest teach you that? She's the only person you listen to."

I didn't respond, trying to compose my racing mind. What had I done?

"The both of you will be sorry," said Isolde. "You've chosen the wrong side, Reginald, and I can't wait to see it cost you everything."

My rage flared again. "I hope the husband you're waiting on is as cold and selfish as Father. Then maybe you'll understand what Mother endures every day."

I turned away before she could retort and stalked down the hall. She shouted something at me, but my ears were ringing too loud to hear. I looked down at my hand, my palm still tingling with the force of the blow.

I am no better than Father, I thought, and the weight of the idea threatened to bring me to my knees as I stumbled toward my chambers.

My animal side, riled and impatient, called to me as I threw open the door to my bedroom. I slipped into my loose white linens before allowing the change to take over. Though I was far from a scrawny boy as a human, my wolf form felt more powerful, the muscles harder and more in sync. My fur was two shades lighter than my human hair—an unusual, coppery brown. Night had fallen, and Kaskilia's two moons were out, the lesser partially covered by clouds, and I sat by the window, my tail swishing with pent-up energy.

I threw back my head in a howl. But instead of making me feel powerful and connected, my attempt sounded mournful and lonely. A few wolves answered, their calls proud and confident.

"Sorry, brothers, not tonight," I said, unable to muster another call.

I stared into the starless night until a knock came at my door. "Who is it?"

"It's me, Reggie," came Mother's voice.

I rushed to lift the latch with my nose. My heart sank, and a low growl filtered through my fangs. A darkening bruise spread from her left eye down her cheekbone.

With a melancholy laugh and a dip of her head, she said, "I lost another one."

"I should not have left you," I said, moving aside to let her in. "I am sorry, Mother. Isolde was..." I cut off with a snarl, disgusted with my sister, but also myself.

"Please don't be angry with your sister," she said as she sat on the bed. "It is I who failed her. I was so worried your father would twist *your* heart into a shape to match his that I gave all of my time and my teachings to you and forgot to tend to Isolde's heart."

"Mother, you cannot blame yourself," I said, giving her bruise a soft lick. "Isolde has made her own choices. I only hope with time that she will see what she has become. But I fear I didn't help tonight."

"You cannot change a person in a day, Reggie."

"No, I... I struck her, Mother."

Mother's eyes grew wide, and she breathed, "Reginald," in a voice so full of disappointment that I rushed to explain myself, my chest aching with guilt.

"I never meant to. She said horrible things about you and Lothar, and I couldn't restrain myself." I heard my babbling, words of a scolded child, and stopped myself. I heaved a great sigh and hung my head. "I am no better than him. I tell myself I am, but I am not."

"Reggie, you are very different from Emmerich," she said, placing her hand on my head.

"Yes, I'm worse. I talk of change and tolerance, yet I do nothing to bring about that change. I lose my temper, just as he does. At least Father is consistent. Whether noble or terrible, intelligent or deceiving, his actions are done with purpose."

"Your father may have great purpose in all he does, but he has little else, Reginald. There is no love in his world, and despite his obsession with the Church of Khaytan and those vile Absolvers, there is little faith, either. He seeks only the power the church can give him in his constant conquests. He seeks power over all, and yet he has turned his back on Maya, who is the true ruler of all he covets. One day, I fear he will be punished most severely, and there will be nothing you nor I can do to help him."

"I don't know why you would even wish to help him when that time comes."

"I love your father, Reginald, as I know you do. He has always been flawed, but he was not always so cruel. Before he took the throne and those hairless priests..." She shook her head and sighed. "The man I married disappears more every day. But you must not do as your brother did and defy him, Reginald. Do you understand? You must take the throne when he is gone and set right all that he has done. Do not incur his wrath for my sake."

"If he finds out what I did in the mine today, I will incur his wrath for my own sake."

"What did you do?" she said, fear deepening her age lines.

"I spared a slave girl."

"By the Great Mother, Reginald, one girl? You did this because of the plight of one girl? Pleasing to the eye, was she?"

"I never said that," I said, but my blustering and snorting likely gave me away. "I implemented more favorable working conditions for the entire mine."

"If you are that starved for female companionship, there are plenty of eligible women in the kingdom. Perhaps Duchess Leticia can introduce you to her younger cousin, Natalia. I hear she's quite well-traveled and loves painting."

I rolled my eyes. "Even if I had an interest, Mother, which I assure you I don't, Father would never allow such a match. She is a fox, and there would be a chance we would have a purely human child. I have no issue with such a thing, but Father will balk at even the slightest chance of it." I scoffed and added, "Besides, she's not rich enough to be a suitable political advancement for him." Mother started to speak, but I cut her off, saying, "No, I'd rather be alone forever than force a woman to love me and pretend I love her."

"But you will dig yourself a grave next to your brother for a slave girl?" said Mother, voice choked with tears.

"The overseer of Marburg will report to me now. If all goes well, Father will never know, and I will have taken steps toward the change I have thus far only envisioned in wistful daydreams."

Mother stared at me for a long time. The fear stayed in her eyes, but her jaw showed resolve as she, at last, said, "Well, if that is how you feel, then I shall not try to steer you from this path. But I will caution you again. Tread lightly. Your father is tough as boar hide, but he is an old man. There will be time to change the world when you sit upon the throne."

"If he has not destroyed it first."

She scratched at the nape of my neck, and I could not stop my foot from thumping the bed. She laughed, but quickly grew morose. "I must go. Your father will be waiting for me."

"Please don't," I said. "Let him stew in his anger by himself and save yourself from further violence. Sleep here in my chambers tonight. There is more than enough room. Take the bed. I can sleep in the reading nook."

"It will only make him angrier."

"Let him feel lonely. Better yet, let him come here to try and retrieve you."

"Reginald, what have I just told you about not defying him?"

"Don't go, Mother. If he rages over it tomorrow, at least I will be there to shield you from him."

She nodded. "All right. Thank you." She stroked my furry head and said, "My noble boy. At least I have done one great thing in my life." She smiled—a genuine smile—and I marveled at how Father could not see that a smile like that was worth more than all the gold and silver a mine could hold.

Maria

I awoke to the cloying scent of soiled hay and a small nose tickling my ear. I blinked heavy lids to see the rabbit faces of Mother, Sarah, and Stephania leaning over me. Even though her grey fur hid her skin, I could see the swelling of bruises covering Mother's neck and face and a raw slash across her cheek. Sarah was favoring her right leg, and Stephania's left ear was bandaged, the tip sliced clean off. But they were alive! A few souls I had not murdered.

Tears burst from me in a gush that soaked my neck. "I am so sorry," I choked out.

"We knew what could happen, Maria," said Mother. "We had to try. This is not your weight to bear."

"No," I said. "Stephania, you were right." Her face blurred through my tears. "It wasn't worth it."

"Maybe not. But maybe it was," said Stephania. "We might have failed, but we proved to Bricriu, and ourselves, that we are not helpless. I think that might be worth the cost. The guards fear us now. I see it in their eyes."

"I hope you're right," I said. "My hope is that even if the cost was far too high, something good can come from this. I think something was set in motion yesterday. Our rebellion brought the Prince of Wolves to Marburg Mine."

Sarah gasped. "You saw him?! And you live?"

I nodded and recounted the tale, mulling it over myself for the first time with a clear head. I left out nothing save for the growing realization that I wanted to meet him again—to see him... and to touch him. By the end, they sat on the edges of my bed, enraptured.

"Are you sure you heard clearly?" said Mother, running a paw over my head as if looking for a bump that might have jostled my brain. "The predator prince spoke Maya's name?"

"Yes. I am certain. And Maya came to me in a dream afterward. She said I would see him again and that all would be made clear."

"I'd love to believe this is all part of Maya's plan, but why would the prince hold our side?" said Mother.

"Maybe the prince does not want to be like his father?" said Stephania.

"I can think of no better explanation, but we can't be certain," I said.

"Do you think Bricriu will follow the prince's orders?" asked Sarah.

"Did Bricriu keep his promise about starving you today, Mother?" I asked.

"No, but we only had one meal. There was no one in the kitchen, and all we found were yesterday's leftovers."

"That's because the bastard fired Gertrude for offering me a sip of water."

"If it were not a sin to desecrate the bodies bestowed upon us by Maya, I would gut that dastardly fox," said Mother, thumping her foot in fury and sending up a cloud of hay, dust, and filth that set me to coughing.

"Don't worry," I said after clearing my throat. "By our hand or not, Bricriu will get what's coming to him."

Stephania hung her head. "Maya's laws or not, he ought to be desecrated, as he did to Gomez. I had no love for the old rabbit, but he was a better man than I thought. He did not deserve that."

I stroked her golden head. "No, he didn't."

She shook her body and raised her head. "At least they've elected Milten to be their new leader."

"That's a wonderful choice," I said. "He is doing well, I imagine?"

"Yes," said Stephania. "He stood up to Bricriu. Told him that the few men who knew where Gomez moved the pilfered gold had died in the rebellion, and Bricriu seems to have believed him."

"Is it true?"

"Milten told me it was, and I don't think he would lie to me. Especially not since he knows I report to you," she added with a mischievous look that was almost hidden by her animal features.

"What is that meant to mean?" I asked with a laugh.

Stephania sighed. "Like I said before, Maria, you know very little of men." She chuckled to herself. "Anyway, Bricriu was absolutely furious, but he didn't lay a finger on Milten. He gave him and the men a month to find out where it is."

"It seems he hasn't yet forgotten the prince's demands," I said. "Let's hope the prince does not remain absent too long, or Bricriu may grow less compliant."

"You want to see him again yourself, don't you?" asked Stephania with that same ornery look. "Want to see if he's as handsome as he sounds?"

"Nonsense," Mother snapped. "Maya might strike you down with soul shock for even implying such heinous things aloud."

I caught Stephania's eye roll, but luckily Mother didn't.

"I wish we could have at least seen the sun before they stopped us," said Sarah wistfully, startling us all.

My heart ached at the look of lost hope on her gentle face. I stroked her fur. "One day, you will, sister. Whether in Kaskilia or Maya's heavenly fields. I will not stop fighting for freedom. But next time, I will not risk the lives of others to attain it."

"What if we risk them ourselves?" asked Stephania.

I winked at her. "Then who am I to stop you?"

I looked at them all with growing hope. We had lost the battle, but the war was far from over.

And for a time, things actually improved.

A few days after the prince's visit, five wagon-loads of new rabbits joined us. The prince was replenishing his family's supply of workers. I was eager to befriend them, but Bricriu did not assign any to my barrack, probably thinking Mother and I would poison their minds. Still, he started letting us sleep a bit longer. In addition to our usual meals, we were given two slices of tomato bread in the morning. On Sundays, instead of laboring in the mines, we scrubbed the barracks clean and organized the kitchens, and some days there was time for leisurely walks through the Cathedral or midday naps. Yet, as I walked hand in hand with Mother or laughed with Stephania, I couldn't help but feel as though the extra scraps were meant to satiate not our bellies, but our hunger for freedom.

One Sunday, two weeks after our failed uprising, I was in the nearly empty mess hall, listening to Milten's tales of searching for Bricriu's gold and his cat-and-mouse conversations with the fox, when yet another group of new Lepores was led down the stairs. The same stairs I had charged to the top of with Paul at my back. I blinked back a tear at the memory of my brother's face, blood gushing from the wound in his head. I tried focusing on Milten's words, but I failed rather miserably. I searched the new faces. They looked terrified. Marburg was a place of legend that made grown Lepores wake up in cold sweats.

"Have you seen Sarah today?" asked Milten, his voice finally getting through to me.

I scrunched my brow. "Now that you mention it, no, I haven't. Why?"

"She said she wanted to talk with me about Frederick," said Milten, his gold-flecked eyes sparkling with amusement. "I think she wants me to introduce her."

"Who's Frederick?"

"Don't worry," said Milten with a chuckle. "He's a good man. He's one of the new workers who came in last week."

"All right," I said with a growing grin. "I trust your judgment. But let him know, if he makes her cry, I'll make him bleed."

"Oh, he already knows all about you," said Milten. "I won't have to convince him to behave."

"Well, I'll look for her when I head back to the barracks."

"Thanks." He scratched at his patchy black beard. "Seems like a lot of ladies are disappearing this morning. I had two men tell me they couldn't find their wives earlier today. Now that I think of it, I haven't seen a few of the men around either. Like Paul's friend Gerald. Have you seen him lately?"

I wracked my brain. "No," I said hesitantly. "I don't think so."

"It's getting overcrowded in here. That new group that just came in will push us above our old numbers. People are getting lost in the hustle and bustle, I guess."

"I guess," I said, scanning the adjoining tunnels for a glimpse of Sarah's black hair. "Well, always good talking with you, Milten. I have to get going."

"Okay," said Milten, leaping to his feet. His face turned bright red at the cheekbones. "Well, maybe we could talk again tomorrow? Or maybe explore the tunnels together next Sunday?"

"If I can," I said, laying a hand on his shoulder before I bid him farewell and headed off to do my own exploring.

The idea had come to me in a dream the week before. I saw myself weaving in and out of tunnels, stopping to dig at intervals as if I was planting seeds, but really, I was testing the soil for weaknesses, for a way out. Ever since then, whenever I had the time or the guards weren't looking, I sneaked around the deserted passages. Whenever I found a secluded spot with soil instead of solid rock, I tried tunneling forward and upward. Sometimes the soil was too soft, and it would create little avalanches that closed up my progress. A few places looked promising, but for the most part, it felt like a foolish endeavor. Even in places where the soil allowed me to create small tunnels, in all likelihood, it might take years to burrow to the surface. But something drove me onward. Something told me not to quit.

So there I was again, wandering through the tunnels. I decided to head for my most promising dig site. I came upon a new recruit, a woman with fiery red hair, on my way, and I flashed her a friendly smile.

"Hello, I don't think we've met. My name is Maria."

I held out my hand, but she suddenly went rigid, her arms stiff at her sides. She tried to skirt around me, but I stepped in front of her.

"Wait," I said, perplexed. "Are you okay? I know it's terrifying when you first get here, but we all..."

She kept her eyes fixed on a point over my shoulder and walked around me, never saying a word. I watched her go, my jaw slack. The poor girl had looked scared out of her mind. I hoped the guards weren't up to their old ways already. Shaking my head, I moved on, zigzagging toward the old, spent tunnels where gold no longer glittered in the veins between the stone. The walls were dark and hollowed out, and I shifted into my rabbit form to better traverse the growing darkness. The excessive mining had made the tunnels unstable here, and as I set to digging, I kept my ears poised to catch the slightest hint of a collapse. After an hour of digging, a sudden rush of collapsing soil forced me to race back down the five-foot-long tunnel, erasing my work.

"Damn," I said, licking my raw paws. Another three days of digging wasted. I would have to find a new place to try.

I returned to the barracks, exhausted from shifting back into human form so soon, and began searching for Sarah. My aunts and Mother hadn't seen her either. I wandered the Cathedral, calling for her and asking around. No one had talked to her since yesterday. Panic squeezed at my heart, but I calmed myself. She would be at dinner. That evening, I raced to the dining hall and sat at our usual table with Stephania and Mother.

"Have you still not found her?" asked Mother.

"No."

"I haven't seen her either," said Stephania.

We waited for five, ten, fifteen minutes. One of the new Lepores tried to sit in Sarah's seat and was screamed at from all sides. The poor girl nearly fell over the bench in her attempt to get away, but I had no time to apologize. I ran from table to table, Mother close behind me, calling for Sarah.

"You haven't found her yet?" called Milten from his table.

"Quiet down over there!" a guard called from the upper level.

Neither Mother nor I ate that night. Sarah did not show for dinner. She didn't return to the barracks for bed.

"We have to tell the guards," I said.

"They won't help," said Mother, face in her hands. "They don't even know who she is."

"We have to try something! We could ask Leopold. He has always been decent to us."

"All right." When Mother lifted her head, she looked older than I'd ever seen her. "But he is the captain. He does not patrol at night. You'll have to wait until morning. And by then, I fear it will be too late." Tears filled her eyes. "I fear it is already too late."

"Don't say that, Mother. Don't lose hope," I said, choking down my own fears.

She just rolled over in her bed and said nothing else. I lay in bed for hours, praying to Maya and struggling to shove away visions of all the horrible things that could have happened to Sarah. When, at last, I drifted into restless sleep, it felt as though I'd hardly closed my eyes before I woke to the sound of Mother's screams.

"Where are they? What have you done with my sisters?!"

I shot upright in the bed. Mother gripped her ratty blanket in both fists, gaping in horror at two new Lepores women, one no older than seventeen. They stared back at Mother with a mix of trepidation and confusion... from the beds where my Aunt Agnes and Aunt Heather should have slept.

"Answer me, you wicked girls!" said Mother, eyes bulging.

I rushed to her side, fearing she'd give herself a heart attack. I hugged her to me and turned to the women.

"When did you come to this barrack?"

The women shared a glance, and I saw fear and a shared understanding pass between them. The eldest bit her lip and stared back at me in silence.

"Are you mute?!" I screamed. I felt as though I'd stepped off the tunnel scaffolding and was plummeting through the air toward stalagmites below.

"The door opened and woke me a few hours ago, Maria," said Stephania. "I thought someone was emptying a bedpan. I went right back to sleep."

"Where are the women who slept here? What did you do with them?" I said, my face heating with fury.

The women averted their eyes. The youngest shrugged.

"I'm going to speak with Leopold," I growled.

But the barrack door swung open to admit two guards.

"Get up," one barked. "It's time for new work assignments. Gather in the center of the Cathedral."

I obliged begrudgingly, leading Mother by the hand as I scoured the domed chamber for Leopold among the hundreds of milling Lepores and guards. At last, I found him standing on a makeshift platform in the center of the room, a rolled parchment in his hand. I told Mother I'd be right back and raced forward, trying to catch the captain's eye. I wondered if he would be as kind to me as before. My rebellion had cost him a lot of men. But I froze before I reached him. The group of fifty slaves standing in a cluster directly behind Leopold were far too large in both height and girth to be Lepores. One of the forerunners lifted his ample belly and scratched beneath its folds. He turned his head to say something to his companion, and the tattoo on his neck confirmed my suspicions. Porcorum. Pigs. Rabbits had been the sole workers of Marburg since it was opened. Why had Bricriu brought in pigs? Or was this the prince's doing?

"Get back in line," said a guard, puffing out his chest in front of me. He stalked forward so that I was forced back among the crowd, but the commotion drew Leopold's eye, and I mouthed a silent, *Help me*. I could not tell by his face if he understood or if he cared, and I hardly heard the work assignments, allowing myself to be shoved into the correct group by the crowd. When I finally stirred from my thoughts, I found myself surrounded by Porcorum, most of them men.

This had to be Bricriu's doing. As the groups headed off to the dining hall for a quick breakfast before work, I rushed to catch up with Leopold, but a Porcorum's fat ankle shot out and sent me sprawling in the dirt. Another hauled me to my feet by the nape of my tunic and said, "Clumsy little thing, aren't you... Maria?"

"Let go of me," I said, shoving him as hard as I could. He barely budged, but he released me with a guffaw.

I scanned the crowd for Leopold, but he was gone. I toiled away the day, assaulted on all sides by tricks from the pigs. They stole ore from my bucket and placed it in theirs. They whispered taunts. I saw other Lepores cowering under their fierce, beady-eyed gazes. I even witnessed one young Lepores hand over a chunk of ore with a shaking hand.

I wondered if the Porcorum were assigned to replenish Bricriu's personal stash or if they just thought having fuller buckets would win them favor with the guards. One thing was for certain: Bricriu had told them my name and ordered them to give me special treatment. Had he orchestrated Sarah's disappearance, too? He had the power and the opportunity. I ground my teeth at the thought, promising to strangle him if he ever got close enough.

But I didn't see Bricriu that day. Or the next. Leopold either. I could not get a spare minute alone. The Porcorum were taking their job very seriously. Under the prince's orders, the guards could not bully us, but Bricriu had found a fine replacement. The pigs treated me worst of all. They didn't steal my food; they knocked the plate out of my hands. They didn't beat me, but I could hardly walk anywhere without being shoved to the ground and laughed at.

Every morning, another friend, cousin, uncle, or aunt went missing. The stress was wearing down Mother as no hard labor ever had. She lost all color in her face, and she walked bent, shuffling with an arm clenched around her midriff. None of the

Lepores who replaced our loved ones would even look at me. None of those lost returned. My world was shrinking around me, threatening to crush me until no air could fit in my lungs.

They also assigned pigs to our barrack, and neither Mother nor I dared to take out the book in their presence, certain they would report its existence to Bricriu. I lay in bed each night, reciting the verses I could remember, hoping to find solace in Maya, but I had no more dreams. The Great Mother offered no answers.

At last, I was able to find Leopold, by pure chance. I was headed for supper when I nearly ran into him coming around a corner.

"I'm sorry," I said.

"It's all right," said Leopold with a curt nod, and then he started to walk away.

Feeling almost mad with the loss of my comrades, I grabbed the back of his tunic and said, "Wait!"

He shrugged off my grip and looked at me with stern eyes.

"I'm sorry, it's just... so many of my family have gone missing. My sister, Sarah, my aunts, my uncles, my cousins. Even some of my friends."

He looked at me with pity but said nothing.

"Please, do you know where they are? Can you at least tell me... if they're still alive?"

He sighed, and his shoulders sagged. "I do not know where they are Maria, and that is the truth. The overseer does not tell me of his plans."

"But you must have some idea. You know about everything that goes on here."

"I did not know of your plans for rebellion," he said, his voice sharp but not exactly angry. "I think you overestimate me."

"So, you will not help," I said, my chest tightening.

"I *cannot* help. I can only tell you one thing, but you will not like it."

"Tell me."

"If your loved ones are not in this mine, they are dead. No

prey leaves Marburg alive. At least not for long."

"Perhaps they are hidden away somewhere?" I asked desperately, hot tears breaking free of my lashes.

"Perhaps. Best of luck to you, Maria."

With that, he left me alone in the vast maze of tunnels. These days, no matter how many souls filled a room, I was almost always alone.

That night, after Mother had shifted into her rabbit form to sleep, I told her what Leopold had said.

"The fox has won," she whispered, her voice scratchy from nights of crying. "He is taking all I love, and soon, he will take you."

I held her to me, rocking her like a child. "He will not take me," I said as fiercely as I could muster.

I got on my knees at her bedside, and together we prayed that those we loved had merely been hidden from us, that they still lived.

I tucked Mother into her bed and went to mine. Stephania had moved to the bed next to mine, and in the dark, we stretched out our hands to each other in a silent goodnight before we shifted into our rabbit forms for extra space on our bunks. I had grown afraid to speak with her too openly for fear Bricriu would take her, too. I did not think he knew of our friendship, and I needed to keep it that way. She had agreed, but we still held short conversations in the dining hall when surrounded by other Lepores. I fell asleep, grateful that I could still call *someone* sister.

I rose in the morning, determined to avoid the pigs and get back to my tunnels. If I found a way out, I would take Stephania and Mother with me, and Milten... if I could still find him. I shifted into human form, stretched, and walked across the barrack to Mother's cot.

"Wake up, Mother," I said gently, leaning down to stroke her grey fur and pull back the cover. I froze with my hand hovering over her head. The ears sticking out of the blanket were brown. I yanked the blanket off, my heart constricting so hard I thought I might faint. The rabbit in the bed opened perfectly round black eyes and blinked at me.

"Who are you?!" I screamed, grabbing for the rabbit's scruff. The Lepores squeaked and dodged my hands, pressing herself against the wall in terror. I didn't care. "Where is my mother?" I demanded, managing to grab her this time. I shook her like a hound, and her body froze up. I could see her small heart thumping wildly beneath her fur.

I stopped shaking her, but didn't relinquish my hold. As she started to come back to herself, I snarled in her face, "Tell me where my mother is, or I will feed your corpse to the pigs, bitch."

"The fox who brought me here took her," said the Lepores, trembling all over.

"When?"

"Not an hour ago."

I dropped the rabbit and burst out of the barrack door. I didn't slow when a guard commanded me to halt. I ran for the dining hall, hearing footfalls behind me. I raced up the steps to the upper level, seeing the two guards stationed at the top but not caring. They caught me under the arms and hoisted me up, kicking and screaming. There was a wagon at the end of the passage, loaded with hay... and rabbits. I saw my mother's grey fur, and I screamed for her. She turned her head, and our eyes met just as the guards at the head of the wagon pulled it out of sight.

"Mother! Mother!" I screamed, the world blurring.

The guards carried me down the steps. A slap on my face brought the world back into bright color for only a moment, and I heard the guard say, "Quit struggling, or we'll have to use force."

I sagged in their arms. What was the point of fighting? Mother was gone. They'd carted her off toward the entrance, toward the light. I only hoped she got to see the sun before they bled her dry and shipped her off to the king's table. I wondered if the prince would have a bite. I had been a fool to think a wolf pup could change anything, could care. Damn the prince! I could not wait on him. I had to see the sun. I had to get out of this dungeon. I had thought the old Marburg was hell. But this was worse. The guards stayed their violent hands, but my fellow Lepores would not offer theirs in friendship. I could not speak to my two remaining friends for fear Bricriu would slaughter them.

The bastard kept his promise, I thought as the guards threw me into a tunnel. I lay with my face on the dirty stone, wetting it with my tears. I did not realize I was wailing until a guard pulled me to my feet and said, "Stop that racket before we have to muzzle you, rabbit."

He shoved a pickax in my hands and pointed to an empty bucket station. I moved as if in a dream, my knees trembling, and did what I had done my entire life. *Clang, clink, clang, clunk.* I stared at the dark rock, the gold vein blurring each time my tears overtook me, Bricriu's words echoing in my head. *I will destroy you and everything you care about.*

There was one thing he had not destroyed. The book. Mother's book. I had to hide it in a better place! It was all I had to remind me of her, and with the Porcorum and the impostor Lepores scrubbing the loose floorboard that housed it each Sunday, someone was sure to notice the hollow creak and investigate eventually.

When the guards announced the midday meal, I pressed myself against the right side of the tunnel and let the others pass me. When the guards looked away, I slipped into a side passage and wove my way back to my empty barrack. I passed only one guard on the way. I dodged him easily by ducking into a pitch-black niche in the rock I knew all too well—the place Gomez had taken Stephania.

Inside the barrack, I crept among the cots until I reached the loose plank under Mother's bed and pried it free. I held the book to my breast, embracing it as I would never again embrace Mother. I tied it to my belly with the bit of rope I used to hold up my trousers. Then I wrapped myself with a few extra rags so the protrusion of the book would not be so obvious.

I rushed back through the rows of barracks and into the tunnels, making my way toward my latest successful dig. My heart hammered in my throat. It had been foolhardy to do this now. Someone was bound to report my absence to Bricriu. He would find out about my tunnels!

I stopped in a secluded passage and closed my eyes. With my nails digging into my palms, I took three long, calming breaths. It was too late to turn back. I had to hide the book.

I had abandoned digging in rabbit form a week before. My paws could only dig in soil, and much of the mine was rock. Stealing a pickax these days was damn near impossible, but I had stumbled upon an old one in these abandoned tunnels as if it was a sign from Maya Herself. I had carved my new tunnel into the rock, and it was slow going. I could barely fit myself into the little niche I'd created.

Just off the side was a small alcove that had once been used as a supply room, but now nothing lay inside but damaged crates and broken pottery. But on the back wall, I found one pot still fully intact, lid and all. I wrapped the book in an old burlap sack I found in one of the crates. I stashed the sacred tome inside the pot among dirt and sand and then sent up a brief prayer to Maya to safeguard this place. I had been gone too long already. I raced back through the tunnels, rushing toward nothing but shackles and horrible loneliness.

* * *

The next week passed in a haze. Without Mother, I was lost. I could not turn to Stephania or Milten for comfort. My grief consumed me. The only thoughts that broke through the black fog were of escape, but with so many strange and unfriendly eyes on me, many days I couldn't get to my dig site at all.

When I returned to my tunnel on a Sunday, a guard's stolen sandwich in tow so that I could skip lunch, I got down on hands and knees and examined the freshly dug passage. The rock was giving way to softer sediment in some places, but I hoped the addition of the stone would help keep this passage intact. There was some moisture in the rock here, and I felt that I might be close to an underground river.

If I could find one, then maybe, just maybe, I could follow it to the outside world. There was a chance I could get caught in the flow, or that water might flood the tunnel. But at this point, the thought of drowning was not all that frightening.

The tunnel was still not very deep, but I could walk a few steps inside it to dig at the back. I set to work, trying to pull out a large chunk of rock that was hampering my progress. I swung the pickax with precision, aiming for the edges of the stone, but the ax stuck fast in a crack. As I tried to pull it out, the old handle broke away from the iron head. I dropped to my knees, panting.

"I'm a fool," I groaned into my hands. "This is all just madness."

A ringing sound made me look up. I scrambled backward out of the narrow tunnel as the ringing grew into an ear-splitting rumble I had heard before. I managed to get myself out into the main tunnel and against the opposite wall, where I held onto a support beam for dear life as the ground shook. I shut my eyes while rocks tumbled and cascaded all around me. A boulder twice the size of my head crashed not two feet from me, and then the whole wall where my foolhardy tunnel had been crumbled with a roar.

I was going to die here.

CHAPTER FOUR
Into the Wild

Maria

The world shook, vibrating my entire body as I clung to the support beam like a child latched to her mother's leg. When the rumbling stopped and the dust dissipated, I opened one eye, then the other. I examined myself for wounds. Untouched. Praise Maya. Then I looked around, and panic squeezed my heart. The main tunnel had collapsed on either side, but above me, the support beam had maintained the ceiling five paces in every direction. Floor to ceiling debris trapped me in the small pocket. But then I smelled the air. Beneath the dry odor of dirt, there was something entirely alien. The atmosphere was warm and moist. A few more rocks tumbled down, and as I waved away the cloud of dust, I saw that the tunnel was indeed flooded—not with water, but with golden sunlight. I blinked. It couldn't be real. It was a miracle!

Brain buzzing with euphoria, I turned in a circle, trying to understand. The side of the mountain had collapsed, and I was at the bottom of a chasm. A shallow river flowed through the stones, and on one side of the cliff, tree roots and vines snaked down. Tears streamed down my cheeks. Such a familiar sensation, but these tears were not harbingers of sorrow and loss but of joy.

"Thank You, Maya. Thank You!" I closed my eyes, held out my arms like wings and basked in the sunlight, breathing deep, memorizing the warmth of sunshine and the smells of everything heated by its rays.

A noise slowly drew me out of the moment.

"Maria! Maria, are you all right? Answer me, *please.*" I knew that voice. I rushed to the collapsed pile of dirt and rock that blocked the tunnel from the rest of the mine.

"Stephania, I am more than all right!" I shouted back to her.

"Oh, thank Maya. I was following you. I wanted to tell you how sorry I am, about your mother. Those damned pigs held me up. When I finally got away, I heard the collapse. Don't worry. I'll call for help. I don't care what Bricriu says; we'll dig you out."

"No, Stephania! Don't tell Bricriu anything! Not yet, at least." A plan was beginning to form in my mind.

"Maria, you'll starve in there," said Stephania. "I don't care if he punishes me."

My elation made my voice breathy. "No, listen. You don't understand. Stephania, I am free! The collapse opened a ravine that leads to the surface."

For a moment, there was silence, and I tried to imagine her face.

"So, you can climb out?" she said at last. "You can truly get free?"

"Yes. But... Bricriu will likely know within a few hours. His spies are bound to report me missing."

"What do you need me to do? Just say the word, Maria." She laughed, a bubbly, almost hysteric sound. "Oh, how I envy you!"

"Don't envy me too much, my friend. I am still a rabbit in a predator's world. Even if I do get a head start and throw off Bricriu's hounds, I could easily be killed in the wilderness."

"I'll try to stall him finding out," said Stephania. "Maybe Milten could pretend to be you in rabbit form. We could keep that white patch on his chest hidden. It's hard to tell a rabbit is male from a distance." She gave that hysteric giggle again.

"No, don't get yourselves into trouble. Let Bricriu find out naturally. It's Sunday. I won't be missed from work duty. That should give me some extra time. What I need you to do comes after he finds out."

"I'm listening."

"He's going to send guards to search the perimeter. Hopefully it takes them a while to find this opening, and my scent will have faded. I'm going to change into rabbit form as soon as I get out of this chasm. That scent should drive them mad and keep them from trying to climb down into this giant hole until my human scent has long been washed away by the water in here. If I can find the stream that feeds into this ravine, I'm going to jump in it and change into human form. They won't have my human scent; maybe I can get away. If the hounds come back empty-handed, that is when you approach Bricriu. Have Leopold bring you to him. Convince Bricriu you have grown to hate me for all the bloodshed I caused. It shouldn't be too difficult. We haven't spoken publicly in a long time, and Bricriu will eat up the idea that his tactics have turned you against me."

"Okay, but how does this help you?"

"I need you to convince Bricriu to send the Prince of Wolves himself after me."

"The prince?" I heard a barely perceptible scoff. "You're still daydreaming of him? Maria, you can't hinge your safety on the prince. He visited once and never came back, and hardly anything changed."

"But he did help. He cared at least a fraction, and that is worth something, especially in a predator with so much power. Things must change. Otherwise, even if I can come back and save you and the others, we will still be slaves to the predator's world, hiding and scrounging for a living. I need to speak with the prince. If he will not help, or if he kills me, so be it, but I have to try. Maya said I would see him again. I think this is what She meant."

"You're going to come back for us?"

"Of course! If I live long enough."

"I will do exactly as you asked."

"Thank you, Stephania," I said, touching the sediment that separated us, hoping she was doing the same. "Oh, but one last thing. Bricriu will likely fear telling the prince he's lost a prisoner. You must spin the idea as though it will let him have his revenge on the prince—make him chase down the wicked rabbit he so foolishly spared. You could also tell him that the prince has my human scent; he took his time sniffing me when he was here." I cringed at the memory. "Bricriu will remember."

"I understand. I'll make you proud."

"I have no doubt. But now I must go."

"Goodbye, Maria. I will see you again; I know it. You are the bravest, most capable Lepores I have ever met."

"Goodbye, sister. I will not forget you. If I survive, I will be back."

I pulled myself away and rushed to the other side of the ravine. If the Prince of Wolves was to chase me, then I would give him the run of his life. I would, after all, be running for mine. If he caught me, I hoped to test him.

I grabbed hold of a sturdy vine that clung to the cliff face. Once I had made sure it could take my weight, I climbed up. The sun was bearing down on me now. My blistered hands shot fiery agony up my arms as I used them to pull the weight of my body. But this pain was nothing compared to what I had endured in my entire life. There was pleasure in this pain. This pain earned freedom.

Finally, I crawled over the edge and used the last of my strength to invoke the change into rabbit form. I curled into a ball, struggling for breath. Though I had been receiving better meals since the prince's visit, I was still emaciated. At least my rabbit side was healthier than my human form, or I might not have been able to stand.

When I raised my head, all pain and exhaustion were forgotten. My eyes watered against the majesty of the sun. At the edges of the bright yellow-white light, I could see greens of all shades. When my vision finally adjusted, my eyes blurred again with tears of joy. I saw the rolling hills of Mother Maya's dream, but now I could smell the grass and the wildflowers blooming in the meadow before me. I coiled my spring-like hindquarters, mustering my strength, and bound into the air, laughing and crying in wonder. It was the first time I had an excuse to binky with joy, and my little body quivered in the moment of weightlessness, a pleasant shake from head to toe with each enthusiastic upward leap.

Dark mountains dotted with rich greens at the base and pristine whites at the peaks beckoned in the distance. There was so much world to explore! I was in the world at last! My heart threatened to burst, spilling my ecstasy in an arterial gush. I flicked my ears in all directions as unfamiliar sounds tickled my brain. Birds chirped in the trees of the forest at my back. Insects of bright grassy greens and earthy browns leaped across the blades, making joyous noises of their own. I had never seen a blue to rival that of the sky, but I was forced to look away as the sun left spots on my eyes. I rolled in the grass, letting it poke beneath my fur, drinking in the scent like life-giving water.

"Praise be to You, Heavenly Mother! Your work is truly marvelous!"

I knew I had to move, but I couldn't contain my excitement. I ran for the forest, my paws leaping through white, gold, and purple blossoms whose scents tempted me to stop. I slowed, realizing that I was ravenous. It felt like a travesty to eat such beauty, but I gorged myself all the same.

It was then I remembered my plan. I scoured the meadow for the stream that fed into the ravine. I headed in the direction of the ravine's trickling waterfall, and I soon heard the playful sounds of water slapping rock. The small stream fed into a tiny pool filled with tadpoles. It was hidden in the high grass, but the scent of water drew me to it.

I jumped in, yelping in delight and shock as the cold water struck my skin. I rolled in it, the smooth rocks at the bottom pressing into my back, and then shifted into human form. It was hard. Almost too hard. I had to scrunch my eyes in concentration to make my ears fall back and turn into hair. I would not be able to shift again today, but I hoped I wouldn't need to.

With renewed energy, I raced for the tree line and crashed into a patch of ferns, taking in the clean air and mingling my laughter with the birdsong. I had begun to lose hope that I would ever look upon the beauty of Maya's world, but now I knew without a doubt that I had been right to fight for this.

But as I thought of all those Lepores I'd lost or left behind, my tears of joy became sobs of sorrow, and I had to rest against a tree, hugging its bark for comfort. I cried for Mother most of all. Why should I be the only one to enjoy this beauty? Mother had taught me that freedom was worth fighting for, but now she would never experience it, never know that I had found it. But the others... I could save the others. I *would* save the others. Let the wolves come. I was ready.

Reginald

The bowstring vibrated as I loosed another arrow. I knew it would go wide. It hit the blue outermost ring—the black sheep of its brothers, all clustered together near the bullseye. I scuffed my boot through the dirt. My mind was elsewhere. This morning, I received two letters—both positive in tone but frustrating in implication.

The first was a progress report from Marburg Mine, as I had requested. The fox, Bricriu, had sent two thus far, both obedient and sunny in tone, but something about them nagged at me. I couldn't put my nose on it, but I had a sneaking suspicion that at least parts of the letters were lies. I had started pondering another visit, wondering how I could do it without arousing Father's suspicions, when I opened the second letter. It was from Edmund, Lady Leticia's guard, who had traveled with me to Marburg. I had started the letter with a smile but ended in a cold sweat.

Edmund said he had spoken to his lady about me, telling

her of the changes I hoped to make when I took the throne. Apparently, Lady Leticia had found my ideas "delicious," and she hoped that I might "ascend the throne sooner than later" and "spare the kingdom further pain." It should have elated me. I had never considered that any of the nobles dared disagree with Father, even on paper, and yet, here was one sending me letters with cryptic lines that might spell a hint of rebellion.

"Sooner rather than later." The sentence ran through my mind repeatedly. Did it really mean what I thought it might? Did others share my views? Was Lady Leticia even a prudent ally? She had a reputation as a bit of a loon, and rumor had it she'd killed two husbands, both of whom had died quite suddenly, perplexing the best healers in Kaskilia. I'd met her on a few occasions, as she was a close, long-time friend of Mother's. She was beautiful, kind (to me, at least), and well-spoken, but her oddity was without question.

I growled deep in my throat. It was idiocy even to ask myself these questions. I was reading things that weren't there.

I notched another arrow. This one at least hit the inner red circle, but I didn't feel I was improving much—years of practice gone out the window thanks to a few words on a page.

"Will you blame the wind or the sun for that sad performance, son?" asked Father, approaching from behind with one of his captains. Today, he was a regal, upright white wolf garbed in a loose purple robe embroidered with gold arrows.

"I accept my faults, Father," I said, standing straighter in his presence despite myself. "I am unfocused."

"Overcome, Reginald," commanded Father. "You are an Ingolf. A hunter by birthright. It is what you were created to do, even in your human form."

Father lived for the smell of fresh blood and the frenzy of the hunt. War and conquest over all. The way of the predator.

Under his gaze, I focused on the target. Unease shoved my thoughts aside, my pulse quickening, as if fearing he might read my mind. I drew, breathed deep, and released, piercing dead center.

"At last, a worthy shot," said Father, sparing me a rare upward pull of his jowls—the canine equivalent of a smile.

I said nothing, only notched another arrow. A Canum guard in human form burst onto the training grounds, calling, "Prince Reginald, urgent message for you, Your Highness!" Skidding to a halt in front of me, he doubled over, panting. He wore the red jacket and blue tunic uniform of Marburg Mine.

"What is your message?" I asked, my heart contracting in fear. I was keenly aware of Father at my side. "We received a report from your overseer this morning, and he said all was well."

The guard gulped in one more breath and then stood erect. "Many apologies, Your Highness," he said, saluting me. "But your presence is requested at the mine immediately. This morning it was discovered that a slave escaped. We are unsure how many days have passed—Lord Winterhall thinks it could not have been more than one—but there was a collapse in an old tunnel that created an opening to the outside. When we found it, the trail was old and muddled by rain, and we believe she switched into her human form to throw us off. We've lost her scent."

"Useless dogs!" said Emmerich, saliva flying. "What good are dogs who cannot track? I ought to put you all down!" He curled his snout and growled at the terrified guard, who fell to his knees in supplication.

"A thousand apologies, Your Majesty," said the guard, his nose mere centimeters from the earth. "If we had been aware of her absence earlier... but there are so many Lepores in the mine. If she had been anyone else, we still would not know she was missing."

"Anyone else? Who was she?" I asked.

"She is the one they call Maria. The one who Bricriu believes helped lead the uprising."

"She lives?" roared Father as my heart filled with ice. "Why was she not served at my table?"

The guard looked between us, his face drained of color. He babbled, no doubt unsure if accusing his prince would result in leniency or immediate retribution. My voice hitched in my throat, but I managed to step between the guard and Father.

At last, my tongue loosed, and I said, "I ordered she be spared, Father."

His face went blank, his yellow eyes an empty void, and my knees threatened to quake.

I rushed on with a lie I hoped would spare my life. "She was not the ringleader. He was killed. But Bricriu suspected she helped with the organization of the attack. I thought if I spared her, she might lead us to the other responsible parties. There had to be more, for such a large-scale uprising. I told Bricriu to watch her closely, to see who she interacted with the most, and then, when he'd discovered all major responsible parties, he was to send them all to us for execution."

"You're a soft-hearted fool!" said Father through a snarl, but the fact that he was shouting at me rather than ripping out my vocal cords suggested some of his immediate rage had dissipated. "There are swifter ways of weeding out the leaders. You should have made an example of her!"

"I do not yet have your mind for proper punishment, Father. I will do better next time." I turned to the guard, my heart still galloping. "But why did Bricriu request my presence?"

"He says you are the only predator who has recently memorized her human scent. He believes that though the rabbit trail has gone cold, her human one might be located in the forests a few miles from the mine, if one knew it."

"I was in human form when I saw her," I said. I could still see her face, remember the odd euphoria her scent had caused. I did not want to find her.

"Your animal side still noted the scent," said Father. "You are a powerful Lobo. You are my son—a wolf through and through. You will fix this mess, Reginald. You will bring her back yourself, alive. Then, when the Absolvers have pulled all they can from her, we will feast on her flesh together."

I had consumed rabbits all my life, but now the notion made me sick. I'd never seen the human faces of the Lepores on my plate before, much less known their names. *Maria.*

But what was I to do? She was just a Lepores. Not worth dying for. Not even worth further angering Father for. I sighed internally.

"Yes, Father."

"May Khaytan be with you and lend you His cunning," said Father, reciting the traditional words spoken before a hunt.

I bowed my head. "Thank you, Father."

"You will take Lieutenant Henry and his men."

Henry was a perfectionist. He'd never failed in a hunt. Father was ensuring I made no mistakes. I'd lost what little trust I'd earned in his eyes.

"I will collect the lieutenant and my squire and then leave at once, Father." I looked to the guard. "Wait for me by the city gates." I thought it best to get the poor man out of Father's reach.

"Yes, Your Highness." He darted off.

I turned toward the castle, but Father said, "Reginald..."

"Yes, Father?"

"Don't bother returning without the rabbit."

* * *

I stood on a low ridge, looking down at a vast crater of dark earth that scarred the green valley. Nearby, a thin stream glittered among the tall grass. The idea that one rabbit had caused the ravine to materialize seemed an act of Sammael—or perhaps Maya Herself was on Maria's side. Her name still bounced around my skull, but my thoughts were jumbled, and my blood was boiling from my encounter with Bricriu.

He'd met me and my party at the gate, still in fox form. He greeted me with a bow and a fanged grin that suggested he was enjoying this far too much.

"I did warn you she was trouble," he'd said. "I fear if word of her feat gets out and she is not severely punished for it"—his eyes had flashed with hunger then—"that the other slaves may follow her example to their own ruin once more."

I hadn't known what to say, and that had angered me more.

I could not protest. Father was of the same mind. It didn't matter what I thought anymore. My influence at the mine had been short-lived. If only I'd allowed the fox to have his way with the troublesome Lepores, my orders for the rest of the mine might have lasted longer. Father was bound to watch things closely now. My chance was gone, and it was all because of a foolhardy rabbit named Maria.

Lieutenant Henry, a prime specimen of a man whose jaw looked as though it could crush iron, pulled me from my thoughts as he ordered his men to transform. They'd stowed their weapons on the horses, which were waiting with Thomas at our planned stop-over point a few miles from the mine. Thomas had gone rather sour when I told him he'd be staying behind, and none of my explanations about the differences in wolf and lynx hunting tactics had been able to sweeten him.

My companions had all left their armor at home, opting for their loose-fitting uniforms designed with hunts like this in mind. I wished I had followed their lead.

I didn't need much coaxing to urge my wolf half out when the atmosphere was already tinged with the excitement of a hunt. My partially metamorphosed animal form remained upright, maintaining a somewhat human frame. It wasn't always easy to jump back to a truly savage form until my muscles were loosened. Reluctant to give in to my feral side, I waited a few breaths to lower my front paws into the wildflower-dotted grass. I had more room inside my breastplate now, and I didn't think it would hamper me too much. We didn't pay our private blacksmith exorbitant amounts of gold for nothing.

I lifted my nose and inhaled deeply, expecting to take in only the scent of clean air and pollen. Instead I received a sharp, stinging sensation in my nostrils, a violent itch, and then my brain flared with recognition at a familiar scent. Maria's scent. Like the mahogany rocking chair my mother sat in when she read me stories as a child. Or maybe scented oils, like those the fiery-haired maidservant I'd lusted after as a young man had rubbed into her skin.

It was impossible. The trail was old, and there was no breeze to waft the scent up the ridge.

"Let's get to that stream," I said to Henry, knowing he wouldn't believe me if I told him I was already on the trail. "That is where the Canum lost her scent."

"Let the hunt begin," he said, sprinting down the slope.

At the stream, I feigned sniffing in circles like the others, though the scent was overwhelming. I could distinguish the exact place on the bank where she'd gone in a rabbit and come out a human. An image of her burst into my head, clear as if she stood before me. Bloodied and bruised, but still beautiful. I shook my head, making my ears flap together. I had to stop thinking of her as anything other than a troublesome slave. She would be dead in a few days, and I had to escort her to her fate.

Despite all the logic I threw at myself, the thought still turned my stomach. It wasn't as though the woman... rabbit... had taken out ten guards single-handed, led her whole family to freedom, and marched out of the exit. She'd escaped on a fluke. Why did she need to be made an example of?

I shoved my conscience aside and sent up a fluting howl, signaling I had the scent. The others rushed to my side, each dipping their noses to the place I indicated.

"I smell only wildflowers," said one.

Henry sniffed long and hard. "I smell it!" he said, scratching at the earth to stir up the scent. "It's faint, but it's there. Extraordinary, Your Highness!"

The other wolves crowded closer, inhaling the freshly disturbed earth. Henry sent up the call, and we formed a loose line, heads bent to the trail. I led, Maria's feet leaving a clear path for me. She had headed into the nearby forest, and I charged into the tree line. The overpowering scents of pine, decaying foliage, and dozens of squirrels and rats, forced me to pause, searching. I concentrated on the memorized scent and picked it up again, more pleasing than any other aroma in the forest.

Hours passed that way, carefully following the faint trail. The odd potency of the scent was wearing off. I couldn't smell the trail any better than my companions now. Had Khaytan Himself granted me enhanced senses at the start of the hunt? Did he want Maria as a sacrifice?

As the day faded away into dusk, the forest grew dense. Tree roots tangled up and burst from the ground in their tussles. Thickets of shrubs, fallen saplings, thorny bushes, and new growth hampered our speed. We lost the trail in one of them. The brambles were so long and the mix of branches so thick that none of us could get inside, but someone else had recently tried. A few freshly snapped branches formed a rough hole, but it didn't go deep enough to see into the heart of the thicket. I shoved my head as far inside as I could. How had she squeezed in there? Was she still inside? The last scent I had of her was her human form. She shouldn't have fit.

"There's blood on these thorns here," Henry said, inspecting the opening for himself.

We split up and circled the thicket.

"Your Highness!" Henry called.

I followed his voice to the opposite side and found him up to the neck in the brambles. He pulled back and shook his grey fur free of stickers.

"The scent changes inside and comes out here. She shoved in as far as she could get, scraped herself up good, and then transformed so she could get out the other side."

I followed his example, ignoring the sharp pricks of the thorns in my muzzle as a familiar thrill filled my chest. She was making it interesting.

The unique smell of a frightened rabbit, like alfalfa grass and sweat, was there. We were getting closer. Henry sent up the call and took off.

She was moving eastward, toward the foothills leading to the Ethereal Mountains. I forced one brown paw in front of the other, fighting weariness. The army had fortified my endurance, but a whole day of running was arduous. Around me, Henry's troops were flagging, tongues lolling out the sides of their mouths.

"Don't stop, men!" Henry called from the front of the pack.

"We're finally close. Let's catch this damned rodent!"

I forced air into my lungs and pushed myself into a sprint as the other wolves yipped and howled to each other in excitement. I ignored the extra weight of my breastplate and focused on the freedom, the intoxicating scent of our quarry, and the euphoria of operating on pure instinct. We ran like true wolves, but the Lepores... the rabbit... *What's her name again?*... She certainly did her animal side justice. Her trail leaped and zigzagged, forcing us over fallen trees and through loose thickets.

The forest went from the bright orange of sunset to the deep purples that served as the moons' ceremonial red carpet. My wolf eyes didn't mind. When she, at last, appeared ahead of us, dashing between two broad trees, my jowls dripped with fresh saliva. I locked my eyes on her dark haunches and used the instinctual burst of adrenaline to reach the outer limits of my body's capabilities. She used the cover of the larger trees to quickly dodge in a new direction, forcing us to skid through the undergrowth to change course. She leaped over boulders and shoved herself through tight spaces.

We drew closer and closer, but still she eluded us. We only caught glimpses of her, springing from one hiding spot to the next. I growled, furious, my strength waning. We would lose the kill. I shook my head, correcting myself. Father wanted her alive. But if she didn't tire soon, it was all for naught. Surely she would. I could tell even from a distance that she was haggard.

Henry nipped at his soldiers' sides, urging them on, but she dashed out of sight, her fur blending with the night. Following her scent, we came to a small peninsula where the Silver River snaked its way through Raven's Rock Forest. At the river's edge, we lost her trail.

"Fan out!" I called.

We poked our muzzles through bushes and under fallen trees. Nothing.

"Did she cross the river?" one of the pack asked as we came together again.

"This river is too deep and swift," I said. "If she tried, she likely drowned. Rabbits can't make that swim."

"Maybe she transformed again," suggested Henry.

"Unlikely," I said. "She's already done it once today, and she's worn herself out. She'd die of soul shock."

I eyed the river's rushing current. Had she really gone in? No, she was too smart for that. Wherever she was hiding on this little spit of land bordering the river, we had her trapped. My adrenaline was dying off, and not only was I tired, I was starting to think of her as a woman again, rather than a rabbit, as my wolf side relinquished control back to my human consciousness.

Two of the Lobo reverted back to their human form to escape the exhaustion of their animal limbs, their Cherbourg uniforms now wrinkled and dirty.

"You two," I said, rising on my hind legs to point at the men, "keep watch here; your human eyes won't do much good in a search. You three, check that side. Lieutenant, climb that ridge and check for movement."

I walked upright to a weeping willow by the riverbank, panning my eyes left and right.

"All this work to catch one rabbit," I muttered, dusting my filthy woolen surcoat with my paw. Perhaps she eluded me because somewhere inside, I didn't want to catch her. But that wasn't an option. Father wanted her, and if I wanted to keep him from shoving his nose deeper into my exploits at the mine, he had to have her.

I licked my fur, brushing away loose bits of dirt as a soft breeze caressed the branches of the willows. The direction of the wind changed, bringing a familiar scent. My ears pricked up and swiveled toward the trees at the sound of soft moaning.

I lowered onto all fours and crept into the trees alone, fearing that calling the others would alert my quarry. A few paces inside the treeline, my paws met loose, freshly dug earth. Below the roots of another willow, there was a hole. I crept to the edge and peered inside.

My black rabbit sluggishly dragged her front paws against the sandy soil. I stared, my human and wolf sides warring. A whole day of running as a wild wolf had heightened my animal instincts, and my wolf side was eager for the kill. It wanted to lunge into the hole and crunch the rabbit's neck. But my human side had regained control while I rested, and I was stayed by her weeping.

Her dirtied paws trembled as she looked at them. Her ears drooped at the tips. But again, she set to digging, slow and hindered by pain and exhaustion.

"Come, Maria, dig," she hissed at herself through her tears. "That's all you're good for. That wolf will eat you if you don't. Rip you limb from limb."

She was broken and exhausted beyond all limits of endurance. Even the beggars in the worst slums at the edge of Silver Creek looked less haggard than this sad creature. But still, she refused to give up her struggle. I found myself awed.

Beneath the rips in the fabric on her back, I could make out deep ridges in her flesh; wounds that never truly healed, exposed by patches of missing fur. She had felt Bricriu's whip more times than I cared to imagine.

I rose to my hind legs again, hoping to further quell the bloodlust of my wolf half.

If I killed her now, while she wept, while I was conscious of her name, of her humanity, I don't think I could forget it, I thought.

I tried to think of something to say, but only a frustrated sigh escaped my lips. Her drooping ears shot up, and she whirled, her large eyes fixed on my fangs. She pressed her back against the wall of her improvised burrow and let out a high, squeaking scream that set my fur on end. Her eyes... her eyes were the same deep azure color as mine. But there was not much humanity in them at that moment. They were glazed, an expression I had seen many prey changelings affect before executions. She resumed her frantic digging with renewed zeal.

"Dig, just dig, burrow faster. Damn this slippery earth," she cursed as the unstable soil fell all around her, refilling the hole she was trying to expand. Still, she dug, glancing back at me as if I would spring at any moment.

"Please, wait," I said, trying to keep my voice gentle and my fangs hidden. "I'm not going to hurt you. But I think you know I can't let you stay here." I held out a paw, praying she wouldn't leap out of that hole and start running again. Father would berate me for a fool, or perhaps even a traitor, if he saw me now, but I didn't care. I only wanted her to quit looking at me like that. Like she was nothing more than a rabbit, and I was nothing more than a beast come to savage her.

"No, I won't let you drag me back to that cursed mine! I would rather bury myself right here," she shrieked as dust fell on her head.

"I'm not taking you back to the mine." A cruel half-truth. I was taking her somewhere worse.

"And why should I believe you, prince of liars?! You talked as though you wanted better lives for us, but you only brought more death." She kicked her back feet, sending a wave of dirt into my eyes. In my upright wolf form, I was thrown off balance, blinded, and my back hit the dirt. I instinctively rolled onto all fours and sneezed. I felt her fur brush mine as she leaped out of the hole and rushed past me.

I watched through blurry eyes as Lieutenant Henry, now in human form, rushed toward us and kicked her in the side. It would have sent a normal rodent flying, but she was as big as a human child, and she fell onto her side, gasping for air. The lieutenant drew the hunting dagger he kept strapped to him at all times and put it to her throat.

"Move a muscle and you're dead, prey!"

She gritted her teeth, drawing in one tortured breath after another. "Go ahead and kill me if it pleases you, butcher. I was never really alive to begin with."

Henry rubbed his beard, considering.

"No, stop! You will not kill her. I forbid it!" I said, grabbing his wrist with clumsy paws and forcing the knife away.

"Your Highness?"

"You heard me! She is my prisoner, and you will do her no harm." Henry still looked confused, and doubtless he would report this to Father, but I couldn't bring myself to say, "The king wants her alive," in front of Maria. I didn't want her to know what awaited her. And... I was ashamed.

When Henry at last sheathed the dagger, I shut my eyes and transformed. Somewhat refreshed, I bent down and took Maria in my arms like a large, furry baby. I carried her toward the riverbank. The two Lobo in human form rose to their feet in surprise. One put his hand to his mouth and simulated a howl. The other three scouts ran toward us from different directions. When they saw our prize, they sent up celebratory yips and howls, nipping at each other and splashing through the river shallows.

The sounds of a successful hunt sparked a small sense of accomplishment in my chest. Maria turned her head to look up at me, her sides heaving. Her eyes no longer held that glazed, faraway appearance, and she cocked her head, as if in recognition. I felt a small thrill, but then she closed her eyes and murmured, "My freedom... is over."

A sharp sting, like a nettle, pierced my heart. I had never known loss like this changeling. I wanted to help her, but I was only going to bring her more pain.

As the others whooped in triumph around me, I bent to whisper, "Maybe not." Then, looking to my fellow Lobo, I said, "Let's go home."

Walking ahead of the pack, I considered my prize. Why did I care at all about her fate? Father had been right. Showing mercy had only led to trouble. She had singlehandedly ruined my chance at proving my ideas for the kingdom had merit. She was just a runaway slave, and yet, I wanted to know her. I wanted to ease her pain. All of my worries seemed irrelevant and childish in light of her emaciated body, deep scars, and sorrowful voice.

My freedom... is over. She had tasted freedom only for a few days. I had had it my whole life, and yet I did nothing with it. Or perhaps Father had stolen it from me, as he'd done her. In some ways, at least, that was true, and it only made me dread handing her over more.

"Your Highness, take this to leash her," said Henry. He pulled off the length of rope tied around his torso like a sash and held it out. "When she regains some of her strength, she may try to run."

I laid Maria on the ground and bound her front and back paws together. She did not struggle, she only stared at me with resigned eyes.

"Beg your pardon, Prince Reginald," said Henry, "but aren't you a bit too soft on her?"

I ground my teeth. Another of Father's watchdogs breathing down my neck. I forced my face into a surprised, offended look.

"Our orders were to keep her alive. She'll die of exhaustion if I pull her along on a leash."

"My apologies, Your Highness," he said, looking satisfied.

"If there are no further questions about my judgment, let's be off," I said, picking Maria up again. "Thomas must have started to miss us."

As the last grey remnants of the sun's light vanished from the heavens, we lit our torches, wary of any threats lurking on the pig trails. The boar clans in Raven's Rock were especially fearsome, earning them more freedom. Even grown bears thought twice about attacking the Andromedae in their own homes.

Maria struggled against sleep, shaking her head so that her ears flapped against my forearms. Her mouth moved as if she was silently speaking. Maybe new curses for me and the pack?

I didn't think much of it, until she closed her eyes and spoke in audible tones, perhaps forgetting where she was.

"Maya, lead us toward Your light. Shepherd us from this world of fear, of pain... of death. Gift us with the warmth of a new form..."

I cringed, ready to cover her mouth but afraid the others would notice.

"What did that heretic just say?" asked a grey wolf behind me. "How dare she speak of Maya in your presence, Highness! You ought to punish her soundly."

I sighed as the company halted around me, snarling or grumbling, depending on their form. This Lepores was still causing me trouble. Father's laws applied to everyone, including me, and these soldiers knew them well. Pity on my part in the face of such blasphemy would be betrayed to Father as soon as we arrived home. I gripped Maria by the scruff of her neck, sneering in her face.

"Silence your blasphemous tongue, prey, or I will rip it out. The Absolvers of Khaytan will deal with you soon enough," I said, shaking her a bit and hating myself all the while.

She whimpered and trembled, her eyes going glassy. The soldiers satisfied, we pressed on as the dense blanket of ashen clouds parted, and Kaskilia's two moons shone brightly for the first time that night. Across the familiar meadow, I could see the dark silhouette of the massive obsidian monument, blacker than the night around it. As we approached, Khaytan took shape, towering fifty feet in the air in the place where He was said to have been born.

The statue was double-sided. The side that greeted us depicted the god in His human form, with spike-tipped angel wings sprouting from His shoulders, His face forever youthful, body forever powerful. On the other side, back-to-back with its human counterpart, there would be an upright black wolf with eyes of diamond, howling up at the twin moons.

At half a day's ride from the capital, the God Stone was a popular site of pilgrimage and prayer for those seeking the blessings of Khaytan. Here would have been an appropriate place to begin our hunt had there been less urgency; although, I supposed it was equally fitting to end our mission here as well. As we approached the statue with our catch, I could not deny that I felt more humbled than usual.

A pair of yellow eyes glowed at Khaytan's feet. Thomas sashayed toward us in lynx form, his fur a mix of fawn and milky white scattered with black spots.

"The mighty pack returns," he said, and I could still detect the bitterness at being left behind. "I see your hunt was successful, but I did expect you sooner."

"No doubt if we'd had a cat on our side, we could have pounced upon her much faster, eh, Thomas?" I said.

"That's precisely what I tried to tell you this morning. Shall I unpack the bedrolls, sir?"

"No, we are leaving Raven's Rock far behind. The boars may already know we were there. We can have some proper rest when we reach the farmlands near Silver Creek. Hitch the horses together and lead us home, Thomas," I commanded, setting the Lepores down a moment to rest my arms. For being the smallest animal to gain a human soul, this starved rabbit had grown rather heavy.

Thomas whined as I'd expected. "Can't we just rest here? We are safe in the shadow of Khaytan's God Stone."

I resisted the urge to roll my eyes. Khaytan was not known for His caring. He possessed His predator changelings to feel the thrill of a never-ending hunt and discarded their bodies when they crumbled under the strain of containing His power. And yet the Church chose to constantly preach about the bountiful gifts Khaytan bestowed upon select followers.

"I gave you an order," I snapped at Thomas. "Men, saddle up!"

"All right, as you say, *Your Highness.*"

"This is no time for your considerable attitude," I said, exasperated, but he didn't hear me. He was mid-transformation, the soft colors of his fur giving way to the mahogany of his human hair, his tiny tail shrinking away.

I reached out my arms, and he handed Maria over. I wanted to prop her upright in front of me so her head would not dangle like that of a corpse, but that would draw curious looks. So, I laid her across the front of the saddle on her belly like a prize.

As soon as all the soldiers had taken human form and mounted up, Thomas brought out some ropes, tying them through the horses' bridles to form a chain. Pulling the rope attached to the lead horse, Thomas led the party back toward more traveled paths and the Cherbourg capital.

I tied the reigns to my arms to help keep me in the saddle should sleep take me. Maria's trembling drew my attention. Every breath exhaled with a slight whimper. I shook my head, frowning. Yes, she had hampered my plans, but I had stolen her dreams just when she'd managed to touch them. Maybe I could offer her a little comfort before delivering her into the hands of death. Tomorrow, she would be tortured and slaughtered, presented at our dinner table, steaming and browned. It was her place to serve, even to feed her superiors when she died, but what she had endured... was still enduring... was not the natural order, it was cruelty. Yes, a bit of comfort could be my gift, my apology.

Unsure, I stroked the fur at the top of her head. Her sniffles ceased in an instant, and her deep eyes snapped to my face with such fierceness I felt she was staring into both my souls. Transfixed, I continued to stroke her head, feeling like a confused puppy.

The fierce gaze turned to resignation before my eyes.

"Stop. Please don't touch me," she moaned.

The disgust in her tone ignited something putrid deep in my chest. "You are mine to do with as I like. Would you rather I hurt you or treat you like a pet?" Yet, I removed my hand. She had cowed me without force; it seemed my natural state of being.

She looked away, at last, turning as far from me as she could, and closed her eyes to sleep. Sometime later, trying not to look at her, I joined her.

* * *

As I returned to consciousness, I still felt exhausted. I groaned, and then realized I couldn't see. I tried to open my eyes, but a silk cloth covered them. My entire body felt numb, arms and legs immobile.

Panic seized my heart. Had the Lepores escaped and tied me up? Had the boars caught up to us?

"Where am I? Release me at once!" I shouted. I received no answer, only a faint echo that made me feel as though I was trapped in a cold, empty crypt.

Then, all of a sudden, I was warmed from within, and sweat rolled down my forehead. A strange light revealed itself, so bright that I was grateful for the blindfold. Even still, I had to shut my lids, tilting my head from side to side, anything to escape the burning glow.

Someone grabbed my head. The flesh on those hands was soft and smooth, imbued with the pleasing scent of lavender. They tilted my head upward, and the light faded. Through the silk folds on my eyes, I saw the silhouette of a woman wearing some sort of crown.

Mother? I thought.

She whispered something to me, in a voice and language I didn't recognize, like a melodious, complex chant.

"What is the value of life?" my mouth asked without my consent.

What is this? That isn't what I wanted to ask.

The woman touched my cheeks with one set of soft hands, then wrapped a second set around my neck. She giggled playfully and then screamed, "Nothing!" as Her now stone-cold hands began to choke me.

I gasped for breath, but none came. My lungs burned, begging for release. Just when I thought I'd lose consciousness, She released me.

"And everything..." She continued, voice sweet once again. "It matters who you ask."

I tried to shout, 'Who are you?' but my tongue would not obey.

"You hold a life in your hands, Reginald," She said as a cacophony of sounds rang out around us—mountains collapsing, waves crashing, cannons firing, bones cracking—and drowned out some of Her next words. "She is... like you..."

The woman shifted again into that foreign language, but this time, I understood their meaning: "What does one life matter to you? Something... or nothing?"

The woman kissed my forehead and then vanished, leaving me alone in total darkness.

CHAPTER FIVE
The Road to Freedom

Maria

My plan couldn't have failed more spectacularly. I cringed against the memory that rushed back as the morning sun woke me. I wallowed in the darkness behind my lids. When I'd heard them coming and transformed in the middle of that damned thicket, I'd had a plan. I'd intended to find a way to separate the prince from his foot soldiers, but they had all stuck together like glue, no matter how many winding trails I made. As they drew closer and my strength waned, I had lost control over my animal side. Overtaken by fear and my instinct to flee, I fell into temporary madness, squandering my one chance to speak with him alone.

I slowly opened my eyes, still unaccustomed to the intensity of the sun, and twitched my nose. Beside me, the prince stirred in his sleep, and I was surprised to see he was in wolf form. I could have sworn when he placed me on his horse he was human... though I didn't get a good look through my tears in the dark. I lay still, pondering him. He didn't look as vicious as his wolf brethren curled around him. His fangs did not protrude through his jowls, and his ears came to rounded hills instead of peaks.

I didn't know what to expect from him, but the signs were good. He had stayed his soldier's hand and spared my life. And he had... stroked me. I didn't feel comfortable being treated like a pet, but it was certainly better than being lashed or beaten... or torn limb from limb by hungry mouths.

I tried to shift into a more comfortable position, but the bindings around my paws made it difficult. My shoulder ached. I rocked back and forth until I got the momentum required to roll over. The prince's squire startled me. Although, he didn't look so frightening, with freckles dotting his boyish cheeks. I vaguely recalled him pulling the horses off the road at the break of dawn so everyone could rest behind the cover of an abandoned farm building with a partially collapsed roof.

Now the sun had fully emerged. I gazed in awe upon sprawling orchards and lush pastures—fields of golden wheat bordered by wooden fences and stone walls. I prayed this first glimpse would not be my last.

The prince's words, whispered at my ear last night, gave me a glimmer of hope. *Maybe not*, he'd said when I'd lamented the loss of my short-lived freedom. But they were taking me to the King of Blood Counts. That much was certain, and unless I did something drastic and made my plea to the prince in secret... I was going to die.

As I watched, his breathing quickened, and his eyes flew open. They glistened like polished aquamarines, finding me instantly. Startled and unsure what to say, I opted for being polite.

"Oh, hello. Good morning," I said. "I'm very sorry for waking you."

He puffed out his jowls with a scoff and said nothing. So much for having manners.

Then, as he rose, he looked down at his paws, and his ears flicked back in alarm.

"When did I...?" he murmured, but cut off when he saw me watching curiously. He cleared his throat and shook from head to tail. He turned to the Felis. "Thomas, am I mistaken, or are these Baron Malcolm Metzger's lands?"

"They are indeed, sir. We're in the farmlands north of the city. We should reach home in a few hours."

"Good, but there's no need to rush. We can rest here for an hour or two." He spared me a fleeting glance. "Untie the rabbit's forelegs and help her to her feet."

The lad grumbled, but he obeyed with a flick of his hunting knife. I started to help myself up, but the boy grabbed my ears and lifted me completely off the ground, kicking and squirming and biting my tongue against a scream.

"Hmmph," he said, looking at me with a scowl. "I thought she'd squeal. They usually do. This one's no fun." He dumped me on the ground with an ornery grin.

"Thomas, I said help her up," said the prince with a mild frown of distaste. "Why must cats always play with their food?"

Thomas scowled and wrestled me roughly onto my paws, his fingers digging into my ribs. I'd had enough bullying for a lifetime, and I decided to teach the boy some manners, kicking out with my bound back feet and connecting with his skinny midriff.

He grunted in pain and cried, "Why you little..." But before he could strike me, the prince leaped between us and snapped his jaws in a warning bite close enough to take off one of my whiskers.

"If you attack my squire again, you will feel my wrath. Do you hear me?" he spoke evenly, but he had made his point.

"Yes, yes," I mumbled, staring at the woken wolves and their perverse smiles. I wondered, not for the first time, if I was delusional. What little compassion this man might have did not extend to putting prey before predator. I stood still and silent, wobbly on my bound back legs, as Thomas used a length of rope to secure me to the tree where they'd hitched their horses. The pack ate rations, their eyes flicking toward me as if pondering whether I would taste better than what they had.

It seemed they'd gotten little rest atop their horses, because they all quickly dropped off to sleep with their bellies full. Even the guard the prince had appointed struggled to keep his eyes open. The prince turned twice on a makeshift bed of hay and grass and then settled down to sleep. It was now or never.

I inched forward, reaching the end of my rope. He flicked an eye open at me but closed it when I sat beside him.

"You're taking me to Cherbourg palace, yes?" I asked in a whisper.

He looked at me through narrowed eyes.

"Yes."

"Why does the king want me alive?"

He only watched me, his animal face unreadable.

"I heard you say the king wants me alive. Please tell me why."

Just when I thought he'd refuse to answer, he sighed and said in a dull voice, "Best that you don't know. Besides, you're not really allowed to speak to me."

"Oh, I see," I said, anger rushing to my head like a gush of steam. His easy arrogance was somehow more maddening than the cruelty I was accustomed to. But I couldn't think too harshly of him. Hubris was no doubt part of his upbringing, but his small amount of civility had to mean something. I had to hope it was a genuine, goddess-given emotion, his natural state. Perhaps I just had to peel back the outer, princely layers that acted as a shell.

I took a calming breath and said, "Well, then I am glad that Maya is allowed to speak for us. I just wish you wouldn't ignore Her. You invoked Her name in the mine so casually, as though you speak to Her often. And then again in your sleep last night. I heard it clear as the night sky. What were you asking Her? Did She respond?"

He flicked his eyes to his sleeping pack mates and then lunged at me, jaws open. I fell back, terrified, but instead of latching onto my throat as I'd expected, he picked me up by the scruff and leaped with me around the side of the dilapidated farmhouse before I had time to let out anything but a gasp. He dropped me unceremoniously on the ground and shoved me against the outer wall with a paw.

I could feel his breath on my face as he snarled, "Are you trying to get us both killed?"

"I hardly think they'd kill their prince," I said with a scoff, trying to calm my racing heart and keep my human side in charge.

"Maybe not with their own hands, but..." He looked toward the back of the building where the pack slept and let his words trail off. He shook his head with a grunt of frustration.

I stared at him, astounded. He seemed truly frightened. Perhaps privilege and status did not save even predator princes from the King of Blood Counts' laws.

"I'm sorry," I said. "I thought my words might bring you ridicule from your pack, nothing more. I thought I was only endangering myself in trying to talk with you."

He reared back his head slightly as if utterly thrown by my words.

"What is it about you?" he snapped with sudden emotion, flashing his teeth. I could not tell if it was anger or pure exasperation. "What kind of spell are you casting on me, witch? Just like before, you utterly confound me!"

"I'm not using any magic against you..." I said.

"Oh, of course not," he scoffed. "Then what overtook my dreams last night? What sorcery brought on such a vision?"

"A vision?" I said, aghast. I lowered my voice and said, "You see Maya in your dreams, too?"

"Ha! You admit you have the power to bring on such visions," he said, eyes wild, but his voice betrayed his fear.

"What? No. The Great Mother has come to me twice. She told me to fr..." I paused, thinking it wasn't wise to reveal that Maya had told me I could bring about the liberation of all prey changelings. I started over. "The second time She came to me was after you spared my life. She said I would meet you again, and I have."

"And you expect me to believe that?" I could tell he was wrestling with himself, trying to keep his volume in check. "You expect me to believe you didn't drug me or bewitch me like one of the Karluk or boar shamans? That Maya Herself came down to me and told me to let you live?"

Tears filled my eyes. "She said that?"

He lowered his paw, releasing me. "You... You're telling the truth, aren't you?" he said, the deep reluctance in his voice suggesting he had preferred to believe I was a witch.

I was still awed by his former revelation. "I had begun to fear I was wrong and was destined to die, but She truly does want me to speak with you."

"And you were ready to accept death? No pleading? No complaints?"

"If it is Maya's will that I die, then I will accept it."

He pricked his ears forward as if wondering if he heard right.

"But you have said yourself, it is not Her will," I continued. "I was right. My escape was an act of divine intervention so that you could be the one to catch me."

"So you are not a witch; you're insane. You escaped from Marburg. You had freedom. And yet you planned all along for me to catch you? Rabbits are truly as dimwitted as they say."

My anger returned, hot enough to make a kettle whistle. He'd grown up with slaves. His family owned thousands of all prey species. Yet he knew nothing of us but false generalizations bestowed on us by other predators. We were all below him. All expendable. All worthless.

"I admit, I don't know why Maya wanted me to find you," I hissed. "You wear a cloak of decency about you, but in reality, you just like making your own rules. You're looking to get out from under your father's thumb."

He gaped at me, incredulous.

"You think your small favors make you different, but you view us the same as your peers do," I said, tears burning my eyes. "You're nothing but a petty bully looking to make himself feel good."

"You don't know anything..."

"I know enough. And even if I have misinterpreted Maya's will and my time has come, at least for a brief moment, I was free. Which is more than I can say for you."

"I'm sorry, what did you just say?" He snorted and shook as though a bee had stung his muzzle.

"You're a prince, and yet you fear saying the name of Maya. Something I will do with my dying breath, regardless of the consequences. You need not labor for your living, and yet you went out of your way to give yourself the task of single-handedly improving Marburg. You do not answer to an overseer, but you answer to a brute who cares little for any life but his own, and I'm quite certain that indifference extends even to his own son. Your whole life, you will be despised by those beneath you and mistrusted by those you would call friends. And so you persecute me for my faith. You call my rationalities foolish, but at least I have a purpose. What is yours?"

"I... you..." It seemed his fury had rendered him speechless.

I tested my luck. "I don't think you have one. But it looks to me as though Maya is trying to give you one. The question is, will you accept it?"

A guttural growl summoned the hackles on his back.

I had pushed him too far. Trembling despite myself under his fierce gaze, I prayed to Maya and tipped back my head to expose my neck, hoping he might be courteous enough to end me quickly. But when he lunged, it was my bindings he ripped. He yanked me off my feet and half-chewed, half-pulled them loose.

"You will get us both drawn and quartered by the Absolvers," he said through a growl bubbling in his chest.

I struggled for words, testing my bruised back legs.

"I must be mad," he muttered to himself.

"No, wolf prince, today, at last, you are acting with purpose. Today, you're truly alive," I said. "Maya smiles upon you. And I thank you."

"Don't offer your thanks yet," he said, ears swiveling toward the sleeping Lobo on the other side of the wall. "And I suppose you may call me Reginald since we are now a criminal pair."

I suppressed a derisive snort but couldn't hold back my tongue. "Oh, how gracious of you."

"Yes, it is, and I'd have you remember it, rabbit," he snapped.

"My name is Maria."

"If you want to survive, *Maria*, stay your tongue and do exactly as I tell you." He spoke my name as if each syllable was an unpleasant chore. "Do not doubt me. Do not second guess me."

He drew a deep breath and stood on his hind legs, surprising me by placing his front paws on my cheeks. I froze in his grasp, angry at being treated like a child but instinctively nervous at being so close to his claws.

"Those wolves will come after you, but only I know what you look like in human form. If you can throw them off your scent, as you did outside the mine, you can blend in... though your tattoo may bring you trouble. Change back, right now."

"You first."

"Are you giving me orders?" he said, wrinkling his muzzle. "What did I tell you? Do as I say and only as I say."

"Perhaps if I say please?" I said, flashing an awkward, buck-toothed smile beneath my quivering whiskers. My dress had been torn to shreds in my mad dash through the forest, and I wasn't thrilled to discover exactly what it might expose when I changed back.

"Why?" he said through gritted teeth.

"I'd feel better about giving up my speed if you gave up your fangs."

"Must you make everything difficult?" he asked. He closed his eyes and sighed, as if I was testing the very last ounce of his patience. "So be it. We will do this together."

I shut my eyes and touched my human side, asking it to come forward. My fur retreated into my body and my torso straightened and grew taller. I peered through one eye and then the other, afraid to look down at myself. I could feel the holes and slashes in my dress by the sensation of sun and wind against random patches of skin on my belly, chest, and back.

My glimpses of the prince in human form had been nothing but shadowy figures and blurred movements. In the mine, I had tried to imagine what a young aristocrat looked like, and I'd come rather close. His large jaw was clean-shaven. His chestnut hair was well-groomed. His nose was prominent but perfectly straight and fairly thin. His muscles properly filled out the armor that had gaped on him as a wolf, and he stood tall and firm, sure of himself. What I hadn't predicted was the catch of my breath as my gaze lingered on his tanned skin and noted the way his hair curled at the nape.

I shook myself internally, cursing myself for a fool, and sent up a silent prayer to the benevolent ram. *Wise Sammael, give me Your temperance and let me not be deterred by the follies of my flesh.*

As I moved my eyes back to his face, I found him staring at me, and I crossed my arms tight across my chest.

"You look much nicer without the bruises. Hair is still messy, though." He flicked a strand of it with a smirk, and I slapped his hand away instinctively. My eyes widened at what I'd done, but I decided I didn't want to apologize, so I hardened my jaw in a silent challenge.

He snorted out a low laugh and shook his head. "I will admit you are quite brave."

When I said nothing, his face grew serious.

"You need something to cover up that sack of a dress. Wait here."

He crept around the dilapidated house on the balls of his feet, and I held my breath, only letting it out when he returned with a light, navy cloak.

"This is Thomas'. He'll be none too pleased," he said, handing it over.

I gratefully drew it tight around me.

"Now, follow my directions exactly," he said, "because if you get lost, you will be neck deep in shite. Do you see that wall behind me?" He gestured across the dirt road we'd traveled last night.

"Yes," I said, glancing over his shoulder at the five-foot stone wall that ran the length of a neighboring field.

"I will lift you over it. Run straight across the field. When you reach the other side, you'll have to climb the fence there yourself or pray there's a way around."

"I can do it."

The hint of a grin twitched his lips. "On the other side of the fence is a main, paved road. That will be the most dangerous place on your journey, you understand? Keep your tattoo covered and don't speak to anyone. Go right on that road as fast as you can without drawing attention, then take a left when it forks. You'll come to an intersection. Take a right, and you will come to a scattered group of residences. Enter through the second gate on the left. There will be a stone house. The man who lives there will offer you protection. You will treat him graciously, and forgo this disrespectful attitude of yours. Understand?"

I scowled at him, but the sound of a wolf whining in his sleep made me abandon my protest.

"Right after the fence, left at the fork, right at the intersection, second property on the left. But... who lives there?"

"A bear."

"A bear?!" I nearly shouted, making him slap a hand over my mouth to muffle my outburst.

"Shhhh, you foolish girl," he hissed, drawing his angry face close to mine.

I tried to speak, but with my lips shoved against his palm, it came out a jumbled mess.

He clenched his jaw and exhaled slowly. "What?" he said, taking his hand off my mouth.

"I said, 'why don't you just roast me now?'"

He rolled his eyes. "He's a vegetarian. Besides, you will tell him that I sent you."

"And he will believe a Lobo prince sent a Lepores to his house?"

He dug a hand down the collar of his tunic and pulled up a golden disk talisman the size of a walnut. On its surface, a rampant wolf howled at the moon, its eyes made of the same red gemstones that were dotted around the edge, commingling with symbols I didn't recognize. He pulled it over his head, grabbed my wrist, and placed it in my hand, closing my fingers over it. "Take this as proof."

It only took up half my palm, but it was heavy. Solid gold. An expensive item probably worth more than my whole family in coin. "I can't take this," I said. "He will think I stole it."

"I should hope he thinks higher of me than that, but if he

gives you trouble, tell him, 'The golden bull whispered to the moons, *Freedom has a heavy price.*' Repeat it back to me."

I did as he said, internally cursing this all as madness. But he was my only hope... and Maya wanted me to trust him, didn't She?

I followed him to the wall without a word, and he hoisted me up with his interlocked hands beneath my bare left foot.

"Good luck," he whispered as I straddled the stone.

"May Maya be with us both." I dangled my legs over the other side, and before I slipped off into the rows of cabbage, I looked over my shoulder and whispered, "Thank you, Reginald."

My feet sank in the supple soil as I raced between fat cabbages. I was tempted to steal one, but there was no time. When the stone fence came into view, I picked up my pace and launched myself at it, grabbing the top with my fingers and planting my right foot on a jutting stone. I hauled myself up to peer over the top but ducked down at the sight of a small horse-drawn carriage. I waited for the sounds of horse hooves and squeaky wooden wheels to fade and then peeked again.

Someone was coming from the left, but they were a shimmering dot on the horizon, obscured by heat haze. I pulled myself up and over and then went right, following the road to the fork, taking a left, just as Reginald had told me, keeping the squire's cloak tight around me and my hair over my tattoo. I passed a half dozen travelers, all on foot, but only a bushy-bearded fellow in a straw hat paid me any mind. When he narrowed his eyes at me, I tried to keep my gate steady and hold my head high. I could feel his eyes on my back, but he never said a word.

Still, when I arrived at the intersection, I was a bundle of nerves, and at the sound of another approaching carriage, I wasted no time in ducking behind a large road marker, praying the coachman hadn't noticed me.

To my relief, he passed me by, but the crack of his whip brought back hellish visions that put a fire to my heels. When the sounds of the carriage faded away, I ran down the right branch of the intersection and didn't slow as the street led into a residential area as Reginald had promised. The houses were far apart and set far back from the road, all surrounded by fences.

I stopped in front of the second left-hand gate and let myself into the yard. The quaint stone home sat on a field of pumpkin patches, and, here and there, fully clothed straw-men stood guard.

As I made my way to the front door, a mouse crossed my path. I watched its soft grey rump with a grin. A large bird swooped down close enough to fan my hair and snatched the poor mouse in its talons, ripping flesh and shaking fur from its beak as it went in for the kill with a quick peck. It ruffled its brown feathers, then bobbed its head at me, its golden eyes curious and daring, as if challenging me to try and take its meal. I jumped back as it let out a screeching call.

Still shaken from the journey, I headed for the front door, wracking my brain to recall the phrase Reginald had told me to memorize. I held the gold medallion in one hand, took a deep breath, and then knocked with the other. I said a silent prayer to Maya and Sammael to protect me from this supposedly vegetarian bear.

The door opened, and a gruff voice boomed, "Hello?"

I looked up slowly, first taking in the enormous boots that had appeared on the threshold, and saw a bald man with a prominent, fat nose and a dense russet beard. His shoulders brushed either side of the door frame, and he was ducking under the mantel to keep from hitting his head. This man wasn't a bear, he was a goliath.

"Can I help you?" the Ursa asked, scrunching his thick brows, and I took an instinctive step back.

I swallowed hard, acutely aware that this man could snap my petite limbs like twigs, probably with one hand. "I'm sorry," I said, sounding short of breath. "Wrong house. I need to go."

I made to turn away, but he grabbed me, his hand enveloping most of my forearm.

"Hang on, what's that?" he said, pulling my hand clutching the talisman closer to his eyes. He snarled at the sight and yanked me inside. He spun me, snatched the talisman away, and pushed me further into the home, nearly slamming me into a roughly carved round table.

He bolted the door and then glared at me over his shoulder. He turned on me, blocking my exit, and said, "You'd better tell me very quickly how you got this." He held the talisman between two fingers, completely obscuring its surface. "Speak now, girl! I don't much like thieves." He reached for an ax that stood near the door.

"No, I didn't steal it! It was given to me..."

My blood went cold as he twirled the ax, examining its blade. "Pardon me, miss, but I don't think I believe you. This is a priceless heirloom. Do you have any idea who this belongs to? What you've done?"

"I have done nothing wrong. The Prince of Wolves himself placed that in my hand freely." I took a step back as he took one toward me, ax blade raised by his head. My next words spilled out in a rush. "Please, I don't know why, but he sent me here to speak to you. He said for me to tell you, 'The golden bull whispered to the moons, *Freedom has a heavy price.*'"

The ax lowered slowly as his eyebrow raised. When he let the handle clunk on the floor and leaned it back beside the door frame, I let out a sigh of relief. Then it occurred to me this bruiser didn't need a weapon to crush me. He closed the distance between us in one stride, and I pressed my back against the table, leaning away from his two outstretched fingers, but there was nowhere to run.

"Calm down, girl. Not going to hurt you," he said, brushing my hair away and running his fingers across my rabbit tattoo. "Well, I'll be damned. Reggie decided to take pity on a rabbit. Sit down over there," he said, voice calm as a summer stream as he pointed to a chair next to a cupboard.

I obliged, happy to rest my aching, cut feet. He placed the medallion on the table, and then he flared his nostrils. I smelled it, too. Something was burning. He cursed and skirted around the table, scrambling for the oven, the flame inside now roaring.

He mitted his hand and plunged it in, pulling out a baking tray.

"Oh damn it. Well, at least it's not burned too badly." He placed the pastry, bigger than my head, on the table, scooting it off the tray gingerly with a thumb. The crust was charred black, but the center filling, though raised and bubbled in places, was a nice russet color. He looked at me a moment, but I didn't have the courage to meet his gaze. I wrapped my arms around my stomach, hoping he hadn't heard my guts rumbling.

"You hungry, girl?"

I flicked my eyes up at him as he pulled out a knife and began slicing.

"I wouldn't refuse you if you gave me the burned crusts," I said, leaning forward in the chair despite myself, my mouth watering.

The man smiled, face full of pity, and slid a whole piece onto a plate. He brought it over, holding it out in both hands.

"Here, take it. But let it cool down a simmer."

I felt my eyes fill with tears, thinking of the last time someone had offered me a pie. I was surprised by the pity in his gaze, and I didn't dare refuse him.

"Thank you," I said, taking it from his grasp. "Maya bless you, friend."

He narrowed his eyes at that, but said, "You're welcome." He poured me a drink from a pitcher on his sanded counter. He placed it on the table while I blew on the steaming pumpkin filling.

"Excuse me. I need to get something," he said. "But you'll be a good girl and wait here, right?"

"Yes, sir." I nodded vehemently, still unsure what to make of him and frightened he might raise that ax at me again.

He walked into the next room, and I took a look about the kitchen. Pots and pans hung on a wooden rack, open cupboards fixed to the walls held plain white plates, and most of the space was overtaken by the oven next to the table, its flume rising out of the ceiling.

The door opened, and my eyes immediately found the flintlock musket in his hand and the two pistols on his belt.

"Oh Sweet Mother, no, please, I told you the truth..."

"Relax, girl," he said, sitting down at the table and resting the musket harmlessly against his chair. "How many times do I have to tell ya I'm not going to harm ya? Scoot your chair over here. Sit with me."

Heartbeat returning somewhat to normal, I did as he asked.

When I was settled, hand clasped around my cup, he said, "I'm sure you would like for me to be honest with ya, miss. So I'll tell ya, there's two things that could happen soon. One, Reginald comes back for you, preferably alone."

"Or two?"

"Those hooded snakes behind Emmerich's damned inquisition come a-knocking at my door, and if that's the case, I'm afraid I might have to hand you over."

"You mean Absolvers?" I asked, shocked to hear a predator use the word 'inquisition.'

"Aye," he said with disgust.

This bear was more interesting by the minute.

"So, why the guns then?" I asked.

"In case giving you to the Inquisitor won't make him happy."

"Oh, well, that's reassuring." I pulled a sour smile, trying to keep my face strong, but my legs had turned to jelly. I might have proclaimed in front of my friends and family that I'd like to see an Inquisitor try and test my faith, and I did mean to proclaim my love for Maya until the bitter end, but the thought of actually being at the mercy of an Inquisitor iced my blood. No changeling survived an encounter with an Inquisitor: those vile elite changelings who shaved their fur and took human form so rarely their paws had morphed into long-fingered, gnarled hands to better hold their instruments of torture. A death at their malformed hands would be neither swift nor merciful.

"Try not to worry about it," he said, picking up his piece of pie in one hand. "If Maya kept you safe for so long, maybe She won't forsake you just yet." He bit into his meal, taking half the slice in his mouth in one go.

My brows reached for the heavens. "And do you actually pray to Maya? Do you view Her as Mother of all, or do you think Her a decrepit old woman bowing at the feet of Her rebellious son, Khaytan?"

He dropped the pie and grabbed my chin, forcing me to look in his blazing eyes.

"Now you listen good, girl. Never insult me like that again, or you'll be in for it. I am no heathen or mindless Covenant follower."

"I'm sorry," I said, freeing my chin with a sideways yank of my head. "It's just I have heard predators invoke Maya's name more in the last few days than in my entire life, and I was curious if it was indeed said in earnest."

He gave a small smile. "Heard Reginald say it, did you?"

"Yes."

"His father might be the reason the whole kingdom's been thrown into spiritual ignorance, but his mother is a fine, smart woman. She taught him the truth. As mine taught me." He gave me a slight nod, scarfed down his pie, and then retrieved powder, shot, and wadding to load his musket.

"Pardon for my rudeness, miss. I shouldn't forget the sufferings of your people at the hands of the Covenant. But if you make me your friend, I might shoot the devils for more than my own satisfaction." He winked at me, a friendly gesture rather than the lecherous sort I was used to. "Eat, before it gets cold."

I followed his example and picked the piece up without utensils, though I had to use both hands. The first bite made me close my eyes. I eagerly took another bite, and then another.

He waited while I ate, tamping a deadly concoction down the barrel of his musket. "You got a name, girl? What's your story?" he asked me as soon as I had finished.

"My name's Maria. I am... I was a slave in Marburg mine."

"Was? Reggie freed you? Wants a pet, does he?" he asked with a shake of his head.

"No, I escaped."

He set his musket down and looked at me with mouth slightly

open. "How by the light of the gods did you do that?"

"There was an earthquake, and a tunnel collapse opened up a way to the surface."

"Sounds like you got mighty lucky. Luckier still that it was Reginald who caught you."

I resisted the urge to roll my eyes and decided to change the subject. "Do pardon me, but what's your name? Are you one of Reginald's knights?"

"Name's Angus. And no, I'm a mercenary."

"Again excuse me for my ignorance, but what's the difference?"

"Knights got obligations to fight for their lords and masters. Mercenaries fight for whoever is paying. But I served with Reggie's father in the army once, same as I did him. And besides that, we're friends."

"So that's where the secret phrase came from? Your days in battle?"

"Well, if you let me finish eating, I'll tell you."

I nodded and watched him finish off the pie. When he'd brushed the crumbs from his chest and beard, he leaned with one elbow on the table.

"This might surprise you, as a rabbit, but not all prey changelings are treated the same. I can tell you tales of many prey changelings who made their mark on history and earned respect from predators." He pulled a strange, pondering, mildly disgusted face. "Of course, they still were eaten if they died in animal form, but it's just the way of nature, I suppose."

He paused to drink from his flagon. I lifted my own heavy cup with care and paused when I got a whiff of the strange scent.

When I pulled a face, thinking poison, he chuckled and said, "That there is a beer, Maria. Somehow I don't think they ever gave you rabbits any."

"No," I said, sniffing again. It smelled like a belch, but somehow mildly sweet. I took a sip, and then a gulp. It was deliciously cold, and there was an odd but pleasant tang at the end. I tipped my head back, chugging it down, and Angus watched me with a mix of trepidation and admiration. As I set down the cup, a burp slipped between my lips, making me blush.

"Sorry, I was just so parched." Warmth spread from my cheeks to the tips of my fingers and toes.

He grabbed my cup, peered inside, and threw back his head laughing. "I think I like you already, Maria."

He got up and refilled both our cups, talking as he went.

"A few years back, Lord General De Draco waged a campaign against the Karluk in the south. The soldiers started calling it The War of the Golden Bulls. The general allowed oxen and bulls to join our ranks in exchange for a soldier's salary and a small cut of land should they return home."

"Well, oxen are almost as frightening as you bears. I saw a few of them once, pulling massive ore carriages out of the mine."

He chuckled. "Glad to hear you still think us Ursa are at the top. But you're right. Usually takes four wolves to take down a bovine. And even then, the wolves should be careful."

He dissolved into a long-winded tale about smaller battles and skirmishes in the war. I got to hear what he thought about De Draco and his captains. He didn't seem to care for any of them save Reginald, whom he talked about as if his crown was a glowing halo, riding at the front of his company instead of hiding in the back, bending down with helping hands to all who served him. He lingered on Reginald so often in his weavings of the battlefield, I began to feel as though I'd seen the prince charging through the ranks with my own eyes, sitting tall and strong with sword raised in a battle cry. He offered details that had nothing to do with swinging swords or leading companies, also. "Always wore his hair a little longer in the army, so it just started covering his ears in soft waves," he told me. "Kept a short beard, too. I told him he ought not to shave it, even when we returned home." He chuckled, staring wistfully at one of his hanging pots as if it bore Reginald's image. "Made him look more dignified."

At last, when he saw my head nodding, heavy with the buzz of alcohol and smothering exhaustion, he remembered the point of his story.

"Don't think less of me when I tell you I can't remember most of the names of those oxen and bison who fought at my side. I remember few wolves, too. But there was one bull I cannot forget. His name was Hubert."

He let the name hang in the air for a moment as if taking time to think on it with reverence.

"He was a white bull. Fitting, for everything about him was honest, free of blemish. It is hard for a man to be both strong of will and humble, but Hubert achieved it. He had the respect of everybody. Even Lord De Draco, for all his pride, had little but good to say of him."

"And what was his job?"

"Ha, well, before the war, he was a prizefighter, and he taught others to brawl. He was also a bit of a philosopher. He was rather small for a bull, but no one made the mistake of underestimating him twice. In the army, in addition to his regular duties as a soldier, he was tasked with training new recruits in hand-to-hand combat, should they be disarmed. He was a patient teacher. Pulled his punches to give everybody a chance. Of course, if you were more of his match in weight, as I was, you would be in for the fight of your life."

"Did Reginald ever fight with him?"

Angus leaned forward, his broad, ruddy face lighting with a huge smile as he propped his chin in his hand. "He sure did, even beat Hubert once or twice. You see, Reggie is smart, knows how to play his strengths. He was quick on his feet, tired him out, and attacked him only when he couldn't swing no more."

"And what sort of philosophies did he view?"

"Hubert thought there was a meaning to all things in life. He believed Maya gave all Her changelings the will to live, but that they should fight for a *right* to live under the sun. Because if there is one thing that Maya does not tolerate, it's laziness."

Maya valued hard work and industriousness, it was true—it was all laid out in the words of Her sacred book—but I wondered if this Hubert had thought less of Lepores who had not fought hard enough, in his definition, to earn a place of equality. That sounded like a tamer version of the predators' thinking, that we were born to serve, that we did not have or could not earn another purpose. Changelings should take pride in their work, yes. That was what Maya taught, but there was no need for inhuman suffering. Lepores had not doomed themselves to their place of slavery. They had been forced there by those who valued themselves over all else and pawned their labors onto others. But I held my tongue, not wanting to challenge the ideals of a friend who, by the way Angus talked, had passed on.

"And what happened to him?" I asked, instead.

"Near the end of the war, we besieged a Karluk village. We broke through their pitiful wall, and some of the defenders retreated. One of the captains ordered our company, Reginald's company, to pursue them."

By the look on his face, I thought I saw where this was going. "They were not fleeing in fear, were they?"

"No, girl. It was a trap. Wild dogs and lions on every side. They came up out of holes dug in the sand. Hubert rallied his oxen companions and formed a wall in front of Reginald and the rest of us, driving them back long enough for us to turn tail and fight the few in back. But when we were free, the dogs closed in on Hubert and his men from behind. I saw them swarm. Saw them leap onto Hubert's back and pull him down. We gave him up for dead, but only a month later we caught a slavers' caravan using him as a pack mule."

He grimaced at the memory, and I said softly, "They had done something to him?"

"The desert dwellers give their war prisoners a choice. But if you refuse to be a turncoat, they take your hands so you can't raise them against them ever again, and then you are made a slave. They'd done a half-arsed job on Hubert's stitches. An open wound in the desert is agony. When we overtook the caravan and saved him, he was praying for death. The wounds were infected, his arms inflamed to the shoulders. But most of us were his friends. Broken as he was, we pleaded for the captains to send him home rather than put him down. We lost that debate, though. The army was still marching, and we needed food. Hubert finally cracked a smile. Said that if anyone should eat him, it should be his old comrades."

I didn't want to hear any more of this. Didn't want to hear how Hubert had tasted. Didn't even want to imagine Angus' teeth digging into a shapeless, cooked hunk of meat, knowing it had been a man he once called his friend. But the look on his face said he wouldn't talk of it, even if I'd asked.

"I'm very sorry," I said. "I did not mean to bring up painful memories."

"It's all right," he said with a half-smile. "Even if a memory is painful, you should treasure it. It still means something."

I nodded, returning his smile, deciding to ponder the happier side of this moment. I had learned of Hubert the bull from Angus the bear while sharing food and beer. What interesting friends I was making.

"Well, since you will be here a while longer, do you know how to play chess?" he asked.

"That's a game, right?"

He let out a loud, singular guffaw. "Yes, it's a game. You say that word like it's new to you."

"Working in the mine, we were never given time for games."

"Well, then, I'll teach you. But first, I'll heat up some water so you can clean yourself. And then we can... improvise something for you to wear. Get you out of those frightful rags."

Reginald

I slunk around the farmhouse, worried that my human foot-falls would wake the pack, wondering for the dozenth time in the last five minutes why I was doing this. What had I done? Had Maya compelled me to help this Lepores?

What does one life matter to you? Something... or nothing? The words from my dream echoed in my head as I wove between the sleeping Lobo toward Jack, who was sleeping standing up in animal form. What did her life matter to me? It shouldn't have mattered at all... and yet, that sounded eerily like Father. Maria's life mattered. All lives held meaning and purpose, but why did hers matter to me more than any other Lepores? Why did it matter more than my pack members'? There was a good chance they would be punished for losing her. And yet I hadn't thought of that for a moment when Maria's oceanic eyes were on me. I felt hot, restless, crazed, like I wasn't in control.

When I reached Jack, I tossed the severed ropes beside me and laid down on my blankets, thinking back to this morning, waking in wolf form when I'd fallen asleep a human. The memory was starting to come back to me. I closed my eyes, pretending to sleep, and called out to my wolf half, trying to touch its memories. While Maya was throttling my human mind, my wolf side, it seemed, had broken free. The images came slowly at first, and then in a rush. *A rabbit on the ground in front of my snout, my fangs bared. Saliva pooled in my mouth as I sniffed the breathing hunk of rabbit meat, yearning for a bite. But the voice of the Alpha made my ears fall and a whine escape me. The rabbit was not to be touched.*

I shuddered at the memory. My wolf side had only burst forth independently two other times in my life, and both had been in the throes of budding adolescence when I had little control over myself. Both times, as today, I had been frightened by the utter lack of humanity in the memories of my wolf half's thoughts. Last night, Maria had been nothing but a hunk of flesh. This morning, she had compelled me to risk life and limb with only her words. None of it made sense. As I shut my eyes, I saw Father's face twisted in fury, the frown lines around his thin mouth now deepening into craters. If he discovered the truth, he would be more than angry. He would be deadly. Mother would have to fight even harder to get my name etched on my tombstone next to Lothar's.

Father thought of Maria the same way as my wolf half. An expendable hunk of meat. If half of me thought that way, and half was a hapless boy swayed by a pretty face... who was I?

Maria's words came back to me as I scrunched my lids against the mounting anxiety tightening my chest. *At least I have a purpose. What is yours?*

The question was not who was I, but who did I want to be?

It looks to me as though Maya is trying to give you one. The question is, will you accept it?

Could I? What would it mean?

A tap on my shoulder nearly startled me out of my skin. My eyes shot open to find Thomas glaring at me.

"I know what you did," he whispered. "I heard you."

My heart threatened to seize, but I forced my face into a snarl. "Then you'd best keep quiet about it, kid, unless you want to explain why you didn't do anything to stop it."

He blustered, and I felt terrible for the fear I'd created in his eyes. "What could I do? You're the prince; I'm your squire," he said, struggling to keep his voice down.

I shushed him and said, "You think the king will wait to hear your explanation?"

He looked on the verge of tears, but he scowled defiantly at me. "Why did you do it?"

"That's none of your business."

"You're going to get us both killed," he whispered, the tears gathering on his lashes now.

"Thomas, have I ever led you astray? Have I ever been cruel to you? Have I ever brought you to harm?"

"No." He sniffed and wiped angrily at his face, trying to banish the tears before they fell.

"Then trust me. Who are you loyal to, Father or me?"

He chewed at the inside of his cheek before saying in a huff, "You." He glanced over his shoulder, checking for stirring tails or opening eyes. "But you can't ask me to lie for you if you're not going to tell me why. I thought you said we were friends."

How could I answer that when I didn't know myself?

I settled on a partial truth, one I thought might make some tiny amount of sense to him.

"She's suffered more than you know," I whispered. "She...

she is more valiant than some soldiers I know. I didn't want her to end up on Father's plate. It seemed an unfitting end. It felt wrong."

"Pardon me if this is mad," he said, voice bitter with sarcasm, "but have you fallen in love with a rabbit? Because I'm not certain I can risk my neck for a mad man."

"Don't be ridiculous. I just... I didn't want Father to have everything his way."

"You did all this... dragged me into a conspiracy that will get me handed over to the Absolvers... just to disobey your father?"

I shrugged. The whole thing sounded so foolish when it came from his tongue. My mind began to bounce from choice to choice, thought to thought, image to image, trying to find the better option, pinpoint where I'd gone wrong.

"You couldn't have had this rebellious streak when you were a lad and been done with it, could you?" said Thomas, running an anxious hand through his wavy hair. "No, you had to wait until you could drag somebody else into it."

"I thought you wanted adventure, Thomas. Excitement. You will be more than my squire in all this."

His face lit up for a moment, but he eyed me with caution. "Co-conspirators?"

"Yes," I said with a grin.

"Outlaws?"

"Let's hope it doesn't come to that."

"But if it does?"

"Then we shall lead a merry band of mercenaries together."

"Deal."

"Thank—"

"Shut your eyes," he hissed.

Startled into obedience, I did as he said. Then his bony fingers dug into my shoulder, and he shook me with all his might. *My, thanks for playing along, Thomas.*

"Reggie, wake up, wake up!" he bellowed in my ear. "The prisoner has escaped!"

As I feigned a confused look, blinking my eyes open, the pack sprang up and swarmed my resting place. Those still in wolf form sniffed the broken bonds while those in human form scanned the surrounding fields. I played my part of the fool, snatching up the ropes, examining the ends, and throwing them down in frustration.

"Damn it," I said. "The cuts are jagged. Looks like she gnawed herself loose." I stood up using Thomas' shoulders for support. "Did you see where she went, Thomas?!" I asked as I returned the favor of a good shake. His teeth clacked together as he pointed down the road the way we'd come.

"I think I saw her running that way!" he said, shooting me a glare when the others looked in the direction of his pointing finger.

"Well, let's not waste time! Come, men; let's go after her," I said. "Henry, stay here and mind the horses!"

"What? I was placed in charge of this outfit, Your Highness. I will lead the charge," said the lieutenant. "Have the squire stay."

The last thing I needed was him sticking his nose into this wild goose chase. He was by far the best tracker here, and he might smell a rat as well as a rabbit.

"I am your prince, and I say I need someone competent guarding the horses. Thomas saw where she went. Come, squire, lead the way!" I transformed as quickly as I could manage, pretending I hadn't done this twice in barely eight hours. I'd have to take it easy when this nonsense was over.

"This way, I'm sure she went this way!" called Thomas.

I felt a tinge of guilt as the pack followed without question, but when Thomas, now a sleek, muscled lynx with black-tipped ears and mischievous yellow eyes, looked back at me with a wink, I was infected by his playful attitude.

We disturbed vegetable patches, scared grazing sheep, and even broke a fence, all looking for our imaginary prey. Eventually, the pack got irritated, and more than one farmer shouted at us with flintlock in hand before they realized who they were dealing with.

Lieutenant Henry certainly wasn't happy when he saw us

coming back without Maria.

"So, not a single one of you could pick up her trail?"

"Maybe she changed into her human form to give us the slip again," said a white wolf. "Only you and the crown prince got a good whiff of that side of her."

"Who was the fool who fell asleep and let her escape?" roared Henry, whirling on the pack. "Which one of you was on guard, hmm?"

"That's not important, lieutenant," I said. "This is my fault. I should have kept my eyes on her. The men are right. I'm the one who knows her human scent best. Thomas and I are going to keep looking. The rest of you return to the castle and promise Father I will return with his slave."

"Are you mad? King Emmerich will have our heads for this."

"He will do nothing until the matter is resolved one way or another. You are prized soldiers. Tell him that I will be back with her."

"But what if you don't find her?"

"We will put a bounty on her head, and someone will turn her in. You are all dismissed."

"But sir, we can't..."

"Lieutenant, I gave you an order."

I knew he wouldn't directly disobey me, but he might keep looking on the way home. Either way, I was confident they had far too much ground to cover and too few supplies in their packs.

Thomas and I saddled up and got on our way—me in wolf form, him a boy once more. We rode in silence until the pack was nothing but dark dots in the distance.

"Well, that was rather entertaining," said Thomas. "Henry was right about one thing, though. King Emmerich will be mighty mad if he finds out about this. I tried telling you."

"He won't. We will have to outsmart him."

Thomas let out a sharp puff of air that said he highly doubted that was possible.

"I'm glad I could trust you, Thomas."

He gave me a crooked grin, but his eyes were dark with

worry.

"Sorry, but I still don't know why I'm doing this," he said. "And where are we going now?"

"Back to the Marburg gold mine. I had some business with the overseer anyway."

* * *

I stood on my hind legs with Thomas under Marburg Mountain, between the vast inner and outer sets of doors, waiting for Bricriu to carry out my latest request. At last, he burst in with four guards and two orderly rows of female Lepores, some petite women, others large rabbits.

I made a show of inspecting them, but a quick scan had already told me this would be harder than I had thought.

There were more than two dozen Lepores here, and none of them resembled Maria in the slightest. I had thought a majority of the Marburg Lepores were related. Families were brought in, and, as was the nature of rabbits, they expanded rapidly, keeping the number of slaves replenished. I had been sure Maria would have many half-sisters and cousins who might share at least some of her features. What had happened here?

"A thousand apologies, Your Highness," said Bricriu, sidling up to me, "but I am still perplexed about the purpose of your visit. What became of Maria? Was your hunt successful?"

I almost silenced him but saw an opportunity in his question. I watched closely as I said matter-of-factly, "She is dead."

Only one face in the crowd reacted in any noticeable fashion. She was blond and obviously young. Her mouth popped open, and then she closed her eyes, head hung.

I took a few steps down her row, but paused, casually looking over an older woman with curly brown hair, not wanting to let Bricriu see my hand.

"How exactly did she die?" asked Bricriu, a smile curling up his muzzle.

"She fell in the Silver River and was caught in the current."

"So she drowned? A pity. I'm sure His Majesty would have enjoyed her."

Tears slipped from the blond girl's lashes and carved lines in her filthy cheeks.

"That is why I'm here. Father will be pleased to hear the rebel is dead, but he was looking forward to roast rabbit, and he finds the females tenderer. I will have to take one of these women with me."

I looked around idly, as if pondering my decision. In reality, I was pondering if the blond would suit my needs. I had no way of knowing if she'd comply with the new plan forming in my mind. I was going to have to risk it.

Bricriu was a lacking overseer, but he was still a fox. I didn't want to test his cunning today. I made a show of things, stopping to sniff at a grey rabbit.

"Perhaps, this one will do, though I'd like something a little younger and plumper if possible."

The grey rabbit's ears drooped.

"Please, Your Highness, take me instead," said the blond, her chains rattling as she stepped out of formation.

Perhaps she will work even better than expected, I thought.

"How dare you give orders to the prince, you daft girl!" shouted Bricriu, storming over with a paw raised for a swipe of his claws. "He will take whomever he likes."

"Yes, which means you have no say either, Bricriu," I said, loud enough to halt him. "Step back and hold your wagging tongue."

He dropped his head and looked away. I then felt I could approach the girl without suspicion. I bent my head and spoke as softly as I could, hoping there was enough distance between Bricriu and us.

"There is a chance you might live, but I need information. If you know Maria, nod your head and say you will come willingly."

She gazed up at me with cautious curiosity.

"I will come with you, Your Highness," she replied with a nod.

"Good, then it is decided. Thomas, please detach her from the line." As Thomas rushed to obey, I turned to the fox. "That is all I require, Bricriu. Send the others back to work."

"Will that be all for today? I thought you were going to do your inspection."

Damn.

I scratched my ear, cursing Maria and all the trouble she was causing. I wanted to reassert my authority here, make sure my plan with the mine was working, but there was no time.

"Have you had any other problems with the workers since implementing my strategies?"

"I wouldn't say so, no."

"Fair enough. My father hasn't complained, and with the amount of gold you've been sending, I'd say everything is fine, as I told you it would be. I will be back later, but otherwise, keep up the good work."

"Well, thank you then, Your Highness," said Bricriu, ears perking up.

I turned from him, not wanting to betray my disgust, and called for Thomas. He led the girl behind me, secured in the mine's sturdy handcuffs. The guards forced the others back into the dark, and the outer doors opened to let us out.

When we stepped into the light, the girl stumbled, a hand over her eyes. I gestured for Thomas to slow his pace and let her recover herself as the doors closed behind us. When she dropped her hand at her side, blinking against the dazzling light, her mouth fell open. Her brown eyes sparkled with tears of awe as she looked left and right, taking in the grass, the sky, the world. Oblivious to us, she fell to her knees and ran her arms over the grass at the side of the dirt path, a smile overtaking her face.

The sight tightened my throat with emotion I didn't want to show and brought thoughts I didn't want to unpack yet. Not here. And yet they came all the same. What had we done to these changelings? We deprived them of the basic natural wonders of light and grass. Despite the infectious laugh that bubbled up from her center, filling the late afternoon air with joyous life, I felt sick to my stomach. My eyes found Thomas, who stared at the girl with confusion and something like dismay.

"She's... never...?" he asked softly, gazing at me in disbelief. I shook my head, and I saw the same emotions I was feeling begin to wage war on his face.

The girl threw back her head and gazed at the few scattered clouds, whispering, "Thank You, Maya. Your works are wondrous."

Hating myself, I said, "I'm sorry, but we must keep moving. Time is not on our side." She looked at me with surprise, suddenly remembering I was there.

"We will be traveling for a while, yes?"

I nodded.

"Oh good," she said, sweeping her hand over the grass one last time before rising to her feet.

"Thomas, please let her ride with you."

Thomas nodded, helping the girl into the saddle first.

"Thank you," she said, her eyes on the horizon.

"Uh, sure," said Thomas, clearing his throat.

He swung himself up behind her, and we passed through the palisade's gate, pointing our horses toward Silver Creek. My plan, which had seemed so clever before, now seemed heinous. Would I really have to sacrifice this girl so that Maria... and I... could live? I could think of no other way. I added that to the long list of questions Maria had aroused in me, all vying for my attention. Right now, I had no satisfactory answers for any of them.

"Pardon, Your Highness," said the girl, pulling me from the hell of my own mind, "but may I have permission to speak?"

"As long as you are respectful, you may speak freely," I said, keeping my face neutral. I did not want to hear accusations right now, and I thought, considering the circumstances, I needed to maintain some level of authority.

"Oh, of course, Your Highness. Thank you."

"First, what is your name, girl?"

"Stephania, Your Highness."

I gave her a nod, worried she might mistake a smile from

my wolf face as a snarl. "Pleased to meet you. You may call me prince, rather than Your Highness."

"Oh, as you wish, prince." She looked perplexed, but after clearing her throat, her expression became pleading. "Prince... is Maria truly dead?"

I took a deep breath, pondering.

"Before I answer your question, I would ask that you answer some of mine."

"Yes, of course. What do you wish to know?"

"Why did you volunteer to come with me, even though you heard the purpose of our journey?"

She looked down at the saddle pommel for a moment, but when she looked up, I saw fire in her eyes.

"Because of Maria. If she were in my place, she wouldn't have hesitated to sacrifice herself for a fellow Lepores. If more changelings were like her, there would be less hate and suffering in the world. She was not my sister, but she loved me as though I was, and I intend to follow her teachings for the rest of my life... no matter how short that may be."

A smile parted my jowls as my throat grew tight again. Perhaps Maya truly had brought Maria to me and intended for me to save her. She was special.

"Tell me, what do you know about Bricriu? Is he hiding something from me? And do not be shy. If there is wrongdoing, it is he who will be punished for it, not you."

"He's a dirty, cheating, lying rat!" she spat, making Thomas' eyes widen in shock before he threw back his head and roared with laughter.

I grinned along with him, but it soon turned into a scowl as she elaborated about a plot to steal gold, Bricriu's punishments after the rebellion, and his unauthorized inclusion of pigs in the mine.

"The thieving traitor!" I growled.

"That is not the worst of it, prince," she said, deep sorrow in her voice.

I clenched my jaw. "Tell me."

"Under your orders, Bricriu could not harm Maria physically. So... he took away all she cared for."

"What?" I roared. "He did not feed her like the rest of you? He did not improve her living conditions?"

"No, prince, he did those things. But... as the weeks went by, all of her family disappeared, one by one. Her aunts, her uncles, her cousins, her friends, her only remaining sibling... and last... her mother."

"What do you mean, 'disappeared?' What did he do with them?" I said, my fury threatening to make me yell. The damned fox thought he'd found a work-around, did he? I'd work around his heart when I cut him open.

"We think... they're all dead," said Stephania, voice thick with tears that hadn't yet fallen. "Maria saw Valorie... her mother... being taken away in a cart with a whole group of rabbits. She was far older than most Lepores get in Marburg, but she was our matriarch. A strong woman, with eyes and hair like Maria's, except hers was grey by the time I met her. I thought she was a crazed zealot at first, I admit. But she was kind underneath, and she held us together. She raised Maria well."

I hardly heard the last bit of what she said. My memories drifted back to the royal box above the Cherbourg public square.

It was less than a week previous. Father had dragged Mother and me to another public execution. One of his favorite pastimes. We were there for the drawing and quartering of a traitor to the crown who had allegedly given up the position of a company of Cherbourg soldiers to mercenaries hired by the Karluks. His death would be a drawn-out spectacle in front of cheering, taunting predators. But to warm up the crowd, hangings of disobedient prey changelings were systematically carried out much of the morning.

It all blurred together, but a tiny woman in her elder years stuck out in my mind. I had not made the connection of her features to the slave girl who had intrigued me at Marburg, but now that Stephania described her, I was certain. It was Maria's mother. Even with the bruising on her face, I was sure. My attention had been drawn back to the scaffold when her crimes were read out.

"This Lepores has displeased her master, unable to produce results in the fields." That had been nothing new, but what he said next had piqued my interest. "She has refused to transform so that her flesh might serve her master as sustenance, despite proper punishments brought against her."

I suppressed a shiver at the memory. She had not gone quickly... nor quietly. She had stood with back straight and chin high, a noose around her neck, and, even in the snarling face of the hairless big cat in his black robes, had refused to transform for the priest.

"I will not allow you to pervert Maya's natural order," she had said. "I will take no part, nor will I feed the king's bloody jaws."

Father, in wolf form to best enjoy the sights and smells, had growled like a savage beside me.

The cat, whose species was unclear without his fur markings, had put a massive, razor-sharp claw beneath her chin and commanded her twice, three times, but she did not flinch, not even when he had his executioners put the noose around her ankles and flip her upside down.

The cat had paced the length of the scaffold with front, malformed paws outstretched to the crowd and shouted, "In the face of such blasphemous denial, the great Khaytan decrees that His priests strip away the humanity of this changeling, leaving behind only the animal psyche and form to feed her masters."

The raucous crowd, who had been shouting threats and perversions at the old woman, grew silent, horrified at the thought... at the possibility. I myself had been stunned. I had never heard of such a thing.

"Is that truly possible?" I asked Mother, but she looked equally disgusted and confused.

Father had let out a laugh like a purr, his eyes alight with perverted pleasure. "The power of Khaytan's Covenant is limitless, Reginald. You'd best remember it."

I'd watched in mounting horror as the priest took a small dagger and sliced a shallow incision in the old Lepores' neck. She winced against the pain but did not cry out. The priest had smothered her in a thick, black blanket and then closed his eyes as he spat out a dark incantation, the crowd transfixed and horrified. He waved his hands, gesticulating in rhythm with his words. His hands signed cryptic, unknowable runes in the air, each movement precise. There were no lights or other visible signs of prestidigitation, but the chanting and the gestures *did* cast a frightening unease over his captivated audience.

I had nearly fallen out of the box as I leaned over the side, hardly daring to breathe. The air itself felt heavy and charged with some sort of current. The priest had finished his foul spell and then removed the blanket with a flourish. I had leaned back in my seat with a smirk. The woman was still in human form, a thin trail of blood darkening her dangling hair and dripping onto the scaffold. *As I thought, impossible. What a ridiculous load of propaganda!*

"Perhaps you had best make sure your friends get their magic tricks down before they perform them in public, Father," I had said, suppressing a laugh.

His claws had scraped the back of my head as he snarled in my ear, "Silence your arrogant tongue before I cut it out in the name of Khaytan."

I had clenched my jaw in defiance, wishing to tell him I was no longer a child he could beat into compliance, but the woman had spoken, making me quiet.

As the cat sputtered and the crowd booed, the woman had shouted, "Ha! Khaytan still cows beneath His Mother's foot when She chooses to bestow Her power on Her faithful. When you find yourself standing before Her throne, you will plead for mercy on your hands and knees, but you will be given none." She had begun to laugh, proud and strong. With a wild yowl, the cat had eviscerated her with his massive claws, and she spoke no more. Father had laughed and howled his approval, but I had turned away, her words ringing in my ears.

I had thought of that day every night since, wondering how much of the Covenant's magic was a sham. The Absolvers had overstepped their bounds, claiming power beyond their capabilities. And yet they still held sway over Father, and thus the entire kingdom. They were far more powerful than I. Perhaps more powerful than Father himself, for they were ever whispering at his ear, and he listened to the pope more than his wisest advisers... or his own son.

"Prince?" said Stephania, pulling me from the memory. "May I please have the answer to my question now?"

I cleared my throat, debating whether I should tell her of her matriarch's fate and quickly deciding it would do nothing but sadden and terrify her.

"Maria is alive. But her fate is in your hands as much as it is mine."

A dazzling smile overtook her features.

"Oh, thank Maya. But what do you mean? Where is she?"

"She is safe for the moment, guarded by my friend, Angus, a true loyalist through and through."

"Angus? Ha, I should have known," said Thomas. "There's a perfect guardian for your new girlfriend. He would never touch her."

"Thomas, what have I told you about using that vulgar tongue of yours in front of a lady. And don't speak on things you don't understand."

"You have to admit, Reggie, he does like men a bit too much."

I tugged Jack's reign with my teeth so he whipped in front of Thomas' horse. "Bite your tongue, or I'll slap your insolent mouth so hard you'll bite it clean off," I said, growling deep in my chest. "Unless you have the nerve to say such things to a man's face, don't speak them at all."

Thomas hung his head and mumbled, "Yes, my prince." He knew the title would irk me, but I had no more time to deal with his childishness. I mulled over my plan. It was almost as reckless as freeing Maria in the first place, but I couldn't deny the thrill. I had never dared trick Father before, never even tried to beat him at his own game. Now the stakes were higher than they'd ever been, yet here I was, at last plotting out my moves.

As Cherbourg's gates came into view on the horizon, I turned to Stephania.

"Is your rabbit fur the same color as your human hair?"

"Yes," said Stephania, brows scrunched in confusion.

"I feared as much."

"Pardon, but why does it matter?"

"Do you wish to protect Maria, as you were going to protect that other Lepores at the mine?"

"Oh, yes, prince."

"Are you truly willing to risk your own life?"

She studied her hands a moment and then looked me dead in the eye as she said, "Yes."

"And you will hold that resolve even in the face of King Emmerich himself?"

"Yes," she said, a righteous fury tightening her jaw and startling me with its vehemence.

"I hope so. I will do my best to ensure you are spared, but I cannot guarantee your life. But if you do exactly as I say, Maria will live. She will no longer be hunted. Do you understand?"

"I understand the danger, yes," said Stephania, only the hint of a tremble in her voice. "And I am willing to face it if it truly means saving Maria. But I do not understand how appearing before the king will do that."

"You are going to pretend to be her. My father ordered her captured. He wishes to torture and then eat her for starting the uprising at Marburg. But I freed her, and now I must still produce a black rabbit. The men I sent back empty-handed will have been interrogated by now, and they'll have divulged all they know about her, including her appearance."

"Why did you free her?" asked Stephania, and I got the distinct impression that my answer would mean either her complete compliance or a heap of trouble.

I bought time by adjusting my reins, using my teeth to better wrap them around my paws. 'I don't know' didn't seem like the right answer. Nor did, 'She intrigues me.' I wasn't sure they were the only reasons, either.

"She opened my eyes," I said. "She showed me how cowardly I have been. She represents... an opportunity."

"For what?" asked Stephania.

Thomas leaned in, eyes burning with curiosity.

"Change," I said.

Stephania smiled. "Maria believed it was Maya's will for you to find her again. I suppose she was right once again."

"Maya spoke to me, too," I said, needing to say the words aloud, to feel their truth. "In a dream. I am unsure exactly what path this is all meant to take, but I feel it leads to great change."

Stephania's beaming smile softened into a wizened one, as if she'd aged well beyond her years in a matter of moments. "I will risk death for even the smallest chance of change, especially if Maria has anything to do with bringing it about. You promise to protect her?"

"Yes," I said, knowing it was the right answer, even if I couldn't begin to guarantee it.

"Then I will take her place."

"But Reggie, she's still a golden rabbit," said Thomas, his conspirator's grin waning.

"That is why you will cover her head with one of those empty feed bags until we reach the apothecary," I said.

"What do you intend to do there? Rub her in charcoal or dye her black?"

"Yes."

"But, the king will know at once. If he touches her, charcoal will rub off. And he's bound to smell fresh dye."

"That is why we tell a simple little lie. Maria, here, was never truly black. She disguised herself when she escaped, to throw us off. You were the one to discover it, Thomas."

Thomas chuckled. "Thanks for the bone, Reginald."

"I thought you'd appreciate it."

"But how do you know he'll believe us?"

"The idea will both intrigue and infuriate him. He won't

question it. It will only make her capture more of a victory." The gates were approaching. "Thomas, cover her head, now."

Thomas obeyed, and Stephania did not protest as the bag obscured her view of the opening gates. We wove through the city toward one of the smaller markets. When we reached the scattering of shops, I carefully maneuvered Jack through a cluster of peddlers' stands to the brick and mortar apothecary on the south end.

"Take her into the alley," I said, pointing to the narrow space between the apothecary and the tailor's shop. "I'll hitch the horses and fetch the dye."

"Let's hope the physician doesn't recognize you," Thomas muttered as he helped Stephania dismount, and the two of them slunk into the shaded cover of the alley.

I hitched the horses and headed inside, Thomas' words making me sweat. But I was the only customer, and the price was a bargain. When I left the shop, I made sure no eyes were on me before I slipped around the side of the building.

"He was old and blind as a bat," I told Thomas. "I think we're in the clear."

"What took so long?" said Thomas.

"He was out of regular dye. He had to make a lead-based concoction. Stephania, make sure you mention that fact when we reveal to my father that you've disguised yourself."

"Isn't that poisonous?" asked Thomas.

"Poisonous!" Stephania squeaked through the bag.

"Precisely," I said. "Change into rabbit form now."

"But I thought you said you were going to try and protect me?"

"I'm doing just that. Now I said change, rabbit. Hurry."

She obeyed, her deathly white skin sprouting golden fur, her legs fattening and growing squat, her arms turning into little forepaws that she held in front of her chest. The bag lifted over her pink nose, hoisted up by her ears.

Even in the shade of the alley, I felt we were exposed. I looked toward the market, still clearly visible a few feet away. People milled about in every direction.

"Come, around the back," I said, coaxing Stephania with a firm paw. Behind the apothecary, amid stores of supplies and heaps of garbage, I was sure we would have more privacy to complete the deed of deception. As long as the physician didn't come around back, we'd be free and clear.

I handed Thomas the ceramic container and the cheap gloves the physician had thrown into the deal.

"I'm sorry, Stephania, but you will need to take your dress off. Thomas will need to apply this to your entire body."

"It's far from the worst humiliation I've faced," she said as we reached cover and I pulled off the bag. I held onto the collar of the ratty dress with my teeth, and she wriggled out of it. "Is this going to sting?" she asked, rubbing at her one droopy ear.

"Far less than everything else that might happen to you. Don't fear the lead. The physician said using it once shouldn't hurt. But close your eyes and mouth."

"I get it," said Thomas, opening the jar. "Emmerich won't want to eat her if there's a chance he could get lead poisoning."

"I knew you were smart, Thomas." I winked at him and then turned to Stephania. "He's far too paranoid to take that chance. It will buy you time. Hopefully, enough for me to get a message to an ally in the palace who can get you out of there. You'll need a code of some sort. A call and response, so you'll know who is on our side."

Thomas took a handful of the pungent paste and smeared it onto the top of Stephania's head.

"Like what?" she asked.

"Got any ideas, Thomas?"

"It needs to sound harmless, in case someone overhears," said Thomas.

Stephania held her breath while Thomas smeared the dye around her nose and mouth.

"How about Stephania asks, 'What do you want with me?' and the other person says, 'To see what a warrior rabbit looks like,'" suggested Thomas, looking proud of himself.

"I like it." Stephania thumped her foot as the paste moved down her neck and chest. Despite that little rabbit-like quirk that revealed her discomfort, she was maintaining her composure under Thomas' dye-slathering hand better than I imagined most women would, which made me wonder what other horrors she had endured in a life of slavery to hold a high chin now.

"All right. It's settled," I said, as Thomas continued down her back and torso. "Stephania, listen closely. I will tell you the same thing I told Maria. You might not trust me, but at this point, I'm your only ally. If you want to survive, take my advice."

"I am listening."

"When you are presented in front of Father, do not even look at him. Remember your place. Only speak when spoken to, and answer his questions with concise answers."

"That's simple enough."

"If you displease him... at least more than he is already displeased... Father will choose to extract information from you himself. If that happens, you are on your own, and the result is death before the sun sets. He is impatient with his dinner."

"Then I will pray for Maya to favor me."

"The other option might be less pleasant," I said, pacing around her so that she could not see my face, pretending to inspect Thomas' work as he covered her fluffy, white-tipped tail.

"Absolvers?" she asked, a shiver running through her body.

"I'm afraid so. Father usually keeps one or two of them around the castle."

She swallowed audibly, and her next question surprised me. "Why do they shave themselves?"

"They fear being skinned alive. With no pelt, it's a less attractive option for those seeking revenge. And there are many."

"The Absolvers skin disobedient prey alive. That's why they fear someone will do it to them," said Thomas.

Stephania gagged, and I glared daggers at Thomas.

"Sammael, spare me," she said. "How can such cruel men claim to be instruments of faith?!"

"They don't follow *your* faith," said Thomas, "the faith of weaklings. Khaytan is strength. Khaytan is power and wealth. Your god is lord of grass and trees."

The zeal in Thomas' eyes, which once might have awoken a desire to hunt in me—to claim my place atop the pyramid of nature—now filled my chest with ice. This was what Father had done with his crown.

"Thomas," I snapped, my hackles rising. "Do tell me what about this woman is weak? This woman who is willing to face Absolvers' instruments and death itself for the love of a friend. I have seen you cower under the gaze of Crimson Guard soldiers when you had nothing to fear from them. It is her god who gives her greater strength than you. Think before you speak, boy."

He scowled at me, his ears turning red. "That Lepores has poisoned your mind."

"Do you wish to betray me to the Absolvers?" I asked.

He shook his head.

"Then let's speak of this no more. I do not wish to lose you as a friend, Thomas."

I ordered him to wipe a cloth against Stephania's mouth and eyes to make sure they were clean, and then we stepped back to view our handiwork. She was inky black from head to toe, but she smelled even worse than before.

"Stephania, as strange as it sounds, you are better off with the Absolvers. They are far more patient creatures than my father, and they will keep you alive until they are certain they've extracted everything they can from you. Should they take you into their dungeons, be submissive and polite at first, but only give them lies they can easily refute. Then adopt an air of arrogance, but not too much. Make it a challenge, but do not drive them to fury. Do not give them too much information all at once. If you do, they will have no more need of you. And you don't want that."

I hoped I had made it plain enough for her. Her face looked rather blank.

"I am quite familiar with torture, prince," she said softly. "But should I stand strong against the pain or act as though I am broken by it?"

I tried to hold back my shock. I had told Thomas this Lepores was stronger than him, but now I wondered if she was perhaps stronger than me.

I cleared my throat. "Show weakness, even if you have to fake it. They will grow frustrated if they feel their methods are not working. They may dig deeper into their considerable repertoire. They are predators, and they want dominion over their prey."

She only nodded her understanding.

"Should we let her dry out a little bit?" asked Thomas, his nose wrinkled against the scent.

"A few minutes in the hot sun will do fine, and then we will leave. Stephania, I hope you are truly as ready for this as you seem. I swear by my crown I will do my best to get you out."

She nodded, raising her head and puffing up her chest.

"If I am to look like Maria, then I will act like her. Let them try and break me. My faith will be my shield."

"Come then. There's no time to lose."

I steered her back into the alley into a corner of sunlight where we could let her dry and air out in privacy, but my hopes of escaping anyone's notice vanished as a slow muted clap snapped our attentions toward the middle of the alley. A melodious laugh froze us all in place.

"Oh my, what a lovely trick, Reginald," said Duchess Leticia Durand, seated daintily on the edge of a large, sealed crate. I stepped in front of Stephania out of instinct, and she covered herself with her paws.

The skirts of the duchess' dress swished as she stepped around crates—a soft green ensemble with a golden bodice and delicate embroidery of curving vines. The long sleeves ended in gold bows and white lace that complimented her petite, feminine features—a thin nose that ended in a button tip and a mouth like an elm bow. Along the edges of the bodice, green ruffles were cinched at the middle to create a frame of flowers that traveled from her collar to her shoes. Her red hair, the same vibrant tone as her fox half, was partially pulled up in a series of small braids twisted into a flower shape and woven with gold tinsel.

"Turning a gold rabbit black," she said with another musical titter. "What fun!"

For all our sneaking around, we'd been recognized. She must have read the question on my surprised face, because the next thing she said without prompt was, "I thought I spied old Jack strung up. I figured you must be around here somewhere. Hope you don't mind me watching, but it's such a joy to watch artists as they work."

I painted on a grin, trying to determine if she was in one of her moods today or if she was actually at her sharpest and playing coy. She had been a familiar face in my life for as far back as my memory stretched, and she had been part of Mother's long before me, even acting as a bridesmaid at the royal wedding.

"Thank you, milady," I said, bowing theatrically with an ornery grin. "I've been practicing." I figured, no matter the state of her mind this afternoon, my best option was to play along with her. Leticia did love her games.

"You're a man of many talents. What exactly are you up to back here?" she asked, her dark green eyes hinting at something hidden beneath the words. I thought back to Edmund's letter. *My lady finds your ideas "delicious," and hopes you might ascend the throne sooner than later.*

"Hoping to avoid a big problem by getting myself in a little trouble," I said.

"In a bit of a mess, are we, Reginald?" she asked, allowing me to lick her hand. Her eyes lingered on the tarnished gloves Thomas had peeled off and now handled gingerly in two fingers.

"Indeed. But I intend to come out of it all white as snow," I said as she curtsied to me.

"Oh, how delicious," she purred with a conspiratorial wink. She rose from her curtsy, and her eyes alighted on Stephania. "Speaking of delicious..." she said, sashaying to the young rabbit and reaching out with gentle fingers to touch her pink nose and the tips of her dyed ears. She seemed to either not notice or not care that a greyish smudge of dye came off on her fingertips.

"In fact, we were just heading back out to get our little rabbit some sun."

Stephania hastily donned her raggy clothing. Lady Leticia grinned and followed us into back to the market. Next to where I'd hitched up Jack, Edmund had parked the duchess' gilded carriage. The driver stood at the carriage door and straightened to attention as we approached. Edmund bowed to me, adding an extra flourish with one leg stretched out behind him and an extra twirl of his hand—a requirement in his mistress' presence, I imagined. "An honor to see you again, Your Highness," he said.

"The honor is all mine," I said, trying not to grin too much at his expense. Leticia liked her playthings to act like the dashing, heavily muscled men in her romance novels.

Leticia was circling Stephania with a finger pressed lightly to her lips. My eye was drawn to a strange trinket on her wrist, an odd, segmented gold bracelet with a circular adornment—a glass covering over a pearl circle etched with gold numbers.

"What a lovely bracelet, duchess. Wherever did you get it?"

"Oh, this old thing?" said Leticia, waving her hand to swish it around her wrist. "My gardener dug it up. Can you believe that? It was filthy, but I had a goldsmith restore it for me."

"It suits you," I said.

She didn't seem to hear me. She stroked Stephania's droopy ear. "Reginald, dear, how much for this one? She's a pretty thing. Even if she is a bit... dirty," she said, rubbing her thumb and forefinger as she gave another of those loaded looks.

She had spied us dying Stephania's fur, and so she must have known the trouble I spoke of was related to the Lepores. Was she offering help? To take the trouble off my hands? It seemed so. But would she rid me of my trouble by making herself a new rabbit's foot charm or by harboring Stephania? I couldn't be sure. I'd heard rumors the Covenant was watching the duchess under suspicion she was a slave smuggler. But rumors couldn't be trusted, and it didn't matter yet anyway. I had to present Stephania to Father before I handed her over to anyone. But perhaps Leticia could help when the time came. I decided to feel her out.

"I'm terribly sorry, milady. She'd make a fine maidservant, but I'm afraid I can't spare her. She's been specifically requested by Father."

"Oh, poo," said Leticia with a little pink pout. "Such a shame to eat something so pretty. You only enjoy it once, and then it's gone. But I suppose Emmerich is not to be questioned, eh?"

My heart skipped a beat and then trotted a new rhythm. Her green eyes were bold, unabashed, but I was sure I hadn't misinterpreted the implications of such a question. Many would not dare speak even that much in public, if at all. You never knew who you could trust.

I took my time, letting a playful grin pull up my jowls, pondering my answer. "For most, that is true. But what sort of wolf prince would I be if I didn't pounce on my father's tail now and then?"

She laughed more heartily than I'd expected, putting her hands to her chest as if to temper her mirth. "Oh, but you are a smart one, young prince. Only by such tests of your strength and stealth can you grow into a king yourself. But I take it this is not one of those moments where pouncing is the best strategy?"

"Not *this* time, milady, no."

"Ah, well, then I shall not pout too much longer."

I opened my mouth to give her a polite goodbye, but a clamor from the inside of a pastry shop cut me off. A tanned youth with dirty blond hair was tossed bodily through a closed window and into the street. An enormous, dark-skinned man with a trimmed goatee leaped after him and snatched him up, trying to carry the boy to safety as four Crimson Guards burst through the shop door and from around the back in groups of two, their swords brandished in their deformed, clawed hands.

"Halt, rebel filth!" yelled the badger leading the pack. His hairless snout was abnormally long, like a rat, and it protruded from the recess of his blood-red hood. He sprang on the back of the large man, digging his incisors into his shoulder. The other three, all shaved cats of various sizes, grabbed for his legs and arms, hauling the two men to the ground. At the taste of blood, they flew into a frenzy, ripping great gashes in the young man's face and biting chunks from the large man's thighs. The boy clutched at his throat, his jugular slashed, and writhed on the ground as his lifeblood soiled the street.

The dark-skinned man bellowed his sorrow and hate, and his body trembled as he forced a transformation into a great black bull. He tossed his horns and kicked out with his back hooves, forcing the guardsmen into a wide circle around him. One leg threatened to buckle from his wounds, but he blew a great puff of air from his broad nose and stomped the earth.

I positioned myself in front of Stephania and Thomas as Edmund moved to guard Leticia, his sword ringing as it left its sheath. The hairless, hooded beasts drew long bullwhips from their belts, snapping them free and twirling them lazily on the ground.

Like vipers, they struck together, their lashes wrapping around the bull's legs and neck, upending him when they pulled the whips taut. The badger leaped forward and forced a vial of something dark down the bull's throat as he struggled against the squeezing chords. The bull shuddered and grew still, his broad chest rising and falling with shallow breaths.

There was murmuring through the crowd, but the badger held up his hands and said, "Go about your business. This concerns only king and Covenant."

I ducked my head and sidestepped behind Jack's neck, not wanting to be recognized.

Leticia sidled up to me and placed her hand on my breastplate. Tilting her chin up so that her lips brushed the base of my ear, she whispered, "Such abominations are a blight on this land. Don't you think?" and I knew she didn't mean the ox and his dead young friend.

"Aye," I said. "Dominion means order, not cruelty."

"So what are you going to do about it, young wolf prince?"

An idea that had already begun to bud in my mind—its roots sinking ever deeper since I'd returned home from the Karluk skirmishes—finally blossomed. It was not only the rabbits of

Marburg who wanted change. Fox duchesses and wolf princes were harboring a secret desire deep in their guts, too. Maria's words came to me, yet again. *Your whole life, you will be despised by those beneath you and mistrusted by those you would call friends.* But perhaps I did have allies. I just hadn't known it. *At least I have a purpose. What is yours?... It looks to me as though Maya is trying to give you one. The question is, will you accept it?*

I ducked my head to whisper into Leticia's hair. "I'm going to pounce."

CHAPTER SIX
The Immortal Game

Reginald

The castle loomed down the wide, cobbled lane. The guards in the wall's towers called to the man stationed inside the castle's inner gate, and we soon crossed into the courtyard. Stephania, walking with her cuffed forepaws attached to Thomas' saddle by a short rope, stayed low between our horses as we rode to the keep. A servant rushed forward to take our horses, and I let Thomas lead Stephania over the threshold. Her ears perked up, and she gazed at the grandeur of the marble, carved stone, and lavish tapestries with wonder and fear.

A quick inquiry of the guards posted in the entryway directed me to Father's study, and I hurried my companions up the stairs. I took two left turns and a final narrow corridor, then stopped to listen with an ear pressed to the dark oak door. I couldn't discern the words spoken, but an adviser was inside. I turned to Stephania and forced a smile. I had to keep her calm. Her human side was brave as any knight, but if her weak, prey mind took over at any point, she might ruin everything I was planning.

"Remember what I've told you. Maria's life, as well as your own, hangs in the balance," I said, taking her lead line from

Thomas.

She nodded, and I opened the door, shoving her in ahead of me with my muzzle. I hoped she understood my coarseness was for show. An armored bear stood watch in the corner, bending his foreleg in a bow as I came in. Father whirled, his leather coat tails flying around him and a hefty silver chain swinging at his wrinkled throat. The Absolver he'd been speaking with dissolved into the shadowy recesses of the bookshelves lined with flesh-bound tomes, but I could feel him watching from beneath his midnight hood.

"This is the waifish thing that caused you so much trouble?" Father asked, the permanent scowl on his human face deepening. His look said I would be berated later, but for now, he bore down on Stephania. "Do you realize why you're here, rodent?"

He lifted her head for a better look, but Stephania kept her eyes low.

"Because I forgot my place," she said, her youthful voice now subdued and grave. "I beg your forgiveness, Your Majesty."

He grabbed her neck, his over-long yellowed nails digging beneath her fur, and threw her to the floor.

"There is no forgiveness here. You have proved yourself useless to me... save in the sustenance of your flesh." He pulled her to her feet by her ears and snarled in her face, "But before you serve the almighty Khaytan with your scattered entrails, you will wish you had never left that mine. You will wish you had remembered your place beneath my feet."

He grabbed her throat in one hand and pinched at her sides with the other, testing the tenderness of her flesh, but his hungry smile turned to a grimace. He leaned in and used both hands to part the fur at the top of her head.

"What is this? Her fur is sticky with something. There are light strands here. Reginald, explain this!"

The rehearsed lie came easily. "I was surprised myself when Thomas first discovered it, Father. She's dyed her fur. Both times we caught her, she had stopped near water. I suspect she intended to wash it off, leaving us to chase after a black rabbit that didn't exist."

"You are a peculiar little rodent," he said, sneering down at a trembling Stephania. "But not as clever as you think." He sniffed loudly. "What is that smell?"

Stephania stared at the floor, her short tail tucked against her body.

"The little fool made her dye from what she could find near the mountain," I said. "I believe it's lead oxide."

Father gawked at Stephania, and then his nostrils flared in fury. His fist smashed her nose and sent her skidding across the polished floor on her side.

"Impudent rat! You wished to poison me with your little trick!"

I rushed to pick her up myself, fearing he might snap her neck. I lightly swatted her cheeks with the back of my paw, trying to rid her of the glazed look overtaking her pupils. She could not lose herself now.

"It is quite a shame, Father," I said, as she blinked up at me, intelligence returning to her eyes. "I, too, would have wanted a piece of her."

Father curled his lip and took a step back, rubbing his hands on his robes.

"I don't even wish to touch her," he said. "But I'm certain Absolver Messene would love to entertain her."

The Absolver slithered forward like a viper, his stone and obsidian holy talismans clicking together. He was in human form... for now... and he might have been a charming man were it not for the Covenant tattoo on his forehead. The ink depicted a wolf wearing a human skull, and its grin was as fierce as his own.

"Aye. I have been studying her with great curiosity, my liege. How unusual for prey to put on such a game. I wonder how she will fair playing mine."

"I tried questioning her about her uprising myself, though I do not have your expertise, Sir Messene," I said. "She is a stubborn thing. I got very little, but I am now fairly certain she had outside help in her escape." I hoped this tossed bone would keep her alive long enough to rescue. "She could be of great value. But she is young and unacquainted with pain. I think your games will prove troublesome for her."

"Fresh meat is the tenderest, my prince. First, we temper the meat, moving it from hot to cold."

"Yes, yes, all very good," Father snapped as he retreated to his desk. "When you've drenched her well, shave her fur with a dull razor. I don't want any more of the poison leaching into her skin."

"As you command, my king. Come along, little prey." He tugged Stephania along by the rope. From the corner of my eye, I saw her look back at me, but I kept my gaze trained on Father, who was resting his scowling face in his hand like a spoiled child who'd had a treat snatched from under his nose.

"Which of those fools is responsible for letting that rabbit escape a second time? I shall have their head."

"It was my fault, Father. I should have assigned the night watch myself, and I should have allowed the men to rest sooner."

Father sat straighter. "At last, you are thinking like a king. You can't rely on anyone else, Reginald. You must get what you want yourself."

Then why must you call to your precious Absolvers before every decision you make? I thought, but I forced my face into happy surprise. He was a hypocrite, but he wasn't wrong. It was time to get what I wanted, and I was going to have to take it for myself.

"I understand, Father. Thank you."

"And you had two successful hunts in as many days. You have not sullied your name." He tipped his head in a minor show of respect. "Perhaps we will have to forgo our rabbit feast, but we will have an execution. Lepores hunkering in every dark hole in Kaskilia will hear of what happens to rebels."

"I'm glad you're happy, Father. I hope I will not upset you when I say I won't be joining you for dinner this evening. I have some business with a few friends in town."

"Yes, yes, that is fine. You may leave."

He unfurled a map on his desk and glanced up at me with a

pleased lift to his eyes and mouth, smoothing his frown lines. I was transported to my youth, a sword in my hand, its tip pointed at the throat of a battle-weathered knight on the ground at my feet. Father had squeezed my shoulder and looked at me with something like a smile. "You have made me proud, Reginald," he had said, and I'd had to fight against the tears for fear of ruining everything. "I shall proclaim you as my son with head held high."

I took a step toward him now, a horrible tightness pressing on my heart and lungs. "Goodbye, Father," I said, reaching his desk with front legs half-raised for an embrace. I could no longer scrounge for scraps of his approval, appeased by the smallest acts of affection, but if there was any hope that he could change, that some shred of his remaining humanity cared for me, then how could I betray him?

"Leave me. I have important matters to—"

"Will you embrace me, Father?" I asked, talking over him, suddenly desperate.

His eyes moved from my face to my outstretched paws, and he raised his brows. Disappointment crept slowly over his features.

"Run along to your mother if you want a woman's comforts," he said, turning back to his map.

My paws fell limp at my side, and I turned away. I stalked to my rooms to pack my things: my longbow, most of my kit, some clothing, and all the money I had saved.

There was a rustling behind me as someone stepped on the carpeted floor of my bedchamber. "So, you're actually leaving then?" asked Thomas. "Am I meant to come along?"

"No, Thomas, not all the way, at least. I need you to stay here. I have other plans for you. And I don't want you to get too involved. I want you able to plead ignorance should things go sour. Which is why I'm not going to be able to answer all your questions, so please don't ask them."

"You can trust me, Reginald," he said, sounding his age.

I turned to him with a morose smile. "I know, my friend. I truly am only trying to keep you safe."

"What do you need me to do?"

"Check the guardhouse and ask around for Sir Albert Truman. If he's not there, then visit his house on the corner of Silver Horse Lane and Steel Row Street. Please tell him I have urgent business with him and to expect me tonight."

"Well that's easy enough. I will be off then." He disappeared around the door jamb.

"Wait, Thomas!"

His head poked around again.

"I will wait for you here. I have letters to write. Then we will be off to Angus'. And please, when we see Maria again, do not breathe a word about Stephania."

Maria

I hovered my finger over the wooden queen's crown. Sighing, I took my king off the board. "I am terrible at this. There is no way I can win now. We should start over."

Angus reached across the table and plopped my king back in his former place, cowering behind his queen.

"Don't give up yet. You could still get a draw."

"What is the point of dragging things out when I cannot win?"

Angus raised a finger. "Ah, the age-old question," he said with a chuckle. "Chess is not just about winning. The game was designed to mimic real warfare. You need to learn how to outwit and predict your opponent. And if you can't win, then at least prevent them from gaining a victory. A living king can retreat from a battlefield and fight another day."

Perhaps he had a point. I had charged into my own war without taking into account all the strategies of my enemies, and I had lost miserably, bringing death to my troops.

"Okay. I want to keep learning," I said, moving my remaining bishop three spaces to block his knight.

He grinned at me. "Good knowledge, Maria, is a deadly

weapon. Better to have it and not need it, than need it and not have it. Why do you think the Covenant exists?"

I studied the board while pondering his question. "The Inquisitors are the king's bishops, and the Crimson Guard their knights. They don't only attack the king's enemies; they collect information for him."

"That's true, but the Inquisitors have their own power. If the king doesn't serve their interests, they can betray him."

"Reginald seems to fear them. Do you truly think his father does, too?"

"I do, whether he admits it to himself or not. Any man with half a brain fears them."

I wondered at that. Did the members of the Covenant fear the king as well? Who was truly at the top?

In my distraction, I didn't manage to draw the game, but I succeeded in prolonging it for a few more turns. Angus gave me an approving smile and began resetting the pieces when a knock came on the door. He gestured for me to be quiet, then picked up his musket and holstered his pistols. I had a sudden urge to dive under the table, but I restrained myself.

"Who's there?" asked Angus, standing to one side of the door.

"The golden bull whispered to the moons, Angus," came Reginald's voice, and my shoulders relaxed.

Angus opened the door and stepped aside. Reginald was in human form again and wore a new, polished breastplate over a fresh uniform. The prince hugged Angus, and the Ursa enveloped him. Reginald pulled away first, turning his eyes on me and leaving Angus to twiddle his thumbs with a flush on his cheeks. Reginald shifted a paper-wrapped bundle under his arm as he crossed the room.

"There you are," he said, smiling at me. "Has Angus taken good care of you?"

"He's the kindest, most attentive host I've ever had the good fortune to meet."

"I'm glad to hear it." He looked me up and down. "I don't

know what that thing is you're wearing, but it doesn't look trav-el-worthy. No offense, Angus, but tailoring isn't your strength. Keep to cooking and ripping off Karluk heads."

I looked down at the enormous tunic that served as a make-shift dress. Angus had tried to roll the overlarge sleeves, secure the extra fabric in bows at my elbows, and hitch up the dragging hem with pins, but it was quite a mess.

"Well I had to try," said Angus with a chuckle. "Can't believe the state you sent her off in."

Reginald shook his head and removed the wrapping from his bundle. It was a white undershirt, a pair of flat shoes, and a long, brown dress with thin straps and a bodice crisscrossed with green ribbon.

"We are in a bit of a rush, so put it on quickly."

"You are giving me a dress?" I asked, mouth slightly agape as I ran my hands over the soft fabric. "Thank you. What did I do to deserve this?"

"It's nothing, just an old one I stole from my sister. It hasn't fit her since she was a child. Come, put it on."

"Right here?" I asked with an eyebrow raised and the hint of a grin at my lips. "Are you in that much of a rush, or do you have other motives?"

He blustered, making me laugh. "That is not what I meant."

"Then perhaps you should be more clear."

"Maria, please be serious."

"Then don't rush me," I said with a smirk as I slipped into the adjoining bedroom.

The dress fit well enough and had a pleasant floral scent lingering in the fabric. The shoes were too big, but they would do. I smelled fresher than I ever had in my life, and I imagined I looked fresher as well. I ran my fingers through my hair, savoring the glide of the silken strands. Angus had let me bathe and brush my hair, and for the first time in a good while, I felt more like a woman than a wild rabbit on the run. When I emerged carrying my old clothes over one arm, Reginald looked rather shocked, and I worried that perhaps the dress did not suit me as well as I'd imagined.

"You... It fits better than I expected," he said. He scratched at his nape and then, with the other hand, ushered me forward, impatient. "Good, now we must leave. Take care, Angus."

As we walked to the door, Angus thrust out his arm to block us and let the gold talisman dangle from his fingers.

"Reginald, I believe this belongs to you."

"No, actually, that is your payment."

"Reggie, friends carry no debts. Besides, it was no trouble. You take good care of that girl, you hear?"

Reginald took the medallion with a smile. "Thank you, old friend." He turned to go and then stopped. "I almost forgot..." He looked back at me. "Maria, could you please wait outside? I need to talk to Angus in private."

I looked around Reginald's arm and saw his squire waiting by two horses, holding a lantern. I didn't like the idea of being left alone with him, but to my surprise, he waved at me.

"Uh, sure," I said, slipping out into the night. I stopped a short distance from the Felis, just out of reach.

"Hello, Thomas. I believe this is yours," I said, holding out the navy cloak. He took a step forward to take it, and then I took a step back.

"Thank you." Looking rather glum, he traced his shoe in the dirt and said, "I am sorry for the way I acted this morning."

"Oh," I said, mouth popping open in surprise. "Thank you. I forgive you. And please forgive me for hurting you as I did."

"You didn't..." he began, brows scrunched in anger, but he stopped himself with a deep breath. "Listen, do you truly care for the prince?"

"Pardon?" I asked, jaw dangling.

"You are trying to make him fall in love with you, are you not? You have done something to make him go through all this trouble to help you. Are you trying to manipulate him into giving you freedom, or do you truly care for him?"

Heat burned from my cheeks to my ears. A Lepores and a Lobo together? And I had thought Angus' stories were strange.

Maya, have mercy. It would be an abomination.

Stunned, I could only stammer, and he fixed me with a cold glare. "If you lead him to destruction, I will make sure you pay with your life."

"I think you're confused, Thomas. I am only following Maya's will, to ally myself with Reginald, perhaps befriend him, nothing more. Nothing improper will ever occur between us, I assure you."

He studied me, searching for truth in my face. "Good." He opened his mouth to say more, but Reginald emerged from the stone house.

The prince gave me an open smile that lit his eyes, and a lump formed in my throat. "Well, you impressed me twice today. I'm quite pleased."

"What have I done this time?"

"Angus is very picky in choosing his friends, but he had only niceties to say about you. Perhaps you truly will be useful in all this."

I gave him a slight frown. "I am not entirely sure what that is supposed to mean, but if I can work to earn my freedom in some way, I will give it my all."

"Oh, but haven't you figured it out yet?" he asked with a mischievous, lopsided grin. "I thought you fancied yourself the smartest one here."

"Thank you for noticing. I would like to think I am clever," I said, returning a playful smirk of my own, "but I'm not a mind reader."

He barked out a laugh, but then he grew more serious, appraising me down his nose. "I have found my purpose, as you put it. I'm going to take the throne."

My heart pounded a random rhythm. "Truly? You mean it?"
"Yes."

"This is not a boyish game to you, is it? Don't promise me change you don't intend to follow through with."

"I cannot promise you change, but I can promise I am serious about fighting for it. I am sick of holding my tongue. Sick of groveling at my father's feet for little more than a twitch of the lips. Weary of watching the kingdom suffer and cower in fear of Khaytan's Covenant and those who would use the predator god for their own ends and cast aside the name of Maya. And I can promise you that you will get to play a part in the fight."

I held back a smile, warning myself to be cautious of this wolf and his charming grin. "You speak well, prince, and I will help you gladly, but I warn you now, I will not be used as a pawn."

He held that lopsided grin for a moment and then chuckled. The rich sound pulled at the corners of my mouth, but I fought its allure and kept my face serious.

"I see Angus taught you the immortal game," he said. "I'm not yet sure what role you will play, but you should know... the humblest pawn can still be elevated to queen."

My heart leaped in my chest, and I felt rooted to the spot. But then he reached out to pat my head, and I ducked his hand with a scowl.

"Thomas will take you to a more secure location," he said as he mounted his Chevaux. "I will meet you there soon."

I watched him ride off into the night, still unsure what to make of him. But I had never been more certain that I was on the path Maya had paved for me. The knowledge brought a lightness to my soul.

Thomas snapped his fingers at my nose. "I said we need to get going."

He helped me into the saddle and then handed me the lantern as he climbed up behind me. We rode off into the night, the lantern dangling from the stirrup straps.

I asked Thomas several times where he was taking me, but his only reply was, "It's best if you see for yourself." When the lights of the city appeared on the horizon, I grew nervous. He would not disobey the prince and turn me in... would he?

When the massive stone wall and its enormous, spiked gates came into clear view, illuminated by torchlight, my pulse galloped in my neck. I braced myself to jump off the Chevaux and transform if he called to the guards walking the ramparts, but he veered off the road and brought us to a line of trees bordering the wall. He trotted the horse to the base of a gently sloping hill and dismounted, holding his hand out for me. I slid down, and then Thomas raised his arms above his head with a yell. He smacked the horse's rump, and the spooked steed ran toward the farmlands.

Startled, I asked, "What was that for?"

"We don't need him, and it will be easier to go undetected on foot."

"Where are we going?"

"Relax, you will see in a moment."

We climbed the hill and then veered toward the place it bumped the wall about five feet from the base, right where it took a sharp turn toward the east. Thomas got on his knees and pulled out a large, square stone to reveal a dark tunnel into the city!

"What is this?" I asked.

"Don't just stand there, climb through," said Thomas.

I got down on my hands and knees and crawled inside. There was plenty of room for me. I could even lift my head without bumping the top.

The tunnel spat us out into a small, wooden box filled with moth-eaten cloaks.

"A closet?" I asked, pushing the musty clothes out of the way as Thomas squeezed in beside me.

Thomas shoved open the handleless door, and we stepped into some kind of warehouse. All manner of barrels and crates lined the walls. Among them, a few cloaked figures huddled next to three candlelit tables, drinking and playing cards. It was a fairly lively place, with groans of disappointment and whoops of triumph echoing in the vast space, but I wasn't sure we were in good company. I saw more than a few knives glinting in the orange light. All those in animal form sported the fangs of carnivores.

"Evening, ladies and gents," said Thomas, his chipper voice out of place here. "Is Diederik around?"

Everything became frightfully quiet, and heads turned all over the room. A fox and two badgers eyed me from the nearest table, and I edged behind Thomas. Then a slender cat with a golden, black-spotted coat sauntered toward us on all fours, her muscles shifting beneath her pelt. She wasn't wearing much save a loincloth and a chest piece made from beads and feathers, and I wondered if that truly covered her breasts when she shifted back.

"Who is asking, and how did you get in here?" she asked. Her tribal Karluk accent made each consonant clipped and sharp, while each vowel was a caress of the tongue.

"I am Thomas, Prince Reginald Ingolf's squire. Diederik used to work for my master, and he has sent me to collect on a few favors." He spoke with poorly masked arrogance, and I wondered if he was putting on a brave face or if he truly hadn't noticed the threat in her eyes or her claws popping free of their padding.

"Did you hear that, friends? A blue blood sent an errand boy to talk with us, and he brought a little snack along with his demands."

"She is not to be harmed," said Thomas, worry finally creeping into his voice.

She scented him and said, "You'll both feel my claws, little kitten." She lowered herself into a crouch. "I don't take orders from blue bloods."

"But you will take them from me," said a gruff voice that drew my eye to a hulking, russet Taurus skirting his broad frame around a far barrel. He was as tall as Angus, but in his animal form he was even broader. I wondered at him, for his arms and chest were shaped with masculine biceps and pectorals, and though his legs ended in hooves, his arms ended in hands the size of barrel lids. He must have been old to possess such a morphing ability, but he looked strong and vigorous as he shunted the cat away and stood before us. A shock of shaggy fur sprouted from between his curved horns and fell into his dark eyes. He wore rusted faulds attached to his hips with a leather band and a wide chainmail skirt piece beneath, like a loincloth. His chest was bare save for a copper necklace that fell across his chest, adorned with bronze trinkets depicting the faces of three stern men. The central visage appeared the wisest and most mournful.

"Pardon Samara's lack of manners, young squire," he said, making Thomas bow in gratitude. "What business does Reginald have with me?"

"The prince is aware that staying holed up in this warehouse grows more dangerous every day. The Crimson Guard is still looking for you, and they've recruited the palace guards to make another sweep for smugglers soon. But if you're interested, the prince is willing to hire you lot as mercenaries again, and you can earn clemency as well as gold."

"Really? So Reginald intends to reward my hard work with... more work?"

"Smuggling slaves from the palace was as risky for Reginald as it was you, Diederik. Look at what happened to Lothar."

"That didn't exactly have to do with slave smuggling, now did it?" said Diederik, crossing his iron-bracelet-laden arms. He even had a few iron rings on his horns that I recognized as slave markers, all bearing the sign of the Taurus, like his tattoo. The biggest bracelet of all, however, looked to be solid silver.

"It didn't help," said Thomas, crossing his arms, too. "Regardless, the prince cannot freely give you amnesty. But don't fret. As before, you will be paid handsomely for your services."

"What's with her? She another runaway slave Reggie's picked up?" the bull asked, waving one of his strange hands at me.

"Yes. He's asking you to look after her for a little while. And load up a carriage with some supplies for your trip. Some salted fish and live birds."

"We'll keep her safe. But what trip are you talking about, and who says we're coming at all?"

"Reginald does. Unless you'd rather wait around here for the Crimson Guard to sniff you out."

Diederik snorted through his fat, pink nose, spraying my face with a fine mist. "And where exactly are we going?"

"The prince will tell you that when he arrives. He asked me to tell you to make preparations. Are you in this or not?"

"You've got a mouth on you, kid," said Diederik with a huff.

"I'll think about it." He turned from us, and Samara slunk closer.

Watching her from the corner of my eye, I spat out, "Excuse me... Diederik was it? Were you a friend of the pugilist Hubert?" I doubted I'd get an affirmative answer, but I didn't want him to leave, especially not with that frown on his face. It didn't bode well. Besides, if he was as old and battle-hardened as I guessed, it *could* be possible.

Diederik froze, and I pressed, "He fought against the Karluks in the Campaign of the Golden Bulls."

He turned around with eyes wide.

"How do you know that name?" he asked, as good as confirming the connection.

"His tale was told to me by an Ursa named Angus."

"Angus, you said?"

"Yes. A rather large fellow, even for a bear. Very kind, though. He's a vegetarian, and I'm quite certain he has a fondness for men. Do you know him?"

Diederik and Thomas burst into hysterical laughter. I was confused, but pleased. What had I said? At least he was smiling.

"That sounds about right," said Diederik as his last chuckle dwindled. "Maybe you and I should have a little chat. Thomas, you got money for those supplies you're asking for?"

"Did the Silver River start flowing backward? Course I do, here." He removed a purse of coins from his bag and threw it at the leader. Samara leaped to intercept it with her teeth.

Diederik rolled his eyes as Samara flicked her tail under his chin. "Just count the coins and get the supplies ready, Samara. You, slave girl, what's your name?"

"Maria. Nice to meet you."

"Well, Maria, since you're to be our guest, would you like something to eat? Don't want Reginald thinking we didn't take care of you."

"Thank you very much. I would be honored to dine with the white bull's friends."

He smiled and gestured for me to sit with him at the corner table. One of his cohorts even fetched me a chair. I felt a small thrill, wondering at how much of the world I'd already seen and how much more there was. Perhaps if I could warm these freebooters up to me, they'd even teach me some of their card games.

CHAPTER SEVEN
Loyalists and Traitors

Reginald

I steered Jack slowly through the torch-lit streets, passing thatched-roof houses of the commoners on my way to nobler dwellings. Neither my mind nor my heart was at ease. I had already scolded myself soundly for a fool for almost forgetting to give Angus the letter. I could not afford mistakes any longer. Not if I was going to go through with the plan still taking shape in my mind.

Albert was the first step. He was a close friend, which was one of the many reasons I had taken him along to Marburg a few weeks before. The third son of a duke, he was entitled to little more than the family name and the small plot on which his grand house stood, so his father had sent him to Cherbourg at a young age to be raised as one of my uncle's prized knights. We'd grown up together, playing in mock battles in Cherbourg's courtyard and then drawing real blood on the battlefield as brothers in arms. If a man as loyal as Albert wouldn't follow me, then I had no hope of success.

When I turned onto Silver Horse Lane, the buildings grew taller and their materials more valuable. Albert's mansion, its walls a mix of cherry wood and polished black stone, stood at the far end. The corners of the roof ended in sedentary stone wolves that snarled and hunched their shoulders like gargoyles. Excitement and dread commingled in my gut until I felt sick. I had never had so much agency over my life, and yet I had never so strongly doubted my every move. I was acutely aware my actions cost more now.

I tied Jack to the base of the short stone staircase and then jogged up to knock on the door. Albert's portly Aries housemaid, Barbara, let me in and then scuttled off to inform her master of my arrival. When she returned, she showed me to the living room where her master was waiting in animal form.

"Reginald, my prince, good to see you." Albert bowed his black wolf head, tucking in one paw. He wore a loose-fitting, flamboyant red pajama set that might have made me chuckle if I wasn't so queasy.

"Thank you for seeing me, Albert. The wife and kids aren't home?"

"Oh, they're here, tucked in bed. They've lost their nocturnal instincts, I suppose. I envy them. Barbara, please pop into the cellar and fetch us a bottle of brandy." He gestured for me to sit in one of the plush seats around the short living room table.

"Thank you, Albert," I said, plopping down in the wide chair designed to fit a curled-up wolf, "but while I appreciate the gesture, it's not necessary."

"Well, get the brandy anyway, Barbara. I've gotten myself in the mood for it."

"Of course, sir," she said with a curtsy, and I studied the goat tattoo on her neck, clearly exposed by her high, tight bun. I wondered if I would keep that tradition. It was an efficient way to keep track of prey underlings, especially in a census, but it had never sat well with me, knowing the mark was made on children.

Barbara shut the door behind her, and Albert climbed into a chair opposite me, sitting with his tail draped over one of the wooden arms.

"Thomas said you had urgent business with me," said Albert,

scratching his shoulder with a back paw. "What is this about?"

I looked toward the door and listened hard for the sound of Barbara's footsteps or swishing skirts. He saw the caution in my eyes and leaned forward.

"What is it, Reginald?" he asked, his ears pricked.

I took a deep breath and then spoke low. "You're one of my greatest friends, Albert, and I would never wish to ask something of you that you weren't... comfortable with. So, if you wish to stop me at any point during this conversation, please do. But you are a resourceful wolf, and one of the few I can trust."

Albert did not protest nor bother with a show of pride or vague promises of acceptance and loyalty. He only nodded to show me he understood fully, and I knew I had chosen the right wolf. I hoped he would agree to my insane plan.

"I would like you to act as my envoy."

He kept his face neutral, but his ear twitched. "To whom?"

"The Clydes."

"The horse clans?" His hushed voice rose an octave.

I nodded. I had expected this reaction. The Chevaux who lived on the rugged islands to the northwest were nothing like the dull-witted mounts we used in Cherbourg. They were educated, independent, and fierce as bears... and almost as big.

"Reginald," he said, forgetting to whisper as he huffed through his snout, "they're savages. Absolute savages. Many Truman men were part of your grandfather's campaigns against them, and less than half returned. Why do you think my mother had so many children?"

I nodded. "I know they are fierce, but..."

"No, I'm not sure you understand. They are *always* at war. If they're not battling with us or the Karluks, they get bored and turn on each other."

Barbara pushed open the door with her ample hip, a bottle of brandy in one hand and two empty glasses in the other. We sat in silence as she poured her master a drink and left the bottle and the empty glass on the table. She offered me bashful smile and a little curtsy as though to say, 'Just in case you change your mind.'

It was the sort of forethought of hospitality that I wasn't at all surprised Albert had instilled into a housemaid.

"Shall I get you anything else, sir?"

"That's fine, Barbara. Once you check that the back door is locked, you may retire for the evening."

"Aye, sir. And a pleasant night to you both, milords."

I wished Barbara good night, then returned my gaze to Albert as he quietly lapped up his drink with a long, pink tongue. But before I could speak, he jumped down from his chair, crossed the room to the window overlooking his street, and closed the curtains with his teeth.

"This is not a sanctioned mission, I take it?" he asked in hushed tones, jumping back into his chair.

I shook my head, forcing myself to hold his gaze. "No, Albert, it's not."

He cocked his head and pondered me before saying, "If you're thinking of making friends with your father's enemies, Reginald, you will have a mighty hard time of it. If your father and uncle don't rip us apart, the horse folk will. Me first."

"Father and Uncle have no desire for diplomacy. The Clydes hate us with a fiery passion, yes, but frankly I don't blame them. My kin have done nothing but try to enslave them. But what might happen if I were to break the cycle?"

"What are you looking to achieve with this?"

I pressed on, encouraged by the fact that he hadn't said no yet. But I spoke cautiously. I still had not decided how much to reveal to him.

"Call me mad," I said, "but I would like to ally with them, start a trade system. They have proven themselves resourceful, battle-tested, and savvy. We're wasting an opportunity for powerful business partners. Their islands are rich in iron ore and peat, and there is probably more we are unaware of. If we want to expand our industry, we will need those iron veins."

He took another drink from his glass and then appraised me with his tail flicking slowly over the armrest. There was something conspiratorial in his eyes that quickened my heart. Perhaps

I imagined it.

"Reggie, if King Emmerich and Lord De Draco find out we have made secret trade deals with their enemies, the most favorable outcome is we will both be jailed, and I don't think I need to tell you that they will attack the Clydes out of spite. Which means all these diplomatic business dealings will be moot. And they *will* find out. Your father has many eyes at his disposal." He leaned closer so that he could speak in a barely audible whisper, "And those hairless rodents of his can disappear into the shadows a lot easier than you think." He flicked his eyes around the room as if expecting a Crimson Guardsman to jump out of a dark corner.

"I didn't say this would be easy. But... it *should* be. In an honorable kingdom, it would be. The problem is our empire has been corrupted, and that corruption starts at the top. There are... less than enlightened people running this kingdom."

Albert's eyes widened, and I expected him to demand I stop there. But he opened his mouth slowly and said in a cautious whisper, "Your father is a very intelligent man, Reginald. Perhaps he is harsh, and he cares little for proper politics, but he..."

"I am not talking about my father, although his eyes have been so darkened by the Covenant that whatever enlightenment he once had is fading fast."

Albert sat straighter. "So you are referring to the Absolvers? But, Reginald, they don't lead the empire," he said, each word careful and calculated.

"Don't they?" I asked, matching his tone. He stared deep into my eyes, and I took a calming breath before speaking clearer than I had yet dared. "They have their claws so deep in Father, I can no longer tell his motives from theirs. My grandfather created the Covenant, and he used it to gradually enslave the prey, but he was never ruled by it. Father lets them run amok. They have poisoned his mind and turned predator dominance into rampant cruelty. Do we really need these watchdogs any longer if they bite the hand that feeds them?"

"Well... you can retrain them when you take the throne."

I shook my head. "They are too strong. They have swayed

the minds of the people, and they will never let me implement my ideas smoothly or peacefully. They will fight me at every turn. You can count on that."

One of his jowls curled in a toothy grin. "You want to put them down?"

"I think it would be best for the kingdom."

"Your father will never allow it. And what's more, your father's administrators and a fair number of the nobles will fight your vision also. The Grimaulds and the Turpins will fight hardest of all, and those are two houses you don't want to mess with. Diplomacy is harder than plundering, and the most powerful noble houses have grown comfortable and fat thanks to your father's conquests. They will back any play he makes."

"I am aware. But I consider this mission to the North a test of my abilities to rule the kingdom. I want to be prepared for when I do take on authority. Which is why I want to be cautious of the alliances I'm making early on."

"You know, of course, that, as a knight of Cherbourg, I am bound to serve your uncle, and the day he acts outside your father's will is the day the earth opens up and swallows us all."

"Yes, but should you accept this mission, you will be gone swiftly, and you won't be absent long, so I doubt he will have time to miss you."

"You want to make an allegiance behind your father's back, and you wish to rid the kingdom of your father's prized advisers? Reggie..." He looked to the door again, though Barbara was surely long gone. I had to lean in to catch his next words. "You're talking of rebellion, aren't you?"

"No, I simply want to make sure that when I ascend the throne, I don't already have ten different bounties on my head. My father does not know how to make allies, only enemies, and their bloodlust will not be satiated when he is gone. Not unless I act prudently now."

"Come now, don't lie to me. We both know you've been acting odd. I was at Marburg. You were taking risks even then."

I leaned back in my chair and rubbed my jaw, giving him

a hard look. "If I were talking of... more radical change, what would you say?"

"I'd say what's been going on this last decade isn't healthy for the country, and change would do some good... but that doesn't mean I'm comfortable doing anything about it. This envoy position you're offering... I'd have to lie to your uncle, and if he becomes even the slightest bit suspicious, he might hang me for desertion when I come back. And that's just the punishment for running off without his say. If he were to find out the cause, that would be something else entirely."

"Uncle's organizing a new summer campaign soon. Aren't you weary of burning border villages and capturing Karluk ports, only to have them taken right back a few months later? Aren't you tired of boiling in the sun in useless skirmishes?"

He shoved his snout in his glass and guzzled the last of his drink before giving me a long stare.

"I hope you know what you're doing."

I couldn't help but smile. "So you'll help me?"

"I'll be your envoy," he said pointedly. "For old time's sake. Who knows? If things go well, maybe I'll let you drag me into a bigger mess."

"You won't need to stretch your neck too far out for me. I promise," I said with a grin. "Tell your family you're coming and send a courier with a note for Uncle citing a family crisis, but don't get much more specific than that. Leave either tomorrow or the day after, but only bring your squire and people you trust. After you've popped in at your father's house to secure your alibi, sail to the port of Angelwatch. There's a Clyde elder there who met with Mother once. His name is Duncan Cormack."

I handed him a sealed letter, which he took with care between his paws.

"So I take it this is my introduction letter? Your seal will get their attention, but what will I do if they simply decide to detain me?"

"You can tell them I would pay handsomely to get you back, and I will if it comes to that. But you might make some friends yourself, maybe sell them some barrels of your family's brandy."

"I don't know, Reginald. The implications of this... it's a big risk."

I had to convince him now, or else I might lose him. I didn't think he'd say anything about this conversation to Father, but then again, the price of talking rebellion was heavy. Most people would do almost anything to get that weight off their shoulders.

"Nothing worth doing was ever easy, Albert. I know you don't want to wage war for the rest of your life. That is, if you ever reach old age. Soldiers rarely do. I'd like for you to help me make something better of this kingdom. I want the mindless warring to end, and most importantly, I want the Covenant's poison leached out of my castle. But if you refuse, I won't hold it against you."

He stood a moment, staring at the portraits on his wall as if asking his ancestors for advice.

"I will need provisions for this little expedition."

"I'm offering you five hundred crowns. Half of which I will give you right now. The other half will be waiting for you at the post office when you return."

"That's quite generous of you, my prince." He gave me a playfully mocking look—one I knew well from our youth—as he said, "Does show how much you care."

"It would mean more if I had worked for that gold," I said with a frown.

"Is that what you're doing, Reginald?" he asked, flicking his ears toward me. "Trying to earn your crown by offering better conditions for those servants at the mine, reaching out to the Clydes, and coming here to conspire against the Covenant and your father?"

"I like to think I'm conspiring to save my father from himself, rather than rising up against him. I wish no harm to come to him. Make no mistake of that."

He nodded with thoughtful eyes.

Hoping to better explain myself, I said, "At the risk of sounding heretical, there was a verse in the old scriptures that said, 'And only those who have achieved something through their own blood, sweat, and tears will be welcomed into heaven. For Maya looked down in anger and shame on all those who prospered from the work of others while doing nothing themselves.'"

At this, he smiled and gestured for me to fill the two glasses on the table. I obliged.

"Looking to earn your way into heaven?" he asked with a sly grin.

"Perhaps. But mostly, I'm looking for a little more heaven down here on Kaskilia."

His grin broadened, flashing all his fangs. "Then let's have a toast. To hard work, worthy secrets, and our little slice of heaven."

I took my glass, struck it against his, and sipped through a smile. I stayed for a short while longer as we spoke about other affairs, then offered him the money and bade him goodbye. There was still one more person I had to see before I took my bags and left.

* * *

The warehouse appeared abandoned in every sense of the word. The entry door hung by a single, twisted hinge. The left side was charred black with the rough licks of flame. The upper window was smashed, and no light from the torches posted in the main streets reached this place. But in an alley not far off, I saw the two loaded carriages I had requested. The lone driver turned his head my way, and I saw his silhouette nod to me before I slipped inside, weaving around the broken door.

The floor was filthy, scattered with rubbish. A puddle of what smelled distinctly like urine sat in one corner. I wrinkled my nose and pushed through the hidden door at the back of the room into a clean, lit entryway where several coats hung on iron hooks. The usual ruckus of chatter and gambling greeted me as I moved into the warehouse proper. Most of the smugglers were huddled at the long table in the center of the room, with cards, coin, and ale spread between them. Diederik rose from his chair and beckoned me with a wave of his enormous, meaty hand.

"Reggie, welcome. Come, you have to see this," he said as he led me to the table. "Your little rabbit is quite the card player."

Maria sat at the head of the table with a pile of coins stacked in front of her. She appraised her hand with her small face scrunched in concentration and her tongue barely peeking between her teeth. I nearly laughed, but it was not only amusement budding in my chest; an unexpected fondness struck me as well. Then a brilliant grin split her face, and my feet stilled. Some of the smugglers around her didn't look as thrilled, frowning into their ales and shooting her dirty looks. Diederik looked back in confusion, finding me no longer at his side. Clearing my throat and hoping my face had remained neutral, I hurried forward.

"Maria, I must speak with you in private a moment," I said. I inclined my head to Diederik. "Pardon me."

I coaxed Maria into the entryway, then closed the door behind us. In such a small space, it was impossible not to brush against her, but I tried my best to keep my hands at a respectful distance.

She looked up at me with mild trepidation. "Did I do something wrong?"

"No, no." I tried to wave away the thought, but my hand struck one of the coats lining the wall and knocked it down on her head. She let out a cry of surprise and tried to tug off the heavy garment, but she tripped over my foot. I caught her as she wobbled like a drunken, headless specter. A laugh slipped between my teeth, and to my relief, she joined in as I freed her from the scratchy fabric.

"Must we really hide out in here?" she asked through a chuckle.

Her hair was frizzed and stuck on end in places, and that feeling of endearment tickled my gut again.

"Well," I said, voice unsteady, "I thought perhaps we'd create some intrigue, but also, I wanted to make sure we stand on the same ground before we speak to Diederik together."

"You... you would like me to do that with you?" she asked.

"Yes. I think you will be a great help. He seems to like you."

"Oh, well, thank you, Reginald," she said, her voice and eyes so genuine in their gratitude that I felt a rush of warmth in my blood, and sympathy tugged at my heart. I had not realized it would mean so much to her. I had only wanted to present a united front. But now I suspected very few changelings had treated her with much kindness, if so small a gesture of inclusion could conjure such a vibrant smile.

"Oh yes, well, it's no trouble," I said, but I found myself pondering ways to make her this happy again. "What I need to know is, do you still have the energy to keep moving? I know it is very late, and you have had a rather harrowing day. I would like to cover as much ground as possible before my father figures out I'm missing, but if you need to rest until morning, we can do so."

She studied me, and her expression shifted into an emotion I couldn't interpret. "Reginald, may I ask... why are you doing this? Rebelling against your father? Was it my words alone that led to this decision, or is there more?"

"Well, I have decided to no longer deny you are a special woman, Maria, but don't give yourself too much credit," I said with a small grin that made her narrow her eyes in a playful challenge. "I have been uneasy in my kingdom since I returned from war. I must admit you did have something to do with all this, but let us say you were a stray spark that ignited a dry hay bale."

"It only takes a small effort to start something big, but it takes a lot more to finish it," she said, serious once more.

"Hopefully, it will only take a small effort to convince Diederik to join us."

"I don't think you will have too much trouble."

I smiled and opened the door for her. I saw Thomas eyeing us curiously and with mild resentment at being left behind. I beckoned him to my side, and his face lifted.

"Thomas, I need you to go out to the carriages in the alley and make sure they have followed my requirements to the letter."

Thomas stood straighter. "Don't worry, Reginald, I'll take care of it."

"Thank you," I said, clapping him on the shoulder before he

rushed off.

If he knew what he was about to miss, he would undoubtedly be pouting, but I didn't want him to know too many details. He'd be far safer if he could truly plead ignorance.

Maria and I stood before Diederik, who raised an expectant brow.

"I think it's time I disclosed the nature of this exploit," I said.

"I'd say so," said Diederik, crossing his arms. "I'm particularly interested in how this plan of yours earns us amnesty. Or was your squire there just flapping his jaw to get my attention?"

"No, he spoke the truth. Is there somewhere we can talk?" I gestured at Maria to show I meant her to come. "I'd rather keep this between us, for now. It will be easier to explain without too many voices shouting questions."

"As you wish," said Diederik, letting his arms fall at his sides. "Come with me."

He led us around a stack of ale barrels to a table in the corner, lit by an oil lamp at its center. I sat down with Diederik, but Maria was left without a chair.

"Are you sure this is private enough?" I asked.

"We will not be disturbed." Diederik smirked and added, "We can whisper if you like."

I sighed but didn't complain further. I leaned one arm on the table and said in a low voice, "You and many of your mercenaries know better than anyone the cruel sting of my father's zealotry and what it has done to this kingdom."

"Aye. I've been a slave under your father's rule. Even some of the predators among us were orphaned by your father's unquenchable blood lust, some stolen from their families as punishment for disobedience, forced to fight in his wars." His eyes flicked between the two of us, lingering on Maria.

"Well, my old friend, I have had enough."

"You want to start smuggling out slaves again? Pick up where your brother left off?" asked Diederik, eyes alight.

"Better," I said with a grin. "I want to liberate the whole kingdom. As of this moment, I have exiled myself and become a rebel prince. I would like you and your brigands to help me depose my father."

Diederik sat back, pushing his mop of hair from his eyes to better stare at me. "You're serious?"

"As the grave. Though I don't plan to end up there."

He let out a breathy chuckle, looking bemused.

"And you want my men to join your opposing army?" asked Diederik.

"Yes, and help me build a bigger one."

"Of who? The nobles will not fight with you."

"We will go to those who hate my father the most. The rebel prey. The Andromedae and the Cervi first, then the Chevaux clans in the North."

"You plan to liberate the prey?" said Diederik, brow rising beneath his tuft of hair.

I let a small smile play at my mouth and chose my words with care. "I plan to undo the false treaty set in place by my grandfather and end oppression of prey."

I flicked my gaze to Maria and found her looking back with joy dancing in her eyes. My next thought left my head entirely, but someone else spoke for me.

"So you plan to start a civil war?" hissed a female voice.

Samara's lithe, spotted body slunk around the barrels into the lamplight. I rose and instinctively stepped to shield Maria from the angry leopardess.

"Samara," said Diederik, voice hard, "when I am having a private meeting, I expect that wish for privacy to be respected."

"It is my job to protect you, and when your guests request my absence, I grow suspicious of their motives," she said, her voice matching his for sharpness. "It seems my gut was right. This is madness." She hissed the 's' sound and curled up her lips to snarl at me, her black-tipped tail flicking like a lure meant to attract my eye while she lunged for my throat.

"I can assure you, I am more clear-headed than I have ever been," I said, doing my best to hide that her gaze made my palms sweat. "I feel it is past time to stop the crimes of my father. I have a logical strategy in place, I assure you, but I ask that you leave me to discuss this with—"

"You're going to fix all of Kaskilia's problems with a civil war? Such foolishness and utter disregard for life could only come from a pampered blue blood," she spat, her giant paws bringing her to the table in two strides. At least she was keeping her voice low, though it did nothing to hide her fury. "If you hate your father so much, why not put a knife in his neck and be done with it?"

"My father killed his own to get the crown, and I don't want to repeat that mistake," I said, hoping she felt all of the ice in my gaze. "The flash of a blade in the dead of night makes me nothing more than a greedy coward after a crown, but if I stage and win a rebellion, it makes me a capable ruler. It will prove my competence to any nobles who would otherwise oppose me. If I kill my father, there will be years of attempted coups and skirmishes to be fought every fortnight. It adds up in bodies, I assure you. With my plan, we attack in one fell swoop. Will there be casualties? Yes, but the rewards will be swifter and greater."

"This is not about an exchange of power from one wolf to another," said Maria, startling me. "If it were, I assure you, I wouldn't be here. Have you ever seen a rabbit and a wolf together, free of bonds or weapons or whips?"

Samara said nothing, only watched Maria with that lingering sneer.

"I would wager you haven't. But if you back Reginald's plan, it will no longer be uncommon. That is what we are fighting for, and that is why I am here. But you can slink back to the shadows if you wish."

"I knew there was a reason I brought you along," I said, looking over my shoulder at Maria. When she beamed back at me, a thrill sang through my blood, and I looked away quickly.

"Look at you," Samara spat at Maria, her voice dripping with so much loathing it took me aback. "You think you understand the way the world works? You think because a wolf has made you his pet, you're special? Well, I see nothing special about you whatsoever. I see only a naïve little girl who, if given her way, will destroy others with a smile, leading them off a cliff by the radiant light of her false hope."

"And you would watch the world burn just to say, 'I told you so,' eh?" countered Maria.

I disguised my surprised laugh as a cough. Samara seethed, looking between us, her mouth working like she could not find the right words to form her disgust.

At last, she scoffed and said, "So it's that simple, eh? The world is colored in shades of black and white? We help you with your rebellion, and if we don't die, we get amnesty and the world is suddenly a harmonious place?"

"Samara, this is a give-and-take world, and it will remain that way forever. But unlike my father and those most loyal to him, I think it can and should be shared. If we follow my plan, we will have already displayed that possibility—prey and predator working together toward a common aim."

Samara looked to Diederik. "Do you really believe a word out of their mouths?"

"Aye, and it sounds damned good to me. We, at last, will have the resources we've needed to overthrow the tyrant, and a leader with a level head and insider knowledge."

Samara humphed and shook her head. "So, we are doing this?"

Diederik grinned at her. "So, you plan to stay with us?"

"I swore I would stay at your side no matter what, did I not?" she said begrudgingly.

Diederik nodded. "You did. And I have always been happy to have you there."

Samara's sneer vanished and was replaced with an unreadable expression. "I expect you want me to keep quiet about this?"

"I demand it, actually," said Diederik. "They will be told when the time is right."

A grumbling growl bubbled from Samara's chest, but as she turned to leave, she said, "As you wish."

When her tail had disappeared behind the barrels, Diederik turned to Reginald once more. "She will keep her word. Samara is many unpleasant things, but a liar is not one of them."

I nodded but still felt a tad uneasy. "All right. Now, let us discuss the plan."

"Wait, Reginald, perhaps it will be safer if you tell me one step at a time, so I don't know the whole plot, and any other spying ears won't know it either."

"No, Diederik. I chose you as my ally for a reason. I will trust you, the way I hope you will trust me. But I wish to remind you, if you go forward with this, capture or failure means death, and most likely an unpleasant one."

"The Inquisitors have already assigned me that fate. I'm not very popular in their circles." Diederik chuckled at himself.

"First, we will liberate the slaves of the Marburg gold mine. The Lepores there have already proven themselves worthy soldiers. We'll increase our numbers, steal a bounty of supplies, and infuriate my father to the point of combustion. It's a win-win."

"Not to mention, we'll be depriving him of his biggest source of riches for a while," said Maria. "It will also make the barons take note and plant the first seed of doubt about Emmerich's heretofore unchallenged power."

I lifted a brow and playfully nudged her arm. "Exactly how much about war and political strategy did Angus teach you in one chess game?"

"It was more than one," she said with a grin, then pushed me back as she added, "But I did organize a rebellion of my own, remember?"

"You're *that* Lepores?" said Diederik, forgetting to keep his voice low. "I thought that Lepores was long dead."

"Yes, she is *that* Lepores, but that story will need to be left for another day," I said hastily, not wanting that discussion to lead to Stephania and her current predicament. I cleared my throat and continued unraveling the plan in a whisper. "Next, we will visit the forest of Raven's Rock and attempt to recruit the tribes there. They like to believe they are independent, but it's an illusion. They still live in constant fear of being hunted by Father's knights and mercenaries. Then, if all fairs well, we may head to Clydalie."

"The troops will love the idea of liberating Marburg. We are smugglers, after all. They will not ask for an explanation or further motive."

"Excellent, then tell them that is our first mission of many. I must go convene with my squire."

I left the table and headed toward the secret entrance that would lead me to the carriages and Thomas. Maria jogged to keep up with my stride. Before I reached the door, she tugged on my sleeve, stopping me.

"Reginald, I'm curious... How did you persuade your father to accept that you had let me go? You went back to the castle with your men, didn't you? He must have demanded to know why you did not present me to him."

My breath caught in my throat. Her fingers were wrapped loosely around my wrist. She was smiling up at me with genuine interest, thinking me a great orator of some sort, to convince King Emmerich to relinquish his anger. How would she look at me if she knew I'd offered up one of her few remaining friends in her place? She would leave my side and never return, and I needed her help if I was to take Marburg. And, if I admitted the truth to myself, the thought of watching her leave was unbearable. I felt I was better when she was at my side, and I had few other positive presences in my life at this moment.

"That's a very long story." I reached out to touch her face, then thought better of it and took her wrist lightly in my grip as I said, "I will explain later. There is much to do right now."

I strode through the door and into the derelict outer portion of the warehouse. She followed close behind, and I could feel her eyes on the back of my head, but she didn't press the issue... for now.

I didn't look back at her as we approached Thomas, sitting tall in the driver's seat of the second carriage, the reins already in his hands.

"Thomas, please get off the carriage and untie your horses."

"What? Oh please, Reginald, can't I come with you?"

"No. I know you think you are ready for war, but I assure you, no one is, and I will not be the one to put you in that position."

"But I am ready, and I want to come with you." His voice was monotone and severe, and I could tell he was fighting hard to keep out the whine that wanted to sneak into the ends of his sentences. "I don't care if the Crimson Guard chases us."

"Well, I care, Thomas. You are the closest thing I have ever had to a younger brother. I can't in good conscience put you in the thick of things. But..." I said, dragging out the word as I lifted my eyebrows, "I do need someone to watch the nobles and report back."

"You... you want me to spy for you?" asked Thomas, his whole face lifting into an expression of pure glee.

"Yes, now climb down. I need to give you something."

He jumped off and took the envelope I offered to him.

"Who is this for?"

"You are to deliver that letter to Duchess Leticia Durand. She is to be your new mistress and caretaker. The address is on it. You do remember the Duchess, don't you?"

"She's not easily forgotten," said Thomas with a smirk.

I resisted a chuckle, for I wanted him to grasp the severity of the situation. "She is one of the kindest noblewomen you will ever meet... if you do not disrespect her. Treat her well, Thomas, and she will do the same to you. Mother, too, may be visiting you in a few days. If she does, you are to inform her and the duchess that I have sent Sir Albert Truman to negotiate a peace with the Clydes."

"That's it, then? That's not hard... but, who will keep your mother safe if you're not around?"

"Mother can protect herself. She's done it for many years."

He gave me an uncertain look and frowned, but then nodded and stuffed the letter in his pocket.

"Good, now give your brother a hug." I held my arms open for him, and he glanced once at Maria, as though embarrassed to show such affection in front of her, but he entered the circle of my quick embrace with a small smile.

"Thomas," I said, holding onto his shoulders and looking

hard into his eyes, "do not tell your parents where you've gone. They must remain ignorant of everything for their safety. Do you understand?"

He nodded, looking, for the first time since I had known him, like a man.

Maria

When the torches of Marburg Mine's outer wall dotted the horizon, Reginald ordered we pull off the road. Reginald helped me down from the first carriage, pulling a hood over his head. His proximity assuaged a bit of my fear, my mind drifting back to his arm shielding me from Samara—a predator hand placed in front of me to protect rather than domineer. He asked Diederik to select the stealthiest of his brigands. Diederik immediately summoned Samara to his side.

"Choose your companions," he said.

The leopard woman puffed out her beaded and feathered chest and picked two female pumas, three deer, and a black bear. Samara and the pumas stayed in animal form, but the Cervi forewent their hooves and armed themselves with bows and hunting daggers. Reginald told them everything he had observed about the three guard towers, the double doors that would lead into the mine, and Bricriu's modest house tucked against the mountain. The others were to wait here among the trees until the torch atop the first guard tower waved twice.

As the small group headed out, Reginald gestured for me to follow him to the edge of the treeline. Surprise put a grin on my face, and the care he took to match my pace made it linger.

"We will need you up front. You can get us where we need to go faster than anyone. You will be well-protected, I promise."

I nodded and sneaked along behind him until we were fifty paces from the wall made of spike-tipped treetrunks braced together and the guard tower nearest the gate. Samara whispered to her company. As she led them forward, Reginald gave me a gentle squeeze on my shoulder to hold me back with him.

"We don't want anyone recognizing our faces," he whispered, his mouth by my ear so that his breath sent tingles along my skin. He pulled up the hood of my borrowed traveling cloak to mimic his. "The longer it takes my father to discover my involvement, the better for all of us. We want him to think this is a random attack by brigands, not part of a greater plan."

I watched, hardly daring to breathe, as the archers crawled on their bellies and the predators stalked through the shin-high grass. Samara paused and flicked up her tail in what must have been a signal, for the archers jumped up and fired at the four guards stationed at the top of the tower as the leopard launched herself at the wooden wall and climbed it faster than I would have thought possible. Three arrows found their mark, and three men crumpled. Samara leaped into the tower's lookout post and clamped her jaws around the windpipe of the fourth guard, choking off his warning call before it truly began. The pumas and bear shimmied up the palisade after her, and then all four predators dropped out of sight. The Cervi archers dropped back into the grass.

A single cry was cut short, a sword rang from its sheath, and a low growl carried over the grass. I clapped a hand over my mouth to keep from gasping in fear as I looked at the second guard tower posted a hundred yards further down the wall. There were at least two guards in that lookout post, but they were turned toward each other, as though talking.

"They have to hurry," I whispered.

Movement in the first tower. A shadow. The torch waved in two quick motions. Reginald kept his hand at my back as we raced toward the gates set into the wall. Diederik appeared on my left as the gate creaked open and the guards in the second tower cried out in alarm. The Cervi archers leaped from the grass and raced through the gate first, unleashing another round of arrows into the second lookout post. One guard tumbled out like a straw doll, and the second screamed as a puma scaled the tower from behind and set to work with tooth and claw.

Reginald, Diederik, and I flew through the open gates just as more men poured from a guardhouse at the base of the second tower and cries of "We're under attack!" drifted to us from the third. Reginald pushed me toward the outer door to the mine as mercenaries rushed inside the palisade and, at Diederik's bellowed command, made a wall of swords and bows to escort us all the way to the mine's outer doors.

A noise inside Bricriu's nearby house hitched my breath. The door creaked open, and a beautiful woman dragged out a squat, ugly man with sparse red hair and a bulbous sack of fat beneath his chin. It took me a moment to recognize the long robe and realize this rounded man was Bricriu.

I knew Samara by her chest piece, which covered very little of her rich brown skin. She pressed a serrated dagger to Bricriu's throat, shouting, "Call off your men! Now! Or I bleed you slowly!"

Bricriu's first cry of, "Halt!" was reedy and trembling. The battle raged on. Samara dragged him closer to the flying arrows and clashing swords.

"Again!"

"Cease fire!" he shrieked as the mercenaries parted to let Samara display him to the remainder of his men, most still rushing over from the third tower. "Put down your weapons! That's an order!"

The guards hesitated, and the mercenaries stepped back, leaving Bricriu and Samara at the center of the frozen action. Samara tossed Bricriu's ring of keys to Diederik, who passed them down the line to Reginald.

"Parley!" Bricriu cried as the guards started to mutter among themselves. "Don't attack! We'll parley!"

The guards finally sheathed and shouldered their weapons in an uneasy standoff. Samara ripped a strip of fabric from Bricriu's robe and restrained his hands. I pulled my hood lower but was unable to conceal my grin from Reginald. He beckoned me to join him as he pulled Diederik out of Bricriu's view.

"What do you want?" Bricriu croaked as Samara threw him down and pressed a bare foot to his windpipe. "I have gold. I can pay you."

"I do not want your money," said Samara, looking as though she smelled something foul. "Be silent, let us take your slaves, and you will live... at least until the king discovers you let his rabbits escape from their cage."

"Oh no, please," said Bricriu, blubbering now. "Emmerich will roast me over a bed of coals."

"I doubt you'd taste good; he is more likely to discard your foul carcass in the rubbish," spat Samara.

The entrance to Marburg was a naturally occurring cave opening in the seemingly vertical cliff face, reinforced with a brick and mortar archway that had two sets of oak doors—one opened outward toward the enclosure and the other opened inwards into the depths of mine itself. I helped Reginald and a goat changeling throw open the exterior doors.

Diederik nodded and pointed to Samara and a handful of his brigands. "You lot stay here and guard the door and the overseer." Samara grunted in acknowledgment, and the rest of our company slipped inside the mine.

Drawing close, Reginald whispered the next phase of the plan. "Maria may have to reveal herself to the Lepores. As much as I'd liked to use our captive overseer to subdue the remaining guards inside the next door, we can't let him bear witness. And we need him alive to weave a tale of a mercenary attack."

"Understood. We can take the rest," Diederik confirmed.

"I would like to continue your old tradition and give the Canum here a chance to join our cause," said Reginald. "We'll move forward and confront the rest. We disarm rather than kill—as much as we can, anyway. We will reveal ourselves only when we've taken total control of the mine."

Diederik threw open the second set of doors, and he and his company attacked the few guards left inside on night duty.

I was surprised to see Captain Leopold clash weapons with Diederik. He had never taken night duty when I was in Marburg. Perhaps Bricriu was punishing him. The two fought hard, but Diederik knocked him onto his back with a violent ram of his right horn. Diederik pointed his spear tip to the captain's throat as his mercenaries subdued the remaining guards.

"Lead the way, Maria," said Reginald quietly.

I strode forward, keeping my hood up in case any more guards were waiting in the dark tunnels ahead. I walked between Reginald and Diederik, leading them through passages I remembered in the blur of my memories of the rebellion. Once we reached the stairs into the dining hall, I moved with more confidence. I led them into the Cathedral, and the sight of the leaning, filthy barracks both pulled at my heart and sickened my stomach.

I held out my hand for the keys, and Reginald handed them over with an understanding nod. I rushed to unlock every barrack as Reginald called out, "Lepores of Marburg, step forward and accept your new freedom!"

Rabbit ears and noses poked hesitantly out of the barracks as I returned to Reginald's side. I saw Milten hop out of the men's central barrack, and I threw back my hood, calling his name.

Even in rabbit form, shock transformed his face.

"Maria!" he called, racing through the crowd of rabbits now spilling from the barracks as the news spread through the cots.

Reginald tossed back his hood, and the barrack guards gasped. But the Lepores only had eyes for me, staring at me like some sort of messiah. Even the pigs gaped at me with something like reverence. For a brief moment, I reveled in it. Then Milten crashed into me, raising up on his back legs to place his small front paws on my biceps, the tips of his ears tickling my chin.

"You're alive!" he said, and we laughed together, my heart swelling.

"More alive than I have ever been, my friend. Where is Stephania?"

My smile disintegrated when his ears drooped.

"No," I said, shaking my head against everything his expression might mean.

He fixed me with sorrowful eyes. "She's gone, Maria."

My heart shriveled—the shock of the news a ferocious blow to my gut. I was too late. Bricriu had taken Stephania like he'd taken everyone else. Perhaps he had discovered the true nature of the ruse she'd played on him for my sake. Tears stung my eyes, but I didn't have time to ask questions now.

When Milten lowered to all fours, I wiped my face and turned to address the whole crowd, forcing down the sorrow for the sake of my mission, a holy fire raging in my heart.

"Lepores and Porcorum of Marburg mine. Your honorable prince, Reginald Ingolf, has decided to offer you freedom, in exchange for your help in the rebellion against his father."

The brigands murmured at my back, and I heard whispers of "Rebellion? No one said anything of rebellion," and "Truly? I thought we were smuggling slaves," and "At last, some real excitement."

"Madness!" shouted Leopold over the mercenaries' mutterings and the Lepores' murmurs of awe. "King Emmerich's power is granted by Khaytan himself. You cannot be serious, Your Highness."

"I am deadly serious, captain!" said Reginald. "But unlike my father, or your traitorous overseer for that matter, I will give you and your men a choice. Either you swear fealty to me, or you die for my father. Choose wisely."

I called to my people. "Arm yourselves with the tools of your underground prison, and should these changelings fight against you for a second time, let them feel our wrath as a hundred crushing blows."

"Prince Reginald, I have always admired you, but now you are acting too rashly," said Leopold. "Maria... you are an unusual Lepores. You are smarter than this. The two of you can't possibly believe you can win a war against King Emmerich with a few starved prisoners and reluctant Canum. Your Highness, please, release me and my men, leave these slaves where they belong, and return to your father having bought our silence."

"You have underestimated these slaves before, captain," said Reginald, "and they are only my first recruits. I will say it one more time: help us or your lives are forfeit."

The captain's chest rose and fell with quick breaths, his

face taut with nerves. Diederik grabbed two of the guards in his brawny arms and squeezed their necks between his biceps and shoulders, hastening Leopold's decision.

"You're offering only the illusion of choice," he said, scowling at Reginald. "But we will join you."

"Good man. You will be guarded, but never harmed, until I can hopefully earn your loyalty. I will begin my efforts tonight, bestowing the same mercy to any of your fellows outside who will accept it."

The captain nodded, and the mercenaries stripped the guards of their weapons and tossed them to the slaves. Milten rushed to pick up a crossbow and pointed it at a guard. An ecstatic cheer rose from the Lepores in a roar of triumph that echoed off the stone and filled my chest with pride.

"Take everything of value," Reginald barked. "Gather all the food, tools, and weapons you can carry."

As the crowd dispersed, I slipped in among them, telling Reginald I would return shortly and leaving before he could respond, taking the quickest path to the old tunnels. I was a bit worried that the tunnel collapse had spilled into the chamber full of old storage pots, but when I arrived, the room was still open for me, though a small pile of sediment had gathered at the entrance. My book was still tucked away in the pot where I'd left it. I put it in a satchel and went to rejoin the company of the Iron Oath.

When I returned, I found some of the pigs hauling an iron chest full of gold hoarded for Bricriu. I directed the Porcorum to Reginald. The chest would be vital for the rebellion. As the company gathered back in the Cathedral, where the Canum were now shackled and gagged in a line, Reginald called for silence.

"Everyone, arm yourselves as best you can. Lepores, stay in the back. I plan to get us out of here with as little bloodshed as possible. Overseer Winterhall will help us with that." He flipped up his hood, and I did the same as he added, "And please, refrain from using mine or Maria's names until Marburg is behind us."

There was a great shuffle and much clanking of steel as the weapons looted from the guards' armory were passed around.

Diederik distributed the stash of rifles and crossbows to the Iron Oath who knew how to operate them, but that left many Lepores with swords so large they could barely raise them. Reginald offered me a dagger that I kept sheathed. As we moved up the stairs to the antechamber, I stepped over several blades in the dirt, abandoned in favor of familiar pickaxes.

Once we had returned to the mine's entrance, Samara yanked Bricriu to his feet, shoving him toward Diederik. The Taurus pressed the barrel of a cocked rifle to Bricriu's forehead.

"You're going to tell the rest of your men to leave their weapons in the grass and step away ten paces. Tell them if they comply, they live."

"P-please, the king is sure to kill me if you take those slaves. W-why should I help?" Bricriu tried for a defiant glare, but his quivering lip betrayed him. "I want some sort of protection if I—"

"The king may indeed kill you, but that's an uncertain future," said Diederik. "This gun, however, will rip open your head if you don't do as I say now."

Bricriu nodded with a whimper. Diederik hurried him to the front of the crowd. Reginald and I blended into the Iron Oath at his back.

Diederik moved the barrel to the back of Bricriu's head. "Tell them now."

"Lay your weapons in the grass and step away ten paces!" Bricriu squawked to the guards scattered throughout the yard, but none dropped their weapons. I held my breath as they held their ground against Bricriu's command.

From across the yard, one of the guards shouted, "Bricriu's a coward! We must stop this!"

"For king and country!" another roared, and then all I could hear were battle cries, rifle blasts, and screams.

Reginald covered my head with an arm, forcing me to stare at the dirt.

"Charge!" he yelled. Then to me alone said, "Stick to my side."

"Restrain as many as you can!" Diederik thundered. "Kill the rest!"

I saw the battle in flashes through shifting bodies and swinging arms. With most of the weapons already confiscated, many guards attacked with swinging fists, only to receive hard blows to temples from rifle butts and sword hilts. I smelled blood and drew my knife, but a wave of bodies kept Reginald and I from the fray. The skirmish ended even quicker than our first attempted liberation, but today, we were triumphant. As the cries of celebration rang out, Reginald's arm withdrew, and I looked around. Samara kicked a blubbering and bound Bricriu back into his house. Every single body in the grass bore a guard's uniform, but there were fewer than expected. Most were struggling in the grasps of mercenaries and Lepores.

"Chain them with the others," barked Diederik. "I'm sure their captain can apprise them of our deal if you take off his gag."

Tears of joy spilled onto my cheeks. My people were free!

As the guards were led away, the rest of the Lepores filtered out into the night. There were murmurs and gasps and cries of euphoria from the slaves as many of them took in the sky and the taste of fresh air for the first time in their lives.

Reginald flashed a triumphant smile as he surveyed the group, and when he caught me watching, he tipped his head, the lines of his mouth softening into something more personal. My cheeks warmed, and I threw my body into his, squeezing hard. "Thank you for freeing my people," I whispered into his chest.

He enveloped me in his arms, then suddenly grew rigid. He gently pushed me away, clearing his throat, eyes focused somewhere over my shoulder.

"This... this is not the time for thanks," he said, standing stiff. "We still have much to do. Your people are not safe yet."

Suddenly embarrassed, I felt my face grow hot, and I studied the ground when he released my shoulders. What had I been thinking? I supposed I hadn't been, and yet I was sad to let go. "I'm... I'm sorry," I said, trying not to think about how warm and strong his torso had felt against mine.

Great Mother Maya, tame my heart, I thought.

A breath from Diederik's bull nose ruffled my hair from behind as he told Reginald, "I saw three turn tail and flee through the gate. Should we pursue them?"

"No. They can only tell the king what we want them to anyway."

A troublesome idea struck me, and I frowned.

"But Reginald, won't the palace guards come here and follow our tracks to Raven's Rock? The forest is expansive for sure, but this is a large company. It would be impossible to conceal all of our marks."

"We want this to look like nothing more than a prison break, yes?" said Diederik after a moment of careful thought.

Reginald nodded.

"We could split the company," suggested Diederik. "I could appoint two of my most trusted companions to act as group leaders along with you and me. We could each take a group of slaves with us and disperse the members of my company among them. That would look like all of the Lepores ran off in different directions without a plan. And with smaller groups all going in wide circles, it would be easier to throw the hounds off our scent, double back, and conceal our tracks. We could meet outside of Raven's Rock and enter together, after your father's soldiers are thoroughly confused."

Reginald grinned. "We'd best get moving then."

CHAPTER EIGHT
The White Queen and the Black King

Ecaterina

I bent over my chicken soup, blowing on the hot broth, but nearly dropped my spoon into the fine china as Emmerich banged into the room at my back. He paced the length of the fireplace, his human face absolutely livid. He worked his mouth, furiously murmuring to himself, gradually turning puce. And while I was relieved he didn't seem to be angry at me... I worried and wondered at what pebble had found its way into his boots. I didn't dare ask and went back to eating.

Hot broth burned my chin as he startled me yet again, bellowing, "Where is Reginald?!"

I turned in my seat, fear gripping my chest, as it did every time Emmerich spoke our son's name in anger. He had spoken Lothar's name that way so many times, and yet I had never believed he would disown him... or worse. I would not make that mistake again.

"I don't know, dear," I said, keeping the shake out of my voice with some effort. "Have you sent a servant to check his room?"

He stopped his pacing and stared at me with disgust. "Are

you truly an idiot, or do you just pretend to be, thinking it endearing?"

I swallowed my pride and held my tongue, and at last he threw up his hands and said, "Yes! Of course I did. He is not there."

"Perhaps he went out for a morning ride. The weather is quite lovely today. Or perhaps he is still with friends."

When he grumbled and continued his pacing, I ventured a grab for more information.

"Why do you need him? If it is an urgent matter, I will have the guards venture into the forest to check his usual riding trail."

"There was a distress fire lit in Marburg Mine's watchtowers in the wee hours of the morning. I tasked Reginald with keeping order there. It seems he's done a piss-poor job."

I breathed a little easier. I had learned to read Emmerich's moods long ago. I had to in order to survive. Reginald was not the true object of Emmerich's rage, only a secondary target. Any violence served up today would be directed at the Marburg staff.

"I am sorry to hear that, dear. Please, my love, sit with me and have something to eat while you wait. You work yourself too hard."

He slowed his feet and looked at me with a touch of softness in his eyes, and the beginnings of a smile tugged at my lips as I saw the man of my youth. He stepped toward me, and then two Lobo knights entered the room in human form, dragging a chained prisoner with them. Emmerich's face hardened to stone, and he turned from me. I let my spoon dangle limply over my bowl, watching as the knights forced the prisoner to his knees in front of Emmerich. For a second, I thought I recognized the balding man.

"Well, well, happy that you should pay me a visit, Bricriu. Would you care to tell me how things are going at my favorite gold mine?" my husband asked.

The name was familiar. I thought perhaps he was the overseer.

"I would very much love to tell you things are well, sire..." the man sputtered, his toad-like chin jiggling.

"But you can't?" said Emmerich, his voice too soft, too tranquil. He flashed the smile that meant the worst sort of trouble, the one that lit his eyes with a rabid glint. "Why, pray tell, is that?"

"We... we were attacked, Your Majesty. Invaded! By mercenaries. They... they freed... all th-the slaves."

My mouth dropped open, but I closed it quickly with a snap. *All* of the slaves? Dear Maya, Emmerich would explode. I did not want to be caught in the blast, but I was unsure how to rise from my chair without calling attention to myself.

Emmerich's pale face purpled again, nostrils flaring. He looked to the knights.

The taller of the two spoke up. "It's true, Your Majesty. We searched the mine. No slaves remained. All of the carts had been emptied of their gold, as well."

Emmerich roared like a bear, stomped to the table, and dragged his arm over it, launching plates, glasses, and cutlery in the overseer's direction. I flinched from his hand as he grabbed my bowl of steaming soup and threw it in the overseer's face. The man let out a piercing scream, his skin beet red. As a silver goblet clanged and rolled over the floor, Emmerich launched himself forward and shifted into a white wolf before his hands touched the floor. He snapped his jaws a centimeter from Bricriu's fat neck. The sound made me search for my own wolf half in my head, preparing to call her forward should he turn his yellow eyes on me.

But he rose on his hind legs, his muzzle curled to show his teeth. "You have failed me one too many times, Bricriu. You're relieved of your post." He turned to one of his wardens standing obediently against the wall. "You, take this rat to the dungeon and tell the Absolvers they are to drop everything and give this fool the punishment of a traitor and a thief. For that is what his actions—or rather, lack of actions—have made him. I wish to see how long he lasts. It might be good for morale to let the men place bets on him."

The knights chuckled, but Bricriu's voice drowned them

out as he pleaded for his life. As the warden grabbed his chains and hauled him from the room, his words became unintelligible, dissolving into high whines and whimpers.

"Tell me you found the attackers' trail. Tell me Lieutenant Henry is there now, leading a pack after them."

The taller knight's grin vanished, and he didn't dare meet his lord's gaze as he said, "It seems the slaves ran in all directions when they were freed. There are many trails to follow, and we aren't sure which will be the most fruitful. Lieutenant Henry has requested more men."

"So this was a rescue mission, was it? Some bleeding-heart mercenaries? A group of prey changelings lurking in the dark underbelly of Cherbourg, no doubt."

"It seems possible, Your Majesty," said the knight, his gaze still on the floor. "The attack itself was well-organized, but afterward, it seems there was little planning."

"Lepores are creatures of very little brains. We will round them up, but it is the mercenaries I want. Lieutenant Henry will have his men. Go to the barracks and get as many knights as you can find. Go to the Crimson Guard captain and tell him to begin sniffing out the names of every mercenary group operating in Cherbourg. I want to know who's gone missing."

"Right away, Your Majesty," said the knight, and he and his companion rushed from the room.

Emmerich whirled on me, hackles still raised.

"Find out where our son is. I want him at that mine."

I rose from my seat, relieved to be dismissed, and bowed my head. "Of course, dear. I will send him to you."

As I rushed to Reggie's room, thinking there was a chance he'd returned during all the commotion, I tried to remember the last time I'd seen him. It had been at least two days, at breakfast the morning before Emmerich had sent him to catch that raving rabbit who'd started an uprising in the mine. I knew he had been in the palace yesterday, though. Emmerich had been pleased with him for catching the Lepores when the other knights had lost her. He'd delivered her yesterday, and I'd expected to see him at dinner, but Emmerich said he had gone out to see friends. I wondered if perhaps he was sleeping off a wild celebratory night in someone's guest chambers.

I threw open the doors to his chambers, lifting my skirts as I rushed over the threshold. One of the young Cervi maids, Helga, was sweeping the main living space, and she jumped when she saw me.

"I'm sorry, milady, I will get this done quickly."

"No, no, it's fine, Helga. But have you found anything that might suggest where the prince has gone this morning? The king has asked for him. Are his riding clothes in his closet?"

"Well, now that you ask, milady, I noticed quite a few things missing from his closet. Along with one of his luggage bags."

I furrowed my brow, a feeling of dread beginning to creep into my chest. I had come to associate that feeling with motherhood—a sort of premonition. Whenever I got that feeling when the boys were young, I would rush off to look for them, and each time, I found them inches from dire trouble... or already deep in the aftermath. Once, I'd found Lothar with a broken bone, Reggie crying even harder beside him. Another time, I'd found Reggie on the roof of the stables, reaching out over empty space to grab an apple from a high branch.

"What exactly is missing?" I asked, rushing into the bedroom portion of his chambers and throwing open the closet with Helga on my heels.

"A coat's missing there, milady." She pointed to a gap in the hanging clothes. "Two pairs of trousers. His riding boots. His biggest luggage case. Undergarments are gone from the drawers, too. I always straighten the drawers once a week, for he just throws things inside them."

I scanned the closet, biting my nails. He had likely packed to spend the night with a friend... but still, I couldn't shake that feeling.

"Perhaps he left a note," I said, mostly to myself. Reginald often left me messages about where he was going, slipped under my door. I wished I could see them as just sweet messages keeping me informed of his life, but I knew what they were deep down. He was letting me know when he would not be around to stand between Emmerich and me. They were unspoken warnings to lay low.

Helga and I searched his bedroom, the living space, and his bath chamber for a slip of parchment with his signature. I plopped down on his chaise and was about to give up and send messengers to the homes of his nearby friends, when a loud knock came at the door. I looked up from massaging my temples to see Angus poke in his head. He entered at the sight of me, wearing a peasecod armor and his plaid skirt.

"Hello, Angus," I said through a surprised half-smile. "Normally, I would ask you whether you deigned to wear anything under the kilt, but I'm rather distressed right now."

He chuckled softly deep in his barrel chest.

"No, milady. I wear it traditionally. Nothing is worn beneath, but everything is in fine working order."

He surprised a laugh out of me. When I had covered my mouth and gotten the giggles under control, I said, "Well, thank you for that, but I really don't have time to talk right now. I..." And then I shot up, sitting stick-straight on the chaise, realizing that Angus would not show up here unannounced without reason. I gaped at him, and he gave me a pointed look that doubled that horrible feeling, tightening my chest and shortening my breath.

"Helga, would you please leave us."

The deer girl rushed to the door and then hesitated, glancing nervously up at Angus. He inclined his head to her and stepped aside to let her pass.

I got up and asked him to shut the door. He meandered further into the room, and I pouted at him, my emotions getting the best of me. My worry had suddenly turned to annoyance and frustration. He knew something, but he wasn't rushing to tell me.

"What are you doing here, Angus? Reginald is not here. He has turned up missing this morning. I thought little of it until I found some of his things missing, too. Please tell me you know where he's gone."

"I'm very sorry, Your Grace, but I don't know anything about that."

"But you must know. You're his best friend." There was a plea in my voice that I didn't bother to hide.

"Maybe he didn't tell me anything, because he didn't need me to know."

I studied him, the feeling of dread making my brain whistle like a tea kettle—a warning. I narrowed my eyes at him. "You're hiding something."

He heaved a sigh and shook his head but said nothing.

"Angus, if Reginald is in some sort of trouble, you must tell me. It is my right as his mother. And if it's something that should be kept from Emmerich..." he grimaced, and I knew I was on the right track, though the thought didn't bring me comfort, "then I am the person best equipped to make sure it stays that way. Do not lie to me."

Angus looked at the floor for a moment before meeting my eyes with another sigh. "He brought a Lepores to my house yesterday. An escaped slave from Marburg. He left with her last night. Didn't tell me where he was going or how he'd found her. I wouldn't lie to you, my queen."

I gaped at him. Marburg? A slave? A woman, no less? By the gods, was it the same one he told me he had spared a few weeks previous? No... she was in the dungeon. The one who started the uprising. What was this?

"Why would he do such a thing?" was all I voiced aloud.

"He didn't tell me that either, my queen. Only asked me to protect her for a time."

"Then why are you here, if you know nothing?" Anger swept over me like a wildfire, threatening to consume all my rational thought in its wake. I snapped, "What use are you to me?" and then instantly regretted it, but I couldn't summon the energy to apologize.

"He left something for you. Asked me to deliver it personally."

He held out an envelope he drew from his coat. I rushed

across the room and grabbed for it, but he raised his arm in the air, bringing it far out of reach.

"Pardon, Your Grace, but before I give it to you, please notice that the seal is unbroken. I'm just a messenger delivering a note; I don't know what's written on it."

"Angus, please don't be unkind with me!"

"It's not that I wish to be unkind with you, but I fear someone else might be with me."

I let out a sigh.

"Yes, yes, I understand. If the guards report your visit to my husband, I will tell him you know nothing. You only delivered a note Reginald left in your mail."

"Thank you," he said, lowering the note and allowing me to take it from his grasp. "You might also mention that if Absolvers visit my property unannounced, they might... accidentally... be shot."

"I don't blame you," I said with a mild smile, fixated on the letter. "A loyal veteran such as yourself shouldn't be bothered with palace politics. Besides, have you ever seen a hairless bear? It's hideous."

He chuckled again and said, "You take care now, Your Grace."

"Thank you. Goodbye, Angus."

I locked the door behind him, then sat on the bed to read the letter. My hands trembled as I worked up the courage to remove the seal. Reginald was chasing after his "change." He had done something rash—even more rash than harboring a pretty slave. I could feel it, and I dreaded finding out the full extent of what he'd done. Letting out a deep, shaky breath, I opened the envelope and slipped the letter out.

Dear Mother,

By now, you have likely learned of what happened at Marburg, and you're likely looking for me. As much as I know it will worry you, I feel you should know, Marburg was my doing. I'm sorry, but I can't tell you here where I am going, and I have no notion of when I will be back, though I promise my intent is to return.

I can no longer stand by while Father poisons the country. I know you told me to wait until I could take the throne peacefully, but there will be no peace that way, Mother. The nobles and the corrupted church will have me act as their puppet rather than their king. I must take my birthright by force if I want to make anything of it.

This is what I want, Mother. It is what I must do. My only regret is that I'm leaving you alone with him. Eventually, he will connect my absence to the growing rebellion movement, and when that day comes, I will be far away, but you may be in the path of his wrath. When that day comes, please remember that you are a she-wolf. Remember what that means. You were born to be an alpha. And an angry mother who loves her child is far more dangerous than an angry man who loves himself.

If you wish to have more answers and do me a great favor, please follow my instruction. In the dungeon, you will find a black rabbit who goes by "Maria," but I'm afraid that now she may be without fur. You must liberate her, Mother. It saddens me that I had to leave her there, for she is brave and loyal, and I led her into a wolf's den to put my plan into motion. I told her I would do my best to save her from Father. Please don't allow me to become a liar. You will know each other by a secret phrase. When she says, "What do you want with me?" you are to say, "To see what a warrior rabbit looks like." Show her kindness, and she might tell you what you need to know.

And please tell Isolde that I do love her, even if she's a spoiled brat.

Your loving son,
Reginald

I squeezed the letter to my chest with tears in my eyes. My fear for my only remaining boy threatened to cripple me, but my chest also swelled with pride. I had raised him to value life, to follow the true faith. What sort of mother would I be if I told him to forget all of that now? Reginald was bravely resisting Emmerich's tyranny, and he needed me to do the same. I would remember my birthright as he fought for his.

I closed my eyes and hugged the letter tighter, whispering, "Thank you, Reginald."

* * *

Finding the dungeon wasn't hard. Navigating its maze-like corridors, however, was a different story. The stone was black, cold, and dank down here beneath the polished floors I had called mine for so many years. I had never ventured through the dungeon door with its enormous black locks, but I knew where the keys were kept.

When I heard the first scream, I mingled one of my own with it, nearly coming out of my skin. More cries of agony bounced off the stone, chilling my blood. I knew I must be near the main interrogation room, and those were Bricriu's screams. When my heart slowed, I continued my search, drawing my shawl tighter around me.

I passed many cells, all of them five-by-five feet and equipped with nothing but foul-smelling buckets and mildewed cots. Most were empty. The few I approached contained still, shallow-breathing creatures tucked under scraps of fabric meant to pass for blankets. I saw a goat with no fur, a castrated deer with no horns, and in one cage, a rabid, blinded badger lunged at me, gnawing at the bars. But I found no rabbits.

What was I doing here all by myself? I would only get myself hopelessly lost. I had come here with little thought, but now as the cold walls drew in on me, I realized there was no way I could steal one of Emmerich's prisoners and not be found out and thrown here myself.

But then I pulled Reginald's letter from my pocket and read his parting words. I puffed out my chest, smoothed my scarlet skirts, and pressed on with a new plan. I was a she-wolf. I was born to rule. I would simply ask one of our guards to help me. They were *our* guards, not just Emmerich's. And if my actions were questioned... I would come up with something.

Of course, then the problem became finding a guard. I turned another corner where I saw some light far ahead. A black-robed Absolver stalked into view. As much as it made my skin crawl to be near him, I waved him down. My heels clicked a rapid beat on the hard stone as I rushed toward him and squeezed his wrist. A shudder went up my spine as I gazed down at the knobby, pink, black-nailed paw attached to the wrist, far too close to my skin.

"You, Absolver! I am looking for a particular prisoner, and I need you to take me to her."

"I am sorry, Your Grace, but I must ask you to leave. These halls are restricted to everyone save His Majesty, select military officers, and Absolvers." He smiled at me, his whiskers stark against his naked muzzle, which poked from beneath his hood in the dull torchlight. He was some sort of wild dog. Perhaps a coyote, but I could never tell for certain when they were pink and wrinkled.

Letting my disgust show on my face, I rose to my full height and said, "Do you forget who you're speaking to, mutt? I am your queen. I have given you an order, and you will obey it!"

He didn't flinch at my harsh tone. In fact, he looked rather uninterested, but to my relief, he nodded.

"Very well, who is the prisoner in question?"

"A black Lepores named Maria. Recently arrived."

"Ah, yes. I had the pleasure of sheering that one myself."

He smiled at me, and there was such lechery in his eyes that I almost struck him across the face without thinking. I managed to restrain myself. My powers were limited here.

"Take me to her," I said, keeping an edge in my voice but making my face more friendly.

He led the way to a corridor I had already passed. The cells on this row were closed with heavy wooden doors topped with tiny barred windows. I had checked all these cells. I thought he was teasing me, but as I stepped closer to the bars and squinted in, I saw a small form cowering in the far corner in the thick darkness. I wondered how many other souls I had passed without realizing it. The Absolver opened the door with a jangling of keys and stepped aside, welcoming me to enter with a wave of his arm.

"Shall I lock the door behind you, madame?"

"Why?" I asked, making my voice cold as a winter's chill breeze. "You think the queen of wolves cannot protect herself against a rabbit? Or is it you who is afraid of her?"

"I simply thought—"

"It is not your place to think for me," I snapped over him, relishing the shocked look on his face. "My husband may ask for your advice, but I don't care to hear it. Leave me the key and go about your business."

To my delight, he could not meet my eyes. I realized then that he was rather young. He muttered, "I'm sorry, Your Grace, but I can't do that..."

"I am far larger than you in my animal form, boy, and I can disembowel my prey with one swipe of my claws or one bite of my fangs." I bared my human teeth at him in a threat. "She will not escape me, and I am perfectly capable of locking a door. And don't try to lie about needing that key for other things; I know how this dungeon works."

"Milady, I don't have the authority to do that, and you cannot force me to."

"You will address me as Your Grace, or your impudence will cost you greatly. You seem to be under the impression I am just a vapid lady of the court. You and your hairless pack may have the king's right ear, but I still have his left, and I'm sure he could get by with one less Absolver if I asked him to."

He whined through his nose—an involuntary sound that made my wolf half wish to lunge in for the killing bite—and then begrudgingly removed the key from the ring.

He cleared his throat, embarrassed. "For you, Your Grace," he said as he held it out on his palm.

I swiped it from his hand, lifted my nose in the air, and said, "Now disappear from my sight."

I tucked the key into my bodice and entered the unlocked cell. There was no natural light at all down here, only the torch burning in the corridor. I left the door ajar so I could see.

The thin beam of dull orange light struck her face, and I put a hand to my mouth. I may have joked with Angus about shaved bears, but a shaved rabbit looked worse. She had only one bucket, and her bed was a carpet of hay. She was curled in an empty corner, avoiding the dried, dead hay and its sharp edges, which would offer no comfort to her naked skin.

She blinked against the dim light and squinted at me with watery eyes.

"What do you want with me?" she asked, one ear flicking my direction, the other aimed at the cell wall, listening for approaching threats.

"To see what a warrior rabbit looks like."

Her nose twitched, and she flashed her bucked teeth in a smile.

"I heard what you said to the Inquisitor. Are... are you Reginald's mother?"

"Yes, I am Queen Ecaterina. And you are Maria?"

She struggled to her feet and took a feeble hop toward me before whispering, "My true name is Stephania. Please say you will take me away from here. I don't know how much longer I can last. Those men, they... Reginald said I wasn't supposed to tell them everything, and I tried not to, but... I let it slip today that our overseer smuggled gold, and as soon as they realize there was no outside help in the Marburg rebellion and I have nothing more to tell them, they will..."

"Shh, child. It's okay. I will get you out of here."

She was trembling, and I hoped my wolf's aura would not frighten her further. I couldn't have her going full rabbit and darting off on me. I took off my shawl and wrapped her in it. Her skin was so cold I rubbed my hands over the fabric to try and bring some heat back to her blood.

"Can you walk?"

"My limbs hurt. They... they put me on the rack."

I made a sound of disgust and pity deep in my throat. "Never you mind, girl. You're a tiny thing; I will carry you. Let's leave this depressing place."

I held her like an overly large babe, her ears tickling my face as her head leaned into my shoulder, and hurried toward the exit. In my head, I ran through all of the things I could shout at an Absolver if they tried to stop me. I hoped I might meet one of the guards to help me carry the Lepores, for though she was frail, she was the size of a young child, and she was beginning to grow heavy. But I saw no one until I rushed around the corner to the final corridor and nearly bumped into the one wolf I really didn't want to meet. Emmerich cocked his furry head in confusion, then he fixed me with his yellow eyes and sniffed at my bundle. His fangs flashed.

"What do you think you are doing, Ecaterina? Put that rebel whore back where you found her, now."

My eyes found the floor, but I scolded myself. This was the only way to help Reggie, to find out what he was planning. *Remember who you are, Ecaterina,* I hissed at myself. I sucked in a deep breath as I raised my face to his and said, "No."

The word echoed off the stone, startling even me with its authoritative depth. My shock was nothing compared to Emmerich's. His jaw dropped, his tongue lolling over his jowls. Recovering himself, he closed his fangs with a snap and growled deep in his chest.

"What did you say?" he said through bared teeth.

I held my head high, but I knew I had to play this very carefully. If I showed too much fragility, he would run all over me. But if I was outright defiant, if I held myself like a true queen, he would treat me as all other threats to his crown.

So, I put on a girlish pout and jutted out my chin in imitation of Isolde, who always got her way with Emmerich. "I said, 'No,'" I said, with a childish whine. "When was the last time you gave me anything? I want this rabbit, and I will take her."

"Ecaterina," he said in the tone of a man pinching the bridge of his nose, and I knew I had played my part well, "I will ask only once." He breathed harshly through his nose. "Put her back, or we will have an argument."

"Then let us have an argument! At least then you'll show me some attention," I said, keeping the pout on my lips. "I am lonely,

Emmerich. You are always busy. I need companionship. All of my maids are formally trained, which means they blither over me and are no fun in general. I want a silly little rabbit girl to spend time with, to gossip with. And I heard this one has pretty black fur." I wiggled Stephania in my arms like she was a plaything.

"Her fur is actually gold," said Emmerich with a triumphant sneer.

"Ooo, even better!" I said, not missing a beat. "How beautiful! I have never seen a golden rabbit. Please, Emmerich, grant me this one kindness. She's already told you all she knows. You don't need her anymore."

"Ecaterina, let me buy you something shiny," he said, his voice softening, though I could tell irritation boiled beneath the surface. "Some real gold, perhaps! You don't need a filthy, hairless rodent."

"She won't be hairless for long," I said with a little sniff.

Emmerich heaved a great sigh. "Ecaterina, I am trying to be nice, but this is your last warning."

"You, nice to me? Hypocrite! You have not shown me tender love since Lothar was born. I am lonely to my bones, Emmerich, and if you wish to continue putting the Covenant above me, so be it, but allow me my little treats. I want this rabbit, and I intend to get her." I stomped my foot, conjuring Isolde as best I could.

"You are acting like a defiant child, Ecaterina. You can have any other rabbit you want, but that one must be slaughtered for her crimes. Give her to me!"

I held myself still even as he growled, bringing his face far too close. I saw surprise flash in his eyes, and I took my opportunity to get in a word before he could explode in a tantrum.

"And what are you going to do about it if I don't? Hit me again? If you dare lay one finger on me or this rabbit, I will lock myself in Reginald's room. You can take a mistress or a serving girl if you need someone to warm your bed. But you can be sure I'll gossip about it when I send letters to my sister. Perhaps I'll even send one to my father!" I leaned in closer, touching the tip of my nose to his shiny black one, Stephania pressed between us, trembling. "Don't forget who I am, Emmerich." I let out a little, "Hmph," and gave him a sneer of my own. He tilted his head, and I heard the breath hitch in his throat.

"Are you blackmailing me?"

"Only if you truly allow such a little trifle as a handmaid to come to that," I said, renewing my pout.

His muzzle wrinkled, baring every single one of his fangs, and a low guttural growl echoed through the corridor, but when he swiped his paw in a furious swing, his claws raked the stone instead of my face.

"Begone! Have your little pet! But if she steps a toe out of line, your next gift will be roast rabbit."

He stormed past me, and I didn't give him a second to change his mind. I walked as fast as I dared down the corridor, up the steps, and out into the light of the castle halls. I grinned the whole way to Reginald's room. I had made Emmerich see only what I wanted him to see. He had no inkling of how I had defied him. I had won.

Helga was still dusting the nooks and crannies of Reginald's room when I arrived, and I asked her to heat some water so we could clean Stephania's wounds. As soon as we finished, we bundled her in a warm blanket to dry her off. I then sent Helga to the kitchen to make her some hot tea.

As I turned to Stephania, my animal side called to me. Curiously, I could sense no aggression in it, so I let it come out. This, of course, made Stephania quite nervous, but I sat docilely on the floor in front of the chaise lounge where she rested, and her trembling subsided.

"Why did you shift?" she asked, eying me cautiously.

"I think perhaps my bold actions today have made my wolf half eager to come out. But don't worry. I won't hurt you." Listening to my animal side, though I wasn't sure it was the best idea, I gently licked her face.

"Then, why are you licking me?" she said with a quiver in her voice.

"I'm being affectionate," I said between licks, moving over

her face and down her back. "I don't particularly have a taste for rabbit, but I'm teaching my animal side not to see you as lunch all the same."

"No, please stop... stop. I said, stop it!" She kicked out with her back legs and connected with my chest, pushing me back. There were tears in her eyes. I whined softly in my chest, scolded and confused, my ears drooping.

"Oh, please don't be upset with me," she said. "I didn't mean to shout. It's just... well there might still be lead on my skin."

"Please do not insult me. I don't play with my food or drink blood like my damned husband. You don't have to make up lies about lead or other nonsense."

"Oh no, Your Grace, it is true."

She started on her tale, and I was too flabbergasted to say a word. She told me about Maria, the one who had really led the rebellion and told me she had escaped and devised a plan to make sure my son found her, for she knew there was goodness in his heart. I wasn't sure how I felt about this Maria. She seemed at once golden-hearted *and* deceptive. It was her influence, it seemed, that gave Reginald his final push, leading him into horrible danger. And yet, she was helping Reginald do what he had long desired. She wanted to improve her people's standing in the country, and I could greatly respect that. As Stephania moved on to her part in the ruse, I began to smile. When she finished, I burst into laughter.

"Oh good Mother Maya! Ha, I need restrain myself before I get a stomach cramp. Oh dear, you've made a blithering idiot out of Emmerich. This moment is worth more than all the gold in his treasuries!"

Her face, which had been amused, soured. "My kin bled and died for that gold. And it certainly wasn't amusing when that Inquisitor ripped my fur off with a blunt knife." I shut my mouth after that. I knew cruelty and suffering, but not like this girl, and I felt ashamed for my outburst.

"I'm sorry, but I promise they will not touch you again." I wagged my blond tail, letting my tongue fall out of my mouth a little. "I think we will be great friends. I will protect you from my husband."

"Is he always this cruel? To everyone, even his family?"

"Yes, even his family. Something his father and first son knew all too well... at the end, at least."

I didn't want to torment her, or myself, with that story, so I turned away. Helga returned, and I sat with Stephania for a while as she drank warm tea. When she kept the tea down, I asked for a meal to be brought to her. Once she had finished, I shifted back into human form, walked to the door, and took the key.

"Stephania, I will let you rest for a while. But I have to lock you in; it's the only way to keep you safe. Let's pray Emmerich won't break the door down."

"Wait, you aren't going to ask me for the secrets Reginald told me?"

"I won't pester you. If you don't trust me yet, don't tell me anything."

"But I have to tell you something; it would help Reginald and Maria."

I closed the door and walked back to her.

"All right, tell me a small detail."

"Right before we reached the castle, he told me that, should you free me, I should tell you he was going south to see if any of the Karluk tribes would fight with him. But I have no idea who they are."

At that, my blood went cold. This couldn't be true. I went to the window and looked out as if hoping to see Reginald riding over the back fields toward the stable, this dangerous quest abandoned.

"They are our most hated enemies," I said to Stephania. "Reginald himself fought against them. They wouldn't welcome him; they would take him and all those with him prisoner."

I tapped a finger to my lip, thinking hard. Reginald wouldn't have told Stephania the truth of where he was going. She was brave for a Lepores, certainly, but he couldn't be sure she wouldn't crack under interrogation. If I knew my son, this was a safeguard.

"This is a carefully constructed lie for his father," I said, wanting her to know she was now my confidant. "He told you this because he knew if the Absolvers got it out of you, they would be misled, and if I saved you, I would have a way to throw Emmerich off his trail."

"I don't understand."

"Reginald's absence has already drawn his father's attention. Eventually, as Reginald takes rebellious action with his new army, and his absence drags on, Emmerich will put the two together. When that happens, you and I will have Emmerich chasing after phantoms, while Reginald's true destination remains a secret."

I knew what I had to do. It wouldn't be easy, and I had to act preemptively.

"Stephania, I will be keeping you company for a little while longer. I need to write a letter."

Once I had the quill and paper in my hands, I still needed to think who I would address it to. I didn't know too many of the Karluk sultans. But there was one I remembered my brother Pascal had some dealings with in the salt trade. When I'd been shocked that a Karluk would consort with a Kaskilian, Pascal had said he was a strict man of business. I searched for his name in my memory, at last remembering: Afolabi.

I decided to be polite with this sultan. I reminded him that he had done dealings with my line of the family. I couldn't tell him Reginald was planning a rebellion; even if he was a man of honor, I didn't want his allies finding out. I hated having to offer him a bribe, but I made him other offers if he wanted to trade. This would hopefully be enough to convince him to be a player in our little game. And all he needed to do was, if questioned, lie and say Reginald had offered to visit his residence.

"Well, I need to make sure this makes it to him," I said, waving the sealed envelope as I rose from my seat. "With any luck, he will answer favorably. But I hope Reginald won't need his help."

"Let's hope so. May I... sleep in Reginald's bed?"

"Of course you may, dear, you are my guest, not my servant.

But if you want to make yourself useful, I can ask the servants to bring you some washing to do, and you can help me with my hair."

She looked optimistic about the prospect, and I was curious to see what her real fur looked like, once it grew back.

* * *

I left with the letter tucked away and a new mission on my mind. I had to provide an excuse for Reginald's absence that would buy the most time. I headed toward the dining room, planning to wait out the half-hour before dinner, but as I drew near, I crossed paths with the two knights from this morning, now dragging two rough-looking fellows between them. One bore the tattoo of a Cervi, but the other's tattoos were voluntary and coated his arms from wrist to elbow.

"Pardon, Your Grace," said the more talkative of the two knights when he saw me watching. He gave me a respectful bow of the head as he wrestled the heavily tattooed one into line. "We've got a couple of fools here who showed up at the gates and decided they'd like to confess to taking part in the Marburg raid."

My heart skipped a beat, and I found it hard to catch my breath.

"Are you all right, Your Grace?" said the knight, as my face paled.

"Yes, just a tad... bemused. May I accompany you? I wish to be there when my husband gives out his verdict. These men have cost our family a great deal of revenue."

"Certainly, Your Grace."

I followed behind them as the Cervi yelled out, "Please, we came to you peacefully. There is no need for these chains," and his predator companion chimed in, "You'll be sorry for treating us this way when we reveal the truth to the king! Maybe he'll put *you* in chains."

The knights didn't bat an eye, only thrust the men into the throne room where Emmerich waited, his paws resting on the gold arms of his throne, his eyes burning with hellfire.

"Come to grovel at my feet, have you?" Emmerich growled as the knights forced the men onto their knees.

"We've come to tell you the truth of what happened at Marburg, Your Majesty," said the predator changeling with a snarky grin that he clearly didn't realize was most unwise.

"Oh? And what would that be?" said Emmerich as I slid into my own gilded throne—its clawed feet resting on the stone of the floor instead of the platform.

Emmerich looked at me approvingly as I glared, stony-faced, at the mercenaries.

"We were hired by someone very close to you to free those slaves," said the Cervi.

"And we'll tell you who it was if you double his price," said the predator changeling. I guessed by his size and mannerisms that he was either a fox or a medium-sized cat.

To my great surprise, Emmerich said, "Name your price."

When I looked up at him, I realized the real game. These men would be lucky to escape with their lives, much less gold.

"Five thousand gold crowns," said the Cervi.

Emmerich bared his fangs. "If your information is not worth that, I will be most displeased."

"Oh, it is, Your Majesty. We wouldn't have risked coming here if it wasn't," said the predator.

My heart was galloping. I feared I might faint on my throne. These men were going to ruin everything. Damn Reginald for not picking his allies more carefully.

Emmerich looked intrigued, his ears pricking forward. "All right. I will meet your piece. Who is this traitor who hired you?"

"The crown prince himself," said the predator with another unwise grin.

I closed my eyes, not daring to breathe, and then remembered to twist my face into a look of shock and outrage. I started to rise from my seat, but Emmerich, to my utmost surprise, beat me to it. He looked like a messenger of death, saliva dripping from his jowls, red veins popping in the whites of his eyes, and a hellish roar bursting through his fangs.

"Throw them on the rack!" he shrieked, leaping from his throne and landing in a crouch on all fours, his white tail whipping toward his head as his hackles rose like spikes. "Take them from my sight! Throw them to the Absolvers! I want real answers! And once I get them, send me their blaspheming tongues on a platter!"

Normally, the sound of Emmerich's rage quickened my heart and weakened my resolve. Now, it brought me relief, while strengthening my determination to make my lies far wilier than those of these foolish men. It seemed that Emmerich had some small piece of his heart left, with Reginald's name branded upon it.

CHAPTER NINE
Forest Guardians

Maria

That night, I had put Marburg behind me for what I prayed was the last time. I glanced back only once, so that my last memory could be of its misshapen back silhouetted by the moon. No gates. No signs that lives had ever been trapped inside that mountain. Just an unimposing, unimportant mound of earth and rock. It would never bring fear to my heart again.

Our group had managed to cover quite some distance, even with our two misleading loops through a maze of fields and a dip in a long forest stream, traveling with the current pushing at our thighs for an hour before climbing out on the opposite bank. A few moments after dawn, Reginald had us stop to take what sleep we could get lying in the underbrush. A few hours later, he sounded a wakeup call, and we gathered to prepare some food from our heavy sacks and trunks of supplies.

Our group included Leopold and a third of the captured Marburg guards. The rest were distributed between Samara's group and Diederik's. No one had thought it prudent to put the chained Canum guards in Milten's group, which contained the highest number of slaves, in case temptation to abuse the situation arose.

As we headed toward our meeting spot at Silver River, I prayed the other groups had all fared as well as we had.

By that afternoon, we'd made it into a familiar portion of Raven's Rock Forest. I thought I saw the very thicket where I'd hidden from Reginald and his pursuing wolves. That evening, we finally heard the gurgle and splash of the river. It glistened in the moonlight. I squinted through the trees, looking for a familiar willow but not finding it.

"Is this the same place where you found me?" I asked Reginald as I settled beside him in the grass.

He had his back pressed to the trunk of a tree with his hands draped over his raised knees and his eyes closed, but he opened one of them to smile at me. "No. I didn't think it prudent to retrace our steps exactly. We are much farther north."

"Oh. Well, why this spot in particular?" I said, edging closer to share the tree.

"Diederik said he recalled a bridge nearby. If it's true, it could save us some time. But he chose this spot because of that distinctive rock there. Do you see it?" His arm shifted my hair as he pointed toward the riverbank, where a rock outcropping jutted over the fast-flowing water.

"It looks like a leaping wolf," I said, cocking my head onto his shoulder to get the full picture.

"Yes. Exactly. That's how we know we're in the right spot."

"So the bridge is a bit farther?"

"Yes, we should reach it early tomorrow. But now, we wait for our friends."

A scoff drew my eyes to Leopold, who was resting against his pack and pulling off his helm with his bound hands.

He glared at Reginald. "Friends, eh? You mean the lot of mercenaries you're paying to help you, the slaves who have nowhere else to go, and the guards you say you welcomed into your ranks but keep chained like slaves? Doesn't sound like friends to me."

Reginald cringed, and I rose to step between them, scowling at Leopold. "He is more a friend to you than Bricriu or the king. You are a smart man, Leopold, you must know that. Bricriu was hoarding gold. The wrath of the king would have come down on all of you, had it been discovered. No doubt, Bricriu would have tried to throw all the blame in your lap. He did not care for you. And you may never have worn chains in Marburg, but you rarely got to leave. You were almost as much a slave to the king's whims as us."

"Bricriu was a pompous weasel, and I am not sorry to be rid of him. Everything you said of him is true," said Leopold. "But how do you presume to know the king and how he would have acted toward us if you had not captured us?"

"I know the king very well," said Reginald. "As captain, your head would be on a pike beside Bricriu's for allowing such a large-scale escape."

Now it was Leopold's turn to grimace. He sighed and looked at his boots. "King Emmerich is the chosen of Khaytan. Whatever ruling he chooses is just."

I crouched in front of him. "Leopold, you are compassionate. I have seen it. If you truly think all of Emmerich's decrees are divinely inspired and not to be questioned, why did you ever show us mercy? Why did you ever deign to speak to me when I was distressed? Why did you give my mother your jacket for warmth when she was beaten? Under Emmerich's decrees, we are filth. We are food and nothing more."

He tried thrice to hold my gaze before giving up with a sigh.

"I have always respected you, Maria. I will hold my tongue. Forgive me for my words, Your Highness, but know I will not stop fighting for the release of my men. I wish to discuss this civilly later."

"You are forgiven, captain," said Reginald. "I promise we will talk. I do not want you in those chains forever, either." Soft exclamations from some of the mercenaries announced the arrival of Diederik's group. Reginald rose to greet his friend.

"No trouble along the way, I hope?"

"Saw a group of palace guards once, but we were already in the cover of the forest, and they were following our first set of tracks. May take 'em all day to figure out we walked backward through them," said Diederik with a chuckle. "They never saw us."

"Excellent," said Reginald.

The Canum guards from Diederik's group were brought to Leopold, the mercenaries greeted each other, and in their midst, Lepores hugged loved ones. The Porcorum gathered in a group unto themselves.

Samara's group arrived an hour later after many had dozed off, myself included. I briefly opened my eyes and forced myself to stay awake long enough to hear that Samara had had no troubles. But when Milten's group arrived a few hours before sunrise, I didn't wake... until angry shouts filled the camp.

"The whole force of the palace will be on us soon!" someone said.

"But if we hold our course and find the Andromedae, they'll think twice before attacking," said Reginald's voice. "We can't let this stop us. Not when we have come this far."

I rubbed the fog from my weary eyes and saw him standing with Samara, Diederik, and Milten in the center of an angry crowd of mercenaries as dawn cast everything in shades of grey. The Lepores and Porcorum hovered at a safe distance, listening in.

"This is not fair to our friends, Diederik," said Samara, looking equally fearsome in her human form with her lean, muscled arms gesticulating her displeasure. "I told you it was unwise to keep the nature of this mission a secret. You owe them an explanation. You should allow them to make their own choice about whether to continue."

Shouts of "Hear, hear!" rose up from the mercenaries as I got to my feet.

"It is true; I am leading a rebellion against the tyranny of my father's reign, and the liberation of Marburg was my first course of action," Reginald boomed over the crowd.

"We should have been told what we were getting into!" someone shouted.

"I could not risk sharing my plan when we were so close to

my father's throne and his many spying ears, and Diederik agreed with me."

"I knew that all of you, once you had the time to think it through, would enjoy the idea," said Diederik. "You enjoyed liberating these Lepores and Porcorum, did you not?"

"You didn't give Haverty and Grom time to think it through, and look at what they've done," said Samara. "They've no doubt gone to the king, and he'll have his armies on us in an instant. They knew where we were going. They don't know it's a full-scale rebellion, but when they tell Emmerich his son freed his slaves, the old wolf will put the plan together."

"What's going on?" I shouted over the frightened and angry yelling of the mercenaries. I stood on my tiptoes to try and find Reginald's eyes. He parted the crowd for me and drew me to the center of the circle with him, his calloused fingers warm around my wrist.

As Diederik shouted to his brigands to get them under control, Reginald bent to speak in my ear. "Two of Diederik's men stationed in Milten's group disappeared last night when they were supposed to be keeping watch—a position they volunteered for."

"Do you truly think they went to your father?"

"The promise of an even greater payday is the only thing I can imagine would make them abandon Diederik." I could see the worry in the tightness of his cheeks.

Fear knocked at the walls of my heart, but I locked it away and touched his arm with as encouraging a smile as I could muster. "Well, it's as you said: we are close to our new allies. We will have a greater force soon. It is not ideal, but... let Emmerich come."

His smile lit his eyes, and my stomach somersaulted as he reached up to touch my cheek, his thumb gliding over my flushing skin. "You give hope wherever you go, don't you?" he said, leaning in closer, and my heart pounded an erratic rhythm. Then, glancing at his hand as though he'd just noticed where it was, he blushed and dropped his arm to his side before rising to his full height.

"Please, listen to me! I did not want to deceive you. If you still wish to leave, you may. But do keep in mind, I doubt Haverty and Grom received a warm welcome at my father's table, nor a single coin. My father does not take bad news well. If you leave, I suggest traveling as far from Cherbourg as you can."

"You might as well come with us," I chimed in, making a few people, including Reginald, chuckle.

"My father's laws made many of you orphans," said Reginald, and a quiet fell over the crowd, "but that doesn't mean you have no family. I wish to strengthen your existing bonds of friendship; they will be vital in the days to come. The very reason I have exiled myself and become a rebel prince is because my father has never cared for bonds of any kind. He has no ties. Not even with his family. And a man such as that destroys all in his path for the conquests of his own selfish desires. I wish to depose him for the kingdom, not for myself."

"And we are supposed to believe that, why?" asked Samara.

"He did not play political games and sway nobles to his side with bribes," I said, raising myself to my full height to look her in the eye. "He is here in the forest among prey and outcasts. He chose to fight with us. To fight *for* us."

"Did he whisper that to you across pillows in the middle of the night?" asked Samara, her full upper lip curled in a sneer.

A choked sound of shock left my mouth before I could stop it, and my ears burned.

"Samara, that is enough," said Diederik.

"I am only trying to enlighten the girl before she discovers the nature of men the hard way," said Samara with a malicious grin. "Just because a handsome man tells you something, little rabbit, doesn't mean it's true."

"Maria is my ally, as I hope all of you are. Nothing more," said Reginald, and the stoniness of his voice was nothing compared to his scowl.

His words were like stingers in my flesh. "Ally" dug its barb deepest, and I felt foolish. Wasn't that what I wanted? When I examined the hurt, I supposed that I had hoped he might think of us as something more intimate. Friends at the least.

Reginald turned to address everyone, even the Lepores and Porcorum who had tried to remove themselves from the brewing argument. "For too long, I have watched my father pervert the church and its teachings. He bleeds our land and our people dry for his personal gain and nothing more. He fills his coffers and lets colleges, villages, and religious monuments fall into ruin. He enslaves the majority of Kaskilia's inhabitants to give a handful of citizens exorbitant wealth. He claims to act in the interest of predators, but even they are forced to come to his throne and beg for everyday needs like new wells or food for their children. And in return, he sends their sons off to war."

Sounds of assent rumbled through the crowd, and someone shouted out, "What will be the difference if you get the crown?"

Reginald allowed a soft smile to peek through his grave visage. "I watched all of my father's deeds in the silence of a cowed child. In my youth, I even strove to follow his example, hoping to please him. I do love my father; I will not deny that. And for all of you thinking I mean to gain the throne through his death, let me set the record straight. I will do all in my power to show my father mercy when we force him off the throne. But take the throne we shall. When the crown sits upon my head, it will also sit upon yours. You will not be forgotten or thrown into the streets. My palace will be an open place for all those seeking aid. Diederik here can have my father's bed if he likes."

A laugh spread through the crowd as the slaves of Marburg drew closer, mingling with the mercenaries to better hear their prince.

"I plan to hold you to that," said Diederik with a grin.

"I expect nothing less," said Reginald, before addressing the crowd again. "I plan to make allies, not enemies, with the surrounding lands, and bring more trade and commerce so that the economy can thrive even with all of the freed prey changelings vying for jobs and land. There will be no Absolvers in my palace, and the ways of Maya's church will be restored."

The Lepores sent up an exaltation, and my chest expanded

with hope. Maya had kept all Her promises to me. Now I had to ensure I kept mine to Her.

Samara scoffed—an ugly, wet sound in the back of her throat.

"You have something to say, Samara?" Diederik asked his companion.

"Yes. It seems to me this little blue blood wants a bigger plate at his father's table, and he's decided to get it by pleasing his little rabbit pet. Why should we risk our lives for a few slaves and exiles who will surely lead us to ruin?"

"Have you truly forgotten your own past, Samara?" asked Diederik, crossing his massive, morphed arms and making her avert her eyes with his look of deep disapproval. "You were a slave and an exile."

Samara gritted her teeth and swished her bundle of tiny braids over her shoulder. "My mother was a tribal princess. I was sold into slavery when the Karluk invaded our lands."

"And you think that makes you superior?"

Samara drew in a breath, gave an almost imperceptible shake of her head, and then thrust a finger toward Reginald. "You truly wish to follow his insane plan? It's childish and foolhardy; the idle dreams of a boy who knows little of the world."

"Yes, I do. I rather miss my childish optimism. Don't you?"

She only scowled at him.

"You had very little to begin with, I see," said Diederik with a mild chuckle. "Well, Samara, *I* believe that is your future king, and I am willing to risk my life for the vision of Kaskilia he's fighting for. So if you'd like to remain with me and the changelings you've come to call your friends over these past years, you will obey Reginald's leadership."

Samara looked around at her fellow brigands. "You all wish to stay and see this madness through?"

A series of ayes called out at her, and one man shouted, "Sounds damned good to me. A real peace accord and a piece of Emmerich and his army to boot? I'll die for that."

Reginald's smile grew, and to my delight, he looked past the mercenaries to the Lepores and Porcorum. "What say you, changelings of Marburg? Will you stand with me?"

My people looked to each other with both trepidation and awe. They were so rarely asked their opinions; they looked to each other for a collective answer. Milten stepped forward.

"As long as Maria stands with you, we will offer our lives to your cause," he said.

I nodded my thanks to him and said to all of them, "This is the will of Maya. I am certain of it. This is how She will fulfill the promises of Her book."

A cheer went through the Lepores, and the Porcorum joined in to start a chant of, "We will stand with Reginald!"

Reginald raised his arms to bring the noise down.

"I am humbled," he said, putting a hand to his chest. "Thank you all. But you must remember that it is not just me or Maria to whom you have obligations. We all have obligations to our fellow changelings as we make this journey. As such, I do not want to see any factions or divisions among you. I am not here to be your overseer, or even your prince at this moment; I am your brother. And we will all be a family."

"And we should kiss and make up if we should bicker?" asked a Porcorum with a smirk.

"Something like that, yes," said Reginald, startling me with a wink as he suppressed a laugh behind his hand. "There is too much division in this country. Too much focus on species. You will work together, train together, eat together. If you bicker, you are to solve the issue among yourselves. I will only get involved if things should escalate to violence. And for that, there will be punishment."

"And what if any of the predators are tempted to eat one of us?" one of the rabbits asked.

"I am a forgiving man, but I will never tolerate fratricide. As I said, we are family now, and families should never cannibalize their members. Is that clear?"

A unanimous agreement went up quicker than I had expected. Even Samara nodded her promise.

"Good. And since we are now a family, every member that

dies will be given a proper burial."

Again there was agreement, and I found myself unable to pull my eyes from Reginald as he scanned the crowd with approval. For the first time, I could easily picture a crown on his head, and it suited him well.

"You need not worry about food, however. Our supplies will last us for a week at least, and there are many resources in these woods—many animals who are not changelings, should a predator's animal side demand meat. When on the march or at rest, we will forage for what we need."

"We'll need to start training our new recruits," said Diederik.

"Would you take charge of that task?"

The Taurus nodded his shaggy, horned head. "With pleasure."

"Any other inquiries?" asked Reginald, but the crowd stayed silent.

"Good. I wish I could let you rest a while longer, but since my father may know of our plans and where we are, I think it best we press on as far into Raven's Rock Forest as we can today."

"The bridge is three miles' march east," said Diederik.

The march was pleasant, the weather fair, and all around me, different species walked side by side. Some even reached out their hands to introduce themselves. I saw a Vulpecula extend his hand to Milten and watched a Porcorum laugh with a Cervi while a badger walked behind them, smiling. It was amazing how quickly barriers could be broken with a leader who encouraged it. The only frowns were on the faces of the Canum guards and Samara. But even Leopold was holding himself straighter, his jaw relaxed, and he, at least, looked like he was beginning to enjoy the atmosphere.

Infected by the comradery, I quickened my step to reach Reginald's side and bumped against him with a playful shove.

"Only your ally, eh?" I asked, grinning through the nervous tightening in my chest.

He chuckled softly, brushing my wrist as he said, "I only said that to make Samara bite her sharp tongue." He scratched the back of his neck as he added softly, "And to ensure no untrue rumors were spread about you or your honor. You are far dearer to me than a mere ally."

"Thank you," I said, my heart leaping for joy.

As we moved farther upriver, the current grew more vicious and frantic, growling at us and producing white foam as it raged over rocks. I thanked Maya when the bridge appeared ahead. Though it was obviously old, it proved sturdy.

As we moved into the forest, I lingered near the back, picking flowers and staring at the sky. A light tap on my shoulder and a familiar voice saying my name brightened my face. But my smile vanished when I saw the bloodied bandage on Milten's head. I hadn't noticed the cut this morning when he'd been in rabbit form, but someone had expertly wrapped it for him while he shifted to human, making the crimson stand out against the white cloth.

"Did one of the deserters do this to you?" I asked, fingers to my mouth. "I thought they snuck away in the night?"

"No, I had a scuffle with one of the Porcorum who tried to force himself on a young Lepores girl."

"You should take this up with Reginald. He won't tolerate such violence."

"Perhaps I will, but... are you certain we can trust him, Maria? You know I will follow you, but each time I look at him now, I wonder."

"What?"

"Maria, why isn't Stephania with you?"

"What?" Ice crystals formed in my blood, pricking me from the inside. "You said she was gone. Taken. I thought... I thought she was dead."

"Well, that's the thing. You looked so heartbroken last night... I went around to some of the women in my group while we walked, asking if they knew any details. They told me it was the prince who took her. They thought she would be with you."

The ice crystals rammed into my heart, and I choked out something unintelligible to Milten before weaving my way to the front of the company. Reginald was not there. Diederik pointed me to the line of chained guards. Reginald was walking side by side with Leopold, deep in a low, private conversation. I planted my feet in front of him, forcing him to a full stop.

"Reginald, we need to talk. Alone please." His face closed up, clearly miffed, but I grabbed his arm and pulled him aside to the shade of some pines, letting the company walk past us, casting curious glances.

"Maria, we are partners, yes, but you cannot undermine me like this in front of—"

"Where is Stephania?" I demanded, my throat feeling raw and bloody.

Color drained from his high cheekbones.

"Maria," he said, shaking his head, "you must understand. I didn't tell you in order to protect you. You have already undergone—"

"Where is she, Reginald?" I said, too frightened to force down the tears or stop the beginnings of sobs that made my chest shudder.

"She volunteered to help you. I did not force her. You must know that."

"What have you done with her?" I said, fists trembling at my sides, commanding myself not to scream.

"She volunteered to pretend to be you. My father expected the escaped rabbit responsible for the uprising; I had to present him with someone, or he would have killed me and hunted you down."

"You made her your scapegoat? Your first act of rebellion was offering up a Lepores as a sacrifice for your ends?" I wanted to strike him, but there were still eyes on us, and I needed them to trust our alliance, even if I felt the new bond between us fraying at the edges. "Is that what we are to you? Pawns to be sacrificed? I warned you I would not be a pawn, Reginald, but I never imagined you had already used Stephania for one even as you promised me a place behind the front lines. If I had known, I would not have even entertained..." I choked off the words. Revealing the depth of my feelings for him would do no good now, for either of us. Whatever had been budding... he had frosted its petals before they could unfold.

Reginald bent his head and closed his eyes, and a tear glittered on his dark lash.

"I admit she was nothing but a pawn when I went to Marburg to retrieve her. My plans were nothing but shades of grey swirling in my head. All I knew was that I had to protect myself... and you." He flicked his eyes to my face. "You had quickly become important to me. Even then."

Despite myself, some of my anger dissipated as I saw true regret mar his face. My pain, however, did not lessen, only morphed into something more terrible—mourning not only the loss of Stephania but also what might have been between us before his actions built this new spiked barrier. I had already come to accept the fate of my mother and everyone else that Bricriu had taken from me. I knew in my heart of hearts that they were dead. Stephania, my sister in arms, whom I had promised to look after... I had hoped that at least *she* had remained safe. "That may be, but you don't seem to know me at all, Reginald. I would die before I let one blow land on Stephania."

Reginald nodded. "And that is why you're nobler than me, Maria. That is why Maya favors you. But I must be the one to strategize. I must be the one to put the kingdom before individuals. That is my charge as a future king."

Now it was my turn to study the ground, but I did so in thought, not in shame. I could not bring myself to say that he'd made the right choice, but as I looked past the hole ripped in both my souls, I understood his reasoning. "That I can understand," I said, "but your cavalier attitude toward the life of prey changelings, as disposable assets, must change if I am to continue vouching for you with my people, Reginald. I thought you were different. I thought perhaps you were someone I could..." Again, I could not put the words into the world and make them real.

"Maria, I assure you, as I talked with Stephania, not only did I realize she was more of a warrior than I, but I also came to truly feel I was walking inside the footprints Maya had mapped out for my life. You planted the seed, but Stephania made me sure. My decision to hand her over, in the end, was excruciating." He sped through his words as he said, "And I took steps to protect her. I ensured my father would not eat her by covering her in lead dye, and I left a note with my mother asking that she liberate her. My mother is a strong woman, and I have little doubt she succeeded. Please, Maria, you must believe me. Perhaps you cannot forgive me now, but you must at least believe me."

"'Little doubt' is not enough. If she is dead, Reginald..." The tears came again, and I was forced to turn away from the stragglers at the back of the company as I muffled my sorrow with a hand.

He reached for me but stopped with his hand hovering inches above my shoulder. He drew his fingers back and sighed. "I am deeply sorry, Maria. But with all my heart, I believe she is alive. My mother will not take a request from me lightly."

As I studied his face, I found no deception now, but he *had* deceived me by omission so many times over the last few days, every time the conversation steered toward Stephania. I ran through each moment in my head, and the urge to hit him returned. But Maya wanted us to find each other. Maya wanted us to stand together.

I held my jaw tight as I said, "I am going to try and find it in myself to forgive you, Reginald. But for now, I need to be alone."

Before I could turn away, he carefully stretched out his hands and held both of mine, encasing them entirely in his palms. I thought of drawing back but couldn't find it in myself to do so. My head was a swirling mess.

"I truly am sorry, Maria. I will do all in my power to earn back your trust."

I nodded, not quite able to smile, and then I left him beneath the pines.

Reginald called to make camp a short while later, and I busied myself helping create a large overhang shelter, using our canvas, tree branches, and ferns. For Reginald's part, he heaved and sweated among his ragtag army, encouraging comradery by calling both prey and predator to his side for aid. He was trying so hard. Not just for my benefit, but for everyone's. I watched him appraisingly but kept my distance, and though he cast his oceanic eyes my way, he did not call my name or join me, respecting my need for space.

Milten, on the other hand, constantly hovered at the edges of my vision, breathing at my neck, always trying to help me haul my load of branches or show me how to place the ferns. I was not in the mood for company, and he began to grate on my nerves, but I did not want to turn him away, too.

Maya was generous; the river was bountiful in trout, and the pigs gathered baskets full of truffles and other edible mushrooms. For our part, the rabbits collected nettles and wild onions, which we then made into a soup. Yet as we sat down for meals, seemingly in harmony, I felt my old resentment toward predators resurface. Here, in the bounty that Maya had provided, was more than enough food for predators all along, and yet they still used us. I couldn't scrub the unfairness of it all from my mind, despite how childish it made me feel.

All the while, my mind reeled with what had possibly befallen Stephania. Even Reginald, who had publicly sworn off consuming our flesh, still used us no differently than Bricriu had. It was clear that predators didn't *have* to eat us, but if we were still disposable to them, how would any liberation change that? There was a lot I had think about. About Reginald. About Stephania. And most importantly, about what Maya wanted of me. I recalled the vision that Maya had sent me about how predators and prey needed each other, and I sought Her guidance.

The next morning, we broke camp, continuing our search for the wild clans. It was a very long march, and Reginald said we wouldn't stop until we found another source of fresh water. Before anyone could raise complaints, Reginald raised his voice in a marching song. I had to stifle a laugh at his horrendous attempts at improvised rhymes.

"Excuse me, Your Highness, but may I offer another song?" Captain Leopold asked, and I could no longer hold in my giggle.

Reginald blushed but looked over his shoulder to smile at me as he said, "Eh, go ahead, captain, I think everyone would appreciate that." A few more laughs carried to us from the crowd. He did not seem to mind if people thought him silly; though, the few times we made eye contact, I knew that he *did* care what *I* thought of him. Despite his lies, I saw someone who was... honest. It left me more confused than ever.

"Thank you," said Leopold with a poorly concealed grin.

When he took up the joyful travelers' song, about crossing mountains and seas to reach a waiting lover, the other Canum's heads raised with the first hints of smiles.

On Leopold's second time through the song, everyone lent their voice as best they could. By the time the day began to fade and we reached a mountain stream, we sang in unison with our footfalls strong and steady. Bridges were being built before my eyes, yet the ravine was still deep, especially between Reginald and me. We were all grateful to refill our canteens, and the area near the stream was suitable for camp.

That night, we all feasted from the leavings of the previous day's bounty. The smells of cooked trout still brought a sense of nausea to me. Even though the predators' food was not from changelings, the smell of meat would likely twist something in me for a long time to come. So much of my life had been spent being treated like a future meal. Reginald wanted us to work together. Maya wanted us to work together. So much had been prescribed to us. So much was now opening up.

When Maya had first touched my heart and mind, it seemed like the natural order needed to be restored. For so long it had been tipped in the favor of Khaytan. But what did the proper natural order even look like? I wanted to correct the imbalance of Kaskilia more than anything, but what would my place as prey even look like in such a world? How much would really change? I tried to push those doubts aside. There was so much good happening around me that to keep dredging up my pain and hurt felt self-indulgent. I looked around at this group and tried to appreciate what had been accomplished so far, and it *did* fill me with a certain righteous pride.

As we sat around our campfire, my heart lightened to the harmony of laughter at silly jokes and the singing of each species' wildest songs. Milten sat by my side on a log, his fingers drifting to mine too many times to be accidental. I drew away as politely as I could, avoiding his eye. He seemed to sense my sadness that I had been trying to keep hidden, but his solution was to smother me with unrequested physical comfort. Reginald sat on the other side of the campfire, the shadows of his face and the dancing of the red light making him look at once sharp and warm. When he gave me a cautious smile through the flames, I steadied my breath and made my way around the edges of the fiery pit to sit at his side.

His lips parted in surprise. "Hello," he said, hanging his head and looking at me only in sidelong glances.

"Hello," I said softly, my body rigid. Eager to respect my wishes to the end, he waited for me to say something first, but I had his undivided attention, his blue eyes on me, softened by days of guilt. Even in human form, they glinted in the orange fire with puppy-like earnestness. "I do not like this odd, gaping space we've made between us. It... well, it goes against everything we're fighting for."

He lit up like the night sky in a star shower, and my heart gave one forceful thump against the walls of my chest.

"I don't like it either. I hate it, in fact. But it is my doing, and mine alone."

"That is mostly true, but I have gotten you into a bit of a mess, myself. I must take some responsibility for the circumstances that led you to do as you did."

"I should say it's a rather massive mess," he said with a crooked grin.

"What? A prince can't get his fine sleeves dirty?" I teased, feeling a little playful. Reginald excelled at drawing that side out of me even in tension.

"I certainly can! Although, to be honest, I've never had to wash out the filth myself."

I laughed, but instead of joining in, he grew serious.

"I apologize with all of my heart, Maria. I loathe what I—"

"Let's not talk of blame anymore," I said, pressing a fingertip lightly to his lips. I had meant it to be one swift movement, to cut off his talk of Stephania—I'd been thinking of it already for days—but my finger lingered as his lips softly pressed back against my touch. I was not sure he was even conscious of doing so, but I could hardly hear the hundreds of voices around us any longer. With a sharp inhale, I pulled my hand away, but his body swayed closer to mine, and I moved to meet it. Just as I drew close enough to see the thin, intricate patterns on his lips, my stomach clenched. Just when I thought I was ready to move on, Reginald's face was obscured by a vision of Stephania, a golden curl falling over her rounded, babyish cheeks.

I leaped up and hurried off as fast as I dared, fussing with my hair as my head and heart screamed at one another. I transformed the moment I escaped the firelight and sprang to the makeshift beds of blankets, grass, and hay. I huddled between a fellow Lepores and a Porcorum, all of us in animal form, and waited for the others, my mind racing as I turned side to side. Finally, I fell into a restless sleep, still plagued by doubt and indecisiveness, still torn between heart and head, joy and grief, duty and desire.

I had a most curious dream. I stood in a stone room, gazing out a window toward the sea. As with past dreams, though I'd never seen the ocean, its name echoed in my mind as I marveled at the sparkle of the sun on the blue, foam-crested waves and the golden hues of the sand. A noise behind me broke my reverie, but I made no attempt to discover its origin.

But next I knew, Reginald stood before me, the sun bronzing the tips of his hair as he blocked the window. He smiled at me with such openness that I became transfixed by the depth of his eyes, charmed by the vulnerable tilt of his mouth. It was a smile I imagined a man should give a woman he cared about. My face warmed pleasantly under his gaze, but when he pressed his lips to mine, I grew scared.

I pushed away from him, and he drew back his head, leaving

his arms around me. He looked hurt, but he did not kiss me again.

I stayed in the circle of his arms but searched the stone room for the goddess. I could feel Her presence, but there was no sign of Her.

"Mother Maya, this can't be," I called out. "Am I destined to fall in love with a wolf?"

Then I heard Her, that voice with a cadence like Mother's, but sweeter and younger, filling the whole room. Instantly my nerves calmed and my heart slowed, comforted by Her wisdom.

"Do you not see that he cares for you? Embrace it; good things will come of it, I promise you."

"But it is not natural. It is not Your way."

"My pious child, do not be afraid to love a man as much as you love me. He is more than just a wolf."

Reginald held me closer, his eyes searching for the source of the voice.

"When you awaken from your sleep, remember this... I did not weave this dream with my own hands; it was born from your mind." Her laugh was beautiful and ethereal—a sound like birds chirping over the babbling of a mountain spring.

I looked up at Reginald and realized I could not sense the wolf in him. My rabbit side was dormant. Unafraid. He was just a man—a man whose embrace warmed my very bones. A man who was honest and noble, who, yes, had failed so many times to do right but was trying so hard. After generations of hardship on this land, he was making up for lost time. Did I want to cost us even more, especially with every tomorrow so uncertain? Standing with him, listening to the waves crashing ashore, I felt safe and appreciated. As the dream began to fade, I pressed myself against him. With the smallest of efforts, he lifted me off my feet. I wrapped my limbs around him, my mouth searching, and then he and the room were gone.

I woke with a lightness in my quickened rabbit heart. But the peace of the birdsong rising to greet the dawn was shattered when I turned my head to find Samara's molten gold eyes peering at me through lines of white war paint. Even in human form, her eyes were hungry and ferocious, and a chill went up my spine at having her so close, squatting at the corner of my bedroll.

I choked back a scream and stammered, "Is there something wrong, Samara?"

She raised an eyebrow and stared in stony silence, not blinking. My rabbit nose quivered, and my legs tensed, ready to spring.

"No, nothing wrong," she said at last. "It's early. You should return to sleep." She stood up and wove between the mats and blankets until she reached her bed. I watched her curl up like her cat half and close her strange eyes, my heartbeat still abnormal.

There wasn't nearly enough distance between us. I felt she was watching me even through her closed lids. I shifted into human form, and some of my instinctual nervousness faded. All around me, changelings lay prostrate in slumber. I put my back between Samara and my satchel and then pulled the *Words of Maya* from among my things. I passed two watchmen on the edges of the camp, the book's front cover tucked to my breast, and continued my short journey into the trees.

I had only begun reading when someone suddenly tapped my shoulder. I dropped the book in a panic. I clutched my chest when I saw Reginald grimacing down at me.

"Sorry! Sorry," he said, showing me his palms. "Easy. It's me." He smiled sheepishly at me.

"You scared me half to death!"

"How did you get your hands on a book?" he asked, still smiling as he bent to pick it up.

He started to hand it back and then read the cover. His eyes widened in awe. He propped it in one arm like a babe and opened it, jaw slack.

"Forgive me for being rude, but may I please have that back?" I said softly, the old fear of discovery seizing my chest.

He peeled his eyes from the inked words to gawk at me. "You... you have the *Words of Maya*, the old holy book? Where did you get this?"

All that escaped my mouth was incoherent mumbling. The Reginald from my dream was still burned in my head like a brand,

and it made me rather stupidly inarticulate.

"Why didn't you tell me about this? Maria, talk to me." It was the hurt in his voice that at last prompted me to speak.

"I was scared," I jumbled out. "I didn't know how you would react. For years, my mother and I have hidden that book from predator eyes. I could not break the habit."

"So it is not only I who holds onto prejudices," he said with the beginnings of a mischievous smile, but when he saw the hurt and shock on my face, he corrected himself. "Of course, you have more reason for yours."

"Thank you." After a pause, I conceded, "I am sorry I didn't share this with you, even though I knew you were a believer of Maya."

"It's all right. I suppose I deserve your lack of trust." A guilty recognition tinged his words. He cast his eyes to the book and flipped a page, then ran his fingers over the words. It was like he was seeing the light for the first time. It was the reverie I'd felt when I first escaped from the mine. Though there remained a chasm between us, I could feel it closing. It suddenly felt surmountable... with effort of course. And Reginald had proved he was willing to put that effort in. I wanted to recognize that.

"Trust isn't going to be easy for many of us." I needed him to understand that. It wasn't just me, and this wasn't just about Stephania. What our kind had endured for generations wasn't going to be wiped away with a few kind gestures and noble intentions. The new yearnings of my heart alone wouldn't fill and cross the divides carved between us. This would be hard, but a stirring in my heart made it seem like it could be—would be—worth it. I met his eyes, and he saw the seriousness in me. I saw it reflected back in him, and even with my feelings stretched and strained, I knew we would eventually have to move forward as best we could. "I *want* to trust you."

"I would like that," he said, smiling at me.

"As long as we promise no more secrets. We cannot lead these people if we aren't united," I said, resenting how breathless I sounded.

"You have given us a great place to start," he said, gesturing down at the book. "I know many, if not all, of our company will rejoice when we show them this. Forget swords, crossbows, or guns, this... is our most powerful weapon. We need to conquer hearts and minds, and this will help immensely."

His words sent a thrill up my spine and swelled my heart until I had to move for fear of it bursting, the last dustings of doubt brushed away by hope. Without thought, I threw my arms around his neck and rose on tiptoes to crash my lips into his, a frantic peck that I quickly staggered back from, my stomach in knots but my skin aflame. He was frozen, lips parted and eyes big as an owl's.

"I-I'm sorry, I—" I began, feeling tears of horrible embarrassment start to well, and then his arms were around me.

As in my dream, he lifted me, and I looped my limbs around him so that I might meld as much of myself with him as possible. This time, when our lips met, he led my mouth in a slow dance, his fingers entangled in my hair.

As my human heart raced, my rabbit side stirred in its hidden chamber, thumping its hind legs in nervousness, but I shushed that side of me. I deserved this one moment of joy. Reginald pulled back just as I did and cleared his throat as he set me gently back on my feet.

Reginald drew back half a step, but he took my hand in his and lifted it to kiss my fingers.

I felt an elated smile cross my face, and then blackness assaulted my vision, and I could not move. When the light returned, Reginald was still there. Though his mouth was moving, I couldn't hear the words. Something stirred my hair by my ear, and then blood sprayed onto the tree behind Reginald. He sank to the ground, reaching out to me, an arrow through his neck. The blackness crashed back in, and from the void, I heard the Great Mother's voice boom, "*Move*, child!"

The sights and sounds of the world returned, and Reginald appeared before me again, unharmed and squinting curiously at me. I pounced like a big cat, shouting, "Look out!" as I slammed myself into him. We tumbled to the ground, the book flying from his hands and landing behind the tree.

Plunk. Plunk.

"Ouch! Maria, what—" He cut off as my finger directed his gaze upward. Two arrows were embedded in the tree up to their fletching.

Reginald shoved me to my feet, shouting, "Run!" but we froze as two men burst from the cover of the trees, arrows aimed at our hearts. They wore patchwork clothing of sackcloth, scratchy wool, and bits of leather. Their cloaks were dyed green, but the rest of their attire was a muddy, unwashed brown. Reginald slowly stood and raised one arm in surrender while the other pulled me against him and tried to coax me behind his back.

With a warning jab of a notched arrow, one of the men said, "Stay still. Raise both hands."

I slowly obeyed, and Reginald released me to do the same. A large stag disturbed the underbrush with his hooves as he trotted between the two men. He lowered his branching antlers, bringing their many sharp tips dangerously close to our heads.

"Well, well, looks like we caught a few Cherbourg scouts," said a deep voice from the center of an oncoming group of deer and cloaked hunters.

The stags were all broad, with impressive racks of antlers, but when they parted to reveal the speaker, he made them look like fawns. The stag holding his antlers to our throats stepped aside for his leader—a pure white creature with twelve bone branches on each antler. He wore a breastplate and an armored back piece fitted for his animal form, all made of tough hides and bones. As he bent his head to appraise us and better show us the sharp tips of his antlers, a talisman of teeth swung out from his neck.

"Ah, Lord Bedford," said Reginald. "It is good to see you again. How have you been doing?" He adopted a teasing tone as if they were old friends reunited, but with my back pressed against his chest, I could feel the nervous trot of his heart.

The stag snorted through his pink nostrils and reared back his head in surprise.

"Reginald Ingolf?! How dare you speak to me like a comrade, Prince of Wolves?" said Bedford, raking a hoof through the soil.

"Please, my dear lord, if you will let me explain. I have come with honorable intentions. I—"

"Silence! I will not listen to any of your pathetic lies. Your father has sent you here as his right hand to enslave my people. Any words out of your mouth are meant to open my wounds and pour salt into them!"

"No, wait! Please, listen, we mean you no harm," I said, drawing Bedford's eyes off Reginald before he could drive an antler through him.

"Hold your tongue, rabbit. I will let you go free after I've dealt with him."

"No, I will not be quiet. Reginald is my friend." My tongue stumbled over the term, but this was no time to question how we might better define what we now were to one another. "I will not sit idly by as you act as judge and jury without hearing his intentions."

Bedford's black eyes bored into me, and he tilted his head in confusion, ears flicking forward.

"Blasphemy!" he shouted, startling me. "A Lepores and a Lobo, friends? What has he threatened you with? You are safe now. You do not have to hold his side."

Before I could answer, a doe ran up to Bedford. She was slim and tawny, her pelt silky, her chest pristine as fresh snow. Upon it rested a necklace of emerald and topaz beads.

"The rest of the prisoners are secured, Father," she murmured into his ear. "But most of them are prey, and only a few appear to be soldiers. They have Canum in chains."

"So, you're transporting your slaves, Ingolf? Foolhardy of you, to go through my forest."

"They are not slaves. You can ask them if you like," said Reginald.

"I said, quiet! We've been tracking you for a while. We heard your marching songs. How, by all that's holy on Kaskilia, did you manage to persuade your servants to accept their captivity?"

"Father, those songs weren't army tunes," said the doe.

I reached out a hand in supplication, taking a step forward as I said, "Lord Bedford, if you will just—"

The stag who had threatened us jumped in front of his lord and lowered his horns as the archers tilted their arrows at my head. Reginald grabbed my shoulders and pulled me back.

The doe reared, shouting, "No, don't shoot her! Father, she is unarmed."

Bedford rolled his eyes but commanded, "At ease." The stag retreated, and the bowmen relaxed their strings.

"Please, listen to me," I said, gently pushing Reginald's hand from my shoulder. "The prince wanted to make you an offer of peace."

"That was the same lie his grandfather used. Why should I believe it now?"

"Father, we have all of them prisoner; maybe we could listen to this one," said the doe, and I offered her a small smile.

Bedford shook his head, making his ears slap his antlers. He sighed before saying, "You, rabbit. Come with me."

"Maria..." Reginald risked his neck by lunging to take my hand.

"I'll be okay, Reginald," I said, turning back to touch his cheek. "They are children of Sammael, as I am. They will not harm me."

He pressed his lips together hard, then nodded. Before he released my hand, he kissed it again. "Please be cautious," he said, ignoring the outraged scowls and stomps of the Cervi.

I followed the deer elder and his daughter to a small grove. As Bedford came to a halt, two female Cervi, their creamy skin covered in tribal paint, flanked me, holding bronze spears. Bedford agitatedly trampled the ground with his hooves as he turned to face me.

"Let's assume for one moment I believe this silly story. That you, a rabbit, are friends with the prince. How did that happen?"

"I was a slave in one of his mines, and he set me free."

"Which mine?"

"The Marburg gold mine. He harbored me. The rest of the Lepores and Porcorum you're holding under guard are my fellow liberated prisoners. The prince is starting a rebellion against his father, and my people have decided to ally with him. He wishes to bring about the old understanding between prey and predator. We came to ask if you would join our cause."

His dark eyes went wide, but then he narrowed them at me and chuckled.

"How foolish do you think I am, little one?"

"Father, please, maybe there is some verity to her tale."

"Silvia, this is a ruse only a wolf could concoct. We are meant to play the sheep and fall into their trap."

I sighed and rubbed my eyes, muttering a simple, weary prayer of, "Oh, Maya, please help me."

Lay hands on the doe, whispered a feminine voice inside my head.

I locked eyes with Silvia and took a cautious step forward. When she looked at me with kindness, I took the remaining two steps with hands outstretched. She looked stunned as I reached for her cheeks, but she lowered her head to me all the same.

Bedford's hoof pushed against my chest—not a kick, more like the shove of a human hand, but enough to knock me back.

"Touch my daughter again, and your flesh shall feel my horns."

"You are blessed," I said, looking into Silvia's eyes and ignoring Bedford as Maya whispered secrets to me. "He does care for you; you should be honest with him. Tell him you are with child."

Silvia's mouth fell open, and she trembled as Bedford turned to her.

"Silvia, please tell me she is mumbling nonsense," he said, voice hard. When Silvia said nothing, his voice lowered with disbelief as he asked, "Is this true?"

I gave Silvia a reassuring nod.

"It is true. I am pregnant," she said, at last facing Bedford. "I'm sorry I kept it from you, Father."

"With whom?" shouted Bedford.

"It is Severin's child."

"That boy is a disgrace! How could you think of mating with him?!"

"That's not true!" she said, matching his tone. "He loves me. He may not be your best warrior, but every time you and Mother were away, he looked after me. He is part of your family now, and you will just have to accept him."

Bedford bobbed his head and stamped his hoof. He opened his mouth, closed it, and then whirled on me. "How did you know?"

"Maya sometimes speaks to me."

"Ha!" There was no amusement in the noise. "A Lepores who thinks she's a prophet. As if the supreme goddess would make time for *you*."

"It is true. I have studied the words in Her book and read of Her deeds. Through the old holy book, I was blessed with Her guidance." That at least got his attention.

"Impossible! The Inquisition burned all those books. I saw it."

"I'm not lying. I have one of the old books."

"Then fetch it for me. I want to see it."

"No."

He approached me, staring suspiciously down his snout.

"How dare you refuse me when your life is at my mercy?"

"Just because you believe you're king of this forest does not mean I will tolerate your lack of manners. If you ask me nicely, I may show you the book. But only on the condition that you will not harm my friends. The prince included."

Reginald

I convinced my Cervi guards to let me sit and positioned myself to block their view of the book. I scooted closer and closer to the tome until I was able to reach out behind me, unnoticed, and draw it against my back. Maria would never forgive me if I didn't keep it safe. I didn't think any of these deer could read, but the last thing I wanted was them trampling all over it or confiscating it.

My mind tried continuously to drift to what might have happened had these forest warriors not attacked. Each time flashes of the kiss came back—Maria's body curled around me, her hair surrounding us, the briefest brush of her tongue between her lips—it grew harder to shove them away. I commanded myself to stay focused. Only my concern for her safety helped me heed my own warnings.

Eventually, Bedford and his daughter returned, Maria now leading them. I smiled as a wave of relief crashed over me.

"Reginald, where is the book?" she asked.

I blinked at her, stunned she would give up its existence to strangers, but I pulled it around my body and held it out to her all the same, saying, "Here. I was keeping it safe."

She thanked me as she took the book and then presented it to Bedford.

"Are all the pages intact?" he said, nuzzling it. "Does it have Lieds thirteen? That was my favorite."

"All of the old stories and prayers are here."

The elder then looked to his people. "Men, be at ease. You may release Prince Ingolf."

I moved to stand by Maria as the Cervi retreated.

"Just how many times do you plan to save my hide?" I asked her.

"Don't thank her just yet. And don't assume I've forgiven your past transgresions," said Bedford.

"I wouldn't make that mistake," I said, braving a hint of sarcasm.

"And just because I've agreed to listen, don't think I plan to lend my people to your suicide mission."

"Difficult doesn't mean impossible or suicidal, Lord Bedford. You, who have resisted my father for decades, should know.

Father has many enemies."

"Good luck trying to unite them to your cause."

"Well, if you and Chief Montague will help me, I'll be half-way there. He is still the shaman of the Red Tusks, isn't he?"

Bedford jutted his muzzle inches from my face and covered me in snot with a sharp snort. "Do not mention that disgusting, rotund pig to me!"

"So that is how you deal with old friends? Dissolving bonds as soon as you no longer need each other for safety? No wonder you are so inhospitable to parleying princes."

"He insulted my honor and made a mockery of our friend-ship."

"Might he say the same about you?" Bedford harrumphed, but I didn't back down. "If you want my father off the throne, you had better sort out your grievances. With your old friend and with me."

"And what makes you think Montague will listen to you? He hates you as much as I do, probably more."

"I'm sure I can convince him."

"Oh, I would love to see that," he said with a scoff.

"*You're* coming around to my side, are you not?"

He snorted again, stamping. "I said nothing of the sort!"

I held in a grin and said, "Look, I'll make you a deal. I will bring Montague here, and we can talk about this politely. A council meeting of sorts. After Maria and I have presented our case before the both of you, if you still think I'll double-cross you, you can band together against me, but promise no harm will come to my people."

"I guarantee no gentle treatment of wolves."

"I was speaking of my band of mercenaries and slaves."

He tapped the ground with his hoof and gave a minute nod of his head. "Very well, then. One of my men will point you in the direction of his camp."

"Great, let us move with haste," I said, placing a hand on Maria's shoulder.

Bedford, however, grabbed the hem of Maria's sleeve in his

teeth and pulled her toward him. My jaw clenched, but I kept still.

"Maria is staying right here. I have no harsh feelings for her, but until you return, she is my hostage."

"Such is lordly hospitality, eh?" mumbled Maria.

"You may take some of your hounds and other predators with you."

I slouched my shoulders and rubbed at my face to hide my scowl. Bedford was doing his best to infuriate me.

"Is this necessary, Bedford? I have done you no harm. I even smuggled some of your people out of the palace... when Lothar was alive."

"You wanted to be a real diplomat. Well, here is your chance. Or are you going to make her do all the work?"

I caught Maria's eye, and she gestured with her head for me to go.

"No," I told Bedford through a sigh. "I will gather my guard and leave."

"Maybe Sammael will favor you, rogue prince. You'd best pray to Him, for I'm certain you are no longer in Khaytan's esteem."

This was going to be difficult, but some of my worries dissipated when I finished telling Leopold the situation. He looked left and right at his men and then fixed me with friendly eyes. "You are a worthy leader, Your Highness. Unshackle us, and you have my word, we will not abandon you."

"Your word means a great deal, captain. It is agreed."

When the shackles clanged to the ground, Leopold selected three of his best men. More had volunteered, but I didn't want to endanger all of them. I refused Diederik's request that he come, too. I needed a leader left behind with the prey in case Bedford tried double-crossing me.

Bedford's man led us through the forest to a hidden trail. He pointed us west, and above the tree line, we noticed a few columns of smoke.

I led my men to the cover of a broken tree. The sounds of

a bustling, hidden village drifted to our powerful ears: happy conversation, hammer falls, shuffling feet.

"So, what's the plan?" Leopold asked.

"Scout the edge of the village, find a straggler, and then get him to listen," I said. "I want to request a dialog with Montague here in the wood, on more neutral ground where we can see them coming."

"But, what do we do if we get caught?" a Canum asked.

"Pray they don't skin us before bringing us to Montague."

Leopold's men exchanged uneasy glances, but the captain himself grinned. "I think we can do this. Five of us versus one or two boars? Easy."

"All right, we will move in single file. If you should notice any strange sound, sight, or smell, scout it out, then report back here."

I kept my ears tuned to the movements of my fellows as we split apart and moved toward the village of mud huts. I could hear Leopold rustle a bush to my left, but I couldn't see anyone. Down the ridge, Andromedae moved about in groups of two and three, some in boar form, others in human form, looking like broader, more muscled Porcorum. I saw two women depart the cluster of homes carrying baskets of washing, but I didn't want to accost women if I could help it. It was starting to look like an impossible task. I heard a Canum head deeper into the forest, which I thought was prudent, but I stayed close to the village, watching for male stragglers to leave the hustle and bustle alone. The broadest of my guards came shortly with a report of two boars bathing themselves in a nearby mud pit. With a low whistle and a whispered command, I gathered the others.

We only walked for a few minutes, and I hoped the mud pit was far enough that any noise wouldn't alert the whole village. I signaled the men to make a wall; we didn't want our quarry running straight to their kin.

The Andromedae couple were chest-deep in the mud, using their noses and tusks to throw the sticky substance all over their bristly, cracked skin. We crouched as a unit and slunk through the underbrush, using the trees for cover.

On my signal, we leaped from cover to the edge of their pool. They raised their heads but did not squeal, and my instincts set my senses on alert. Something was wrong.

Nonetheless, I pressed on, saying, "Morning. We mean no harm. We'd like to have a chat." I held up my hands, palms out.

The male boar raised his belly out of the mud and said, "Well, well, what's this? A bunch of little puppies come out to play?"

"Pardon to disturb you," I said. "We've come for a parley with your chief. I ask only that you act as messenger and tell him to meet us here. There will be no need for violence."

"A likely tale," said the sow before bellowing out a squeal so loud that roosting birds fled in fear.

"Hold her down! Leopold, with me!" I called, already shifting for better agility. I had no desire to be gored.

The guardsmen transformed in a blink, a few hems popping. A black bloodhound and two grey wolfhounds leaped into the mud, knocking the sow to her side. One hopped on her back and held her down, and the others clamped her legs in their teeth to try and stop her kicking. Leopold pounced on the boar, but he bucked him off and landed a strong kick that sent Leopold sprawling in the mud, darkening his creamy, wiry coat. The boar lowered his tusks and charged at me as I charged at him from the side. I managed to dodge in time, but he turned his massive bulk and came straight back at me.

Fearing my legs would be hampered by the sucking mud pit, I sprang out, slipping on the bank, and ran through the forest, leaping over a fallen tree. I could hear the hog snorting and his hooves digging up the earth, giving chase without any thought to his mate. I pushed my legs to their limit, hurtling toward the nearest tree. At the last second, I threw myself to one side, and the hog rammed the tree face first. He shook himself once and then turned toward me, but the black hound pounced from behind, tackling the hog to the ground. He tried to sink his teeth into the Andromedae's bristly shoulder for better grip, but the hog bucked until he tossed the hound into the tree.

Acting like a wolf wasn't working, so my human brain took

over. I grabbed a large rock in my mouth and chucked it at the boar's belly. By sheer dumb luck, I hit him square in the ball sack instead. He wobbled on his legs, then collapsed on his side, squealing in pain. I edged closer as I said, "I'm sorry for your pain, but this would not have happened if you had let us speak with your shaman, as we asked. We just wanted peace."

"The only peace you will get from us is Maya's last whispers," the hog grunted.

"At least remember to tell your shaman the truth of why we came, yes?"

"Go to hell, spawn of Khaytan."

"I'll take that as a no then." I gestured to my companion, then howled to the rest of the pack, hoping they would have time to get away.

I took one step and froze, ears pricked forward. My call to my companion was too late. A javelin pierced his chest, and he went down with a whimper. I crouched low, and a second javelin whizzed over my head.

"Run, Your Highness," the black hound said through clenched teeth and a nasal whine as I slunk toward him.

I appraised his wound for the space of a heartbeat and knew there was nothing I could do for him. I leaped over him and tried to cut through a dense cluster of trees, but a fat tribeswoman threw a net over me as I passed her tree and yanked me off my feet. I struggled in the net and bit at the fibers, but couldn't get myself free as she dragged me to a man who pulled me out of the net. I tried to bite their hands, but the man lifted me by the scruff like I was a pup, and the woman tied my paws to a sturdy pole. They carried me off like dinner ready for the fire, the pole braced on their shoulders.

They brought me to the village, and I searched the group walking around me, all of them flipped upside down. I saw no sign of Leopold and the other hounds, but it brought me no relief. At the heart of the village, in a muddy, makeshift square surrounded by huts, Montague awaited me. I knew him by his headdress of bone and foliage—rodent skulls grinning at me from among fern fronds and leg bones that looked long enough to be canine. His belly sagged over his broad loincloth, which dangled to the dirt. His wild, curling hair was mostly grey, scattered with its original chocolate brown. Despite his age, there was obvious strength in the muscles of his arms. His chest was covered in old, white scars, and his Andromedae tattoo had a similar look, the black ink faded and patched, as though he'd taken steps to try and remove the marked skin.

"What have you brought for me, son? A lost wolf dog?"

"They tried to attack me and my wife while we were mud bathing, Father. We caught five of them, but one was killed."

I growled low in my throat at the news but silently thanked Maya that Leopold and the others were all right.

"Pity to have lost one so quickly, but we'll skin them all just the same. Let's start with this one; his unusual coat will look marvelous on my bed."

"Thank you, Montague, but I'd rather keep it," I said. "I am Reginald Ingolf, and I came to talk to you."

He spat in my face and drove his fist into my gut.

"You are the son of the white wolf, and you wish me to believe you came here to do nothing but talk? Pah! Don't insult me, pup. I'll cut out that waggling tongue."

He struck me with a flurry of blows, shouting, "Come to slaughter my children?! Want to put me in shackles?! Filthy wolf!"

I snarled and whined and snapped against the pain, tail tucked between my legs, my head woozy from dangling upside down.

"You wolves think you're the mightiest of creatures. Pah! Look at you now, pup!"

"May I castrate him first, Father?"

Montague laughed. "Of course, my boy. And you can feast upon your spoils tonight, too."

Montague's son shifted into his human form, smiling ear to ear, and I saw the resemblance in the dark, curling hair and the wide nose.

"No, wait!"

Montague's son held out his hand, and another man placed

a large knife in it.

"Please, listen to me. I am leading a rebellion against my father. I freed the slaves of Marburg and then came to Raven's Rock to seek your help, to see if you would join my ranks and take back the kingdom. We will have true peace once more and restore Maya's order."

Montague's brow creased, and he blocked his son's path with an arm, saying, "Wait; stop!"

He edged closer to me, eyes roving over my face, then moving down to my chest where my medallion hung hidden in my fur and caked in mud.

"You truly are Prince of Cherbourg," he muttered.

"Yes, yes. And I am not lying about anything else either. I came so that we might help each other."

His smile broadened. He clapped his hands and called out to his people, "Hear that, my children? We've caught ourselves a royal wolf and his pack." Montague chuckled, and his entire village burst into hysterical squeals of laughter.

"Your crown must have squeezed your head too hard, little prince, for you to be stupid enough to come here. But I don't believe you're yet deranged enough to come with only a handful of men. Where is the rest of your army?"

"I hardly have one, just a few mercenaries and freed slaves. But currently, they're being held by Lord Bedford."

He let out a phlegm-laden scoff and wrinkled his broad nose. "If that old fool managed to subdue your pack, perhaps you really are a bunch of new rebels."

"He's probably lying, Father. Let's just kill him and be done with it."

"No, if he speaks the truth, there may be a bounty on his head." He tore his eyes from me to give his son a pondering look. "And his words bring back images of my recent dreams." He snapped his head back to me and said, "You say you released workers from a mine?"

"Yes, I did. There are Porcorum among them. Distant cousins, perhaps?"

"Unimportant. Tell me, was there a black rabbit with deep blue eyes among them?" he asked, eyes sparkling with anticipation that he tried to conceal with a stern frown.

I was stunned, and a little wary, but I decided I had no choice but to try and appease him with the truth. "Yes, yes, there is, and she's a dear friend of mine."

His brows raised, and he rubbed his chin as he muttered, mostly to himself, "In my dreams, a golden light shines from her chest, as though her heart is a beacon."

"Bedford is holding her hostage," I pressed. "I was to come to you so that we could discuss an alliance together. He holds the rabbit you speak of as collateral in case I tried to flee. He knows she is... special to me."

He squeezed my head between his chubby hands.

"If you're lying to me, I will make you suffer worse than any demon of your depraved god."

I nodded, and he gestured to his son. "Cut him loose. Tie a collar around his neck. He will lead us to his camp."

"But Father..."

"Please trust me, my son, and do as I say. Bring the rest of his pack, too. Throw muzzles on them."

The collar was fat and made of thick leather. Montague's son pulled it much too tight and then cut my paws free. My tail slammed the earth first, and then the front paws came free, and I rolled onto my feet, unbalanced and dizzy. The chief's son yanked my rope lead and grinned at me. I bit back a growl and begrudgingly walked forward—the Crown Prince of Cherbourg walked on a leash like a mongrel pet.

A rock whizzed from the crowd and cut my shoulder. "Auch!" I grunted as the shaman chief laughed. "You're enjoying this, aren't you, Montague?"

The bastard took the leash from his son and yanked, nearly suffocating me.

"Every second of it. Now get moving!"

CHAPTER TEN
Wild Diplomacy

Ecaterina

Stephania fixed me with watering, worried eyes as I locked her in my private chambers. This special space had been set aside to make myself beautiful and sip wine with my handmaids but not to sleep or get too comfortable. Reginald's room wasn't safe for Stephania anymore. Emmerich had ordered it searched yesterday when two days had gone by without a trace of him. I insisted I had already searched it, but as Emmerich's rage and paranoia grew, my word was not enough. It rarely was.

Now I hurried down the corridors to answer a summons from my dear husband. A rare occurence. He expected me to be at meals and in his bed at night, but other than that, he cared little for where I was or what I did. The dam was about to break. I was sure of it.

I curtsied to Emmerich when I entered the throne room. He was in wolf form in his throne, his tail draped over one armrest. His gums greeted me as he snarled straight ahead, ignoring me. He was brooding. I stayed quiet and took my seat, eyes downcast and demure.

"Do you know who I have just met with, Ecaterina?" he

asked, eyes still on the back wall where his unnamed guest had no doubt recently departed through the door.

"No, dear. Is there news of our son? I'm so worried something ill has befallen him."

"Something ill is sure to befall him soon," he snarled.

I steeled myself against the ice that attempted to crystallize in my chest. These past few days, I had kept a close eye on Emmerich, making sure I happened to find myself in places I knew he'd be. When he let me, I trailed behind him quietly, only speaking when he looked to me. I told him I missed Reginald and that I was worried. I reminded him of days I knew he thought of fondly, at least at one point in his life, like of how proud he had been when Reginald had caught his first hedgehog in the yard during his very first hunting lesson; things of that nature. I asked him to please find our son and told him I was sure that if anyone could, it was him. He had softened his voice to me and even smiled at me many times, and I hoped I was speaking to the last remaining shred of his heart that still cared, prolonging his disbelief of the mercenaries' accusations. But it seemed I hadn't succeeded.

"You received bad news?" I asked, summoning a sob to my voice.

"Two nights. That is how long those whimpering mercenaries have withstood torture, and still, their tale remains the same. And yet still, my son has not shown his face. What am I to believe, Ecaterina?"

He didn't look at me, but he said my name without any bite. Perhaps I could still sway him.

"Do you think the band of mercenaries has harmed him? What was the name of the group the Crimson Guard said disappeared two days ago? Iron Oath? Do you think they kidnapped him and used him to break into your mine? Perhaps those two they sent were supposed to get a ransom from you, but they feared you would kill them straight away if they told you the truth, so they spun this tale, hoping to get gold from you that way."

His wrinkled muzzle softened as he pondered my words. "Perhaps," he said slowly. "I must get to the bottom of this. I am going to the mine myself. Now."

He jumped from his throne, and I followed him as he stalked upright through the chamber, shouting to the nearby servants to ready him a carriage.

"Emmerich," I said, holding up my skirts to free my feet as I followed him, "might I please accompany you? My head is spinning with questions, and my mother's heart is aching. Please, let me come with you so that I do not have to wait for answers. I will stay out of your way, I promise."

He paused and studied me with yellow eyes. "All right," he said with a nod, and then continued toward the main hall that would lead us to the front entrance.

I hurried after him, saying, "Thank you, dear."

We passed Isolde's piano room along the way, but it stood silent. I had thought it best to keep her and her conniving tongue out of the way while this business with Reginald played out. I'd sent her to my sister's in the countryside with the promise of meeting a young suitor there whom Patricia had mentioned before.

Our carriage was waiting for us right outside the doors, and I slid in after Emmerich, helped inside by Sergeant Claude, who bowed and said he would be accompanying us. I knew the man in passing thanks to Reginald.

I settled in for a lengthy, silent journey, letting Emmerich scowl out the window as I tried to compose myself and gather my thoughts. I worried my letter to the Karluk sultan hadn't yet reached its destination, but I had paid triple for a speedy, direct delivery. So perhaps all would work in my favor. Still, it would be better if I could prolong his belief that Reginald was in trouble rather than the cause of the trouble. But how to do it?

I sat pondering how best to approach the matter. I waited an hour, until his huffs of frustration grew further apart, and then I reached out and stroked his furry cheek with my fingers, as I had always done in our youth. He stiffened, but then turned to me slowly as I scratched behind his ears. It was not hard to summon tears. Touching him like that brought beautiful memories now tinged with pain, for I knew that we could never return to that place of love. He might warm to my touch on a day full of distress, but there was no warmth for me in *his* touches anymore and nothing but mild interest and sexual longing in his eyes when he looked at me.

Blinking the moisture over my bottom lashes, I said, "Emmerich, Reginald loves you. He would not betray you. Please, believe that. Believe *me*. Something terrible has happened. I can feel it in my mother's heart, and I am so afraid. Please, find whoever has taken him." I hardened my voice as I said, "Turn all your wrath upon them. Do not let them get away with it."

He stared at me for a moment and then pressed his forehead to mine, my nose touching the soft fur of his muzzle as he nudged me. "I will not let this stand, dear. You can rest assured of that. Don't fret, my pet."

He drew away quickly, leaving me short of breath with a lump in my throat. What a mess. I knew the monster that lurked within him. I knew it had driven away both our sons. And I would help Reginald in his quest with my dying breath, but... I was still weak to any tenderness Emmerich deigned to give, and my heart ached for who he once was. I let the rest of the journey pass without conversation, hoping I had done enough and praying there was nothing to find at the mine.

When the carriage rolled to a stop, Emmerich jumped out and then rose onto his back feet, not glancing back. Sergeant Claude helped me from the carriage, and I rushed after my husband toward the cluster of knights standing in the center of the entrance. It was so strange to see the dark prison flung open like that, but with no more souls to keep locked away, the knights had decided to let in the sun.

"Sir Henry, report!" Emmerich barked.

The knight bowed and then stood stock straight as he said, "Still sniffing out the muddled trails, Your Majesty, but with each passing hour, they grow fainter. Thank you for the additional men. I have evenly distributed them over all paths. I believe we will sort out the true direction before the trails go entirely cold."

Emmerich curled his lip and huffed, but said, "Very well. I've come to observe things for myself. I need answers, and no one seems capable of delivering them." Henry paled, though Emmerich's voice was level. Emmerich didn't spare him a second glance as he turned away and snipped, "I do not want to be disturbed."

Henry bowed again and waved his men back. "You heard the king. Disperse."

Henry himself retreated into the dark mouth of the mine through the second set of doors, and I took a few paces back toward the carriage, allowing Emmerich a wide berth but refusing to be shunted away fully. Claude stayed by my side. Emmerich side-eyed us but did not protest. I stood still and silent, watching as he lowered to all four paws and sniffed the ground in wide circles that started at the palisade gate.

Then he moved in a straight, sure diagonal line to the entry doors, where he froze. He scratched the earth around the left door where the padlock dangled from the handle. He bared his fangs and then let out a furious yell that stood my neck hairs on end. It morphed into a howl, and then something exploded inside him. I could only watch in open-mouthed horror as he bit into the earth and yanked up great chunks. He tore into his own haunches, drawing blood, snarling and snapping and spinning in place. When at last he wore himself out, he stood on all fours with tongue lolling and sides heaving.

He rose to his back paws slowly and said over a growl deep in his chest, "Reginald was here. He stood here... with a rabbit! A fucking rodent! He charged the doors with it."

"Emmerich, you don't know if—"

"Traitor! Shame of my flesh! I will tear out his heart with my teeth and take back the life I so foolishly gave him!" he thundered, blood dripping from his jowls and his hindquarters.

I tried again but positioned myself slightly behind Sergeant Claude. "Emmerich, how can you know he wasn't chained? Wasn't forced?"

"Chained by a rabbit?! If that is true, then I should still drink his blood and end his shame!"

"A whole group of mercenaries attacked this mine. The rabbit may not have bound him, but even a Lepores can hold a pistol to someone's back. Please, Emmerich, don't leap to conclusions."

His sides heaved, and his eyes were wild, dilated with rage. He licked the blood from his teeth and snarled, "I will get to the bottom of this one way or another. My mouse of a son was here, and I intend to sniff out exactly which group he was in when he left."

I wrung my hands but felt a smidgen of relief. Perhaps that meant he was considering my suggestion as a possible truth. "

But as he stalked toward me on his back legs, my instincts coaxed me further behind Claude. Emmerich bared his teeth at me and said, "If I discover your son is plotting against me and you knew anything about it, your heritage won't protect you. I'll spill your blood like any commoner and drink it from my finest chalice. Do you understand?"

"I have nothing to fear," I said, holding my chin high, though old habits screamed at me to cower. "I have not acted against you, Emmerich, and I can't believe Reginald would either."

"Whether he is captured or heading a band of rodent rebels, this is your fault. I should never have let him hang on your skirts, nor let you fill his head with all your simpering, female emotion. Now he is either a captive of prey or a traitor to his pack. A shame to his race, whichever is true."

He returned to all fours and called for Henry as he raced through the outer gate. I followed at a safe distance, between the knight and the sergeant and saw the faint indentations of small paws and sandaled feet here. Emmerich was careful to step around each track with his large, padded paws, his dark nose brushing the dirt and trampled grass. He growled continuously, thrown into a frenzy by the lingering scent of so many freed slaves no doubt. Each sniff was an affront to his crown. But surely these tracks were too muddled, too old, to glean anything of use. I knew I could not discern between them for more than a few paces, and I was no inexperienced pup.

He, however, walked determinedly east and followed one of

the many branches of tracks. My heart stopped when he went rigid, his growl sliced off at the end. My muscles coiled for flight, as I waited to see if the mutilation would once again be self-inflicted or directed at me. Slowly, his hackles saluted the sky, rolling from his head to his tail, and the growl that began in his gut deepened as it reached his chest. Sergeant Claude and Sir Henry inched together in front of me. I sent up a quick prayer to Maya to bless them for their chivalry, but I doubted they could stop him if he truly wished to rip out my throat.

Emmerich's growl reached a fever pitch, and he chomped down on the air so hard he drew blood from his gums. His body quivered, and his hackles stood like razor-sharp spikes atop a fortress gate. With another growl bubbling in his throat, he turned one eye to us, blood staining his fangs.

"Sir Henry," he said, his low, deadly voice shaking with the fury that vibrated his muscles, "this is the path you will follow. Call all your men back from their useless wanderings and follow this trail to completion, no matter how many rivers, valleys, or forests it leads you through."

"Yes, Your Majesty," said Henry, dropping to one knee and exposing his neck in a bow, as was expected when swearing fealty to the alpha. "Thank you. I will not fail you. Khaytan is with us."

Emmerich said nothing, only snarled down at the trail. Henry tipped his head up and said with such hesitation that I wasn't sure he'd manage to finish, "Your Majesty... what am I to do if the prince is... if he is not a prisoner when I find him?"

"Chain him, shave him, bring him home, and throw him on my dinner table."

When the tears came, I didn't stop them, nor did I try to control the fearful shake in my hands.

"Emmerich, please. There is some sort of misunderstanding here. Reginald loves you."

"Love," he spat, rising on his hind legs. "Love is a word, Ecaterina. It has no meaning. It will have no part in my decisions for how to deal with a rebellion."

I sucked in a gasp. *At last, the final walls have fallen away, and you admit your lack of humanity aloud.*

"Your Majesty, if I may speak," said Sergeant Claude.

"If it is of use," snapped Emmerich.

Claude bowed his head and said, "Your Majesty, this does not make sense to me. If your son was to start a rebellion, I believe he would go south, not east."

As my breath was stolen from my chest, Emmerich's ears pricked up. "Why?"

I dared not move, even blink. What Claude said next could either ruin my plans or play right into them.

"On our journey to Marburg, your son spoke of policy and politics. A Grey-Lodge guard asked him what he would do when he inherited the throne, to make conversation along the journey." Emmerich's eyes flashed, but he said nothing, and Claude pressed on after a brief pause to compose himself. "Prince Reginald spoke of... of making peace with the Karluks, to establish a new trade market."

I felt for the poor sergeant. I could tell he was not sure he'd made the right decision in telling Emmerich a lesser evil of Reginald's in an attempt to convince him he was not responsible for this larger evil of rebellion. I wasn't sure if the decision was wise, but I thanked Maya that he said it and prayed my letter would be read by the sultan in time.

"At last, someone who is of use to me," said Emmerich. He gave Claude the slightest of nods. A great honor. Then he turned to Henry. "Change of plan. Split your men. The majority will follow this trail, but send a small group of knights to interrogate the minor sultans who operate on the borders of the Karluk territory. Ask them if they have received any word from my son or negotiated with him."

"And if they don't cooperate?" asked Henry.

"If you don't know what to do, what use are you to me?"

"I understand, Your Majesty. It will be done just as you say."

"Good. Ecaterina, we are leaving."

I wiped my face clean and followed him to the carriage. I put my foot on the step, but he filled the doorway and snarled down at me from inside.

"Remember, woman, if I discover you have lied to me or acted against me in any way, I will toss your corpse in a hole and let the worms and crows do what they like with you."

I shielded my eyes with my lashes and hung my head. "I have never acted against you or our kingdom, Emmerich. And I never will."

He moved aside, and I kept my eyes downcast as I settled inside, holding back a sad grin. If he had known me at all, he would have killed me then and there. For he should have known that I would gladly die for my son a thousand times over, while for him, I would shed little more than a single tear.

Maria

I sat cross-legged in the grass, flipping tenderly through the pages of the holy book. Bedford watched me with one dark eye, occasionally craning his head to try and read over my shoulder, withdrawing each time I caught him. Silvia curled her legs under her and lay beside me. I whispered the beautiful poems of Lieds into her silky ear.

Sometime later, Bedford's scout appeared through the trees.

"The Andromedae are coming," said the scout.

I smiled and rose in hopes of greeting them, thinking Reginald successful, but Bedford shoved past me. I fell on my butt and nearly dropped the book. Silvia helped me up with a gentle push of her soft head at my back.

"Well, well, if it isn't my old friend. Your little spy ran off in a hurry," said a congested, bass voice.

I couldn't see around Bedford and his guards.

"Montague," said Bedford stiffly. "I can't say it's a pleasure to see your undulating form. You just keep adding more... layers."

"Bedford, you dumb brute, let me through!" I yelled, pushing my way between furry deer bodies.

I stumbled out the other end and steadied myself with a nervous grin. There were more boars than I had expected. Those in human form were armed with large nets and bundles of throwing spears, and they looked very much like the Porcorum I was accustomed to. Then I noticed their shaman—a morbidly obese old man whose status was only betrayed by his feathered headdress. He gawked at me with beady eyes straining to open their widest. I wrinkled my nose unconsciously and took a step back, disturbed by his stare.

Unperturbed by my accidental rudeness, he stepped forward and dropped to his knees at my feet. I felt my jaw drop but was unable to stop it.

"It... it is you," he said, voice trembling as he clasped his hands together at his chest. "The blessed daughter of Maya, come to liberate us from the tyranny that entraps us." On his knees, he turned to his clan and gestured for them to join him, saying, "Bow, all of you bow before your benevolent prophetess."

One by one, the Andromedae fell to their knees or lowered their tusks to the forest floor.

I was so utterly confused that my arm hung limp as a rag doll when he took my hand and kissed it.

"Praise be to our Mother in heaven for sending you, angelic one. I am your loyal servant to command as you please."

"Uh, that is... kind of you," I said, carefully extracting my fingers from his grip. "But I'm afraid I—" My gaze found Reginald leashed like a beast. His tongue lolled out of his mouth, and he raised his paw to try and make the human gag gesture, flicking his eyes toward Montague. But though I agreed with the sentiment, I couldn't laugh while seeing him in that state.

"How dare you treat your prince that way?!" I shouted at Montague. "After he came to you in peace and extended a hand of friendship! Release him immediately!"

"He came into my..." the Andromedae shaman began and then dissolved into grunts and confused mutterings. When his babbles ceased, he asked, "He is truly your friend?"

"Yes! Now you let him go this instant!"

"Yes, yes, of course. Son, you heard her! Let the prince go."

The Andromedae leading Reginald freed the collar with a begrudging scowl, and I breathed a sigh of relief. Reginald padded over to me and stole my breath by rubbing his cheek against mine. A warm and delicious sensation bubbled up from my center, and I hugged his neck, wishing there weren't eyes on us.

"Please do forgive my rudeness, Prince Reginald. You must understand why I didn't believe you were so close to our dear oracle," said Montague.

A soft growl escaped Reginald's muzzle, but he cut it off quickly, taking a deep breath. "If you return the body of my fallen comrade, I will consider us even... for the most part."

"You killed an envoy?" I said, my fury swift and biting.

"They surrounded my son. We did not know. Please forgive me and my people our transgression, but I did not expect you to send dogs as your messengers. We thought we were in danger. But... of course, you know best."

I tried to keep my bewilderment out of my face. He was speaking to me as if I were a noblewoman or a holy leader. I had no idea why, but I thought it best to keep up the ruse in this dangerous scenario, though the fanatical adulation was both irritating and a bit frightening.

"Allow the Canum an honest burial, and I will extend forgiveness, as Reginald said. And release my other friends," I said, pointing to the Canum still chained among the pigs.

"As you wish, dear Maria," said Montague, practically kissing the earth.

I jumped, unable to stop myself. "How do you know my name?" I turned to Reginald. "Did you tell him?"

"No. It was he who asked me about you. He wanted to know if I traveled with a black rabbit."

Leopold and his remaining men were unleashed. They walked to Reginald's side with gracious nods to me.

"I am so sorry, my brothers," I heard Reginald whisper to the Canum. "I should have thought of a better plan."

"You live with your mistakes, Reginald. At least you tried.

We could have fared far worse," said Leopold, but I was only half-listening, for at the same time, Montague was saying, "Maya sent me visions of you. Three, to be exact. In my dreams."

"The Great Mother speaks to you in dreams, too?" I asked, stepping closer, my heart racing.

"Yes, dear woman. For many years. It is why I am blessed with the title of shaman."

"Please, rise. I am just another humble servant of Maya, as you are. There is no need to treat me... this way."

He rose, but he said, "You are more than that, Maria. You are the key to the future of the kingdom. The key to tipping the scales out of Khaytan's unnatural favor."

I felt both honored and terrified by the implications. "Please, tell me of your dreams."

"At the time, they made little sense to me, but I knew they had to be important. In the first, I saw you as you are now, a woman with dark hair digging and scraping at a wall of stone with hands like iron." He looked down at my fidgeting hands and observed the rough calluses and the dark grit that had stained my nails. No scrubbing could get it all out anymore. I impulsively tucked them into my body, embarrassed, but then corrected myself and let them hang confidently at my sides. I would not be ashamed of my past.

Montague smiled warmly and continued. "In my next dream, you dug with unrelenting fervor until you emerged from the crushing darkness—desperate, frightened, but alive. You changed into a wild, black rabbit and ran from the pursuing ghosts of your old life. Even when the hateful spirits had caught you in their clutches, you abolished them. Your heart shined gold in your chest and purchased your freedom."

I remembered it more as dumb luck, a frantic dash through the wilderness, and the near loss of my human mind, but I realized he had seen a vision of my escape from the mine, my capture, and the freedom I earned from Reginald.

"My third dream was more curious, for it was shrouded in fog. I saw you in the form of a dark-haired lady, but your rabbit spirit still shone through the veil, imprinted over your human half like a shimmering ghost. I say this dream was strange because it frightened me. You were seated at a high table, a place of honor, standing unafraid before a nobleman... no, not a man... but a titan. He looked like a stone that had been hewn from the Ethereal Mountain itself, arms as broad as a tree, even the hunters of the sky worshiped him. He wore no crown, for the strength of his spirit commanded more respect than any symbols of authority created by mortals."

I had no memory that matched this dream. Was it my future? How could that be? Maya had shown me the choice of a future with Reginald, shown me the possibility of a future where prey and predator were once again in balance. But... who was this titan? What was his role? What place had I reached? Where did I go from there?

"That is all? There were no more?" I pressed, hearing the childish disappointment in my voice but powerless to stop it.

"That is all I have been granted."

"How are we to know you haven't misinterpreted your dreams? How do you know they are even from Maya?" asked Bedford. "You are hardly reliable these days, Montague."

I had almost forgotten he and his fellow Cervi were there at my back. Montague glared over my head at the white stag and jabbed out an angry finger, mouth opening to spout angry words.

"My gentle changelings," I said, holding out an arm to each of them, "I propose we hold our short council now to remove any tensions between us and to allow Reginald to tell you of his plans. As he told you, Bedford, you can choose to join or stand separate from us, and we will not hold it against you. But please, don't let this divinely presented opportunity pass you by without consideration. And do show us courtesy and let us leave peacefully if you decide not to answer Maya's call."

"Let us make it a wild council and come together in animal form, in a show of trust," said Reginald. "Let us honor the diverse skills Maya and Her children granted us in a time of greatness and harmony."

"I think it's an excellent idea," I said, staring pointedly between Montague and Bedford. I made sure Bedford could clearly see the book I held at my hip.

"That can be done, certainly," said Montague. "But we have three prey leaders here, and you only have one predator chief."

"No, he is my second," said Reginald, placing a paw on Leopold's front haunch. "And for my third..." He paused, and I could see him weighing options with care. "Why not have another woman present? I think that only fair. Leopold, can you please fetch Samara? And ask her to come in animal form."

My mind flashed to this morning, her golden eyes on me, looking hungry. "Reginald," I said, scooting closer to him to speak in low tones, "are you sure about that? She doesn't like either one of us. She might cause trouble on purpose."

"She is not our enemy, Maria. But if we do not treat her with respect, she may become one. And she is one of the last predators I would want against me. Let us extend her an olive branch."

He spoke with such surety that it calmed my spirit. I nodded. "All right."

"We have come to an agreement. The three predators are selected." Reginald nodded to Leopold, and he retreated into the forest to fetch Samara. Reginald turned to the prey leaders. "Where should we hold this meeting?"

"I have a small pavilion across the river," said Bedford. "We can go there."

"Perfect," said Reginald, smiling at the two leaders. They frowned at him, and Bedford rolled his eyes, but the looks they threw at each other were fiercer and uglier. Their people were no different—the deer stomping their feet and flaunting their antlers or bows, and the boars lowering their tusks, snorting, or slapping their clubs into their open palms.

As we waited for Samara, I sidled up to Silvia and murmured, "Could you perhaps stay here when we leave and ensure they don't kill each other to try and please their childish leaders?"

She laughed softly and nodded. "I will try my best."

* * *

Bedford's pavilion was a thing of pure beauty, a circular stone structure with five columns as its supports. It was obviously man-made, but nature had adopted it. Moss and vines snaked up the columns and over the roof, and magenta flowers dotted its surface nestled amid the greenery. We all walked up the short, stone steps onto the cool floor and aligned ourselves between the pillars: a wolf, a rabbit, a leopard, a stag, a hound, and a boar. I couldn't contain my smile, cherishing the weight of the book tied around my waist with a light cord, its title concealed against my fluffy belly. This felt ordained, and I imagined the Great Mother smiling down on us, prey and predator working to find an accord.

Reginald sat on the stone floor directly across from me, between Leopold and Samara, and he wagged his tail when he saw my bucktoothed smile.

"Maria, since you are the one truly responsible for our being here, why don't you lead the council?" he offered.

I flushed. "Thank you, Reginald, but I have no experience with such things. Perhaps it would be better for you to—"

"No, please, prophetess, lead us," said Montague.

"I would find that favorable to a predator leading as well," said Bedford. "Their voices have been the loudest for far too long."

I took a calming breath, my stomach fluttering with a mixture of flattery and anxiety. "In that case, I—"

"Prophetess? She is no prophetess," said Samara, her claws popping free of their beds. "Carrying one of the old books does not make her divinely inspired."

I jolted as if stung by a bee. How long had she known of the book? Had she been trying to take it from my pack this morning?

"How dare you!" said Montague. "She is the greatest prophetess of our time." He turned to me, his small hooves clicking on the stone. "Does not the Great Mother whisper directly in your ear, child?"

"Yes, I have been blessed to see Her in my dreams, and re-

cently... She has begun to speak in my ear when She deems fit."
I lowered my gaze, feeling at once inflated and very small. "I do
not know why She has chosen me, but I will carry out Her will
as best I can."

"She lies!" said Samara. "She is only trying to make herself
important. She has the holy book, by what means I do not know,
and she is using her knowledge of its language to deceive you!
There is nothing special about you, Maria. And you cannot convince me of it. I am not swayed by my genitals, as our prince is."

"Samara," growled Reginald, "you are acting like a child. Do
not make me regret bringing you here. If you want your voice
heard in this council, you will be civil!"

"I will not tolerate lies," said Samara, wrangling her voice to
a more even tone. "Especially not those that mock my order. I am
a priestess. I have served both Khaytan and Maya faithfully and
in equal fervor since my youth. She is nothing but a Lepores with
eyes for power and princes."

"Then tell me how she knew my daughter was with child by
laying hands on her brow?" said Bedford.

I looked at the majestic stag in surprise. I had not imagined
he would come to my defense, but he looked absolutely livid on
my behalf as he glared at Samara down his muzzle.

"And tell me how she knew that we were about to be am-
bushed by our friend Lord Bedford here this morning when she
was not in animal form and has no combat training?" said Reginald. He pulled his gaze from Samara and asked me, "You had a
vision, didn't you? Your eyes went distant, and then you pushed
me just before the arrow struck."

"Yes, Maya warned me we were in danger. I... I saw the arrow
strike you. I've never had a vision while awake like that before,"
I explained. "I am still learning what Maya wants of me and in
what ways She touches my life."

"But you gazed upon Her visage?" asked Montague. "Was
She as lovely to behold as the old scriptures say?"

"Even more so, my friend," I said with a giddy smile.

"What did She tell you in your dreams?" asked Montague,

his marble-like eyes as wide as they would go.

"I would very much like to hear of them, too," said Bedford.

"And I," said Leopold.

Samara scoffed, but no one paid her any mind. I saw hope in their faces, and it allowed me to speak with authority.

"While I was in Marburg, She saw my heart and knew of my plans for the rebellion I started there. She came to warn me that I was swaying toward imbalance, wishing prey to find dominion over predator. She showed me a world wherein Lepores overtook the land and ate everything without discrimination. They fell into ruin and starved. The Great Mother held me in Her arms as I lamented and told me, 'to tip the scale too far in either direction leads only to death.' That is why we are here, my new friends—to discuss our grievances and our hopes in a polite manner and truly listen to each other with open hearts. That is why we must come to an agreement of some kind—to find a better, balanced tomorrow for all our peoples, where we put aside our animal differences and come together as humans. We must remember the equilibrium of the animal world, but come to remember that we are all united as humans, and we all deserve respect."

"The problems of this kingdom cannot be solved through discussion," said Samara.

"We are discussing so that we might be united in the fight to come," said Reginald. "Maria and I are not as naïve as you like to think, Samara. We know the costs ahead."

"Do you?" she hissed. "Have you experienced any hardship in your pampered life, prince?" She flicked her yellow eyes to me, "Have you seen any part of the world but the dark of a mine and the path to Raven's Rock? You have suffered, yes, but you understand little of the world. How do you plan to lead anyone?"

"I have fought in war, and I have fought battles in my own house. You know little of my father if you think he made my upbringing pleasant or pampered," said Reginald. "And Maria not only led a rebellion with practically no resources, but she also led us to this meeting. She is the reason the prey leaders are gathered here. She has the power to unite."

Samara scoffed. "It is too little. This continent is broken, and Emmerich is too powerful. We would do best to leave altogether, sail to distant lands."

"What are you truly afraid of, Samara? Do you not want change?" Reginald asked.

"What I want is for you to stop acting as if you know me and what I want." Samara turned her eyes on me and added, "And I want you to stop acting like you have divine answers. You have given me no reason to think you special."

"Why do you always use that word? Special?" I said, stung by her words as usual, though I wasn't sure why.

"Yes, Samara, I think it best that you sort out your irrational grievances with Maria here and now," said Reginald. "You have been harsh with her from the moment you met her, though she has given you no reason to be."

"No reason!" shrieked Samara. She shook her head at me in disgust, but she sounded a great deal calmer as she said, "Do you have any idea how many years I have spent with prayers and rituals and more prayers? Every night I would watch the stars, and every morning I would wake up early for the sunrise, hoping, begging for a miracle or even a faint whisper of Maya's voice. Or some guidance from Khaytan on how to take back my life, to show strength. But I heard nothing. I sought the Great Mother for comfort in a time of darkness. When he— " She cut off with a gasp and looked around nervously, as if she had said something she shouldn't and then quickly corrected, "When I was powerless and alone, stolen from my people."

I looked around and saw the men frowning. They did not seem to have much pity for her or her explanation, but I recognized something in her voice, in the way her shoulders slumped. She lost some of the fire in her heart as she reflected on these things. I had seen these signs among the Lepores women in the darkest times, when Bricriu lorded over us without rules. I'd seen it in women drawn into dark corners, their screams muffled as men took what they wanted from them without their consent. I wondered if Maya was placing answers in my heart, though She didn't speak directly, for I was certain Samara bore a pain she'd never let anyone see. A pain that came from the mysterious "he" she'd spoken of. I was pulled from my thoughts as she fixed me with burning eyes.

"And you say that you've spoken with Her?" she said, her voice rising an octave. "That She sends you visions? And you even have a book that the Inquisition would burn and maim and kill for?" Her voice became a cracked whisper as she said, "What makes you so special?" I thought I saw the beginnings of tears in her eyes and felt moisture gather in my own. This woman knew great pain, as I did, but I thought perhaps hers was a different kind. Though, I had heard her speak of enslavement before. Hadn't Diederik said she was a slave, a stolen princess?

Samara's voice grew stronger as she continued, "How have you prayed more than I? How have you been more faithful than I? Does Mother Maya favor the children of Sammael? Does my simultaneous worship of my predator god lose Her favor?" Her tone bordered on hysterical as she looked deep in my eyes and said, "Tell me! If you have all the answers! What does Maya tell you?! What does Her book tell you?"

I sat up on my hind legs and looked down at the book strapped to my belly. I ran my front paws over its cracked leather, and tears for my mother stung my eyes. I heard her voice, carried from a day in my early childhood when her hair still had some of its original rich color. *This book is meant to be shared, Maria, not hidden here in this dark hole. If you ever get the chance to spread its joy, do it.*

I hopped diagonally across the stone circle and stopped before her. My rabbit legs tensed, and my whiskers shivered, but I forced my eyes to stay locked with hers.

"Perhaps you should ask Maya Herself, dwell in Her scriptures and search for the answers to your questions," I said, shimmying the rope over my fattening haunches so that the book fell on the stone between us.

Samara's mouth fell open, exposing her thick black gums and the yellow teeth nestled within. She panted hot breath onto my face as she took a tentative step back, as though I was tricking her. I pushed the tome to her with my head. She raised a paw as the book slid toward it, as if it might burn her.

"Do you want it? Here, you may have it," I said. "I only ask that you return it when you have found the answers you seek."

She lowered her paw and swiveled her eyes over my head at all those watching.

"But I... I don't understand. Why are you giving it to me? Surely it is priceless to you. To your family."

"Yes, my mother dedicated her life to protecting it. I would give my life for it."

"Then... why?" she asked, voice just above a whisper as she gazed at the book with longing. "I have not been... I have not given you reason to trust me with your one and only treasure."

"Who am I to deny a dedicated follower of Mother Maya the chance to live in Her word for a time?"

Her paw trembled as she retracted her claws and reached out to hook her toe pads under the cover and flip it open. She carefully turned the first two pages and then closed her eyes in a sigh that sounded to me like a sob.

"I can't read it."

"I can teach you."

A strange expression crossed her face, and in her animal form, I couldn't be sure what it meant. To me, it seemed frightened and hurt, as if her pride was a physical part of her body and I had stabbed it with a hidden dagger.

"I do not need *you* to teach me anything," she said, holding her chin aloft. She gingerly closed the book and pushed it back to me. "I do not need your charity, little rabbit. The book is yours. Keep it."

I sighed, apologizing to Maya for failing in spreading Her message as I had hoped. But perhaps I had made a crack in Samara's shell. Even her last insult had not held as much bite. Carefully, and with some difficulty, I picked up the book with my front paws so that I could hop back to my place between the prey elders.

Bedford fixed me with a perplexed look. "That was very gracious of you. But I'm afraid if you live in a self-made world of idealism, the real one will disappoint you. Peace with predators may not be possible, no matter what we do."

I wilted, wondering if he was right, but then Samara spoke up, her voice full of her usual spite but powerful nonetheless. "That is not true. Did she run from me? Did I harm her? Our animal sides do not hate each other, and they can be controlled. My grievance with Maria has nothing to do with her prey half."

I had to laugh, a breathy sound of disbelief.

"Thank you... I think," I said. "I am glad you are no longer opposed to the purpose of this council. But, Samara, if you were to resent me for some insult or pain I had caused you, I could understand, and I would do my best to earn forgiveness. But I can remember no wrong done to you. Remind me if I am wrong. But if your grievance, as you call it, stems from greed or envy or pride, that is something you must fix. I cannot extend my paw in peace in any greater way than I have just done."

She sat straight and tall, tail twitching like a snake around her feet. "That is fair. I may not like you, and I still think you are a fool. The stag is correct. You are too idealistic, and I would not have my friends led astray by your foolhardy optimism. But... I have come to respect you today, Maria. And I do... appreciate the gesture you made." She said it as though the sentiment might gag her, but I smiled.

"Thank you, Samara. And, if I may say one more thing. Maya does speak to you; you just don't know how to listen. She's everywhere, in all of Her creation, including the people you care about... and even those you don't. But you must truly love and appreciate those things to hear Her whispers in them."

She inclined her head stiffly but said nothing.

"I think that's a marvelous start," said Reginald. "But unlike Maria, me and my people have wronged you, Lord Bedford, and you, Chief Montague. So, I would like to address both of you and earn your forgiveness if I can, so that we might unite for a cause that is greater than all of us."

Both nodded, urging him to continue.

"First, please understand that the alliance I am presenting is no trick. I mean what I say. Please, do me the courtesy of taking me at my word."

Montague grunted assent, but Bedford remained stony.

"I come to you two because you are great leaders who love your people. I have seen it in the fierce way you battle my father's unrelenting onslaught. But as strong as you may be, the nobles are cunning, and they have far more resources. If you want to earn some freedoms for your people, you will need the lessons I have learned about the monarchy."

Bedford harrumphed. "I think I have more wisdom than you on this topic, youngling. I was part of the original accords. I lived in Cherbourg and took part in the politics there."

"Then pray tell me why are you here, Lord Bedford? With all your wisdom, you had not foreseen my father betraying the peace and imprisoning and slaughtering so many prey. You weren't able to act quickly enough to take your family and wealth and flee to a place where you would be accepted, or at least tolerated. Because my father is a difficult man to understand. But I have spent my life learning how he thinks. My survival depended on it. Forgive me if I am too blunt, but do not hate me because I am a wolf. Instead, love me because I am the healer who will cut out the infection."

He held Bedford's gaze, clearly viewing him, as I did, as the most formidable obstacle.

"Lord Bedford, we have had a most tumultuous history. My father burned your house, tortured you, stole your lands, and forced you into seclusion here. Since then, he has hunted your children and kin. I can't apologize for him, but I will do it for myself... for I reached manhood long ago, but in my father's presence, I was a child. I knew his treatment of your kind and all prey changelings was unnatural and cruel, and yet I never tried to sway him. Never tried to exact change on my own, until now. And I am sorry."

"If your brother is any example... I understand your inaction,

Reginald," said Bedford, sounding morose. "If I am honest, and if I allow Maya to bring peace and grace to my heart, I know you are not my enemy. And if Maria, with her connection to the Great Mother, truly feels you are a friend to her, then... I think you could be an ally to all prey kind. I believe I can set apart my hatred for your father from my feelings for you, but it may take time. And I would still like to discuss your strategies before I fully promise my people to your cause."

Reginald bowed at the waist. "Thank you, Lord Bedford. We will have many opportunities to speak as long as you like. But now, may I give you a token of alliance?"

Reginald shirked off his medallion with some help from Leopold and clasped it in his teeth as he approached Bedford.

"What do those symbols mean?" said Bedford, bending to inspect the trinket.

Reginald draped the gold chain around one of Bedford's branching horns and said, "I'm sorry; I don't know. My mother never taught me this old wolfen language. But to you, it could mean whatever you want, such as courage and honor or..."

"Tolerance and brotherhood," I suggested.

Bedford looked at me, then returned to face Reginald. He wasn't too generous with his emotions, but he nodded and said, "Perhaps you could remove my other necklace, prince?"

Reginald's ears perked forward, and I smiled. Bedford was asking Reginald to remove a symbol of his vengeance against wolves. Reginald clasped the wolf's teeth medallion carefully in his teeth and tugged the twine knot free. He placed it at Bedford's feet.

"I accept your apology, Reginald," said the stag, "and ask you forgive me for my own mistakes."

"Consider them wiped clean," said Reginald.

He turned to the boar and flashed a toothy grin that allowed his tongue to loll out the side, and I had to bite back a giggle at how endearing he looked.

"Chief Montague, you and I do not have much of a history, but your great skill as a shaman and the prowess of your people in Raven's Rock are well known. I would be honored to have another beloved changeling of Maya to consult with. Maria is a wonder, but she does not have your battle experience. I have Leopold to aid me in that area, of course, but I do not think he would protest having someone of your skill join our strategical planning. Would you, Leopold?"

"Not at all," said Leopold, inclining his head to Montague. "I would be honored to hold council with you, Chief Montague."

Montague let out an appreciative series of quick snorts, flicking his thin tail. "If we reach an agreement here today, I will look forward to it. But that remains to be seen."

"Of course," said Reginald. "And let me say now that I am sorry for all wrongs done to your family, and I am sorry and embarrassed for how poorly I handled my excursion into your village today."

"Ah, that is forgiven, prince. In all honesty, if you had simply marched into my village, you would have been gutted before you ever saw my face. And as for the sins of your father, I will no longer hold those against you. My stubborn friend, Lord Bedford, has spoken great wisdom in his choice to do so, and I will follow suit. Maya's clear favor for your alliance with Her great prophetess is more than enough reason to follow you into battle."

"Thank you, my new friend. I'm afraid I didn't bring another gift, but I wish to bestow one on you as well," said Reginald.

"Do you have any particular talents?" the boar elder asked with a playful, snorted laugh.

"Well, I can carve wood."

"Then I ask you carve me a staff, with an owl at its head. And in return for your labor, I will give you a bow, made by my cousin, the most skillful craftsman in my clan."

"Ha, I wonder if it's even half as good as anything carved by my bow makers," said Bedford with something like a smirk. His tone was playful rather than insulting, but I worried the embers of the fire between them would reignite because of the half-hearted slight.

I took a step forward, ready to get between them, but Montague only snorted and said, "Hmm, you cannot prove this sort of thing with words, only with actions. Or, in this case, competitions." He lifted his snout in a strange grin, and Bedford swished his tail and laughed.

"Let us make it a friendly but fierce competition then, you old, fat, puffed-up pigeon," he said.

"Challenge accepted, you blustering oaf," said Montague through another chuckle.

"A marksmanship competition it is!" said Reginald. "It will give you both a chance to train some eager students. But we will have to start working on new weapons for your people. Your bronze ones won't do. Against my father's steel, they will buckle and break."

"It is all we have, thanks to your father's decrees!" blustered Montague. "The predator nobles keep us sequestered to these forests, and bronze is the only metal they allow us to keep. All the time, they tax us and confiscate whatever iron we manage to harvest."

"And every now and again, they demand some of your strongest children as thralls. But as difficult as your life here has been, and I will never deny it is harder than anything I have ever endured, it has been good to you," said Reginald.

"And how is that?" thundered Bedford with a scowl.

"It has made you strong. Yes, you have suffered and sacrificed much. But look at what you have gained." He made a sweeping motion with his paws. "You have made the best of what little you had. You love your families more fiercely, for you work and struggle side by side with them each day. Even your friendship together is strong. It may have bent, but your laughter here today shows it is not broken. The bonds you forged in your life here are too strong to break. You rely on no one, which is why in these forests, you are freer than the nobles who harass you. The high lords sire children only to satisfy their sense of pride and come begging to my father for gold to satiate their greed."

Tears came to my eyes. "He is right!" I said. "If it had not been for the sacrifices made by my family, I would be nothing more than a scared girl who knew nothing save how to dig a hole in the ground. Families will always sacrifice whatever they have for the future of their children."

"And so will we," said Montague with pride.

"Here, here!" said Bedford with a smile.

"Shall we tell our people the good news?" said Reginald.

"Together," said Bedford.

"But first, I must ask..." said Montague. "Won't your father send his people to track you down? Has he put a bounty on your head yet?"

"Not that I'm aware, Montague. I have done my best to keep him in the dark about my involvement in Marburg's liberation, but my absence will make him suspicious. Though I've taken precautions to lay false trails, he will eventually figure it out. We should remain vigilant."

"Your father's bannermen will find a cold grave here," said Montague with a malicious grin.

"If they do come, we must make sure none of them report back," said Reginald. "But we should still try to capture some of them alive."

"You're not thinking of forcing them to defect to your side, are you? I think that would be a terrible idea," said Bedford.

"Not true. My company was also forced into service," said Leopold. "Don't forget Emmerich is a very unpopular king, and next to him, working with Reginald is an honor."

"Thank you, Leopold," said Reginald. "And worry not, chieftains. I know most of my father's men. I'm sure I can find ways to persuade them."

"Perhaps they should be reminded that Emmerich is not, and never was, the anointed son of the gods as he claims to be," said Samara.

"I think there are far more predators who long for the old ways, the true ways of Maya, than Emmerich would have us believe," I said, thinking of Gertrude.

"Can you agree that we should try and recruit all we can and grow our numbers?" said Reginald.

"We may try it," said Bedford.

"I will agree for now also," said Montague.

"Then let us part feeling accomplished," said Reginald, "and share the good news."

Reginald led the way without hesitation. As I watched his confident stride, I wondered what it must be like to take charge as naturally as breathing and to be so self-assured that you never glanced back to see if your companions were following, even if they were potential enemies moments before. Samara and Leopold followed quickly with the same predatory ease. I looked to my prey companions with soft smiles and walked between them at the rear.

"Linger here with us for a moment, Maria," Bedford whispered to me when I tried to pick up the pace and close the distance.

I slowed, widening the gap between predator and prey, and turned my ears to the stag. "You wish to say something in private, Lord Bedford."

"Does your dedication to your people surpass your newfound... loyalty to the prince?" he said in low tones.

I scowled at his implications, but I supposed it was a fair question. I took it seriously and searched my heart for the true answer. "Yes. All I do is for my people and the restoration of Maya's kingdom. Those come above all else for me."

Bedford nodded his approval. "Then you will understand why I say the three of us must remain cautious and vigilant, as is the way of our kind. I believe Reginald says what he means and believes in the vision the two of you have imagined together, but should he change his mind at any point, I don't think it wise to assume he will remain loyal to us. If it meets his ends, he will betray us, for all predators place themselves first, entitled by their place in the food chain. I ask that you remember that, Maria. All our lives may depend on it."

I bit my lip. Even if Reginald lost zeal for our cause, I couldn't imagine that he would harm me or my people in any way, but many other examples of predators I knew aligned perfectly with

Bedford's thoughts. But Maya had chosen Reginald, and in my mind, that made all the difference. I chose my words carefully.

"I understand your caution, Lord Bedford, but Maya brought me to Reginald through my dreams. She sees something within his heart, and in honoring Her will, I have seen it myself. Reginald has humbled himself to me several times in the short weeks I've known him. He is not without flaws, but when they are pointed out to him, he acts to remedy them rather than letting pride rule him. His heart is honest, and I believe he will stand by us." I had to hold back a startling flood of affection that overtook me and threatened to shake my voice, but I cherished the hidden feeling, letting it flower in my chest. "I think our focus should be on protecting our prince and strengthening in his heart his desires for true fellowship. Rather than throw up walls against him, let us open his eyes to our culture and our ways so that he might understand us better. I believe he's more than willing to learn if we offer teachings and acts of friendship."

"Maria is right. If Maya has brought the wolf prince to us, we should not only avoid petty conflict but seek to truly unite," said Montague. "Let us intertwine our roots and welcome him into our fold... while keeping one eye on him at all times."

Bedford studied us both with mild annoyance, likely sensing he would often be the odd man out in our discussions. Then, he fixed his enormous eyes on me and said, "Do you really believe you know his intentions?" He finished with a scoff forced through his muzzle.

I was sick and tired of being thought of as a foolish girl in the throes of puppy love. I raised myself to my full height, spared one glance at the predators' distant backs, and forced my companions to a halt by stopping short. I did my best to speak in the voice of my mother, strong and assured.

"I know why you are suspicious. It is true. I do not know him as well as I would like. I intend to remain his close partner in all of this. I have no doubt I will uncover his truest feelings and intentions and prove to you that, though he may not fully understand our plight or yet look on us as truly equal, he can be taught, and his intentions are pure."

Montague smiled. "Spoken like a leader."

Bedford inclined his head to me. "I will await your final verdict, and abide it."

I repeated my words to myself like a pledge as we hurried our pace to rejoin the predators. I vowed to keep my mind open to all possibilities so that should Maya whisper the truth to me, I would hear it. The thought of learning more about Reginald thrilled me. I did not wish for our first kiss to be our last. I thought perhaps it was time to get as close as a woman could get to a man... for hadn't Maya given Her blessing?

CHAPTER ELEVEN
The Price of Love

Maria

Sweat dripped into my eyes, my skin roasting beneath the sun's rays, as I raised my quarterstaff diagonally across my body to block Milten's practice blow for what felt like the hundredth time. A familiar burn had leaked into my shoulders during the lesson, but it was nearly impossible to summon memories of Marburg's dark tunnels here in a sunlit clearing. Those images haunted me in the dead of night.

I retaliated with a swift blow that managed to tap the shoulder of Milten's gambeson, and he grinned at me. "Good one," he said, striking faster than I'd expected and rapping me in my side. The thick gambeson absorbed the blow, and I smirked at him, "Oh, you wish to be serious, do you?"

He arched a brow in a good-natured challenge, but before I could deliver on my mock threat, Diederik called, "That's enough for today. Put down your staffs!"

Milten and I propped our staffs in the grass and leaned on them, shoulders sagging with relief. Everyone faced the front.

"You all did well for your first lesson. I think I can make warriors out of you yet," Diederik said.

I still wasn't used to hearing his baritone voice coming from human lips. When we'd first entered the clearing and found him waiting on us, I'd done a double-take. He was exceptionally broad in human form, but the similarities to his animal half ended there. His red hair was cut short, but his mustache was so long it extended far past his full beard. He'd forgone his bronze talisman necklace and wore a fox-skin draped over his shoulders instead. A layer of fat lay over his muscles, but I could tell that he was built like a boulder beneath.

I was astonished how well his skin and hair had aged. To have his animal side evolve as it had, he must be one of the oldest changelings I'd ever met or read about. Yet, the only pronounced wrinkles were at the corners of his eyes and mouth, and though some grey had washed out the vibrancy of his hair, it still held its ginger tone.

"You may keep your staffs with you until our next lesson to practice the movements on your own unless I hear of any childishness involving them. Remember, they may not be blades, but they are weapons, not playthings."

I nodded my understanding along with the rest.

"Return your gambesons. Then you are dismissed."

Milten helped me slide out of the gambeson, and after we'd dropped them in the pile, we headed back to camp together, strolling into the shade of the canopy. I was giddy with the prospect of seeing Reginald for our midday meal. He had asked if we might discuss our next steps for the rebellion, wishing to tell me his budding ideas before bringing them to anyone else.

"Ugh, I shouldn't have eaten so much last night. I think I may be sick after that," I said, rubbing my belly.

"And I shouldn't have drunk so much of that blueberry spirit of Bedford's," said Milten, making a queasy face.

I laughed, and his weary eye sparked with fresh life. I looked away quickly.

The promised archery contest had been a rabble-rousing celebration, with all sides cheering on their own competitors but sitting mingled among all species, sharing food and drink. I had cheered myself hoarse after Reginald bested the Cervi champion with a swift display that landed three arrows inside bullseyes in the space of three breaths. The urge to throw my arms around him when he returned to his seat was immense, but with so many eyes on us, we shared long glances and brushes of the hands instead. I counted it as one of the most joyful nights of my life, and I hoped that, even with a war on the horizon, I could have many more like it.

I was smiling dreamily at the memory when Milten said in a low, breathy voice, "You look beautiful with that flush on your cheeks."

Stunned, I blinked at him, stopping short in the underbrush. He returned my gaze with glossy eyes.

"I mean, you've always been beautiful," he said, "but out here, in the world where you belong, you're gorgeous."

My smile was tight and awkward as I looked away. I had come to realize Milten found me... appealing, but I hadn't realized the depths of his feelings until now, feeling his desire on my skin like a burning ray of light shot from his eyes.

"Thank you, Milten. You're sweet."

I turned from him and continued on the path tramped down by the other Lepores' feet. They'd left us far behind. I'd only taken a few steps when Milten took my arm in a light grip.

"Wait, Maria, won't you stay here with me a moment?"

"I'm sorry, Milten, I really must get back," I said, eyes dancing over his face. "I... I promised to join Reginald for a strategy meeting."

To my further discomfort, a dark scowl crossed over his face for a moment. He tried to rectify it, but his voice was dull as he said, "All right."

I smiled at him with a sheepish shrug, and he dropped his hand from my arm. "You can walk with me if you wish."

An ugly scoff scraped his throat. "Oh, thank you."

Swallowing down a lump in my throat, I kept my gait steady. He paced me and said, "Do you shirk off all compliments, or just mine?"

"What?" I said, incredulous.

Now it was he who wouldn't meet my gaze. "I'm sorry. I didn't mean to be rude. It's just...you know I've had feelings for you since we were young, don't you?"

"Milten, I'm not sure this is the time to talk about this," I said, using my quarterstaff like a walking stick.

"That's not an answer," he said, voice very small.

I sighed and stopped, trying to hold my nerves at bay. Matters of the heart shouldn't be taken lightly, I knew, but I had inadvertently let this go on far too long already. "I have suspected your feelings for some time now, but I was never certain." He watched me with large, vulnerable eyes, and I steeled myself for what I had to say. "I think you're a good man, Milten, and you are a dear friend, but I do not feel the same way."

"I see," he said, looking off into the trees with a scowl. He heaved a harsh sigh and said, "I suppose I will have to turn my attentions elsewhere."

Perplexed, I scrunched my brow. "Why do you feel the sudden need to take a partner?" I asked, hoping I could get to the bottom of this uncharacteristic anger shadowing his normally genial face. Then perhaps we could move past this awkwardness quicker.

"I am the elected male leader of our people. Not that that means much with *Reginald* running the show." He spat the prince's name like it was a curse. "I am supposed to be an example and a pillar of our culture, and yet I have no woman to call my own."

"Your leadership has little to do with who lies in your bed, Milten. I don't understand your—"

"Gomez had too many to count," he snapped, cutting me off, though he still didn't look directly at me.

"You aren't Gomez. Thank Maya," I said. "That is not the leader we need now."

"The men are starting to whisper. I hear it," he said, as though I hadn't spoken. "I thought it would be most logical and most favorable if you and I became a united leadership. But I suppose you have eyes outside your species."

My spine stiffened, and I used it to hold myself tall and strong. I would not deny it. Who was he to question my affections? I balled my hands into fists, staring directly into his eyes, and he stumbled over his next words, wilting like a scolded boy still too defiant to hold his tongue.

"I see how you and Reginald look at each other. I hear how he talks to you. It's unnatural. It goes against Maya. I am the match ordained for you. I feel it."

"How dare you place your own desires in the Great Mother's mouth?" I said, keeping my voice down by gritting my teeth. "And how dare you accuse me of things you don't understand. My attractions are none of your business. And I do not owe you my hand."

"Maybe not, but you owe it to your people to keep yourself pure."

"And how exactly does lying beneath you keep me pure, Milten?" I demanded through a snarling lip.

"It means you don't muddy your faith and your bloodline by lying with wolves!" he spat back. He held his staff in a white-knuckled grip, twisting his hands over it as if trying to restrain himself from breaking it over his knee. "You are a symbol now, Maria. A symbol of Lepores strength and faith and vitality. Don't you understand that?"

My disgust scrunched my face, and I gawked at him. "You truly have no idea what I am fighting for, do you?" I said, shaking my head.

"How am I supposed to know your thoughts if you shrug me off each time I attempt to steal a moment of your time?" he asked, throwing up his hands so that the staff dangled precariously from one hand.

"I'm not keen on any more of my time being stolen, thank you."

He turned from me in a huff, stabbing the staff into the ground and leaning his hands and head atop it. His dark hair shook along with his head, and he closed his eyes with a deep sigh.

"I don't want to watch you throw away all you've achieved for that pompous canine," he said.

"Pompous? You know absolutely nothing about him, Milten," I said in a low voice, my jaw tight.

"And how much do you know?" he said, whirling on me with wild eyes, throwing his arms out in a grand show of frustration. His staff struck my shin hard, making me crouch and hiss through my teeth in pain. The ache raced up to my hip, and I rubbed gingerly at the welt already forming.

"Maria... oh, Maria. I'm so sorry," said Milten, crouching before me, eyes wide with worry.

He reached for me, saying, "Let me look," but I shooed him away.

"I'll be fine. It was an accident," I said.

"Let me make it up to you," he said, sounding like himself again.

I sighed, weary in more than my muscles. I shook my head. "There's no need, Milten. I just need to get back to my tent. I'll see you later." I limped off, never looking back and not intending to seek him out any time soon.

I soon heard the sounds of our new bustling community ahead. Reginald had set up our camp midway between Montague and Bedford's villages, and now the Cervi and Andromedae tribes walked among our hodgepodge of former slaves, mercenaries, and mine guards all turned rebel soldiers. I swatted branches out of my way as I limped back to my tent, hardly paying attention to my route and keeping my head low so as not to be engaged by passersby.

When I came to the fallen log that marked the path to the water hole, I had to pause and retrace my steps. I passed the dining area with its table that was nothing more than a great tree trunk shaved flat on both sides, then came to the rows of tents and makeshift shelters strung with humble possessions old and new. At last, I saw my patched burlap tent among hundreds nestled in the clearing. I set my sights on it and listened to the swirling thoughts in my head, trying to make sense of them.

I was angry and tired and hurt in more ways than one. I had always counted Milten as a dear friend, but it seemed he only wanted one thing, which I had never given any sign of wanting from him. The worst of it was his reasoning! He needed me to wed and bed him so that he could remain leader and live up to Gomez? *Pah! How about trying to be his own man?* Had he not thought of that?

It was all infuriating, and I felt foolish for not seeing it coming.

My tent was only five paces away when a familiar voice rang out. "Maria!"

I barely held back a groan. "Yes, Samara?" I said, turning to face the towering tribal woman, her dark skin glistening with a natural golden sheen.

"Are you injured?" Her thin brows kissed as she scrunched them in concern.

"Oh," I said, taken aback, having expected some biting quip. "It's nothing really. Just a little swollen." I rubbed my leg to show her the afflicted area.

She squatted beside me and ran a callused finger over my inflamed skin. "Training injury?"

"Not exactly."

She looked curious at that, but said, "Quarterstaff?"

"Yes, how did you know?"

"By the shape of the welt," she said, rising to her feet. "I can make you a salve that will cool the heat and ease the swelling."

"That would be very kind, but I don't want you to go to extra trouble."

"No, it would be a good supply to have in camp," she said. Though her tone was all business, something softer spoke to me from her eyes.

"Yes, you're right. In that case, I will await you in my tent."

She nodded to me as I opened the flap of my new home, but she stopped me before I could enter, saying, "What did you mean, 'Not exactly?'"

I turned to find her face unreadable, but I decided that sharing my embarrassment with her might help draw aside the final curtain preventing her from truly seeing me as an ally.

"A man I thought was my friend accidentally struck me in a moment of anger."

She made a humph sound that, for the first time, wasn't directed at me. She gazed off in the distance and crossed her arms. "You're sure it was an accident?"

I nodded.

"What was his reasoning for his anger?" The way she said the words suggested she expected anything but a reasonable answer.

"I refused his hand in marriage."

Her scoff was thick with disgust. She glared at the idea for a moment and then turned to me with a distressed look. "It wasn't Reginald, was it? Because I certainly don't want to follow a man who—"

"No! No, Reginald would never do something like that. This was a Lepores I have known all my life, Milten. For centuries, our people have always had a matriarch and a patriarch, but they have never been required to be married. Yet, now that Milten has achieved new status as patriarch, he insists that he and I should be married. He says the men will think him weak if he has no woman in his bed." I scowled and swallowed down the rage that threatened to make me shout. "Should not a partnership be made for love? Not rank or perceived obligation?"

She studied me so long I almost apologized, thinking I had managed to offend her in some way. But then she said, "It should be as you say, out of love, but that is very rare. It is the way of most men to take what they want and never ask your desires. Not really, at least. Most push and prod as if they already hold claim on you and are just trying to make you see it for yourself. The worst of them take what they want without warning. From my experience, it is difficult to find one who truly sees you as an equal, your own person, rather than a prize to be won. Even rarer to find one who has romantic feelings for you, or whose feelings you can genuinely return."

I nodded, mouth slightly parted with realization. "Yes," I said softly. "I always thought it was just a way of Lepores, to have a relentless urge to mate and incessantly seek after women, manipulating or stealing their prize."

Samara looked at me with understanding and took a step toward me that seemed entirely unconscious. "I assure you it isn't just Lepores."

I studied my feet, pondering hard as I said, "Reginald has never pushed me to do anything. Well," I laughed, "he did push rather hard to get me to quit running my mouth and flee the day he freed me. But, he has been very courteous and has always let me state my opinion. He has even sought it out on many occasions." I caught myself, remembering who I was talking to.

I was quite surprised when she said, with a brow raised, "If that is true, then perhaps I was misstaken to protest your friendship and make the assumptions I did. Pardon me."

I was so stunned that a strange, garbled sound came out in place of real words. I tried again. "Thank you. Apology accepted."

She smiled at me. It was a tiny smile that didn't exactly light her eyes, but I was amazed. I beamed back at her.

"Thank you for talking with me as a woman, Samara."

She inclined her head to me and said, "You're welcome. It may take me until tonight or tomorrow morning to gather all I need for the salve, but I will return with it. If you are not here, I'll leave it inside your tent."

"Thank you."

I ducked inside my tent, but before I let down the flap, she said, "Maria..."

"Yes?"

"Might I now accept your previous offer... to teach me to read Maya's book?"

My smile overtook my face. "Of course, Samara! We can begin lessons tomorrow afternoon. After my training."

"I will be here."

I shut my tent and listened to Samara's footsteps retreat as I thanked Maya for my new friend. Next, I asked Her blessing for what I was about to do. The truth of my words to Samara had watered a seed that had been fighting to bloom for a long time. At last, I decided that it was time to take action and fulfill that desire, for no one other than myself.

Reginald

It was only midday, and I was already in a foul mood. Leadership from a burlap tent was proving far harder than lordship from atop a throne. I'd barely risen and begun to prepare for the swordplay lesson I was to lead when one of Diederik's rams had come running to my tent. There was a brawl between a Vulpecula and a Porcorum that had become dangerous when their animal forms sprang free. Luckily, I'd thrown my wolf half into the fray and broken it up before any fatal injuries were imparted, and punished them both soundly, for the cause had been petty. I'd earned myself a bruise over my ribs and a pounding headache for my trouble.

When the bushes rustled on my path to the waterhole, I almost groaned, expecting more needy pleas that would keep me from my plans with Maria—the one bright spot ahead of me on a gloomy day. Instead, Maria herself appeared, leaves caught in her hair.

"Were you hiding in the bushes?" I asked, tail wagging.

She let out a girlish, delicate laugh. "Only for a moment."

Fresh pink flowers bloomed on both her tanned cheeks. My hidden human half reacted, my heart picking up a trot as I wondered what exactly was on her mind. I stammered, "Are... are you all right?" pointing at the welt my scanning eyes had found on her leg.

"Oh, it's nothing. Milten didn't mean to," she said, making me blink in confusion and surprise. "Samara volunteered to make a salve to cool the swelling."

I let out a swift, surprised laugh. "You really do charm everyone you meet," I said. "I'm glad to hear you're getting along."

"Did I charm you?" she asked, barely above a whisper, looking at me through thick lashes.

My heart galloped. She had never looked at me so forwardly before, mostly stealing sideways glances I felt more than saw. But I was in my wolf form for one, and more importantly, I still had my doubts that a romance between us would work, though I prayed I was wrong. Our human halves melded effortlessly, but our animal sides had been opposed for centuries. I had been telling myself soft touches and occasional kisses were harmless, but she was looking at me in a way that sent pleasant but dangerous shivers down my back. I gave her my best, friendly smile and said, "Of course. I set you free even though it meant my head, didn't I? You turned on the charm nicely."

She smiled back and said, "I came to ask if you'd like to have an early dinner with me. I thought we could... talk."

I blurted out, "Uh, of course," as I tried to steady my pulse and warn myself to be cautious.

"Wonderful. Let me go fetch our meal. Could you meet me by the pavilion?"

"All right."

She flashed me another grin, this one excited, and ducked back into the bushes. I obeyed, utterly perplexed, and reached the pavilion in a matter of minutes. I sat and appreciated the subtle wind blowing through the trees and the melody orchestrated by the birds. It was a lovely summer's day, and I was exhausted. I happily dozed off as soon as I lay down on my stomach.

When Maria returned, she awoke me from a rather blurry dream. I fluttered my eyes open and saw she'd changed into a new outfit: a green linen shirt and fitted woolen hosen.

"That shirt suits your complexion," I said, feeling awkward but wanting to pay her a compliment. "Where did you get that from?"

"Thank you," she said, sitting down beside me with a basket and beginning to spread a blanket. "Silvia gave it to me."

"I thought you rather liked the dress I gave you."

"I do like the dress you gave me. But the hem got torn, and

I needed to try something new. Do you not care for a woman in men's clothing?" She raised a brow, and I wondered if it was a trick question.

Unsure what she wanted, I opted for the truth. "Not a problem with me. But speaking of clothing, what are mine doing in a bundle over this blanket?" I asked.

"I brought them back for you, so you can change when you transform back to your human half."

"Change?" I said. "Maria, you've made a habit of asking me to transform whenever you like." In truth, I had hoped to stay in wolf form to better control myself when caught in her new, more intense gazes.

"You've had rest. I will be behind the trees to give you privacy."

As she headed into the forest, I shouted, "I didn't say yes!"

She didn't even glance back. I groaned but shifted nonetheless. She was even more of a puzzle than usual today. I put on my own hosen, shoes, and wine-red shirt, my eyes searching the trees, feeling watched and exposed. When I finished, Maria rejoined me on the blanket.

"What do you have there?" I asked, looking at the covered basket in the middle.

"Nothing fancy, but I asked Silvia for help, and her aunt offered us some fresh bread with potatoes and goat cheese," she said, uncovering the basket.

"Goat cheese?" I asked in surprise. "Are you aware that the deer only have cheese once a year?"

"Oh." She looked guiltily down at it. "I was not aware." She fixed me with a poignant look and said, "How sad that such a simple commodity is a delicacy to them, exiled here and forced to move their homes constantly to avoid being hunted. Don't you think?"

"Well, yes, I suppose it's unfortunate their human sides are deprived delicacies, but I hardly think that's their biggest concern. And I think their animal sides allow them to enjoy their nomadic lifestyle."

"You believe they enjoy the place they've been given in your father's hierarchy?" Her dark brows came together in a slant as sharp as her voice. "You think it suits them, do you?"

"Maria, please," I said with a scoff I couldn't keep from slipping free. "That is not what I said. My father's hierarchy could not even be called a pyramid. It is two blocks placed atop each other, with predator on top and prey below, with him sitting atop both. That is not the natural order. But deer naturally choose to—"

"Natural order?" she said, her mouth a hard line. "What exactly is the natural order, Reginald?"

Her mood had shifted so violently in the blink of an eye that I was left scrambling to figure out what I'd done. I struggled for a fully formed answer to her question. I heaved a sigh and found I could not quite meet her eye. I did not want to fight with her, and yet she seemed to be placing great importance on my every word, so anything I said might be construed in ways I hadn't expected.

Taking a calming breath, I straightened my shoulders and said, "You talked of Maya's desire for balance in the world, Maria. That is what I meant by natural order. Predators were made to hunt prey, whether as a pack or as independent hunters. Prey were meant to stick together and move from place to place so that the world's natural resources are never depleted in one area."

Her jaw softened, and she sat back, leaning on her hands as she appraised me with cautious eyes.

"But how do you fit our human sides into that assessment?"

"That is a question that has plagued our people since the very day Maya imbued us with the duality of spirit," I said with a frustrated huff. "You expect me to answer it here and now, in the midst of a picnic?"

She cocked one brow and tilted her head the other way to balance it out. "I suppose that's fair. But answer me a different question then." She pulled the basket toward herself and added with a minuscule smile, "Or you don't get a picnic."

I found myself studying the curve of her mouth, the corner tilted up, lips parted. Every day her face grew more confident, more expressive, and I found myself more intrigued with each new expression. I cleared my throat.

"Then ask it. I'm hungry."

A stern line replaced the charming, crooked smile as she asked, "Do you believe predator changelings should have natural dominion? Do you believe only they are fit to rule a kingdom?"

I bit my lip against my gut instinct: a simple yes. I didn't want to fight with her. A serious fight with her on a matter such as this might prove deadly for me. I was not naïve. I knew that Montague and Bedford's alliance would not have happened without her. I would likely have been roasted on a spit without her. And as I mulled those thoughts over, I realized they shattered all my preconceived notions.

"What?" she said, studying me with curiosity. "What are you thinking?"

I smiled at her. "I'm thinking I've been a fool."

"That is not a word I would regularly apply to you, Reginald," she said. "What makes you say that?"

"Because I have always thought that predators were the only races meant to rule. We are stronger. We are often cleverer."

Her mouth turned down in a scowl, and I hastened to finish my thought.

"But! I held that notion without having known many prey. I have equated your human sides with your animal sides too closely. You are a natural leader, Maria. You have shown me that again and again since I met you. If not for you, I would likely be nothing but a pelt on Montague's bed."

She wrinkled her nose in distaste, but a smile broke through, and she actually chuckled. Then she fixed me with bright eyes, the smile replaced by contemplation. "And without you, I would be just another dead slave sent to your father's table," she said softly. She stared down at the blanket and cleared her throat before saying, "Please, we shouldn't let this delicacy go to waste." She pushed the basket closer to me, then pointed at the knife inside.

It took me a solid fifteen seconds to realize she wanted me

to serve the food. I almost laughed. No one in my entire life had ever presumed to request such a menial task of me, and yet the realization of that felt ludicrous all of a sudden. I sliced the bread from side to side, then cut the cheese and uniformly placed each wedge between the bread. I broke the sandwich in two and offered Maria her half.

For the sake of politeness, I waited for her to begin her meal before I started on mine. After the first few bites, however, the silence weighed on me.

As she chewed, she toyed with her hair, and I caught that enticing scent again, the one I couldn't place. It made me lean toward her, hoping to soak it in deeper. Her eyes flicked to my face, and she flushed as she moved into the welcoming circle I created with my arms.

As she leaned her back into my chest, and I pressed my cheek into the rich silk of her hair, I realized that I only experienced the smell when we were alone.

My breath caught in my throat as she tilted her head back to offer a look full of desire. Called by her eyes, I caressed her mouth with mine and then withdrew quickly to resist the temptation to fall sideways onto the blanket with her wrapped in my embrace. To give my mind something else to ponder, I asked, "So, what exactly happened with Milten?"

She observed the treeline with a sigh. "He insulted me, and then accidentally struck me by flinging his staff around like a child in a fit of anger."

My brow creased. "I thought that you two were friends."

"So did I," she said with a stony look. "But apparently, he just wants me for a wife to bolster his status with the men of our clan." She scoffed deep in her throat, while I choked on my last bite of sandwich.

"He asked for your hand?" I said, the depth of my anger startling me.

"Yes."

A dreadful, gut-sinking possibility crossed my mind, and I said hastily, "And you said no?"

"Of course. It wasn't exactly a romantic gesture." I could practically hear her roll her eyes, though I could only see her profile.

My stomach sank. I hadn't realized how strong my aversion would be to Maria being with someone else. Then the guilt struck as my warring mind questioned whether, by offering her small affections, I was holding her back from a relationship that would make her happier.

I swallowed hard and tried to sound nonchalant as I said, "Well, is... is that something you want, though? A relationship with a Lepores?" I tried for a smile and failed as I added, "Given the next suitor's advances are more thoughtful?"

"No," she said, whipping her head around with a frown. "I do not wish to be with Milten or any other Lepores." Her face softened as she touched the stubble on my jaw. "You are the only man I have any desire for."

I was transported back to adolescence, sweaty and flustered in the intense heat of her attention. "Well, did you and Milten court in the past? Is that why he dared to be so bold?"

She frowned again, and I sighed internally. Her emotions shifted more than the tides today. I got the distinct impression I was being tested, and I was failing miserably.

She turned away from me as she said softly, "I have never been with anyone in that way."

"I didn't realize," I said, genuinely surprised. "I would have thought you had had at least one romance in your life. I imagine you have always been greatly admired."

She shifted in my arms to face me with an amused grin. "What else do you think of me? Now I'm curious."

I gulped. There were many ways to go wrong here, but knowing what I did of her, I thought she would most appreciate a genuine analysis, rather than empty compliments.

"I think you are strong of will. Admirably so. You have a fire within you that is fueled by both your faith and your determination, and if Marburg did not put it out, I don't think anything ever will."

She beamed at me, and I breathed easier, feeling more confident as I said, "But, I think you should be more open. You work very hard, but you don't spend too much time with others."

She looked at me with an intensity that shot lightning through my blood. I saw something carnal in her eyes, and as much as I longed to return it, I looked away. Knowing it was likely foolish but needing to stop her looking at me that way before I did something risky... or harmful, I said, "Especially not with men, as far as I have noticed. Your caution is well-founded, I'm sure, but even with the men in your clan, you act very timidly. If Milten is any example, you likely have many admirers and simply don't realize it. And if you never give them a chance..." I shrugged, not looking at her.

"Let's talk about your love life, shall we?" she said, her voice sharp but not as cutting as I'd expected. "I don't know how things work among the nobles, but I can assume that since you are the king's son, most aristocrats would be more than happy to marry their exuberant daughters to you. And yet, you're unmarried and unbetrothed."

"Yes," I muttered.

"So you never cared about the matches you've had. Why? Did you worry they only desired you for your wealth and influence? Did the match feel disingenuous?"

I looked down at her and found true empathy in her eyes. "How do you read me so easily?"

"I feel... connected to you," she said with a shrug. She met my eyes with such confidence all of a sudden, it took me aback. It was as though some outside force had filled her to the brim with strength.

I swallowed hard, entranced by her eyes and the confident set of her shoulders.

"Do you feel the same of me?" she asked. Her blue eyes were veiled by her lashes, but still, they bored into me, searching for what, I didn't know.

"Yes," I said slowly. "I feel it's why we have been able to form new alliances, why our numbers grow every day."

She studied me hard as she said, "I want more to come from our relationship than just alliances."

I thought I knew what more she wanted. I had found myself wanting it ever since I'd held her that day in the forest, her mouth hot against mine, our bodies entangled. But it was a dangerous desire. Something I might not be able to give. Perhaps I could give her something else. Let her know that I valued her, even if I couldn't be all she wanted me to be.

"What are you smiling about?" she asked, a smile of her own filling out her cheeks.

"Wait here," I said, an idea striking me.

I rose and hurried to the other side of the pavilion. With all this talk of predator dominion and prey in positions of power, I wanted to perform some sort of gesture to let her know I viewed her as a leader. As an exile in the forest, I could not offer much, but it had occurred to me that I'd given gifts to the other prey leaders at the council meeting and not to her. I had not shown her that she was equally important and that I saw her as capable.

I gathered a fat handful of white and pink flowers from the pavilion's bounty and then hastily knotted them together into a circle. I hid it behind my back and returned to her. A gentle smile settled into the lines of her face and brightened her eyes as she patiently watched me approach.

"Maria, you are right. We are more to each other than co-conspirators or even friends," I said and sat on the blanket beside her, still concealing my gift.

Her brows lifted expectantly, and her smile grew to show her teeth.

"We are equals," I said. "And I am sorry if I ever made you feel otherwise. Without you, I would be prince of nothing. With you at my side, I have a growing army of rebels, and with your help, I know we can win back our kingdom and shape it how we wish."

"Reginald," she said in a breathy tone.

"Wait, please let me finish."

She nodded.

I took a deep breath and said, "I promise you, when Maya leads us to victory, you will have a place among the nobility of Kaskilia. I cannot offer you a real tiara or any real signs of nobility now, but let this serve as a reminder of my oath."

I pulled the flower crown from behind my back and placed it atop her dark hair. Her eyes widened, and she stroked the blossoms with her slender fingers. Glistening tears spilled over her lashes.

"Reginald," she said, but her voice trembled so much she had to start over. "Reginald, that is the kindest thing any man has ever done for me."

I felt myself blush and cleared my throat, suddenly self-conscious. I scratched at the back of my neck as I said with an awkward chuckle, "It's only a bundle of flowers. I promise I will give you something much nicer when I can."

"I don't need any more gifts, Reginald," she said.

I watched her hand come toward my face and was powerless to move away as she buried her fingers in my hair.

"What I need is you," she whispered, her hand coaxing my head closer.

I closed my eyes at the warmth of her touch, but then a jolt of guilt sent me scooting away.

"Maria, we can't," I said, my voice too harsh in my throat.

She drew back her hand as though I'd bit it. "Why not?"

I let out a scoff-like laugh. "Let me count the ways!" I shook my head, feeling half-mad. "Maria, we are too different. What we have been doing, even the smallest gestures of affection... though they feel wonderful, they are dangerous. I fear what might happen if we... go further."

"I do not want to join our animal sides, only our human spirits. We don't have to fear soul shock."

"Maria," I said with a desperate exhale, trying to convince myself as much as her, "I am worried I will harm you. With each passing day, I grow more attached to you, more amazed by you, but perhaps it would be safer to stop now. Continuing will only make things harder. I wish to keep you by my side through all of this, but perhaps what we must remain is cherished friends."

"Reginald, you admitted you've never found genuine connection with women who are like you. Why must you be with a predator? Why must you be a slave to your animal side when you know there is a chance you and I could find genuine connection together?"

I stammered, having no answer. I found myself drinking her in, my eyes roving everywhere I'd been afraid to let them linger before. I'd known instinctively from the moment I let her free outside that abandoned farmhouse, risking my men and myself, that she could become important to me, that I could love her if I let myself. Something about her called to me. She fascinated me, delighted me, understood me. I shut my eyes against the thoughts and her probing, hopeful gaze.

With hands clenched into fists so I would not reach for her and whole body tensed so I would not lean in, I said, "What if my wolf side sprang forward on its own? It's done it before. If I harmed you, I... I don't know what I'd do."

"Reginald, I trust you. As I have never trusted anyone save my mother and Stephania. I feel... we are meant to be," she said, voice as soft as spring rain. "Please, if your only hesitation is your fear of your wolf half and not... a lack of desire for me, then..."

I could feel my will cracking already, but when she came forward on her knees and brushed her mouth against my ear, it shattered. I inhaled the scent of the flowers in her crown, mingling with that maddening aroma from her hair. My blood warmed at the sensation of her breath on my skin, and when she asked, "Do you desire me, Reginald?" I moaned deep in my throat.

"Maria, I do desire you," I said, forcing myself away, half off the blanket. "But... even if our animal sides can lie dormant, what would it mean for this rebellion if something should tear us apart? What would become of our cause?"

She chewed at her lip and gazed up at the sky, as if asking for answers or strength. "Reginald..." she began at last, and I clung to every word, wishing with every fiber of my being that she would say something that would allow me to act as I wanted, that would shatter all the reasons for my hesitation. "I have had little joy in my life, and even less freedom. Do not misunderstand, I had many happy times with my family and my friends, but all of it was tainted by cruelty and hunger and the constant knowledge that our lives were not our own. I have always had to worry for not only my own life but the life of my loved ones, and it has always dictated my actions. Most everything I've done in my life was done out of necessity. Even our mission together. That is something I *must* do."

She fixed me with shining eyes, her chest rising and falling with heavy emotion. "But this. You and I. This is something I *want*. This is something my heart begs me to do, for me and for you. I think we could lift each other up, Reginald. I think we could be beautiful. Please, if you have similar feelings, let us try."

My heart skipped a beat and then pounded so hard she surely heard it. My ears warmed, and my hands itched to touch her in new ways. Struggling to find my voice, I nodded, lost in her gaze.

She moved first, but I came most of the way, the two of us crashing together in a kiss that was at once forceful and trembling. As she drew patterns on my scalp and back, I let my hands memorize her form. She had grown stronger over these last weeks, and she was not quite so thin, but she still felt tiny in my arms. But not fragile. Her muscles were taut and strong beneath her soft skin.

I hushed my fretful mind and listened only to my body and the thumping of my heart. The taste of her mouth was like pure ambrosia. All logic fled my brain to make room for something far more carnal and instinctive. My fingers explored the lower hem of her shirt with an unspoken question. When she answered by slipping her own hands beneath my tunic, I grabbed the green linen and pulled it over her head. With my forehead pressed to hers, I watched my hands explore her soft skin from collarbone to hips. Putting her mouth to my neck, she wrapped her arms around me and tugged at my shirt. I drew back to help her bring it over my head and then melded myself against her once more. She smiled against my kiss, her hands lighting little fires over my chest.

Slowly, we fell onto the blanket, her body atop mine. The scent of her skin and hair... it was chrism, as though I was bathing in holy oil. But then, the demons came, tempting me with their sinister whispers.

My blood grew cold, and I stiffened. My wolf half, sensing *her* rabbit half, wanted to bite her, to savor her flesh in a very different way than my human mouth.

I forced it aside as she murmured, "Are you all right?" I kissed her for answer, firmly locking the door to my wolf side. I would not hurt her. But if she asked me to, I would gladly nibble softly here and there to arouse her further. I would kiss her wherever she wanted me to, hold her in my arms until she was drained, satisfied, and still craving.

I needed to feel her entire body against mine. In unison, without words, we shed the rest of our clothes and surrendered to each other. And for a time, we were enveloped in each other's warmth, feeling the beautiful ecstasy of our union. Her soft moaning and playful giggles were music to my ears. And every time she called out my name, I lost myself to passion.

In the end, I sighed, releasing all the burning lust I had held within me. I lay beside her, staring at the sky and feeling the dull warmth in my muscles. She drew her head up from my chest and whispered in my ear.

"That was the single most beautiful moment of my life."

I beamed at her, and then she closed her eyes and rested on top of me. For a moment, I was left in silence, feeling her chest rise and fall with the rhythm of her breath. But one of the demons had stuck around, planting doubt.

Was her love worth risking everything I had left?

I looked at her as I pondered, remembering how she looked when I first met her, beaten and emaciated. Her cheeks were now a soft red, and her smile, while faded, still had me hungering for her kiss. Then I touched her cheek and found it was wet.

I returned my gaze to the sky.

Yes, it was worth it.

Maria

I awoke with Reginald's hand clamped over my mouth. I grunted out a muffled protest, and he pressed a finger to his lips. He said something, but I couldn't hear it. Blackness overtook me, my back sinking into the warm grass of the clearing as another vision took hold. Soldiers in the blue and gold colors of Cherbourg marched in formation toward our camp, and then, with a flash of light, the tents were ripped to pieces and blood-soaked corpses lay everywhere. They were coming!

The blackness returned and then faded to reveal Reginald's worried face. His clothes were rumpled, the shirt pulled on backward in haste.

"Did you hear me? I think my father's men are here," he whispered.

I nodded vehemently, and he released my mouth.

"Yes," I whispered back. "Maya showed me another vision."

His eyes went wide, but he said nothing, only threw the picnic blanket around my naked shoulders and took my wrist to lead me behind one of the pavilion's pillars.

I quickly summoned my rabbit form, and he nodded his approval. I listened, crouched in the pavilion's greenery. Footsteps and voices reached my long ears.

"I thought I saw movement. Let's go see what it was," said a man's voice.

I itched to run, but I couldn't lead them back to camp. Reginald seemed ready to fight. But I couldn't tell how many there were, and he had no weapons.

"Let me act as a decoy," I whispered, an idea forming.

"Not a chance."

"Reginald," I hissed, "I will be fine. You need to warn the others. You need your weapons. I can best serve our friends by leading these men away. I'm small, I'm fast, and I'm smart. I can do this."

His eyes searched me, so filled with worry it tugged at my heart, but he nodded with a harsh sigh. "All right. There's no use arguing with you anyway."

I brushed my whiskers against his cheek, then left him to creep toward the tree line, my brain scrambling for a cleverer solution. Before ducking into the trees, I wrapped my blanket around a tall shrubbery, disguising it to look like a person. I looked back at the pavilion, and Reginald had vanished. As the Cherbourg soldiers' forms appeared on the other side of the clearing, I slunk further into the forest and hid. I peeked out from behind my tree and saw them step onto the pavilion, searching.

To draw their eyes to my decoy, I stomped a nearby dry twig. Bang! Bang! Two shots rang out in quick succession.

"I shot it, but it didn't drop," said one, crashing into the forest. A heartbeat later, the other said, "It's a farse! Search the area!"

They were looking to collect corpses, not prisoners. Heart thrumming like hummingbird wings, I crawled through a patch of tall grass, keeping my ears tuned to their movements. When they had their backs turned, I dashed past them, but my paws on the underbrush made them whirl around. Three more musket blasts sent splinters of bark flying and made leaves leap into the air not two feet from me. I stumbled sideways and rolled through the dirt to regain my footing—unsure if I'd tripped or been shoved. The pounding in my chest told me I was still alive, but I felt a burning pain in my leg. I banished it from my mind. I had to keep running... but I was leaning left.

Suddenly, the rhythm of the pursuing footfalls changed, and I heard snarling. Movement to my left drew my eye. A wolf wearing a gold and blue bandanna around his neck paced me, swerving closer as he growled, "Come here, little rabbit!"

"Eat filth, patriot scum!"

I leaped through a narrow space between two thick trunks, but my burning leg buckled beneath me on the landing. Rolling end over end, I crashed through the underbrush. I tried to get back up, but, dizzy and aching, fell back to the ground. The wolf pounced, his front paws forcing the breath from my lungs as he landed on my back.

"Nowhere to run now, little prey," he growled. "Where is the prince?"

"I will never tell you."

He reared back for the killing bite, but his low growl became a wet gurgling. Warm liquid gushed onto my neck and face.

His weight increased and then suddenly lifted, and I rolled over to see Reginald wielding a bloody sword, flanked by Samara, whose golden eyes scanned the trees, her spear held at the ready.

"That was one of their captains," Reginald told Samara. Then he crouched and said, "Maria, are you all right? Is that blood his or—?" His face went ashen when his inspecting hands reached my hind leg.

"She's injured," he said over his shoulder to Samara. "Can you help her?"

She patted the satchel secured over her shoulders, and I could see herbs poking out beneath its flap. "I'll have to crush and mix them, but I can make her medicine. My instruments are in my tent."

"Then we go there," said Reginald.

I chanced a look at my leg and felt woozy at the sight of my muscle tissue exposed by a short but wide gash. The deep wound steadily seeped crimson into my fur.

Screams echoed from the direction of the camp. "We have to help them!" I cried, struggling to rise.

"Maria," said Samara, her face suddenly in front of mine. "I know it will be difficult, but if we are to make it to my tent in the thick of the fighting, you must change back. If you cannot run, your rabbit form is useless in a battle."

Using her hypnotic eyes as a focal point, I concentrated with all my might and felt the change begin slowly, at my crown, and then speed up as it moved to my toes. I rose from a crouch and shifted my weight to my right leg as I stood, leaning on Reginald. Samara forced her spear into my hands.

"You know the basics of this, yes?" she said.

When I nodded, she said, "Good. I do not need it." As she smiled at me, her teeth elongated to fangs, and her braided hair receded into her skull, lightening as it became a gold that matched her eyes. The fur traveled down her body and grew spots as her limbs shortened.

"More of them, headed this way," said Reginald. "Hurry!"

Samara completed her transformation as they burst through the trees—two men and two wolves. She jumped in front of me, muscles taut beneath her pelt as she let out a shrieking growl that pierced my eardrums and brought the wolves up short.

"It's the prince!" said one, and they all gawked at Reginald.

The thickest one, still in human form, shouted, "Traitor! You are no prisoner!"

"We have our orders," said the black wolf beside him.

"Please, I am not a traitor," said Reginald. "I only seek the peace of the past. I do not wish to hurt you. Call off your strike against those innocent, unarmed changelings." He gestured through the trees where the shrieks had grown more horrendous and the clang of steel more prominent.

"Innocent?! They are prey!" shouted the broad man.

"Prey lover!" said his slenderer fellow.

"Blasphemer!" spat the black wolf. He lunged along with his grey companion, and Samara met them both with her claws, swiping faster than my eyes could follow, her ears flat to her head. The black wolf lunged for her neck while the grey went for her shoulder, but she danced between them and then pounced the black wolf in a shredding, slicing embrace.

The two soldiers charged Reginald, and I adopted a shaky, one-legged fighting stance, holding the spear like I'd learned with the quarterstaff. Reginald met the broad man's blade with an upswing that knocked him back, but the other attacked from the side, forcing him to dodge and then counter with a wide swing that left his side open. I saw the broad knight take notice and jab his sword toward Reginald's ribs, but I struck out with my spear and pierced through his hand. He dropped his weapon, and Reginald ran him through.

Samara's hiss drew my eyes to her. The black wolf lay dead, but the grey wolf clung to her, his teeth seeking purchase in her haunches as she spun wildly to shake him off. Reginald was deep in a duel with the remaining knight, so I hobbled forward as fast as I could and tried a jabbing motion, hoping for more precision. The unpracticed movement was clumsy and weak, but I managed to sink the spearhead partially into the wolf's shoulder. He sprang back with a yip. Samara pounced and severed his spine with her fangs. I turned back to Reginald to see him kick the remaining knight to the ground and knock him unconscious with his sword pomel.

"Let's move!" he called, and we followed him toward camp.

I supported myself with an arm leaned on Samara's silky back, fighting wooziness. The satchel she carried in her mouth dragged over the earth. When the trees parted, I gasped in horror. The campground was in chaos. Bedford and Montague's forces were easily distinguishable by their patchworked uniforms and bronze weapons, while the mercenaries were identified by their steel and dirty visages. Lepores and Porcorum ran in frantic circles, trying to avoid swinging blades and gnashing teeth as they headed for the trees, but not all of them had made it, and many were still caught in the fray.

"Stay with her. I will find my tent," said Samara. She dropped her bag of herbs at my feet and rushed into the thick of the battle.

I slung the satchel over my shoulders. Reginald pulled me behind a tree and took my face in his hands. "Stay here. Keep your spear at the ready. I cannot sit by and wait while my people are slaughtered."

My heart filled with love for him as I realized it was the first time he'd referred to all the species gathered here as his collective people. But I only said, "Neither can I! Let me fight with you."

"You are hurt, and though you are brave, you are unprepared for this battle. Another day, another fight, my love. I promise. Go with Samara when she returns." He pressed his lips to mine in a quick, hard kiss and ran off with sword raised.

I watched from behind my tree. Reginald didn't stray far from me, but he wielded his sword mightily, and one, two, three foes fell before him. He waved down Lepores and Porcorum, calling them to him and rushing any Cherbourg soldier who sought to stop them.

I ripped my eyes from him and scoured the field for Samara. With her bright color and dark spots, she was easy to distinguish among the shifting bodies. She sliced through a man's jugular with a claw and then leaped on a wolf who had a squealing Porcorum by the leg. She couldn't use her teeth, for they held a small, cloth bag, but she made a pattern of slashing and running on, leaving bloody trails and giving our warriors an advantage in her wake. It wasn't until she was almost to me that I noticed Montague was following behind her, surrounded by a ring of his men. As Samara reached the tree line, Montague's men made an opening for him to slip through after her, belly first.

I stepped out to reveal myself, but the sudden movement made the world blur. They rushed to me, and Montague supported my back to keep me from falling.

"Come, Maria, we must get you to a safe place."

"Climb on my back," said Samara.

I clung on like an ape as she dashed through the trees, following Montague's wheezy, shouted directions. He puffed and panted behind us until, at last, we reached his village and a home with a red door.

They laid me on the cot, and Montague tied a cloth around my leg to staunch the bleeding.

"Quickly, change back and boil some water," he said to Samara. "We need to clean it. Do you have any surgical tools?"

Samara shifted with a grunt of effort, then rolled out the cloth bag to reveal stone, bone, and steel instruments. She pulled handfuls of herbs from her satchel and headed to the fire pit outside.

Montague pulled out a frightening set of scissors and knives. Before I could say anything, he stuffed a gag in my mouth.

"My apologies, Maria," he said as I let out a muffled cry of outrage, "but I must act quickly. This will hurt, so bite down."

I did as he told me. Montague's hands were sweaty as he inspected my thigh. He clucked his tongue and muttered, "It's broad. Not sure a stitch will hold." When his finger pressed inside the wound, I shrieked and threw back my head.

"Well, you're lucky, Maria. We won't have to dig out a musket ball. However," he winced at me, "we will need to cauterize the wound."

I tried to scream, "What?" but the gag made it a nonsensical, high-pitched sound. Samara reappeared and pressed a hot cloth to my leg to clean the wound. The pain was minimal, but my heart hammered. When Montague came back with a glowing rod, I scooted away from him. Samara squeezed my hand and met my eyes. She said nothing, but she didn't have to. She would not let go until I did. I bit down on the gag and stared at Montague. I thought I could endure it, but the moment the burning metal touched my skin... I passed out.

Reginald

Distant voices became shouts as I returned to the battlefront, breastplate digging into my shoulder where the gambeson had worn down. I approached the line of trees where dozens of Bedford's hunters were shooting arrows at Father's wide line of pikemen.

Five Cervi corpses lay piled up as a temporary barricade for their fellow archers, having fallen to Cherbourg's harquebusiers. Heartless, but necessary.

Taking cover behind the corpse wall with one of the bowmen, I looked out into the clearing that had once been our camp, now a field of destruction and blood. Spearmen and musketeers overturned our tents, impaling and shooting anyone in their way. I heard the slide and click of a reloading windlass crossbow. Diederik threw down his painted tower shield in front of me, his furry chest pressed to my back in an odd embrace.

"Someone give the prince a helmet!" the Taurus shouted, while I stared down the bolt-tips stuck in the oak of his pavise inches from my nose.

At Diederik's back, some of the Iron Oath mercenaries were

still equipping themselves from what they had salvaged from camp, and one of the badgers threw me a barbute as I ducked under Diederik's morphed arm to join them. I struggled with the chin strap a moment, then whirled at the sound of growling armored wolves charging into our midst. One jumped over Diederik's shield and clamped its jaws on his shoulder. I rushed in and thrust my sword into the wolf's unprotected belly.

As the wolf's corpse fell, Diederik picked up his bronze mace and brought it down on the head of another that had lunged for my unprotected thigh. Not even the forged steel on its skull could protect it from the crushing force; it collapsed without so much as a whine.

"We need to regroup. Who's leading the Red Tusks while Montague's with Maria?" I shouted over the din of battle.

"Montague's eldest son, I would think. Let's move. But put on a tabard before someone mistakes you for one of your father's men," said Diederik, snapping his fingers to one of his people, who threw a green tabard over my head and held my sword while I fastened the cord mid-run. As we neared a ditch between two groves, I took back my sword, ready to aid a company of Andromedae who were taking a stand, using the ditch as cover. Even the lumbering boar failed to break the phalanx, and many of the javelins thrown by their human brothers glanced harmlessly off the enemy's armor.

We arrived just in time to prevent them from being overwhelmed. I slashed into a pikeman's arm, disarming him, then kicked him in the shin. He collapsed, howling. Raising my sword to parry and counter another man's swing, I heard another musket volley. Two bullets whistled past me, but I grunted in pain as a third slammed into my armor, denting and then piercing it, so the ball embedded in my side, sending fire through the muscle.

I glanced down long enough to assess that I would live, then looked up to see four harquebusiers drop dead with bronze spears in their bellies. Two others threw down their unloaded weapons and ran. They didn't make it very far. Red Tusks caught one in their nets and a javelin caught the second in the head. Montague's son dislodged the corpse's spear, then whistled and waved for us to follow.

"Quickly, some of Maria's people are ahead. They need our help!" he shouted, and our two groups rushed to follow.

We dodged through the trees until the scuffle came into view ahead. A group of Lepores were locked in a desperate melee with a pack of Lobo. They swung their spears and quarterstaffs as valiantly as they could, but their tunics and padded gambesons afforded them little protection, and most were already bleeding.

I slashed into an armored wolf's leg, then raised my sword to finish him off but was knocked to the ground by a lean bear. My sword was pinned against the soil, as the Ursa's weight crushed the air out of my lungs. He roared in my face, teeth bloody, and raised his large paw.

"Die in the name of Khaytan, rebel!" he shouted.

Just before the claws slashed my neck, Diederik slammed the edge of his tower shield into the bear's face. He fell on his side, grunting in pain but quickly rose to his hind legs. Leaping to my feet, I decided to let Diederik end him. There were other enemies to fight, and the Lepores were quickly succumbing.

A Lepores' back bumped into me as his thrusts failed to deter an approaching lynx. I launched a flurry of disorienting swings and slashes, hoping to force the cat to open up his side as he juked, but the cat deftly dodged each blow by leaping back and then pouncing forward again with incredible speed. But he did not anticipate the Lepores, who struck out with his staff, planting a firm blow against the lynx's ribcage. The cat collapsed.

I turned my head to find Diederik. The bear still stood his ground, but his strength was waning. His next blow did little more than scratch the bull's bronze talismans, and Diederik parried the second with his horns. On the counterattack, the Taurus brought his mace down on the bear's skull. Blood gushed, and the changeling came down with a thud.

"Diederik, on your left!" I shouted.

The Taurus swung out at the Lobo who tried to rush him, but both blows went wide. The wolf spun around the shield, ducked a swing of the mace, and bit into Diederik's leg. The Lobo yanked back, planting his paws to try and pull the leg from under Diederik, but the bull stood firm. A Lepores woman in a dirty gambeson and leather cap brought her staff down on the wolf's back, dazing him. Diederik finished the job.

I took another glance around. The field was clear of enemies, the last two falling with arrows in their necks. The battle, however, was far from over. We were at risk of falling to attrition. Most of the Lepores in this company lay dead, and only a handful appeared capable of continuing. I pulled two deep gulps of air into my heaving chest and spat, my arms already shaking.

"We cannot hope to continue like this!" I shouted, "Everyone who is still able to fight, follow me. We must find whoever is directing this attack."

I led my small band forward, putting the clearing and the tent village at our backs. The air here was befouled by smoke; a kettle had been tipped over, setting one of the larger tents ablaze. From beyond the trees, we spied a platoon of Cherbourg men reforming, their lances and crossbows at the ready. Their blue uniforms were stained with dirt and blood from a battle with a small band of Bedford's Cervi, the last of whom was run through the heart with a lance even as I caught sight of them through the dense foliage. I signaled for everyone to be quiet and advance slowly, hoping I could catch them by surprise.

A runner dislodged the lance from the deer carcass and handed it to a knight atop his horse in the middle of the formation. I held up a fist to signal my men to pause. This man in blued field armor had to be one of Father's lieutenants, but I couldn't recognize him from this distance.

He scanned the trees where we stood. I had to act fast; even if the knight's helmet restricted his vision, it was likely one of his men would spot us. We looked to be outnumbered, and a frontal assault might end badly. But before I could formulate a command, one of my Cervi archers drew an arrow and shot it at the knight's horse. The mount neighed and reared, the arrow embedded deep in its shoulder.

Our cover was blown, but the lieutenant's greenhorn men fired their muskets in the general direction of the arrow's origin without discretion or order, hitting none of us and covering their ranks with a cloud of smoke, adding to the confusion of the knight's thrashing horse. The men began to cough and call to each other as their leader struggled to calm his mount, and a few broke ranks to avoid the horse's hooves. I shouted the charge and ran right behind Diederik, his heavy pavise providing cover to us both.

"Your men are with you, Reginald. We can do this!" he thundered as he ran.

As we surged forward, I heard an additional blast of gunfire and momentarily halted. I assumed they had not had time to reload. Peering around Diederik's shield, I witnessed the lieutenant lift a pistol barrel away from the head of his prostrate horse and realized he had put down his own mount. I doubted it was out of compassion toward the horse's suffering. As he stepped over the dead beast, it was clear all that mattered to him was pushing forward, and so I urged our company to close the distance.

Our soldiers met their line head-on, and with their formation in disarray, the phalanx proved ineffective. Most of the men in the center line couldn't even raise their pikes in time to meet our assault. Now we had a breach, and we were determined to push through. Their crossbowmen misfired in the chaos, with only a few bolts hitting their marks, and we fell upon them before they could reload.

Two hulking mercenaries to my left shoved the pikemen who dared face them to the ground. Diederik mimicked the action on my right, and the crash of his shield caused a wave in the enemy line as several men lost their footing. One swordsman crossed his blade with mine, but he could hardly retaliate before Diederik struck him on the side of the head with his mace with a wide swing that forced me to sidestep to avoid being hit as well.

I barely had a second to react when the knight materialized before me, his broadsword glancing off the side of my helmet. When I parried his second blow, I caught the hatred in his eyes even through the narrow slit in his visor.

"Reginald, you traitorous mongrel," he spat, and I instantly recognized him as Lieutenant Henry, the man tasked with Maria's capture and shamed by her escape. "I will have your head!"

"Keep pushing the line! Keep pushing the line!" I shouted at my men.

Henry wore heavy armor, but trying to tire him out was not an option. I was already exhausted. His next blow sliced into my gambeson sleeve and left a light but stinging cut. In a stroke of luck, I saw an opportunity to grab his sword arm, and, summoning what strength I had left, I smashed the pommel of his own weapon against his face.

The blow dazed him long enough for me to dodge to his left, switching my double-handed sword grip to the blade so I could use it like a maul. I pummeled him over the back of the head, once, twice, three times. He staggered forward, but one of his men steadied him with a shoulder in his back. He whirled around and riposted, but I easily ducked under the blow, then scarred his faceplate with my blade. He stepped back and tripped over the legs of his dead horse.

Henry's sword flew from his grip and crashed into the underbrush. He groaned, dazed and immobilized. I smiled. The fight was not yet won, but some of his men had seen him fall.

"Soldiers of King Emmerich, your leader is vanquished! Lay down your arms, and you will be spared!" I shouted at the top of my lungs.

"The prince is indeed a betrayer," shouted one of the loyalists. "Khaytan will never forgive this. Fight to the end, brothers!"

"Lieutenant Henry has fallen, and Captain Hugo has not returned!" another warrior cried. "The fight is lost."

The first man's pleas had been ignored or absorbed in silence, but the second's outcry infected many more. Throughout the line, several soldiers dropped their weapons, pleading for mercy. My soldiers promptly pushed them down, but delivered no killing blows. At last, in Maya's name, we had triumphed today.

Christopher Vastag

Ecaterina

Emmerich had slipped out of my sight again when I went to relieve myself. I think he was growing sick of my feigned neediness, always tagging along. But now, more than ever, I needed to stick with him, even if he didn't know I was there. I needed to know what he knew. I'd caught him whispering with an Absolver in an unused hallway yesterday. He'd held a meeting with the leader of the Crimson Guard the day previous. He had eyes and ears everywhere, and right now, they were all tasked with sniffing out Reginald. I knew men had been sent to the Karluks, but I didn't know if my letter had been successful. What I did know was that Sir Henry and his men were still following the trail their alpha had set them upon. If they found something, would they send a messenger back for orders first or attack on sight?

Reginald had been missing over a week, and Emmerich grew more furious and broody by the day. It was dangerous to be near him. I headed to the garden to calm my nerves and rethink my strategy, but as soon as my heels hit the cobblestone path that wove between the lush shrubbery and vibrant flowers, I froze. Emmerich and his bastard brother stood muzzle to muzzle, obviously deep in a hushed conversation.

Two armored soldiers followed at their heels. My presence would not raise an alarm, but they would no doubt bow if I got too close and give me away. I hung back, pretending to sniff the hydrangeas and inspect the pear tree until they sat on a bench next to one of the hedgerows. Seizing my only chance, I crept up behind the bushes, feeling like a foolish schoolgirl spying on her secret love.

"Gregory, have you gone senile? An entire army battalion disappeared without a trace, and you think Reginald is not involved?" said Emmerich through clenched fangs, doing his best not to shout.

"I received word they'd followed the trail to Raven's Rock," said De Draco. "You know that is dangerous country. We cannot be sure Reginald has anything to do with their silence. Your anger is getting the better of you. You seem to ignore the fact your son may be a captive, as if that is more offensive than him betraying you."

Emmerich let out a huff through his muzzle but said nothing.

"The wild clans of the forest despise us, and we them. Any soldiers caught there would be attacked," said De Draco.

"The very idea of them winning is preposterous!" said Emmerich. "Those damn clans fight amongst themselves too much to form a united front. Even if they did, they could never hope to defeat so many of our soldiers with their antiquated, rusted weapons... unless my damned son is helping them."

"Underestimating your enemies will get you nowhere, Emmerich. Besides, I saw that letter from Sultan Shariff Afolabi Ghafur."

"And you did not realize it reeks of lies? You expect me to believe my son could travel south in the company of hundreds of slaves and thieves, and no one but this minor sultan would notice him?"

"Why would the sultan lie? Just to anger you? It seems imprudent, seeing as how he has few resources compared to his wealthier fellows."

"Do you know where some of his scant resources come from?" said Emmerich.

"The queen's brother has had dealings with him before, I know, if that's what you're implying."

"There is treachery in my house, Gregory, and I will uncover each and every source."

I sank lower behind the hedges, quieting my breath with a hand.

"Emmerich, your nose smells treachery everywhere. Now you've turned it on your own house with the same ease, and I admit, I find it troublesome. Your family is your refuge, Emmerich. Do not forget that."

"That is why I wear the crown and you are the general, brother."

De Draco sighed. "You will have to accept my apology, Emmerich, because I won't be sending any more of my changelings to Raven's Rock. I'm deploying my armies to march on Sultan Afolabi Ghafur. He will be thoroughly questioned."

"Brother, you are being an idiot! Led like a sheep to the edge of a cliff by a rival shepherd."

"Maybe it is a trick, but we can't take the chance Reginald is negotiating with the Karluks. Besides, the sultan has been troublesome lately. Two rats, one bite."

"How is it that my son cannot even be a man in my house, but the moment he leaves, he pulls all the right strings to dissolve this kingdom into absolute anarchy?" Emmerich let out a low growl.

"I have not betrayed you, Emmerich. I am simply pursuing a secondary path to help and protect you." I could not see their faces any longer, but the long pause that followed made me think they were sizing each other up.

"The only order I did not follow was to tell the men to kill Reginald on sight. That is not how you treat your flesh and blood, Emmerich."

"So, you're going to let him kill your men with impunity?"

"That battalion was largely comprised of inexperienced greenhorns and cheap mercenaries. The only knight in the bunch was that fool Sir Henry who let the Marburg Lepores leader escape."

Emmerich huffed. "What of Sir Albert?"

"What about Sir Albert? He took a short leave to visit family in Alemanni territory."

"That's probably a lie. You know he's a close friend of Reginald. Why didn't you interrogate him?"

"I'm sorry, Emmerich, but I can't casually distrust my captains as you do. Besides, Albert has grown rich, meaning serving you is in his best interest, and he's still loyal to me. But since you're so afraid he's one of Reginald's pawns, I'll relocate him and his family to a province away from the capital. At least until this little problem is resolved."

Satisfied De Draco had staved off Emmerich's bubbling rage

for the moment and perhaps even talked some logic into him, I slipped away from the hedgerow. I headed to my chambers and found myself, not for the first time, eager to see Stephania. The girl was smart and tough beyond belief. Yet, she still held some of that lovely sweetness so prized in young girls. Talking to her was easy.

She smiled and curtsied at me when I entered, a broom in her hand and a sky-blue kerchief over her head, where her golden hair had returned in short, bright fuzz.

I sank onto my couch with a sigh, massaging my temples, absolutely exhausted in mind and body. But at least I felt my exertion had purpose, and I was not pounding at a brick wall, as I had been when I'd sought to draw Emmerich's affections from his cold veins and tried to keep peace with my bickering, unhappy family.

"What troubles you today, Your Grace?" asked Stephania, propping her broom against the wall and coming to sit with me.

"I've overheard news that may be cause for celebration or the start of serious trouble. And I am uncertain how to assure it tips one way or the other."

"News of Reginald... and Maria?"

I gestured for her to be silent and rose to peek my head out the door. Though he denied it, I was certain that Emmerich had commanded the guards to adjust their routes to station themselves by my room far more often than before. But the hallway was clear.

When I returned, I told her in a whisper, "I told you Emmerich distinguished Reginald's scent from that giant mess in Marburg and set his dogs upon it."

"Yes," she said, breathy.

"Well, the battalion that followed it vanished in Raven's Rock. Emmerich is convinced it's Reginald's doing, and I'm inclined to think he's right. It makes sense he would recruit prey leaders after liberating Marburg. He is allying himself with those who hate my husband most first. And it seems he's had a victory. General De Draco still believes my ruse with the Karluk is a viable lead and doesn't suspect me, but Emmerich is no longer convinced. It will grow more and more dangerous for both of us over the next few days, and for that, I am sorry. But I am glad in my heart despite everything. For now, I am certain Reginald is alive and well and making progress with your friend Maria's help."

"Well, let us take comfort in this moment knowing they are safe for now. Praise be to Maya."

I smiled at her. "Yes, praise to the Great Mother. And may She continue to safeguard them."

"May I relieve some of your tension, Your Grace?" she asked, pointing to my shoulders.

"Yes, please, dear."

She walked behind the couch and kneaded her fingers into my shoulders.

"Your son is strong, Your Grace. And Maria is the strongest person I know. They will succeed. I feel it."

"I wish I could share your undying faith, child," I said with a sad smile. "But I have already lost a son to my husband."

Her fingers paused on my shoulders. "I am sorry, Your Grace. That must still pain you. I cannot imagine."

Tears stung my eyes as my eldest boy's slender face swam in them. "I shall tell you of Lothar," I said, my voice cracking.

"Emmerich was a softer man back then, at least with us. Lothar deferred to his father in his presence. He and Emmerich always went hunting together, and that's where it all went wrong."

I drew a deep breath; this was the hard part.

"Emmerich had just changed the laws, and prey changelings in animal form were fair game. Wolves just love hunting deer, and this began a conflict with Lord Bedford, the local leader of the Cervi clan. It got worse when his own sister became a victim."

"Lothar wanted to diffuse the conflict, he felt responsible for what had happened. There were too few prey elders in court who held sway at the time, and the king and the Church of Khaytan soon pushed them out entirely. Soon afterwards Bedford was exiled, some of his family were enslaved, including his eldest daughter, Willa. She became an object of my son's fascinations."

Stephania was a smart girl, the subtle nod of her head and frown on her lips made it clear she understood the relationship was one-sided.

"He tried to help them and only made things worse?"

"It was discovered my son was smuggling slaves out of the castle, in an attempt to win Willa's affections."

It was difficult reliving the shock of seeing my poor son's mutilated body. I took a deep, unsteady breath and said, "When the Crimson Guard found her, she was sitting next to his corpse, crying, the both of them naked. Before the guards could grab her... she brought the dagger to her own throat and killed herself."

Stephania came to sit beside me, studying her hands and shaking her head.

"And your husband denounced his own son to avoid a scandal?"

"He'd not been able to punish him himself," I said, my lip curled in a snarl. "He had to do it in death."

We were both silent a long moment, and then Stephania said cautiously, "Pardon, Your Grace, but please, can you assure me that Reginald is not doing the same thing his brother did? I need to know Maria is safe."

I reached out and took her hand. "I told you, my dear, Reginald was my second chance. Reginald came to admire Lothar for standing up against Emmerich's cruelty, but he always saw the folly of his actions with Willa."

Stephania's shoulders slouched with a heavy sigh, but then she rubbed away her tears, and her smile slowly returned. She nodded to me, and I was glad I hadn't lost her trust.

"Thank you for listening," I said.

"Of course, Your Grace."

"I want to do more, if I can. But I need more information. Please, can you think of anything else Reginald said that might hint of his plans?"

"No, I'm sorry."

"Did he meet with anyone on his way to the palace?"

She perked up. "Yes! Well, it was accidental. It was a duchess."

"Duchess Leticia Durand?" I asked with rising hope.

"Yes! That was it. She and Reginald... they spoke oddly. They spoke of trivial matters, and the duchess was oddly flirtatious."

"That is just Leticia," I said with a mild chuckle, though my heart sank with disappointment.

"No, but you see... they spoke of very little, and yet, they spoke slowly and cautiously. They stared at each other in such a way that it was like they were actually holding another conversation with their eyes. There were many conversations like that between the Lepores at Marburg when we were planning our rebellion."

If Reginald had chosen Leticia as an ally in this, I applauded his taste. I had to know for sure! Perhaps Leticia was afraid to contact me, for fear of her message being intercepted.

"That is very helpful, Stephania. I think you're onto something. Tomorrow, I will sneak you out of the castle, and we will pay her a visit."

I kissed her cheek and wished her goodnight before forcing myself to get up and head toward Emmerich's bed chambers.

CHAPTER TWELVE
War Crimes

Ecaterina

I always felt lighter when I left Cherbourg, and I imagined it was the weight of eyes lifting off me—Emmerich's being the heaviest burden. I relaxed into the carriage's cushioned seat with my shoulder leaned against the window for a pleasant view of green pastures and rolling hills. Stephania sat across from me with the tip of her petite, rounded nose to the glass. Her wonder at simple things never ceased to put a smile on my face, and lately, it had come to affirm in my soul that Reginald's ends were just.

I reached forward and showed her how to roll down the window with the crank on the door, and she closed her eyes with head hanging out of the carriage and inhaled the scent of summer flowers. The drive to the southern town of Mount Green passed mostly in silence. We rode through an unseasonably heavy rain shower, and I pitied the driver, as well as my three-man escort of personal knights, loyal first and foremost to my father's house. They were the only guards I could trust on such a daring errand, as I had known both them and their fathers since my youth. Upon my marriage, I'd had ten in my charge, but Emmerich loved finding reasons to dismiss them.

It was past noon when the long stretches of vineyards appeared outside the window, marking our arrival into town. It was a beautiful place, but one could only fully appreciate it during autumn, when the vines drooped and the air was rich with ripe grapes ready for harvesting. The vineyards were all dotted by quaint houses for the servants and farmers, and in the distance, the owners' mansions and expansive villas rose high over it all, usually on hilltops. Leticia's villa was at the heart of town, and I leaned my head out of the window with Stephania as its walls came into view.

Stephania gasped, and my smile vanished, my blood going cold. Inside Leticia's gate stood a black prisoner carriage and a red coach bearing a Crimson Guard banner. What did they intend to do? Take the duchess herself prisoner?

This was going too far. I set my jaw with a clack of my teeth, resolved that whatever those serpents were here for, they were about to leave empty-handed. I reached under my skirts, thanking Maya I hadn't worn a hoop, and drew my slim dagger from my garter. Stephania's eyes went wide when I handed it to her.

"Hopefully you won't need this. But stay inside and keep your head down."

"And if they come in after me?"

"Run them through the neck."

I slid out as gracefully as I could manage without an arm for support and shut the door. My knights rushed forward.

"Your Grace, please, it's dangerous," the eldest, Sir Jonathan, began, but I held up a hand.

"I'm going to see what this is about. Danger be damned. I am no damsel."

Jonathan searched my face, his grey mustach twitching. "Aye, that I know well." He pressed a fist to his chest in fealty. "As you wish, milady."

The three knights followed me past the gate, flanking me on each side and in back, hands ready at their weapons. My mouth twisted in a snarl when I skirted around the prisoner carriage and saw the duchess, in nothing but an emerald silk robe, being dragged out of her home by a wrinkled, hairless elite badger who had her by her auburn hair. Her guards rushed after her, but they were struggling to break through the badger's companions—two bears and several wolves. Her men were outnumbered, and the Crimson Guard stopped them on the stairs.

"Unhand me! How dare you?" Lady Durand shouted, throwing an elbow into the badger's stomach. He grunted but did not relinquish his mouth's hold on her hair.

"What is going on here?" I yelled.

Leticia strained to look up at me, her head yanked down by the badger and her bare feet slipping in the mud. "Oh, Ecaterina. Thank the gods. They broke in while I was in the bath! Of all the indignities! They say I've committed a crime, but all I did was wash my hair. I suppose they're jealous they don't have any."

The badger growled and threw her into the mud, ripping a chunk of her tresses out with his teeth, his crimson hood falling down his back. He sprang atop her and hissed, "Yes, and if you don't tell us what we need to know, duchess, you may find yourself without that precious fur of yours."

The change had already overtaken me, my wolf side called forward by my rage, and I let her come happily with no regard to the ripping fabric and popping seams of my fine satin dress. I gnashed my fangs as I dropped to all fours and raised my hackles with a growl.

"Speak to her that way again, and I'll rip out your throat."

My knights drew their blades. Leticia's guards had ceased their scuffle with the Crimson host, but they did not sheath their weapons. Their gazes bounced between their paused opponents and me, waiting for a final verdict.

"Your Majesty," said the badger, one paw on Leticia's throat, "we hold the authority here. We were given absolute power over the management of traitors by the king himself. And the duchess is guilty of sheltering dangerous heretics, if she is not a heretic herself."

"Did I give you permission to open your mouth?" I snarled. "You may have jurisdiction, but under a direct order from royalty, you'd best bend the knee. I don't care why you're here. You have five seconds to release her and leave these premises, or I'll consider *you* the traitor. One..."

"You are overstepping yourself, Your Majesty. The queen has no authority over Lord Khaytan's Absolvers, and we are the hand with which they enact His will," said the badger, crouching low, still pinning Leticia to the ground. The duchess had ceased her struggles and was waiting with eyes locked on me, her muscles tensed to spring.

"Two... three..." I said, my eyes never leaving the badger as I wriggled out of my ruined dress. As my wolf side prepared for a fight, I began to hope he wouldn't back down.

"Your Majesty, we cannot defy Khaytan."

"Four..."

"This woman will be given a trial."

"Slaughter them all!" I roared.

As my knights clanked behind me in their armor, I sprang through the mud and sank my teeth into the badger's leg as he leaped off Leticia and tried to run back to his larger friends. He whipped around his own body to try and bite my ear, but with a snap of my head, I tossed him into the mud and sprang atop him. I clamped my jaws around his neck, relishing the half-forgotten sound of vertebrae cracking between my teeth.

My knights and the house guards crushed the Crimson Guard between them. They died choking on their blood, heaped together in a crimson puddle that darkened their robes a shade. One wolf slipped free, ducking under Sir Jonathan's arm, but one of Leticia's men gave chase and slashed his leg with a rapier. He finished off the hairless Lobo, then spat on his corpse as he cleaned his blade. I found myself taken with the mahogany tone of his long hair, striking against his blue uniform.

"Dastardly cowards, not quite so divine now are you?" he said before rushing to his mistress.

I followed suit and sat at her side while her handsome guard helped her to her feet. She winced when she pulled her robe ties tight around her waist.

"Leticia, are you all right?" I asked.

"Yes, I am fine. Thank Maya for you, Ecaterina. Those bastards were hounding me for weeks. This time, though, they refused my bribe."

"I'm glad you're safe." I rubbed my head against her side, and she threw her arms around my neck.

"What should we do with the bodies, Your Grace?" the mahogany soldier asked the duchess.

"Just hide them in the basement for now, Edmund."

"No! Put them in their coaches and set them ablaze. We want as little evidence as possible remaining."

"We may have just rattled a wasps' nest, Ecaterina," said Leticia, fussing with her mud-encrusted, damp hair.

"Perhaps," I said, speaking in a careful tone, "but right now, Emmerich is occupied with Reginald's strange disappearance."

She flashed me that ornery smile of hers—her mouth tilting upward along with her right brow, revealing only half her teeth. "No need for secrecy here, Ecaterina. I know why you've come. And you're right." She giggled. "Reginald is causing a *much* bigger stir than a few missing Absolvers."

"So, he did contact you?" I said with a growing smile of my own.

"Come with me, dear."

"Wait!" I turned to Jonathan and said, "Could you please fetch Stephania? Give her warning before you open the door; she's likely terrified, and I gave her a knife."

"Oh, she is here?" said Leticia as the knight hurried off. "Wonderful! I'm anxious to see her again. I met her once before, you know. Such a brave young girl, facing Emmerich that way."

"Well, yes, she told me, but... how did you know about—"

"From a rascal lynx, who has proven quite the handful. At least he's doing a good job keeping mice out of my cellar."

"Thomas is here? But I thought he had gone with Reginald."

"No, your son sent him here with a message and charged him with looking after me," she said with a sly smile. "Apparently, I do need protection."

Sir Jonathan delivered Stephania to me with a bow, and Leticia clapped a hand over her mouth at the sight of her hair. She pouted and ran a hand over Stephania's fuzzy head, clicking her tongue for the shame of it.

She led us inside to the upper level of the house. Leticia's villa looked more like a wooden castle, with pyramidal roofs painted in a sooty grey. The interior was inviting, but humble. She had little in the way of fancy decorations, and her furniture was largely utilitarian.

What she did have was an extensive collection of glass bottles, all of varying sizes, shapes, and colors. She occasionally liked to tap them with her immaculate nails to listen to the sound. You soon learned that it was a grave offense to disturb her collection. I'd seen her demand a duke's fingers for touching them, though I'd managed to talk her down from *that* political disaster.

We gathered in the dining room, which opened directly into the kitchen. Here the ivory-painted walls were lined with ceramic jugs, each with expensive wine and spices.

My stomach rumbled at the sight of a duck roasting in the sizable fireplace. The aromatic scent of onion soup wafted in from the swinging kitchen door. I hoped it had plenty of vegetables in it for Stephania.

Thomas burst through the door, wearing a pair of brown pants and a felt hat.

"Your Grace! I came as soon as I realized. I couldn't hear properly from the—" He froze at the sight of myself and Stephania, then rubbed his eyes as if worried we were mirages.

"Your Majesty," he said, dropping to a knee.

"Hello, Thomas. Good to see you."

He rose and gaped at Stephania. "You're alive! Incredible. I mean, I had hoped you would be, but... well, I guess I owe you an apology."

"Oh. Thank you, Thomas," said Stephania, voice timid as she curtsied.

"Thomas, please set the table and fetch the soup pot," said Leticia. Then she turned to Stephania and crouched to draw her into a hug. "Stephania, I, too, am delighted you're all right."

Stephania stood stiff, stunned, but when Leticia held on for a few moments longer, a smile grew on her face. "Thank you, Duchess Durand."

"Oh please, call me Lady Leticia."

Stephania nodded and then tilted her head as she stared into the Vulpecula's light green eyes.

"What is it? Do I have something in my teeth?" asked Leticia, noticing Stephania's strange look.

"Oh, no! Pardon me for staring. It's just that your eyes... they remind me of someone."

"A good someone, I hope."

"Oh, yes, very good."

Leticia rose with a grin and said, "Ecaterina, I think you should leave her here. She won't be safe around Emmerich."

"I know, but I worry that will make him suspicious. I've told him she's my personal handmaiden, and he tolerates her well enough. I fought hard to have her, and if I just give her away, that will look odd. He's already beginning to mistrust me in all this."

"Well, I'm not sure if he's begun to suspect I'm savvy to Reginald's plans, but he is suspicious of me as well." Leticia shrugged with another ornery grin. "I *was* offering sanctuary to a few rabbits." She sat with a flourish, as if she had skirts to tame, though she still wore only her robe, which had begun to gape open at the top again. She pushed back her matted hair with a dignified sniff and turned to me with a gentle smile.

"How are your children doing?" I asked. Brow furrowing, I looked around the room and said, "And where *is* your husband? Why did he not come to your aid?"

"My sweet babies are fine. My husband, however, is not." Her voice went icy, a cruel tilt misshaping her left brow as she turned to me with a malicious half-smile. "He's maggot food right now."

"Leticia! My word!" I said in shock, though I couldn't deny a tinge of amusement tickling my lips. "Is this the second or third one you've poisoned?"

"Second, because, like the first, he was very cruel to me," she said with a little girlish sigh. "I'm only grateful he gave me the children I so desperately wanted. Oh well. I might marry Sir Edmund next. You've met him. The devilishly handsome one in the blue uniform. That dark burgundy tint to his hair, my gods." She made an *mm* sound as though she'd just tucked into a roast. "He's very polite, and he knows his place."

A laugh escaped me, though it felt foreign. "Frankly, Leticia, I'm a little envious. You have no idea how many times I thought about murdering Emmerich."

"You should have been born a duchess, my friend... and a fox." Her smile warmed as she turned to me. "I can marry whomever I like. I had the sense to pick husbands who were less powerful than me. Even if their families had reason to question my stories of fever and prolonged illness, they wouldn't have dared risk saying anything only to be proven wrong." Her brow made that arc again. "And, in a way, it was true." She tittered, and I shook my head—with disapproval or awe, I wasn't sure.

"I've suddenly figured out why you don't let people touch your glass bottles," I said with another brief laugh. In truth, I'd suspected it for a while.

Thomas had begun pouring soup into our bowls. I saw that it was chicken soup, with noodles and carrots.

"Don't put any chicken into Stephania's bowl, Thomas," I said, sniffing the hot liquid. I dipped my tongue in for a quick lap and licked my jowls appreciatively.

The knights and servants soon joined us at the table. Leticia had made it a rule that as long as there was food to be had, no one would go hungry in her house. And this, I thought, was a nice moment, predators and prey gathering at the same table to eat their meal. But I knew that everyone here had manners and fine breeding. A scene like this was much harder to replicate in the real world.

When the fine silver spoons were scraping the bottom of the china, Leticia looked across the table and said, "Stephania, dear, you haven't eaten very much. Why not serve yourself another bowl of stew?"

"Thank you, Lady Leticia, you're very gracious, but I could not possibly eat anymore," said Stephania, bowing her head as she placed a napkin in her lap.

Leticia nodded and then looked over the whole table, saying, "Then I ask that you all depart and leave me with my guests. Except you, Thomas. There are political matters to discuss."

With a loud shuffling, the guards and servants made their way to the door, but Edmund hesitated beside his mistress. After a moment, he sighed and got up, but as his foot crossed the threshold, Leticia said, "Edmund, darling, are you forgetting something?"

He turned his head, bit his lip, and smiled when he saw Leticia patting her cheek with her eyes closed. Edmund returned in four long strides and kissed the noble vixen's cheek, not once but thrice. Her smile shifted into a frown, and without warning, she jabbed a fist into his stomach, saying, "Don't get too far ahead of yourself."

Edmund, who hadn't even flinched at the blow, bowed with amusement gleaming in his eyes, saying, "Pardon me, but you know I find it hard to control myself around you, milady."

Leticia raised her chin and smiled at his low bow, his head hovering above her lap. With a growing smile, she said, "All right, you can stay. Close the door and sit down, please."

Normally, I found Leticia's games amusing, but I was in a rush. "So, since you are here, Thomas, I assume Reginald asked you to tell us something important?" I asked the squire.

"Well, I was to deliver a letter to Lady Leticia, requesting her alliance, and if she agreed to consider it, I was to tell you both that Reginald sent Sir Albert to negotiate a pact with the Clydes."

"I was rather afraid that he might," I said with a sigh.

"Hang on, Ecaterina; let's look at the larger picture here," said Leticia, making Thomas blush as she leaned over the table, letting her robe gape wide. "Where is Reginald right now? His letter to me was rather cryptic."

"He's in Raven's Rock, probably negotiating with the wild

clans who live there," I said. "From what I can tell, it is working. Yesterday, Reginald defeated a battalion Emmerich had locked on his trail. De Draco admitted he'd sent mostly expendable conscripts, but that is still an accomplishment."

"So, we are now in the midst of a civil war," said Edmund, his face and tone unreadable. "All because the prince fell in love with a slave woman."

"And how would you know that, Edmund?" I demanded in a huff. "Were you the one who accompanied my son to the mine?"

"Yes, I offered to be his bodyguard when he went to hear the overseer's report." He turned to Stephania. "Thomas says you're close with this Maria. She burrowed under his skin, didn't she? Was it planned?"

Stephania stared at the ground, rubbing at her neck tattoo. When she raised her eyes to look at us, I noticed they were wet and glossy.

"So, this is all our fault then? All because we wanted to be free. You think we wanted to start a war and get people killed?"

"Stephania, stop torturing yourself. No one is blaming you," I said.

"Well, you're right. I don't have to be sorry. So what if Maria wooed Reginald? So what if she asked him to start a war against his father? That simply means she did something none of you could. Go ahead and blame us if you want. I'm proud that I followed my sister's wild dreams." She sniffled, rubbing away her tears.

Stricken, I stretched out to nuzzle her shoulder. Leticia clapped as though it was a fine scene in a play.

"Bravo, bravo! Such fire, such passion... Maya and Sammael look down on you with pride, I'm sure," she said, placing a hand over her chest. "You are following in the footsteps the Great Mother laid out for you."

"Come now, duchess, surely you don't believe everything is subject to divine providence?" said Edmund.

Leticia reared up like a cobra. "Edmund, are you questioning my faith?"

The man dropped his eyes. "No, milady, not at all."

"I should hope not. Everything that happens is because Maya allows it to happen. I should know." She turned from him and studied the china. "When I was a young lady, I used to hear the goddess in my dreams. But you know what happened?"

"She is no longer speaking to you?" asked Edmund softly.

"Correct! And do you want to know why?" Her chest rose and fell with rapid, angry breaths, but still, Edmund nodded.

"When I inherited my titles, I cowed under the black hoods of the Absolvers. I allowed a number of my citizens to be executed for heresy, knowing they were innocent. Do you know how the old scriptures work, Edmund?"

"No, milady. My parents taught me only the ways of Khaytan, and I never met my grandparents."

"Let me tell you then. Sammael knew His mother's laws, and to maintain Her balance, He sometimes asked His prey children to sacrifice themselves to keep the peace with His brother. But the Inquisition preaches that Khaytan deserves all Sammael's children. First, they silenced His word and blinded us all to the balance He brings, and now they are silencing Maya. I will not stand for it."

"My mother used to force us to listen to Grandfather's stories," I said with a sad smile. "Looking back, I am sad I didn't pay closer attention. He spoke of legends learned from friends as well as enemies. In his old age, he didn't care to distinguish between the two."

"People like that are a blessing to the world," said Leticia, "but I am sure he did not have an easy life."

"No, he did not. He remembered the old times, and those were the stories I clung to. Stories of when Kaskilia was young but not innocent. Back then, the gods as we know them simply did not exist. Even the Great Mother was no more than a name whispered on the wind. Back then, changelings held loyalty to no one outside their clan. They didn't care to listen to any animalistic spirit apart from their own. The Andromedae worshiped a pig as big as a bear, with golden tusks that dug trenches to protect his children. When the Chevaux lived free, their totem was a stallion with wings. The warring families never agreed on anything. It was a time of even greater bloodshed than we live in now. A harsh world where there was no art and no civilization as we know it. Only animal brutality. But something changed. The Great Mother made Herself known. She taught us how to allow our human sides equal part. Without Her and Her teachings, we would still live in that harsh world. But now the Covenant is disregarding Her. They have tipped the scales so far it will benefit no one in the end. It must be stopped." I shook my head at the ceiling.

"May I please add a rational argument to this discussion?" asked Edmund.

"Go ahead, Edmund. We are not stopping you," I said.

"Let's assume for one moment, Your Majesty, that your son succeeds. He unites the warring clans, allies with the Clydes, and takes his father's throne. What then? Do you think those prey factions will accept him as their ruler? Or that he will be able to control them? I'd wager they'll want revenge for their oppression."

"I see. You believe the prey chieftains might start a genocide against all predators," I said, tilting my head side to side, pondering the possibility.

"That will not happen," said Stephania. "Those prey are fighting for their freedom, not to cause more violence. Even if the king's cruelty has blackened some of their hearts the way you suggest, Maria will bring light to them. You can be assured of that."

"Pardon, but that is ridiculous! You believe your sister... or cousin... or whoever she is, can manipulate chieftains who outrank her in every respect?" asked Edmund.

"You would do well not to underestimate her," said Stephania. "Look how far she's already come."

"You never used to speak like this, Edmund," said Leticia with a pout. "You used to believe anyone could achieve anything.

Yourself included—second heir to a minor noble and still become a knight. Shall I reconsider my decision to wed you?"

The knight looked down, wringing his hands. From his face, I thought perhaps his worry was more for his lady's involvement in this trouble, and I didn't want them to argue. I already liked the young man more than her past husbands.

"Edmund, I appreciate your views," I said. "But at this point, such a massacre is unfounded speculation. Consider instead what happens if Reginald does rally a prey army. Emmerich will use it as an excuse to turn all the nobles against his son." My own words sparked a new thought. "General De Draco knows it. He isn't concerned at all about this war, for he knows the nobles will want to repel any invading army, especially one comprised of prey. If we don't help Reginald, he will never win. And nothing will change... except perhaps for the worse. I don't think that's what you want, Edmund."

Edmund let out a long sigh. He glanced at his duchess then back to me, clearly pondering more protests.

Before he could speak, Leticia said, "Your blithering is of little use now, Edmund, darling." She shot him a cheeky smile. "We killed Crimson Guard soldiers today. We stand with Reginald, or we are eventually found out and given a swift trial."

He blinked at her, as if the realization of what he'd done half an hour before had only just struck him. He feigned stabbing himself in the chest with an invisible dagger, wincing and clenching his teeth in mock pain.

"Yes, I suppose we've really done it now," he said. "But, milady, I was only doing my job to protect you. We can deny any knowledge or involvement in this. Please, there must be some other way than facing down Emmerich yourself."

"It's too late, Edmund. We have to participate, even if it is only to deny Emmerich any reinforcements."

"That is exactly what we must do," I said. "We need to persuade the nobles not to support my husband. If we succeed, Reginald will have the crown, the barons will still have their armies, and we avoid the chance of any genocide."

"And how exactly are we going to do this without the Covenant finding out? They have eyes and ears in every wall," said Edmund.

"Oh, for Maya's sake, how did you ever become a knight?" Stephania burst out.

I was thrown for only a moment, and then I smiled. She had at last cast off her protective shell. Leticia smiled at her as well. Edmund, however, wasn't amused. He flared his nostrils and slammed his fists on the table.

"You think I am afraid to die fighting my enemies?" he protested. "It is not about that in the slightest. If I betray my king, he will punish everyone I know and love, and then torture me to death under the eyes of Khaytan, who will surely torture me further in the afterlife."

"Have you gone daft, Edmund?" said Leticia, walloping him on the back of the head.

He rubbed the afflicted area and frowned, but said nothing.

"You presume far too much. Bricriu, the mine overseer who stole from Emmerich under his nose, was my cousin. But did Emmerich torture me for his treachery? No, he did not."

"That's because—"

"Enough," said Leticia. "Honestly, Edmund, if you'd like to remain a coward, please leave my home." She turned to my handmaiden without waiting for his reply. "Stephania, I think I know how Maria persuaded Reginald. If our prince cannot tolerate Emmerich as a father, why should we tolerate him as our king?"

Stephania grinned, but Edmund looked crestfallen. His shoulders slouched, and he stared at nothing in particular. For a moment, he shut his eyes, letting out a long sigh. But when he turned back to Leticia, I saw genuine love in his eyes, and his face opened up, enthusiasm returning.

"I will follow you into any danger, milady. Besides, I can't let Albert be the only one stretching his neck out."

"Albert hasn't yet been accused of treason," I said. "Neither my husband nor Gregory knows where he really went. Gregory only asked him to temporarily change his residence. In his own way, Gregory is harsh, but he's smart and methodical. He will do everything he can to avoid a civil war."

"I don't think asking him to help us will work, Ecaterina. He would never betray his brother," said Leticia.

"True, but the moment he realizes Reginald is a serious threat, he will try to persuade Emmerich to negotiate terms. For the moment, however, we need to talk only with our closest family and friends."

"And how shall we communicate, Your Grace?" asked Edmund. "With pigeons? Your husband might not be taking Reginald seriously now, but the moment he does something brash, the powder keg will explode. You could be caught in it. The king might lock you up and deny you any communication."

"I am aware of the danger; believe me," I said. "Using pigeons is a sound idea. I will keep them where he least expects."

"Ha, you've thought of a nice little trick, Ecaterina?" asked Leticia.

"Yes, indeed. It involves springs and levers. And thankfully, I know a very good locksmith."

"Should I send a message to Reginald then, Your Grace? He might like to know about this development," Thomas asked me.

"No, Thomas, we will only contact Reginald when he returns with a proper army. But as for right now... Leticia, call everyone back and crack open a wine barrel. I think we should celebrate."

Reginald

With a jolt, I awoke, trembling like a leaf, my brow frigid with sweat as my heart hammered against my ribs. Already the nightmare was fading, but I still heard the ring of steel in my ears. I looked to Maria, still curled up at my side, breathing peacefully. Restless, I kissed her temple and cheek and then slipped out of the tent, pulling on a shirt as I went. I paced in front of the finely crafted Cervi tent Bedford had offered me after we'd moved our remaining troops closer to his camp a week previous. But I needed to stretch my legs further and hurried through the camp toward the denser part of the forest, as if to outpace the uneasy feeling left by the dream. My thoughts, waking and sleeping, were troubled as of late.

Seventy-eight changelings loyal to me had fallen, but it was nothing next to the three hundred or so troops that my uncle had lost. My first inner dilemma had been quashed rather quickly, thanks to Leopold. After the battle, there were many prey who had died in animal form. I knew the promise I had made in my early speech to my new followers, but I could not help but think that the meat could feed many hungry mouths.

Before I could fully decide that I didn't dare risk alienating my new allies, and possibly Maria, Leopold took a shovel and began the first pit for the body of a slain boar. As he dug, he invited Montague to say any prayers he wished over the body, and the family came to mourn. Leopold spoke to all of them with great respect, and when the burial was done, he bowed low to them—a gesture they returned. Before he was finished, the rest of our patchwork clan had begun to follow his example. I was astounded by the level of solidarity in our camp. Everyone had to return to Maya eventually, but I was resolved not to make light of a single death. Every soldier lost was a reason for mourning. I would not be my father.

The supplies and equipment we had taken from the fallen would be useful should Father send another wave after us, but the hundred prisoners proved difficult to manage. I had known they would be a harder-won group than Leopold and his men, but I hadn't expected the zealous hatred they harbored for me the moment they realized whatever rumors they'd heard were true. My alliance with prey was all they needed to know to wish me a slow, torturous death.

Even though most of them were young recruits, their blind loyalty to my father and uncle was astonishing. When asked exactly what King Emmerich or General De Draco had done for them, the only answers I got were vague pronouncements such as, "King Emmerich showed us the light and put predators in their rightful place as rulers." They were fresh-faced, untested, and barely out of their training... or perhaps 'indoctrination' would be a better word.

When we moved north, closer to Bedford's village, I'd changed tactics. We needed a larger camp now that the Andromedae were moving with us, so I had the prisoners handle the construction work while everyone else foraged for food and continued their battle training. I told my people to treat the captives nicely and to offer them a kindness here and there to try and befriend them.

Most of our captives were omnivores—bears, badgers, some foxes—so it wasn't hard keeping them fed. The few wolves, however, had already proved rather picky, and I was worried they would do something brash soon. I'd placed the Iron Oath gang in charge of watching over them, for I didn't want to keep them in chains. I didn't want them to feel like prisoners of war, but men offered a second chance.

Just before I ducked into the treeline at the edge of camp, I looked toward the new construction. Neither Samara nor Diederik was on shift at the moment, which made me a tad uneasy, but they couldn't be expected to stay all day. Diederik had left a dozen Aries, a half dozen Cervi, and a handful of Taurus to watch over them this morning. All armed. The prisoners worked in human form, hauling logs and binding branches into thatched roofs.

Everything looked to be in order, but still, as I headed into the trees for a jog, I went in the general direction of the construction, thinking I might drop in to chat with some of the prisoners. But as I drew closer, the thought only made me feel weary. I decided to return after a run. I wanted to be alone with my thoughts.

I veered deeper into the trees, starting the pace slow to get myself warmed up. A rustle in a thicket made me crick my neck and reach for a sword that wasn't there. I heard a loud snap, a crunch, and low, guttural sounds that were all too familiar to my wolf half. He knocked at the door of his cage in my head, wanting a piece of whatever meal the wolf in the thicket was enjoying. I knew it was a wolf. Even in human form, with my wolf half scratching at the door of my consciousness, I could sense it. Smell it even.

I crept closer, wishing I could transform to give myself the advantage of fangs but worried that I might partake without human thought. And something deep in my gut told me this secret meal was not a simple squirrel or lizard. Heart pounding, I bent slowly to pick up a heavy fallen branch. I slunk around the thicket, trying to see inside. A few paces to the left brought me to an opening in the brambles where one or two bodies had crashed through. I nearly heaved at the sight. A massive brown wolf with a mangled ear tore into the belly of a small, dark-haired man I recognized instantly as Milten. His large eyes stared at me without sight, and yet I felt them imploring me as his head jiggled with the force of the wolf ripping out his innards with its teeth.

My nausea was replaced by rage, and I flew at the wolf with a wild cry, crashing through the dense, thorny tangle of branches with no regard for the pain. I brought the hefty stick down on the wolf's back before it realized what was happening, and it yelped as its body buckled. But it came up snarling, and when it fixed its dark eyes on me, I recognized them. Lieutenant Henry! No wonder this wolf was enormous.

I smacked him in the muzzle with another swing before he could lunge, and then I shouted, "Murder! Iron Oath, come at once! Murder!"

Henry leaped and grabbed the other end of my stick before I could react. He shook his head violently, and I struggled to hold on. I kicked out and struck him in the ribs. The stick slipped free of his jaws, but the sudden switch in momentum nearly put me on my butt. I stumbled back, and my sleeve caught in thorns. Henry lunged for my throat this time, but I swung with all my might, and he dropped to the ground with a high whine. He tried to rise, but he crumpled, and I dove atop him, sitting on his back and trapping his thick neck in a chokehold.

Two Aries and a Taurus hacked away at the thicket with their machetes and hatchets. The goat changelings gaped in horror at Milten's body, and then the Taurus looked to me, saying, "Are you all right, Prince Reginald?"

"Yes, I am unharmed, but chain this Lobo immediately!" I said as Henry struggled against me, trying to turn around and bite me in the face. I clamped a hand over his muzzle and squeezed my bicep harder into his throat. The Taurus rushed to my aid, pulling a heavy set of shackles from around his neck and clamping the largest ring around Henry's neck. I held onto the iron collar to drive Henry's head into the ground while the Taurus fought to secure his thrashing limbs.

"I have done nothing wrong!" said Henry. "I am a Lieutenant of Cherbourg. It is my right to satiate my hunger with the flesh of underlings."

"You lost your title the moment your battalion was defeated, you fool," I snarled, watching the two Aries carry Milten's mutilated body from the thicket with mournful looks. My arms were covered in the poor man's blood, transferred from Henry's bloody neck and chest.

"You are an exiled, traitorous prince," said Henry. "You have no right to rob me of my titles!"

"Do not talk to me about betrayal," I snapped.

"Why, because you know I'm right? You betrayed your kin, your family, your father, and for what? To be subservient to your prey slaves?"

"No! Because you have betrayed the laws of Maya and the laws of nature. You did not hunt this changeling's animal side to satiate hunger. You killed his humanity out of spite! You knew full well he was the Lepores' male leader, didn't you?"

"Leader! Ha! A Lepores leader? What nonsense. I broke no laws. I followed the teachings of Khaytan, the one true god. A true predator has no remorse, and you will hear none from me!"

"Muzzle him," I said through gritted teeth, thrusting him from me as the final leg shackle went on.

The Taurus shrugged to say he had no muzzle and then

punched Henry in the face hard enough to knock a tooth free.

"That'll work," I said, rising to my feet and handing the Taurus the lead chain.

"What monstrosity is this?" said Diederik, drawn to the commotion. Apparently, he'd been about to begin a training lesson, for a number of Lepores trailed him. The two women in the group sent up dreadful screams of lament and shut their eyes against the sight of Milten's body being laid outside the thicket. The three men who'd freed him from the brambles knelt in the grass beside their leader, heads hung in shock and mourning.

"One of the prisoners slipped free of our watch, sir," said one of the Aries, his head bent so low he had to stare at his own belt buckle. "We... we failed, and we will accept punishment."

The other Aries and the Taurus nodded their agreement both at Diederik and me.

"The only one who will be punished is former Lieutenant Henry," I said, jabbing a finger at the Lobo. "He will be judged by us and by Maya."

"I will be praised in Khaytan's fields and given a place of honor in His eternal hunt," said Henry, earning himself another blow from the Taurus mercenary.

More changelings were gathering now, in all forms. I saw Bedford's mighty antlers over the heads of all gathered, and soon he and Montague, who was in human form, cut through the crowd. By that time, we'd dragged Henry out of the thicket, and Milten's wounds had been covered by someone's offered jacket.

"By Maya, is that the Lepores leader?" said Bedford.

"Yes," I said with head hung low.

"Burn that brute!" said Bedford, lowering his horns at Henry. "String him up and light him ablaze! I told you keeping these men prisoners would only lead to tragedy."

I sighed. "I should have kept them chained until they proved more cooperative. No one regrets that choice more than me right now." I shook my head. "We will hold a trial—"

"Trial?!" blustered Montague. "No trial is needed! You caught him in the act! We send him to his precious predator god with a thousand ancient curses on his head. Today!"

A roar went up from the Lepores and the Andromedae who'd gathered.

"Please, we have to maintain a level of—"

"Reginald? What's going on?"

Maria's voice, which usually filled me with warmth, sent an icy spike through my chest. I rushed forward to try and block her view of Milten's corpse, but she pushed through the crowd before I could reach her. Her eyes found me first but quickly looked to her people gathered around the body. Her face went ashen, and I stepped toward her, thinking she was going to swoon. But she kept her feet, her eyes swiveling from Milten's blood-covered body to Henry in chains. She passed me as though she didn't recognize me and fell to her knees at Milten's head. She hugged her own middle and bent forward to press her forehead to his, shutting her eyes and letting out a cry that shattered my heart.

Her tears wet his hair as well as her own, and then she tipped her head back to plead with the sky. "Why him? Why would You take him?" She fixed her shimmering eyes on me and moaned, "I had not yet made things right with him." She looked down at his lifeless face and shook her head, lips parted in horrified disbelief. Then she turned to Henry with more pain than anger on her face. "Why would you do such a thing?" she said in a ragged whisper. "What grudge did he bear you?"

"Do not talk to me, evil witch! You poisoned the prince's mind. You are the reason for all death that occurs in this foolish rebellion. If I had known for one second you would be this much trouble, I would have slit you open from head to tail the minute you crawled out of your hole."

At that, loud jeering erupted from the crowd. A rock flew from an unseen hand and struck Henry in the shoulder.

"Such arrogance!" said Montague, belly and extra chins quivering with rage as he stomped closer to Henry. "The prince has offered you clemency for your previous crimes, and you bite his feeding hand. And now you speak of murdering a blessed prophetess of Maya. Shame upon you!"

"You are all fools! She is not divine; she is a whore. I need no clemency. I am no criminal, unlike all of you. I follow King Emmerich's divine commands, and I will do so with my dying breath."

More cries of outrage made me brace myself for a possible stampede. If Henry wasn't careful, not even a formal, humane execution would be granted him. The prey would trample him to death. I stared into the crowd, hoping to stave off the rowdiest among them with stern, individual looks of warning. Instead, I saw that as more of the Iron Oath mercenaries gathered, they brought prisoners tagging along with them, now chained to avoid more chaos. Henry's comrades were watching his display with stoic looks. I was not sure if that was exactly a good sign, but at least they were not shouting in his defense or spouting more obscenities at Maria.

Hoping to show them that we followed strict but fair laws here, I raised my hands high over my head and boomed, "Everyone, please be quiet! This man will be punished for his heinous crime here today, but we must not fall into chaos. We must follow proper protocol." The crowd quieted, but the air was taut with furious stares and hunger for violent revenge. I turned to the chained lieutenant. "Henry, your lack of remorse will not serve you. Please, remember your humanity. I know it lies within you. Will you not repent and pay restitution in the form of servitude to all those affected by the death of this man?"

"He is a rodent, and I will never repent for enacting my divinely bestowed predator right," said Henry.

Again, I looked to his gathering comrades, but none showed any similar passion in their faces. Many gazed on with detached or stony expressions, likely fearing the repercussions of agreeing with their captain, but I saw some of their features twist with distaste as they listened to his rants.

I sighed at Henry and asked, "Will you forever remain loyal to my father, despite the woe he has brought to this country, predators included?"

"Until my dying breath! That man built this land into a prosperous empire, and you want to destroy it for your own greed!"

"Greed? If this were about greed, I would have rallied no-blemen, not exiles and nomads, for noblemen are the only ones who truly prosper in my father's empire. Do you forget the many petty thieves he sentenced to die for stealing scraps of food? Or the battles in which he abandoned our injured, leaving them to bury the dead and act as a rear guard. Those were predators he sacrificed to his greed for land and conquest. Yet, when I asked your former enemies to show you mercy, to mend your wounds, and offer you food and shelter, they did so. And this is how you reward their hospitality?"

"I can't say I cared much for their hospitality, but at least I re-ceived one fair meal," said Henry with a malicious, fang-bearing grin. He looked at Maria and sneered, "Your friend was delicious. My only regret is I didn't get to eat his heart."

Maria turned away and tucked her face into her shoulder, a hand rising to hide her face as she closed her eyes in a pained cringe.

"Enough! Reginald, please end this charade. Just execute him already!" said Bedford, stomping a hoof.

"He will be given a formal execution by sword tomorrow," I said. Henry growled low but said nothing, and I continued, "Tonight, he will be shackled in a secure location. We will not become a mob. Can we all agree on that?" I looked to my fellow leaders, including Samara, who had slipped in quietly a moment before and sat cross-legged beside Maria in silent solidarity.

All of them nodded, though Bedford said, "If we must, but moving forward, I propose we establish different sorts of punish-ments to better suit the level of monstrosity in a crime."

"Fair enough," I said.

"I think for this criminal, his animal skin should be offered as tribute, to make a coat or blanket to warm Milten's loved ones," said Bedford. "That is the old way."

"No, my friend, in the old way, that was only allowed when the predator himself offered up his skin on his deathbed, and that was to his own children as an inheritance."

"But the old laws only suit the predators. I agree with Bedford," said Montague. "This should be the new way."

"But we have not allowed our predator fellows to consume prey who died in animal form," I said, keeping my voice level and calm so as not to offend Bedford or Montague accidentally. "We buried them all after the battle with my father's men. So how can we ask our predator fellows to offer up their animal halves?"

"The new laws must suit all of us, without distinction," said Maria, making everyone swivel their heads to her in surprise, "for the old ways won't work in our new community."

"Maria is right, as usual," I said. "We will hold another council in the coming days to make a written law for our rebellion that will carry into formal law should we succeed in overthrowing my father. But let us not drag out Henry's confinement or allow anger to build and lead to disruption. In the morning, he will be given a soldier's execution for his heinous crime and lack of repentance, and then buried."

I did not open it up as a question, and thankfully, no one protested. The crowd simmered down and dispersed. The elders went back to their duties, and Milten's close friends carried him away. I sat with Maria there by the thicket and held her until her eyes were spent of tears.

Maria

I placed a bouquet on Milten's grave, overwhelmed by a feeling of powerlessness. I had wasted an opportunity to restore a friendship, thinking I had all the time in the world. He was gone so suddenly. Any of us could share a similar fate. I had always lived under a looming shadow of death in Marburg, but in those dark tunnels, it was more like a distant friend rather than a frightening entity. But now that I had far more to live for, it was a sinister shadow, and I felt it was creeping up on all of us.

Wiping away the last of my tears, I said, "Goodbye, Milten. I ask Maya to give you our blessings. We will miss you."

I turned around into Reginald's chest, and he caught me in the circle of his arms. I had thought he would want to hide our affections, but he showed no hesitation in showing familiarity toward me.

Samara cleared her throat as she stopped beside us. She had said nothing for or against my relationship with Reginald, and her face was unreadable now as always. She had wiped her cheeks clean of white paint for the ceremony, and she looked particularly sun-kissed as she offered me a blue flower. I stepped away from Reginald and rose to kiss her cheek as I took the gift.

A small smile pulled at her lips as she whispered, "Maria, I heard Maya's voice today, and She asked me to tell you that Milten's rabbit soul is alive, and She will give it a good life."

Overcome, I hugged her and squeezed as tightly as I could. She patted the top of my head and then extracted herself gently. She disappeared into the thick crowd of Lepores waiting for their turns to approach the grave. I took Reginald's hand, and we moved aside.

That night, after Henry's execution, we feasted in Milten's honor. His name crossed many lips, and Henry's was uttered by no one. Reginald had ordered his grave unmarked as punishment for devouring a human form, and we all took that to mean that he would forever remain nameless among us.

Bedford was a gracious host, offering kegs of an alcoholic drink brewed from blueberries. With our spirits lifted, the camp was filled with songs, and Leopold acted as lead performer. The senior guardsman knew how to spin a good rhyme. He sang about the stars and spectral riders racing chariots through the heavens.

When I woke the next morning, a dull ache filled my head, and my mouth felt like cotton. I looked over at Reginald, asleep on his back with one arm thrown over his head, and smiled.

A week ago, after passing out from Montague's hot brand, I had awoken hours after the battle was won with Reginald hovering over me, face pale and tightened by unendurable worry. When I smiled at him, he had breathed a great sigh and snatched me up in his arms.

"Oh, thank the Great Mother, you are alive. If I had lost you... I could not have withstood it." As he covered my face in kisses, he'd told me that he loved me, and my joy had spilled over, uncontainable.

Now, I bent over and kissed his mouth, and he rose toward consciousness with a soft groan.

"I'm going out," I said, my tongue calling for water.

As I moved to slip out of the tent, he grabbed my ankle and playfully tugged me back with a cheeky smile.

"Don't go," he said with a theatrical moan. "Don't leave me by myself to nurse this headache."

"That's precisely why I'm going out," I said with a laugh. "I need to escape into my animal half. Her head is clear, and it has been too long since I let her roam. And there is work to be done, as always."

He rubbed at his eyes and sighed. "All right, I'll join you in a little while. We cannot all be as hardworking as you, my love. Not all the time."

"Be careful. All your compliments may begin to go to my head," I said with a snort of a laugh and a wink.

I left on my loose nightdress and shifted into animal form before leaving the tent. Outside, the whole camp was a mess. The ground was even littered with party-goers unable to get to their tents for a rest. I saw Samara in her customary perch in a nearby tree, sleeping in leopard form. I passed Diederik's tent as he was leaving, tying the cord of his trousers with his evolved hands, and bid him good morning.

When I arrived at the creek, I gulped the cool water, relishing in the peace of the forest—just the sounds of the birds and the flowing water.

But then a rustle in the bushes to my left disrupted the melody. I perked up but was not afraid. I stood on my back legs when a silver fox emerged, heading for the creek bed. I tried to conjure a name, but I could not remember any silver foxes in our party. The only Vulpecula I'd ever known with that coloring was...

I gasped. "Annabelle?" I said in disbelief.

The fox raised her head, and as I took a few hops forward, I saw the light green color of her eyes. It was her. Our former overseer. The only one in Marburg history who had treated us with kindness. I had come to count her as a friend before she'd vanished.

I showed my front teeth in the widest smile I could manage and held out my front legs. "Annabelle! I don't believe it."

The vixen crouched at the sound of my voice, and I thought I'd startled her. "Don't you remember me?" I said. "It's Maria. From Marburg."

Head raising, she ran at me, but there was only hunger in her eyes, and my smile vanished. I turned to run, but on my first hop, she collided with me, and we rolled through the grass. She came out on top, and her fangs snapped for my neck, forcing me to bite back, leaving a bloody mark on her muzzle.

"Stop!" I screamed, but she lunged again, and I only just managed to wriggle out from underneath her by kicking wildly with my back legs. I turned tail and kicked again, striking her in the head. She yipped, and when I heard the bushes rustle, I skidded to a stop and looked back. She was running the other direction, following the creek upstream.

"Annabelle, why?"

She froze and turned back at the sound of her name. She took a few furtive steps forward, sniffing the air. I summoned all the energy I had to turn back to human form. I didn't care if I was barely dressed. I had to make sure she remembered who I was.

But my transformation only terrified her. Five paces from me, she yelped and turned to flee. I took a running leap and grabbed her tail. She hissed and growled, trying to bite my hand, but I laid my whole body atop hers, pinning her.

"Diederik, Leopold, someone, please come quick!"

Diederik crashed through the underbrush horns first and, without any questions, took Annabel in his arms, keeping her head pressed to his brawny chest, fingers wrapped around her muzzle in a firm but careful restraint.

"What is wrong with this fox? Has it gone completely feral?" Diederik asked as Annabelle thrashed and bucked in his grip, trying to claw him.

"I don't know. But tie her up somewhere and fetch me my dress. I don't want to appear in front of the whole camp in a damp nightgown."

Diederik left me alone with my thoughts. I had never expected to see Annabelle again, but this? She wasn't even herself. She didn't speak, only yipped and growled.

It was Reginald who returned with my dress.

As we walked back together, he said, "I saw you caught a fox. But, who is she?"

"She's my previous overseer, Annabelle. But she acts like she's gone mad."

"The previous overseer, you said?" His brow creased with concern.

"You know her?"

"Not personally. But it was a rather big deal when she disappeared from Marburg. I was told rather recently that the former overseer was the half-sister of a Duchess Durand. I hope to make the duchess one of my allies. She has never liked my father."

"I'm certain it's Annabelle. I see it in the color of her eyes, her fur... she even has that scar on the tip of her nose. She earned it fighting off a Canum who tried to rape my cousin."

"Maria, I believe you. Just let me think for a minute."

I let him ponder, for we had reached camp, and I saw Diederik had tied Annabelle to a tree. He had one of his Vulpecula mercenaries with him, in fox form. The mercenary stepped close to her with ears up and friendly, tail swishing, but Annabelle screamed in that high, yowling, haunting way of foxes, and he jumped back from her.

I rushed to fetch her some food and returned with goose eggs. She growled when I drew close, but when I dropped the eggs before her and stepped back, she tucked into them, one eye keeping watch on all of us.

Montague arrived, supported on the new owl staff Reginald

had recently completed.

"Who is our new guest?"

"An old friend. But I fear she may have lost her sanity," I said.

Montague tilted his head, scratching his chin. He had me hold his staff, then cautiously walked up to her. She barked at him and shied away, but he drew a beaver skin sack from his pants pocket and shook it so that whatever was inside rattled as he hummed a low chant.

"There is something terribly wrong with this Vulpecula," said Montague with a look of horror. "I cannot perceive her human aura. It's as if half her soul is vacant... dead."

"Dear gods... it can't be true. I... I saw it fail with my own eyes," said Reginald, a hand over his mouth and gripping his cheeks hard enough to make divots.

"Do you know something of this, my prince?" asked Montague as I handed back his staff.

"I..." He shook his head, gawking at Annabelle in horror that mimicked Montague's. He started over. "My father forced my mother and me to attend a public execution. There was a... a woman there." His eyes flicked to me but could not hold there, and I narrowed my own. "She refused to repent or transform into prey form, so the Absolvers claimed they were going to perform a ritual that would split her soul, erase her humanity, and leave only a savage animal. But... it didn't work in the square. I saw it fail."

I gasped. Such a thing went against Maya in a way I had not fathomed possible.

"Madness! Heresy of the worst kind!" shouted Montague. "Only Khaytan Himself would have the nerve to permit an undoing of Maya's work."

"You think they succeeded?" I asked, barely above a whisper.

"It... it could be. They would not have been so confident as to try and perform it in public if it hadn't worked before," said Reginald. "But to use it on the sister of a duchess... that's even riskier."

"Isn't there a way we could find out?" I asked. "Montague,

you're a priest. Maybe you could make a ritual of your own, try and connect with whatever is left of her soul."

"Ah, Maria, I am a shaman for prey. For this, you will need a predator shaman."

"I'll fetch Samara," I said, and took off.

I found the tree easily enough and shouted up, "Samara! Samara, please wake up."

She opened her eyes and yawned to flash all her fangs in a low roar.

"What is it, Maria?" she asked lazily. But upon seeing my face, she clambered down to a lower branch and jumped off, landing on her feet in front of me. "Is someone injured? Are we under attack again?"

"No, but we need a predator shaman immediately. I found a vixen today. I knew her once, long ago. She was the first predator friend I ever made. But... something has happened to her. We fear she may be the victim of the Inquisition's latest abominable ritual that has stripped her of her human soul. Montague has already examined her."

Her eyes widened. "Show me this vixen."

When we arrived, Reginald and Montague were gone, likely to inform Bedford, but a small gathering of gawkers had formed around Annabelle. I shooed them off with an angry scowl so Samara could approach.

When Samara and Annabelle locked gazes, the fox tensed and froze. Samara maintained steady eye contact and lowered herself to her belly, moving forward in a slow crawl. She moved with great caution so as not to frighten the vixen, but still, Annabelle trembled on her rope lead. However, she stood in place, as if hypnotized, not yipping or backing away.

When Samara was close enough to stretch out and touch noses, she mewled. Annabelle made a soft whine in response. It went back and forth for a little while, but I couldn't say if it was a true conversation or simply Samara gaining trust.

When Samara carefully backed off and turned to me, she said, "Well, at least she's trying to communicate. This will take some doing, however. How confident are you in handling her, Maria?"

"She is a friend, but she's already tried to turn me into lunch. I'm a little scared to get close to her."

"Maria, you're not going to survive this war if you can't suppress your fears, regardless of how much Maya is looking out for you. This fox is terrified. I think you can provide comfort."

"All right. Carry on. I'm listening."

"First, put a muzzle on her. I know that might be harsh, but it must be done. She's a wild animal now, she will not respect you if she's not afraid of you. Once she understands you are in charge, then you can show her compassion."

"And then what?"

"Take her to your tent and keep her there until I return."

Finding a muzzle was the easy part. We'd fashioned some for the more unruly of our prisoners. But putting it on Annabelle was a completely different story. She jumped and snapped her jaws with more ferocity the closer I got.

I tried approaching slowly and with calming sounds, but when I grew frustrated, I remembered Samara's words about respect. "This is for your own good!" I shouted and stomped toward her with shoulders back. She cowered and snapped at my ankles, but I swatted her muzzle soundly and pounced on her. After a short wrestling match, I got the job done. She had calmed down a little bit but now refused to move. In the end, I had to pull, drag, and eventually carry her to the tent. Samara arrived shortly after, now in human form and wearing her colorful skirt and beaded chest piece. Her long hair was braided and adorned with bronze rings. One cheek was painted with a sunburst while the other bore a crescent moon.

She put down her bag and sat across from me. The vixen started squirming and fidgeting again, but I tightened my grip and held her in place.

"Annabelle, relax. Samara won't hurt you."

"Good, very good. Now remove the rope from her neck and tie it around her front paws, then take the muzzle off."

"As you like."

While I was doing that, Samara took out a bundle of herbs, then placed them in a brass bowl. She struck two flints together and caught the dried plants on fire, releasing a thin, white smoke. Samara raised the bowl and waved it through the air.

"You may want to hold your breath," she said. "Go stand near the entrance. This smoke isn't poisonous, but this ritual is not intended for prey. It may affect you differently, even knock you out."

I did as she told me. This tribal magic was completely foreign to me, but I would save my questions for later.

Samara waved some of the vapors into Annabelle's face and moved the bowl under her nose. The vixen's eyes became glossy, and her head nodded and swayed. The shaman then put out the burning herbs and held the fox's head. The pair locked eyes, and then Samara started chanting in a strange dialect.

"*Makadunyiswe umama womhlaba owadala umhlaba wethu, makadunyiswe ingelosi enika izingane isinkwa, nosathane onobuqili onconyelwe ukubagcina besaba.*"

She repeated these phrases over and over. Then uttered the only words I could understand. "Open your mind to me. Show me the things you have witnessed."

For a moment, nothing happened. Then Samara's hands trembled, vibrating Annabelle's head. A thick stream of saliva poured from Annabelle's mouth, and blood spilled from her eyes. I fought the urge to rush forward, unsure if this was meant to happen. Then Samara dropped Annabelle's head, and the shaman's eyes opened to reveal only the whites, her shoulders twitching, arms shaking. Annabelle convulsed on the blankets.

Unable to sit still, I dropped down beside Samara and held her shoulders.

"Samara, what's wrong?!"

Her pupils rolled back into view, but she didn't move, and though she looked at me, she didn't see me. I turned my attention to Annabelle, taking her in my arms and wiping her eyes and mouth. Thank Maya, she was alive, but she was trembling uncontrollably. I held her tighter and patted her back.

"Samara, please wake up! Are you all right? What's happening?"

She blinked rapidly, then crossed her arms over her chest and let out a few raspy breaths. She shook her head as if to clear it and said, "Yes, I am fine. Give me a moment. I need to relax my heart." All her usual confidence had fled her voice. She sounded melancholic and defeated.

I sat as patiently as I could, lowering Annabelle to the blankets. Her breathing was quick and shallow, but she did not shy from my touch when I patted her head.

"Maria," said Samara. "I saw what was done to her. Montague was correct. Her human half is dead. Irretrievable."

My blood went cold. Not only was it a heinous act of pride and cruelty to even attempt such a thing, but if the Absolvers could truly achieve this, it would bode greater ill for the kingdom than any of us realized was possible.

"I'm sorry," said Samara. "I should never have had her relive that memory. I never imagined people could be so depraved."

She blinked back tears, never letting them spill. I, however, could not contain mine. They rolled down my cheeks, and I brushed them away in silence. Memories of Annabelle came unbidden. Her smile when she'd managed to scrounge up more blankets for us. The day she'd stopped a guard whipping Mother and walked her back to the barracks herself. The confident set of her shoulders as she unleashed her wrath on a guard who'd been caught drawing a woman into a dark tunnel. The memory that hurt the worst was of the night when she sat outside our barrack and talked to me through our lookout hole. She spoke to me as though I was a friend. The simplicity of her questions about my day and my interests and my worries had been the sweetest gesture anyone had offered me. It made me feel normal. It made me feel almost free. Now, I hugged the fox that once was my friend and whispered in her ear that everything was all right. She whined and licked my cheek.

"I think I may have awakened her memories of you, at least," said Samara. "Her mind is still intact, so some of it is retrievable. But I'm sorry to say her condition is worse than we feared."

"How could it possibly be worse?"

"I saw a dark blotch in her head. I think it might be a cyst or a tumor; I can't say for sure. But I'm afraid your friend is dying."

I rocked with Annabelle pulled into my lap, unsure whether to cry, scream, or break something... or in what order. Such pain and suffering, all for the machinations and political games of a few superstitious fear mongers.

"How long does she have left?"

"A month, maybe two if she's lucky. But really, she could have a convulsion and die at any moment. It's a miracle she survived this long."

The first sob broke through my defenses. I set my jaw and decided I would do everything in my power to make her final days more comfortable. It was all I could do.

"My apologies, Maria, but I need to go. I have a terrible headache."

"Thank you, Samara."

I sat in the tent, brushing Annabelle's fur. It relaxed us both. After a while, she opened her eyes, and I was certain if she'd still had her humanity, she would have smiled.

She lay her head on my shoulder, and I hugged her with a small bit of relief. I offered her a drink of water and looked up when Reginald entered. He sat down with me and gave me a humble smile.

"You've been in here for a long time. Did you have anything to eat? Shall I get you something?"

I shook my head, no. In truth, I hadn't even paid attention to whether I was hungry. I stared at Annabelle, avoiding his gaze.

"Maria, talk to me. What's wrong?"

"You know it's true? You talked to Samara?"

Now it was his turn to avert his eyes. "Yes."

"They couldn't just torture and kill her," I snarled through gritted teeth. "That's cruel enough. But to rape someone's soul and then leave them to die a crippled, confused animal... it's unthinkable."

Reginald frowned and looked away, shaking his head. When he looked back to me, I recognized a familiar feeling I'd harbored many times: vengeful anger.

"My father has a lot of explaining to do. This is a war crime against one of the noble predator families. It will not be taken lightly in any circles." He gently took my chin and tilted it up. "Maria, I promise, when I am king, the Covenant will be the first thing I abolish."

I nodded, managing a small smile. "Thank you." After a few steadying breaths, I added, "You said that she's Duchess Durand's sister and that you think she's an ally. We should tell her about this. You should send a messenger—"

He cut me off with a shake of his head.

"Why not? She could help us."

"This isn't the first time I've asked you to trust me, Maria, but I'll ask again. I cannot risk sending any messengers if there's a chance Father might intercept them. I will inform the duchess eventually, but now is not the time."

"But—" I cut myself off this time, closing my eyes to shut away the rushing thoughts. "You're right, I suppose." I sighed. "What should we do now?"

"Keep moving forward. We will hold the council meeting to establish our laws tonight."

"All right. I will be out in a little while."

CHAPTER THIRTEEN
The Coming Battle

Reginald

I sat at the head of the log table with Diederik on my left, a seat waiting for Maria on my right, and Bedford and Montague across from me in places of equal honor. Bedford, though, had declined an actual chair, keeping to his animal form as usual. After a few minutes of sipping the mushroom, carrot, and wild onion stew, Diederik nudged my shoulder and pointed through the trees. Maria approached with head high and face clear, leading Annabelle on a leash.

The changelings at the table whispered among each other, pointing fingers. Maria took her place at my side, smoothing Isolde's freshly washed dress with dignity, the leash wrapped around her wrist. Despite the determined set of her shoulders, I read her weariness in the lines of her face and felt it in my own bones. I rapped the back of my knife against my glass to call a quiet.

"I have been thinking hard and long," I said, projecting to those gathered among the trees, "and before we establish our laws in writing tonight, I wish to propose our first action of attack. I believe that with a bit of strategy, we can overtake the city of Dogsport. It is a vital trade city for my father's crown, and a siege upon it would cripple his resources and allow us a means to sail to the isles of Clydalie, where I have already sent a trusted envoy to spread our cause. And if we are lucky, it will eat away at some of my father's blind trust in his Absolvers and their Crimson Guard to protect him."

"So it is true then? You are opposing not just your father, but the church as well?" one of the Ursa from Uncle's regiment asked.

"The Covenant, or rather the Inquisition, has no right to govern the people of this land, and they have told you a great lie. That Khaytan alone rules heaven, that His brother Sammael is weak and irrelevant, and that Maya is an old, powerless figure."

The murmurs turned to shouts and wild gestures. But I was quick to call things to order.

"Everyone be quiet! Listen, I know you are afraid of taking on such a great risk. That you have families you would rather return to. But now, we are your brothers and sisters. Of course, this will be a hard battle, but it's a righteous one that will mean a better tomorrow for all of us."

"Have you not seen the vixen I am caring for?" said Maria, rising to address our people and gesturing at Annabelle, who lay curled at her feet. "She was a noblewoman. The Covenant stripped this predator's humanity, as they have tried to dehuman-ize prey for years. No one is safe from the Covenant."

The crowd shifted as heads turned to each other, savage cousins who had served a kingdom, willingly or not, that they were now asked to betray. Whispers began, each voice looking for affirmation.

"Reginald, this is preposterous!" said Bedford. "Your army is too small to conquer Dogsport. To form a force large enough, we would have to leave pregnant mothers to care for the young and old, while the rest march off to war."

"I think a prudent question is, why not raid another, much smaller harbor town to commandeer ships for our voyage to Clydalie?" asked Leopold. Prey and predator alike murmured agreement.

"Understand, my father's pride is at stake as much as his

kingdom," I said. "He will do whatever it takes to end this war quickly. He may already be assembling a force. Dogsport is closest, only a day's march."

"We can push back any armies he sends after us," rumbled Bedford. "All we need to do is keep vigilant and organize properly."

"And what if he sets fire to this forest with has his men waiting around the edges for the fleeing souls?" I shouted, shaking my head. "This sacred forest is nothing but a fraction of his timber and iron supply. It means next to nothing to him. We must leave this place and besiege Dogsport with all available fighters."

"Again, why Dogsport?" asked Leopold.

"I have already told you. That city is important to my father! All he has ever done is steal from people: their land, their friends, their freedom. Now it's time we did the same to him. The city has a large garrison, yes. But if we defeat it and abolish all my father's assets there, those troops will not bother us again, and my father will know we are not children playing games. We are sending a message in fire and blood. The only kind he understands."

"You plan to sink the fleet, don't you?" said Maria, cocking her head at me. "Not just take a few boats to sail away."

"Exactly."

"But what if we are outnumbered?" Diederik interjected.

"The longer we wait, the more likely General De Draco and King Emmerich send their full force to slaughter us all," said Maria, standing. "I say that instead, we lead the old wolf away from your homes and teach him a lesson he won't soon forget! Some of us will die and rest in Maya's arms. But those who don't will see Emmerich grovel at the feet of prey!"

A new ruckus erupted, this one powered by jubilant cheering and stamps of determination rather than fear.

"I'll take the risk to see the white wolf lick the dirt at a Lepores' feet," said Bedford, voice lifted by a smile as he bowed his antlers to Maria. Then he looked at me. "Let us set our pact in writing tonight, my prince."

* * *

The meeting—another sacred gathering of our animal forms in Bedford's pavilion, this time with an audience—had gone better than I'd expected. We'd need a few more days to fully draft our community's new laws, but with my logic and Maria's reminders of Maya's love for balance, our company agreed that prey may offer their dead to predators, and vice versa, but the grieving must receive compensation. Those who partook would offer full condolences, respect, and prayers to Maya, a sign of understanding that nothing can be taken for granted.

Maria had seemed to read my every thought. She jumped in as smoothly as if we rehearsed it, each of us building off each other's words. I had never experienced such a link with anyone, save perhaps Angus. It delighted and excited me, and as everyone journeyed back to their tents, I gently caught her cotton tail in my mouth. Her head was slow to turn, but there was no worry in her eyes, only curiosity.

"Reginald, what are you doing?" she asked in a soft voice.

I released her and gave her my most playful grin, my tongue barely poking out of the end of my muzzle. "I just want a few minutes alone with you."

She followed me into the forest, and I headed for a place I'd passed many times on my runs.

"Reginald, where are you taking me? We won't be able to see anything if we transform this far from camp." She shot me a sly smile and said, "We are out here to do more than talk, yes?"

I chuckled. "Don't worry. There is a clearing up ahead, and there's plenty of moonlight."

A few minutes later, the trees parted, and we came out into a lush meadow bathed in the white light of our twin moons. I nibbled the tip of her ear and then regretted it, for I had to fight down my wolf half. The smell of her animal form elicited thoughts of chomping and tearing rather than playful wrestling reserved for pack members.

"Hey, stop it!" She lightly slapped my cheek with her paw

without fear, and sobering my wolf half grew easier as I gazed into her eyes.

"I'm not sure you thought this through," she said through a giggle. "We have no blankets."

I sat in front of her, my tail thumping the grass. "The earth is soft, and we can stay warm if we cuddle, my little bunny. Besides, does not Maya tell us to grow close as we can to nature?"

Her chest expanded, holding onto the breath a moment before letting it out with a laugh. "You have a persuasive tongue, my prince," she said with a wink.

"It has other talents as well," I said.

"Hurry and change back before we offend the Great Mother," she said with a light chuckle, though her eyes showed true concern.

The magic of transformation always held me captive, but the shift from a black rabbit into the woman I loved stole my breath. Her raven hair sprouted as her ears fell back and tumbled in soft waves over her shoulders and back, her naked form revealing itself in a gentle wave. Her petite curves more pronounced with each passing day, no longer starved thanks to three square meals a day.

She rubbed at her arms. "I'm cold. Don't dawdle. Come warm me."

I closed my eyes, welcoming the shift, but the door in my head slammed shut. The hinges filled with ice as a chill overtook my spine. A voice I knew well snarled from within my skull. *Hello, son.*

I gasped and squeezed my eyes tighter, gritting my teeth as my legs trembled. The voice was so real. So close. I could feel him—a set of dark tendrils snaking through my brain, constricting and probing. *No, no. You're not here. Get out my head!*

The tendrils retreated an inch. *You can't shut me out, Reginald. Traitorous pup!* The tendrils dug in, erupting a searing pain in my skull. *Open your eyes!*

As much as I fought them, my eyelids peeled open. Maria was smiling at me, though her brows scrunched in confusion.

"Reginald, how long are you going to keep me waiting?"

My eyes were no longer mine, but they briefly studied her face before drifting to the ink on her neck. Malign, poisonous hatred seeped from the dark presence in my head, like suffocating smoke. I ground my teeth and dug my claws into the earth, trying to choke down the hatred that made my limbs shake with rage.

The slave from the mine! The whore rodent whom you crept with through the night, attacking my mine and stealing my slaves. For this pathetic creature, you betray your pack?!

"Reggie, are you all right? You're shaking..." said Maria, bending down to try and meet my eye, her hand extended as she took a tentative step toward me. I turned my head from her as my father screamed: *I will have you slaughter her with your own teeth!*

"Reginald, look at me!"

I whined, head turned, biting down until my gums bled. I could feel Father sinking deeper, taking control of my limbs. He had a power I had never dreamed possible. Even in my own mind, I was not safe, and Maria...

I tried to call a warning, scream at her to run from me, but the only sound that escaped was a low growl.

"Reginald, what's wrong?" asked Maria, sounding near tears.

At the pull of an unseen string... I jumped. Her scream was silenced as her back slammed the earth, me atop her, driving all the air from her lungs. My claws ripped into her shoulders, chest, and thighs, and her eyes flew wide as she drew in a ragged breath and screamed in agony.

The scent of her blood cast my conscious mind farther from the iced door that held my human side hostage.

"Reginald, stop! Stop, please!" Her small hands beat against my head and pushed at my neck, trying to drive me back, her legs thrashing uselessly beneath my weight.

Her pleas became a scream as my teeth plunged into her right breast, tearing and mauling. Her eyes rolled back, but her hands still buried deep in my fur, pulling with waning strength.

"I am not your savior, slut! I am your king and your undoing! You will die for your crimes against me, slave." The words came out in my voice, but I had not uttered them.

Blood traveled in branches across Maria's chest, pooling in her collarbones. She fixed me with terrified eyes and whispered, "Please, Reginald..." Her hand traced my cheek and head, smoothing down my ear in a caress.

My head jerked from her touch and reared back, fangs bared for a killing blow to her throat, but inside my mind, I charged the door with a battle cry. I slammed against it with my shoulder, screaming, *She is not your slave! You are no king! And you have never been a true father to me!* Trapped inside my head, I backed up and slammed against the door again, crying, *It is she who is your undoing, and I will be there when she takes your crown from your head!*

Rage flooded me—my hate, my poison. I threw it all at my father as I crashed into the door again. With a mighty crack, the ice fell away, and the door flew open. As the transformation back into a man overtook me, the dark tendrils retreated as though burned, and it was my father's screams of pain that filled my ears. I came back to myself to find my arms wrapped around Maria's limp body, her blood slick against my skin. I tasted it in my mouth and spat it onto the grass. I rose with her in my arms and ran.

Maria

I was lost in a swirling grey abyss—grey skies over dark rocks on an island overlooking charcoal waters. The stone beneath my feet bled, and the air stung my nose with sulfur. Had Maya abandoned me here? Surely this was Khaytan's realm.

An old white wolf with eyes glowing ruby and jowls spewing foamy saliva leaped on me from the darkness, knocking me on my back. His claws dug into my chest as he shouted, "Traitorous slave, evil witch, vile temptress, foul usurper, I will taste your flesh and let you rot with the worms!"

Between my screams, I pleaded with the Great Mother to

make him stop, but she didn't answer. The wolf buried his fangs in my neck, and as I wailed in agony, his hair turned coppery brown. Reginald?! Reginald was attacking me, biting me, killing me.

I shut my eyes, continuing my fruitless prayers. It could not be true. Then the weight lifted, and Reginald gazed down on me with baleful eyes, whining. He licked my wounds, and the pain drifted away, like morning mist under the sun. A bright light shone from behind him, its glow so powerful I had to shield my eyes, and that's when I awoke, my arm raised to cover my face.

A small ray of sunlight passed through a tear in the tent and hit my eyes. When I raised myself to a seated position, I gasped from the stinging, fiery pain in my chest. The sharp inhale only deepened the pain and left me heaving for breath. It felt like someone had stabbed me in the chest. I suppressed my scream to a sharp yelp and stared down at myself.

Beneath my nightgown, my breasts and belly were wrapped with thick bandages. Memories flooded me. Reginald shaking, his eyes devoid of their humanity and luster. His claws raking burning lines in my flesh. His snarled words of hate at my ear, piercing me as deeply as the teeth he sank into my chest. My breath came in short gasps, tears burning my eyes as I tried to make sense of it.

"Maria, please calm down," said a voice to my right. When a hand touched my shoulder, I whirled, screaming, and raked my nails across something soft. I gasped when I realized it was Samara, now clutching her scratched cheek.

"I... I'm sorry, I..." My mind was spinning, and the pain was urgent, fragmenting my nerves and focus.

"It's all right," she whispered. She was crouched in human form at the side of my bed. Her face was devoid of paint, and the bags below her eyes suggested she'd slept poorly on the floor.

"Reginald," I choked through quickly welling tears, "he attacked me!" The truth of it hurt, as if the words were razors in my throat. "He lost control of his wolf form. He—"

"I know," she said, putting a hand on my leg. "He told me

everything. It was more complicated than that."

"More complicated?!" I shrieked. My swirling mind told me I was a fool. I should never have pursued a relationship with a wolf... or at least been more cautious. It seemed his animal nature was stronger than I had imagined. "He acted like a brute. A savage! He lost control. How can I tell my people he means us and our kind no harm when—"

"For gods' sakes, keep your voice down! I understand you're hurt, but do not be brash. You will put his life in danger with such talk."

"He put *my* life in danger," I said, my jaw dangling. I scoffed in disgust, betrayed by my lover and my friend in the space of what felt like minutes. "You are taking his side because you are a predator, just like him. He spun some lies, and you believed them. Or you think he was blameless because it is his right, his nature?"

Her mouth popped open, expression flat, stunned. Then she raised her eyebrow, and her lip curled in a furious snarl. I tried to scoot away, but she gripped me tightly, her nails digging into my shoulders.

"Have you utterly lost your sense? Just a predator?" she spat. She looked down at her hands and released me with a huff. "Tell me, Maria, do you want to be just prey?"

I shook my head, my tears laden with shock and fear and confusion my body couldn't contain.

"Then listen to me, and never insult my intelligence again!" She closed her eyes on an exhale, and when she reopened them, they swam with sympathy. "Forgive me for shouting. But the wolf who attacked you last night was not the prince." She cut off my scoff with a raised finger and a pointed look. "He was not in control of his body. His father, King Emmerich, possessed him."

"Now it is you who insults my intelligence," I said through a stern jaw.

"I have seen it before."

I studied her face—grave and even fearful. I found no deception, and I swallowed hard, unsure whether to be relieved or terrified.

"To explain, I must tell you a story about my homeland... and my mother."

I nodded for her to go on.

"The continent where I come from has many names. In your tongue, some have called it 'Plains of Eternal Summer,' but though the sun is bright, it is not a fair and shining place. In the dry season, when the rains come late, even family members might slice each other's throats for a cup of water. There were always horrible wars with neighboring tribes in dry times."

I nodded to let her know I was listening attentively.

"My mother, Temitope, had many titles: Blind Warden, Sightless Guardian, Spirit Seer."

"Was she actually blind?"

"Temitope lost the use of her eyes, but she could see more than most. Each nation and tribe has its priests, shamans, witch doctors—people of wisdom who hold communion with the divines. Even among the most revered magi, my mother was special, but she jealously guarded her secrets, even from her daughters. I learned what I know by spying, and I received numerous punishments when caught." She spoke of the woman reverently, though to me, she sounded harsh.

"My mother always entertained important men in her bedroom—envoys, warlords, chieftains from rival clans. Their eyes would change overnight. They would enter our home as arrogant fools, and by morning, they followed at her heels like cubs, but their eyes were wide with fright. It was as though she had torn out a piece of their soul, and they knew it. They danced to her tune, praised her as though she was Maya incarnate. For a long time, I wanted to be like her, to use men like playthings." She gestured with her fingers in the air as though stringing puppets. "Until I realized the truth of how she did it. I found ancient scrolls that detailed the ritual, and the depravity, the arrogance of it, turned me away."

Samara's eyes drifted toward the floor, and when she spoke next, her voice was raw, some of its usual power drained by a pain I couldn't see but felt all the same. "She caught me among her things, and less than one moon cycle later, a Leo warlord had claimed me as his own, and Mother never came for me. I had disobeyed too many times. So I was left with a man I could never control, never sway, never love, and I was *his* puppet." Her fists gathered up my bedding, her arms shaking as she restrained her emotion.

I ran my hand down her arm, and her muscles softened.

"I am sorry for all you have suffered, my friend. But I must ask... how are you certain Temitope's magic worked?"

"How do you know the Covenant's magic works? Because the proof is right here before your eyes, even if you parade her around like some tamed animal." Samara pointed at the silver vixen curled on a blanket in the corner of my tent.

She might have struck me across the face, so great was my shock, and so quickly was I cowed by the words. I had never meant to... display Annabelle that way. I had only wanted to keep her close, so she would not be alone.

"How do you know the Covenant is using similar methods?" I asked, not meeting Samara's eyes.

"There is a way I can be certain, but I will need to speak with Reginald again... after you talk to him first."

I hugged myself with one arm, rubbing my left hand over my right bicep. "I don't know if I can." I shut my eyes against images of his fangs tearing my flesh, but that only made them more vivid. I felt tears coming.

"I know what it is like to feel powerless beneath a man," Samara said, barely above a whisper. "I know what it is like to have your freedom taken in ways you didn't think possible, as though it was drained from your very veins." Her golden eyes found mine and held me tightly. "And I am sorry for your pain."

She put her arms around me, mindful that any light touch to my chest might spark more hurt. At the sensation of her warm skin on mine, I felt as though a piece of Mother's soul had found a home in this woman's body. I let her wipe away my tears and hugged her tight.

"But, Maria... Reginald did not act in malice," she said into my hair. "It was not his tongue that lashed you or his fangs that harmed you. Not truly. I know it is hard to believe, but if you cannot trust him right now... please... trust me. If I believed he had purposefully attacked you in any fashion, I would have acted as judge and jury myself."

I pulled back from her, trying to understand. I realized since I woke, I had only been thinking of Reginald the wolf, but now I turned my mind to the face of the man I had thought I loved. I thought of his words, his promises, his actions. It was difficult to reconcile the two images. "I will go talk to Reginald," I said.

She smiled and nodded. "I will be there shortly."

Outside everything was calm, the camp still in the faint light of dawn. I slunk to Samara's tent, and never before in human form had I felt more like prey. The idea of anyone seeing me with these wounds, and the explanation that would have to follow, was more than I could bear. At the tent, I pulled the flap away and stepped inside. A shape lay beneath a blanket. I touched it tentatively, and Reginald rolled over. I stepped back, shocked. His eyes were ringed with purple, and his cheeks were covered in dust and tear tracks. He reached a hand toward me, rattling a chain around his wrist, and then pulled it back, biting his lip.

"Maria..." His voice was low and hoarse. He shut his eyes against tears. "I am so sorry."

"Reginald, what have you done to yourself?" I asked, pulling back the blanket to find his feet chained the same as his hands.

"Nothing compared to what you've endured," he said. "But Maria, please believe me... I was not in control of myself. I put on these chains so I could not be overtaken again."

He rolled away from me, curled in a ball, and anger shot through me. He was acting pathetic, as if he'd been the one attacked and betrayed.

"Reginald, sit up and face me. You are a prince. Do you want our people to see you like this?"

"I am a prince no longer," he said. "I gave it up the moment you showed me the truth of myself outside that old barn. Even then, when I'd barely met you, I wanted to help you thrive, wanted to be with you enough to risk everything. I'm crazier than I thought."

I crossed my arms over my wounds. "Please. You act as though I'm the only woman you've ever had."

"I've had other women," he said, rolling over and sitting up. "But you... you are courageous, intelligent, and selfless. No, Maria, you were not my first love, but you are the one I needed. I tried every day to make myself worthy of you, and I will continue to do so, even if you cannot forgive me. I should have stopped him the moment he made his presence known."

My mouth parted to let out a soft sob, my heart in a vice. I turned away, covering my face.

"I want to believe you, Reginald. I know in my heart you would never call me those ugly words, even if your animal half overtook you. I know those words, at least, were not you. But I am scared."

He reached out slowly, giving me plenty of time to turn him away, but I let his fingers brush my face and then leaned into his palm.

"I'm scared, too. If my father can take my mind whenever he wants... I cannot be with you. I cannot lead these people. I cannot bring about the change I promised."

"Samara is coming. She says she can uncover the truth of what happened. But for now... I think we should let you out of those shackles. Someone could come asking for you any minute. This is a secret we must keep to ourselves, or all we've done could be undone in an instant."

"You would be alone with me without them?"

"You... you stopped him last night, didn't you?" I thought of his fangs coming for my neck and then drawing back, his eyes widening with fright rather than malice. "You can stop him again."

He brightened a fraction and pointed to the key just out of his reach. By the time I freed him, Samara had ducked her head inside the tent, her bowl of incense in hand. Unlike with

Annabelle, when Samara put the smoke under Reginald's nose, his body stayed straight and strong, and his eyes focused as they locked with Samara's. Both their pupils expanded as the shaman chanted.

When it was finished, Reginald rubbed his forehead, and two drops of blood dripped from his nose.

Samara sat back and smiled. "This is better news than I'd hoped. As frightening as this invasion was for the both of you, I believe you've crippled our enemy with his own attack."

"So, Emmerich truly took his mind?" I asked. "You're certain it's the same magic your mother used?"

"Yes, the very same. Reginald speaks the absolute truth," she said. "But he fought back hard." She nodded encouragingly at Reginald. "The walls of your subconscious are dense. It was difficult for me to breach, even when you were allowing me to see your thoughts. I imagine Emmerich had a lot of help from his Absolvers to do what he did, but even then, when you pushed him out, forcing him back through the barriers of your will, I expect he didn't return to himself unscathed."

"I don't understand," said Reginald.

"Neither do I," I said.

"What Emmerich did required incredible power of will and years of practice to execute properly. When you fought back, he was outmatched, even with his hairless beasts helping him. I imagine you damaged him in both mind and body by banishing him, just as soundly as besting him with a blade. I expect he will be incapacitated for days, maybe weeks. I wouldn't be surprised if you put him in a coma. I doubt he'll try overtaking you again any time soon."

"So, I managed to push him out of my mind permanently?"

"Well... not permanently, but now he understands the risk, and you understand how to banish him."

"But wait, if the king is crippled, we can simply march on the capital, and you can claim your birthright." I smiled at Reginald, hesitantly reaching to touch his shoulder.

He took my hand but shook his head. "This doesn't change

anything. Father's councilors will keep this a secret, and if he doesn't recover soon, they will name a regent. No, the only way I can win the crown is with a coup."

"Do remember, Maria, we can't tell the clan elders what happened. And if we change the plan unexpectedly, they will ask questions," said Samara.

I nodded. There was no way around that. I turned to Reginald. "I'm sorry I didn't believe you. I—"

He cut me off with a shake of his head. "There is nothing to forgive, Maria. I hope only you can forgive me... and not fear me."

I wrapped my arms around his neck and kissed him deeply, cherishing the warmth and comfortable familiarity of it... but deep in my gut, I worried that perhaps Samara was underestimating the will of the king.

Ecaterina

Lightning flashes lit the distant hills, the weather as volatile as the mood in the castle. I had woken in Reginald's room, warm and peaceful, but I had walked into a war zone at dinner, my servants bloodied and bruised.

"We inquired when the king would arrive for breakfast," one of the kitchen attendants confessed when questioned. His battered eye looked ready to pop from his head.

"I will get to the bottom of this." I turned to my lady in waiting, Felicia. "Fetch these poor changelings the doctor."

I marched to Emmerich's chambers in a hot fury, but my blood chilled at the sight of a dozen armored guards standing outside the door... Crimson Guards. Panic seized me. I'd thought I would hear whispers of the missing guards buried at Leticia's estate before anyone uncovered their deaths and my involvement.

One of the mangy beasts noticed me and blocked my path, his eyes shifting under the red hood covering his helmet. I froze.

"Pardon, my queen, but the king is indisposed at this moment and doesn't want any company."

I tried to keep my face stony as my lungs re-inflated. Something else was afoot.

"How dare you impede me in my own home? I assure you such commands from the king don't apply to me. He will want to see me. I demand you let me through!"

"There has been an attempt on the king's life, and he desires to see no one. The betrayal of the prince will lead to many changes around here, Your Grace. Everyone will be questioned thoroughly before the king returns to his duties."

"If the king has been harmed, I must see him!" I said, allowing my fear at the guard's implication of an inquest to spill over into my inquiries for Emmerich. "Even more reason why I would want to see him. And do not speak on things you don't understand. Reginald is your prince, even if he is not within these walls." I jabbed a finger into his plated chest, but he didn't so much as flinch.

"Arguing with me is fruitless. And if you force the issue, we will arrest you, until the king asks for you to be released."

"Fine," I said through a snarl, blood boiling. "If you refuse to follow my order, you will answer to your Lord General."

"General De Draco is on the list of people who are permitted to see the king. You, however, are not."

I swallowed down bile. I had never been spoken to with such disrespect in my home. Yet this guard acted as if he feared absolutely no repercussions. Something had shifted. Emmerich was no longer lapping up my lies.

"We shall see," I said, holding my head high while my stomach sank.

I retreated to my room and stayed there for two days, only venturing out to try and speak with Gregory, to appease him and figure out exactly what was going on.

But the general was tight-lipped about the king's condition, saying only that he needed rest after an assault. He clammed up when I asked how on Maya's green earth someone got to the king in his own chambers. None of it made sense. I then had my maids bring me news and meals to Reginald's room, barricading myself inside with Stephania. According to palace gossip, Gregory held a meeting to inform the prominent nobles in the capital about the assassination attempt. He had been named regent until the official investigation was concluded.

After that, everything had been far too quiet. Until a pigeon delivered a message from my brother Pascal in Dogsport. I opened it with trembling hands, and Stephania read over my shoulder.

Sister,

I fear my pen may cause you pain in more ways than one, but I must know the truth so that I can protect you. My spies spotted Reginald and a large force of prey soldiers in the forests of Raven's Rock near the city. I fear Reginald has allied himself with the elders there, Bedford and Montague. I have told no one. What do you know of this? More pressing, what should I tell Emmerich should this come to light?

This message was already two days old. Reginald might have already put his soldiers to good use.

Stephania beamed, and I was partially infected by her joy. Reginald had rallied a force around him with no help from a crown. I had an inkling of what he planned to do, though, and it twisted my heart with dread. I prayed he might land the first blow in this brewing civil war... but what would that mean? When his true intentions came to light, no one would be able to remain neutral. I would be expected to pick a side, and Emmerich was no fool. It would be damn near impossible to convince him that I had played no hand and would not stand by my son going forward. My only chance was to find him before anyone brought him word of an attack. Maybe I could appeal to whatever reason he had left.

A thunderous banging on the door made the servant squeak, and Stephania latched onto my skirts like a child.

"Open this door in the name of the king," said a deep voice.

Deciding it was unwise to anger them any further, I obeyed.

A dozen guards stood in the hall, with Emmerich at their

center, wearing his red sleeping robes, hair disheveled and face sickly pale, like he'd just woken from a nightmare.

"Traitorous bitch!" he screamed, his fury momentarily straightening his weakened, bent form. "Throw her on her knees!"

Two knights grabbed my arms as I shouted, "Emmerich, please. This is outrageous. I've done nothing wrong."

Emmerich only shuffled into the room, wincing with each step, while the knights pressed on my head and shoulders, forcing me to the ground.

"Your Grace!" screamed Stephania, still clinging to the back of my dress. It was the sound of a frightened child calling for her mother, and I burst into tears, trying to turn my head to see her, to reach out and touch her face, but the knights tightened their grip. A third knight came forward and dragged her off me, but the moment he tossed her aside, she ran for me again, tears in her eyes, shouting, "Let her go!"

The knight's knuckles cracked against her mouth in a back-handed blow, and she collapsed, spitting blood on the rug.

"I know what your son has been up to," Emmerich drawled. "And I also know he's with that Lepores whore." He glared daggers at Stephania, and I knew the ruse was over. Emmerich reached me at last, his face twisted in a grimace of pain and hate. "So, your brother is in on this little rebellion, too, eh?" he said, bending slowly to snatch up the letter he must have already read and resealed with some Absolver trickery.

"That is ridiculous. He sent me that note because he feared your wrath would turn upon me, since Reginald has escaped you, and wanted to warn me. It seems he was right. You have lost your mind!"

He leaned in and breathed his coppery, blood-tinged breath in my face in a ragged rhythm, straining to keep his back bent.

"So your little message to his contact among the Karluks was just... what? A misunderstanding?"

I dropped my eyes as the old terror crept into my veins, threatening to freeze me in place. My eyes met Stephania's—her face covered in tears and blood—and I ground my teeth.

"Pascal had no knowledge of that," I said, glaring at him as I once glared at prey, freezing them with fear before I pounced. He blinked, taken aback, and I smiled, thinking on Reginald's words. *I was born to be an alpha*, I snarled to myself. I opened my mouth to tell Emmerich that yes, I'd led him astray, and no, I did not regret it, but Stephania shouted over me.

"She only sent that message because I told her that's where Reginald was going. She wanted to find out for herself if it was true."

"Stephania!" I cried in shock. "D—"

"I did what Reginald told me," she cried. "He freed my friend. I owed him a debt."

Emmerich straightened and looked between us. He seemed to take my dangling jaw for outrage rather than horror.

"This is true?" he asked me, a dare in his eyes.

I stammered. "I... it's..." I shook my head in confusion, a thousand thoughts warring for first position in my brain. If Stephania took most of the blame, perhaps I could still help Reginald... but Emmerich would surely slaughter her, and I couldn't bear the thought. I knew he'd make me watch.

"She... she's not being entirely truthful," I managed at last. "She's trying to protect me."

Emmerich sneered in disgust. "Prey think only of saving their necks."

"She said she thought she'd overheard Reginald talking with a mercenary contact about the Karluks. I... I wanted to investigate further. I didn't know what was going on, and I worried you would act brashly. I thought I would find the answers first and then come to you with them. I was hoping Reginald would be proven innocent."

"You are a damned fool, Ecaterina. A fucking imbecile. I will deal with you later."

He held out a hand to the closest knight, who handed over a dagger. He snapped his fingers in Stephania's direction, and another of his mindless soldiers forced her to her feet and brought her to him. Beneath his gaze, her eyes went glossy, the rabbit side hidden within petrified. Emmerich unsheathed the dagger, panting like his inner wolf.

"As for this little prey," he wheezed, voice low and deadly. "I never liked such garrulous behavior from my food." His bloodshot eyes widened, crazed.

"Emmerich, stop. Please! She's just a girl. She obeyed an order from her prince. That's all."

"Silence! I allowed you the company of this rat to get you out of my hair, but it was clearly a mistake to let it whisper in your ear all day. I will put an end to that whispering for good."

Emmerich snapped again. One of the knights forced Stephania's mouth open, gripping her cheeks, and then stretched out her tongue with metal pliers.

"No! No, Emmerich, don't! I beg you!" I cried, struggling against the grips of his brutes. Stephania's chest fluttered with frantic, shallow breaths, her eyes searching for me, a low whimper in her throat.

Emmerich's hand trembled, but he brought the knife down in a sawing motion. I closed my eyes through Stephania's first wail, and then something struck my knee. I looked down at the bloodied organ beside me and gagged, my heart threatening to stop.

The knights dropped the crying girl, and she writhed on the floor, her hands to her mouth. My captors let me go when next I tugged against them, and I sprang to her side, pulling her into my lap.

"Stephania, I'm so sorry," I said, bending to press my forehead to hers, so my tears wet her face. I stroked her short hair and screamed, "Somebody get the physician! Staunch the bleeding!"

"Stop wasting your pathetic tears on a worthless slave," said Emmerich. "You spared none for me in my time of need, I'm sure."

If Maya had descended at that moment and tossed him straight into hell Herself, it would not have been enough.

"Damn you! You malignant monster! I love this girl like my own child! *You* haven't loved me for decades," I shouted through my sorrow.

My words struck Emmerich across the face and drew out a bellowing roar. "Your child? You would call that rodent your child!"

"What other child do I have?" I screamed back. "It's your fault my first son is dead, my second abandoned me just to be away from you, and you've taught my daughter to hate me!"

"You're mad. You're as much a shame to this family as the sniveling boys you raised. I'll kill you before I let you bring the wrath of Khaytan upon my head. I swear it on the great wolf's name. I'll kill you!"

He raised the knife over his head, bearing down on me, and I squeezed my eyes shut, turning to shield Stephania with my body. But then I heard Emmerich wheezing and shouting in pain, and the knife clanging on the hardwood. When I looked up, he was gripping his chest, staggering back in a near faint, but a knight was on hand to catch him.

Two more men rushed past, lifting the king up and carrying him away.

"Get me to my chambers. Fetch the physician," he mumbled.

I waited only two breaths after they carried him off before lifting Stephania and running for the kitchens. The other servants would help me. After all the crown had done to them, despite the constant fear of what might be done next, there was still so much compassion in prey. They understood pain, and so they sought to lessen it in others. They would help. And I, in turn, would help them.

CPSIA information can be obtained
at www.ICGtesting.com
Printed in the USA
LVHW012124240722
724287LV00001B/72

9 781624 751554